Undercover

Book 4 in
After the Fall Series

A Novel

By David Nees

ISBN 9781696252041

Manufactured in the United States

For Carla
My encourager

Grateful thanks for to my beta readers: Chris, Regina, Kathi, and Kermit. Your insightful comments are key to turning my rough agate into a polished (gem) stone. I appreciate your generosity of time.

A special "thank you" to my friend, Eric. You have the writer's perspective and that is so helpful to me.

I owe a special thanks to Dr. Jordan Peterson. He is unaware of his contribution to this tale, but his insights helped me put some thoughts and words into one of the characters in the story. I'm sure you'll know which one, when you get there.

And thank you, Carla and Catherine. Proofreading is hard to do and it takes away from the joy of reading a story. My work would be riddled with errors but for your help

Cover art by Onur Aksoy. You can find his work at https://www.onegraphica.com/

Undercover
Book 4 in *After the Fall* series

"Once you've lived the inside-out world of espionage, you never shed it. It's a mentality, a double standard of existence."—John le Carré

"Whoever fights monsters should see to it that in the process he does not become a monster. And when you look long into an abyss, the abyss also looks into you."—Friedrich Nietzche

"The beginnings and endings of all human undertakings are untidy."—John Galsworthy

Chapter 1

Jason sat close to his small campfire. The old Native American saying, probably apocryphal came to mind, "White man builds a big fire, sits far away, Indian builds a small fire, sits close". He smiled. Small fires were good; a lot easier to maintain, you didn't have to collect as much wood, and they drew less attention.

He was in a grove of oak trees nestled in a dozen acres off of the highway. Not far enough to feel comfortable, but it was the best place he could find. There were fewer stands of woods in the farming country through which he traveled. The tall trees kept out most of the sunlight, leaving the forest floor less choked with bushes, especially the irritating wild rose which grew so abundantly in the eastern forests.

His trek to Charlotte had been uneventful so far, but he didn't want to let his guard down. The world outside of protected towns was still a dangerous place. One ran into fewer people, now four years after the EMP attack, but the federal government had still not achieved anything like an overall, unifying presence. Cities were on their own with smaller outlaw groups continuing to prowl around the countryside looking for opportunities.

His sense of caution had caused him to camp off the highways that he used as modern-day trails. The roads were littered with abandoned vehicles, long looted of any valuables, but walking was easier, despite the hard pavement. The roadways were not choked with undergrowth so he could make good mileage each day. At night he would head off into whatever stand of woods he could find and set up camp where he hoped he would not be seen.

His thoughts were interrupted by a small sound. A soft crunch of leaves. It was subtle. A cracking twig or stick would have sounded like a rifle shot in the still of the night. This sound was quieter. If his senses hadn't been on alert, he would have missed it. But there it was.

His rifle was leaning against the tree a few paces from where he sat. *Can't reach for it. That'll alert whoever is out there.* Jason didn't doubt the sound was human in origin. No animal would make such a noise and few would approach a campfire.

He stretched and yawned in an exaggerated manner, slid another stick into his small fire and then turned as if looking for more wood. He got up and stepped back, hoping if whoever was approaching saw him, he would look like he was getting more firewood. He slipped into the darkness.

When he was beyond the light of the campfire, Jason turned and crept to one side from where he had disappeared. When he was sure he would be flanking anyone who approached, he took his 9mm out of its holster, crouched down, and waited. *Patience always wins out.*

There it was again. More soft crunches. It sounded like more than one intruder. Jason had no illusions. People approaching surreptitiously at night, not announcing themselves, were up to no good.

He shielded his eyes from the fire so it wouldn't affect his night vision. Soon enough he saw a shadow in the brush across from the clearing where he had set up his camp. Two figures, barely more than shadows, emerged with a third trailing behind them. They looked around, their bodies hunched over, expressing caution and fear as they slowly advanced towards the fire.

"Where'd he go?" Jason heard one of the men ask.

"Shhh," came the response.

"Rifle's still here. Think whoever was here run off?"

"How'd he know we was coming?" another replied. "We was quiet as mouses."

The men looked around the campsite. Jason had set up his cover tarp and ground cloth, laid his backpack on it, and had pulled his cooking gear out of his pack.

"Looky here. He's got some food. Those army pouches, whaddaya call them?"

"MREs, the first man replied."

"Could use some of that," the second voice said.

"He left his rifle. Looks like a good one," the first man said.

"What if he ain't run off?" The third voice said. It was a lighter, younger voice, not as gruff as the first two.

"If he ain't, he's in for trouble. We're taking all this. Who knows what else's in the pack?" the first voice said.

They brought the food and pot over near the campfire.

Jason spoke now. "Got you boys covered. There's two of us. You make a move, two will die and the third won't get three steps before he'll join you."

The men froze and looked around wildly.

"He got a partner?" one of them whispered.

"Can't. We'd seen him," the second man replied.

"Put your weapons next to the fire and lay down on the ground. Now!" Jason's spoke with a sharp voice. "Feet towards the fire, face down. Put your hands on the back of your head."

The men still didn't move.

"Do it now and you probably won't die. Don't, and we'll shoot you."

"It's only you," the first man said. "We didn't see anyone else. You're bluffing."

"You willing to bet on that?"

"You can't kill us all 'fore we get you. Now why don't you just leave and we'll let *you* live."

"You don't want no trouble from us," the second man said.

The two men had turned towards the sound of Jason's voice. They were still holding their rifles.

"Why don't you show yourself. Seems like we got a standoff here. Now what're we gonna do about it?" the first man said.

"You boys are in a tough spot. I can see you but you can't see me. I can't let you go. You'll be sneaking back up on me. Don't want to kill you, but if you don't do what I say, I will."

"We do what you say, you'll just kill us anyway. I ain't interested in lying down and getting shot in the back."

"Do what I say and you got a chance to live."

The third one didn't say anything. He looked smaller, younger than the other two.

Suddenly one of the men brought his rifle up in Jason's direction. Jason fired and the man's rifle went off into the air as he fell. The other got off one shot before Jason's next shot hit him in the shoulder. He dropped his rifle and cried out. The younger man dropped to the ground at the first shot and cried out, "Don't shoot me!"

The second man was reaching for his rifle as Jason approached. Jason shot him in the head. The first man had been hit in the chest. Jason looked at him. He wouldn't live long. The third figure was just a boy, lying on the ground, whimpering and asking Jason not to shoot him.

"Your two friends are dead and dying. Why shouldn't I shoot you?"

"It wasn't my idea. I didn't want to rob you. It was them that made me."

"But you came along."

"They woulda shot me if I didn't go along."

"Why are you with them anyway? You don't look like much of an outlaw."

"I met 'em on the road. I was afraid of being alone and they said we'd do better together."

"Doing what?"

The young man hesitated.

"What is it you were doing?" Jason repeated his question.

"I guess you could say we was robbing people." He hurriedly continued, "Not killing them, just taking stuff to stay alive."

Jason thought about the other young men he'd come across who'd taken up with bad people. Things had not ended well for them. *Bad decisions can lead to dying.* Now here was another.

"Get on your knees," Jason commanded.

The young man rolled over. He still had his hands in the air.

"Put your hands on the back of your head. I'm going to put my gun in the small of your back. You move your hands, I'll shoot you in the spine. You'll be paralyzed and your guts destroyed. Not a good way to die, slow and painful."

Jason frisked the boy. He only had a sheath knife on him.

"Sit down," Jason said. He collected the three rifles and laid them on the other side of the campfire.

"How'd you find me?"

"We smelled the smoke. Followed it into the woods. I thought we might get something to eat. I didn't figure they'd try to rob you."

"And try to kill me. You know that's what they had in mind."

"I think they was hoping to run you off."

Jason took some paracord and tied the boy's hands behind his back. When he was done, he went over to a log and sat down.

"What should I do with you?" Jason asked aloud.

"You let me go, I'll be on my way. You won't see me no more."

"Not sure I believe that. Where'd you come from?"

"Charlotte."

"Where are you headed?"

"Somewhere's else. Charlotte's not a good place. Run by the mob. They make you work hard and beat you if you get out of line."

"So, you set out to be an outlaw. That it?"

The boy shook his head.

"But you came sneaking up on me, looking to steal what I have."

"That's what they wanted to do. I thought we'd just beg some food off you."

The boy's face brightened in the firelight. "Maybe we could travel together? Help each other out?"

"I'm not going in your direction."

Jason got up to inspect the men's rifles. There was a bolt-action 30.06, a lever-action 30-30 and a bolt-action .22. It was not a powerful collection of weapons.

"Which one's yours?"

The boy pointed to the .22.

"You got rounds for it?"

The boy nodded. "Maybe forty in my knapsack."

"What else is in your pack?"

"Sleeping bag and ground cloth, change of clothes, pot, and canteen." He paused to stare into the fire. "Don't have much, really."

Jason went over to the boy. "What's your name?"

"Chuck. Chuck Bigger."

"Well Chuck Bigger, I'm going to tell you a few things and you need to listen carefully. Your life will depend on it."

The boy nodded, his wide-open eyes, reflecting the firelight.

"We're both going to leave here. Can't stay with the dead bodies. They'll attract animals. I'm going to let you live. You're going to head north and I'm going south. If I see you after we separate, I'll kill you." Jason leaned closer to the boy. "Don't think I'm bluffing. I just killed both of your friends. I've killed more men that you can count on your fingers. If you mess up the chance I'm giving you and come back at me, you'll die like these two and be left for the animals."

Chuck was now shaking.

"Do you understand me?"

The boy nodded rapidly, too afraid to speak.

"Now here's the other thing I want to tell you. If you go to Hillsboro, you'll find a town that's run by civilians. I won't give you a recommendation. You'll have to convince them to let you in on your own. But if you're willing to work and contribute, you can find a place there and you won't have to be on the road where you'll likely get yourself killed."

Jason stood up. He unloaded the rifles and threw the 30.06 and 30-30 into the brush. After that, he pulled a second MRE out of his pack and started heating it. He untied Chuck and told him to eat.

After eating, Jason retied Chuck's hands, packed up his gear and then yanked the boy upright. He buried his campfire under dirt and then set out through the dark woods pushing Chuck ahead of him.

When they got back to the interstate, Jason untied the boy. He handed him his empty rifle. "Now, you remember what I told you?"

Chuck nodded.

"Okay. The first thing is you leave," Jason said, pointing north. "And you don't come back."

"You don't have to worry. I'm thankful you didn't shoot me. I'll go to Hillsboro and try to get in."

"You do that. If you make it, you'll be one of the lucky ones. I killed a couple of young men like you that had made bad choices. I have no problem killing bad people. People who threaten me or my family. But if you don't pose a threat, I'll leave you alone, even if I think you're not going in the right direction." He paused for a moment. "You understand what I'm saying to you?"

The young man nodded.

"Good. Make good choices and maybe you won't wind up like those two." He pointed back to the woods from which they emerged. "But keep this in mind as well. You'll have to work in Hillsboro. It isn't a place for the lazy or those who want to cheat."

Jason waved him off and watched him walk away. *Already the killing begins*. Jason felt a weight come over him. The cycle of killing—having to kill—which never seemed to end, was a heaviness that burdened him. It felt like an ominous start to his mission.

When the boy was out of sight, Jason turned and headed south. *Looks like I'm in for a night of walking*, he thought.

As he went along, his mind drifted back to the encounter that precipitated his current trek; a surprise visit from some not very upright citizens of Charlotte.

Chapter 2

Kevin Cameron studied the two men sitting in Steve Warner's office. Steve had been elected to a full term as mayor of Hillsboro after filling in when Jason Richards had resigned the position. He had called Kevin to attend the meeting. Kevin was in charge of the militia, which had been separated from the town's police. Kevin worked directly under the authority of the mayor. His militia was in charge of defending the city against external threats.

"This is Joe Nicoletti," Steve said, pointing to a thin man with dark, slicked back hair. A scar ran down over his left eye which gave his face a sinister, unbalanced look even when he smiled, as he was doing now.

"And this is Alex Jasco," Steve continued. He gestured to the man sitting next to Nicoletti. He was a large man, well over six feet tall and weighing over two hundred pounds.

"He goes by the nickname, 'Ears'," Joe said.

Kevin sat quietly, not saying anything. Nicoletti looked like the hood he probably was. Kevin had seen enough of his type with Stansky during his reign in Hillsboro. Jasco, or Ears, looked like a bodyguard, muscle for someone in power, Nicoletti in this case. *Take more than one 9mm bullet to stop that guy.* He had the type of body that a .45 was made for.

"Why Ears?"

Kevin directed his question to the man. He made the chair he was sitting in look small. That didn't seem to make him uncomfortable, though. He was used to being oversized and seemed untroubled with his effect on others. He was imposing, no doubt, but Nicoletti was the one to worry about. Kevin was afraid he was not bringing good news to the town.

Ears just smiled and pointed to his two appendages, scarred by years of contact, probably from boxing.

"Mr. Nicoletti has traveled here from Charlotte," Steve said. "I asked him to wait until you could join me to hear what brought him all the way to our town." Steve nodded to Nicoletti to begin.

The man shifted forward in his chair. "Mr. Tagliani sent me here to talk with you about some overdue payments we're owed. Joe Stansky, who I assume you know, stopped paying the money he owed to Mr. Tagliani two years ago and Mr. Tagliani wants to make his account current."

Here it is, Kevin thought. *We knew this day might come. Now we've got another challenge to deal with*. He sat quietly. Steve would have to take the lead as mayor. He was there to offer his support as well as his insights *after* these men had departed.

"And who is Mr. Tagliani?" Steve asked.

"Al Tagliani," Nicoletti relied. "He's in charge of Charlotte."

"And why would Joe Stansky be paying Mr. Tagliani?"

"We had a business arrangement. Stansky paid Mr. Tagliani for the right to operate in Hillsboro on his own. Think of it as a franchise fee."

Nicoletti turned as Kevin gave out a short laugh.

"It was a legitimate business arrangement," Nicoletti said. "But he stopped making payments after the power went out."

"What you say brings so many questions to mind," Steve said. "Let me start by first asking why is this the town's problem?"

"We know that the town played a role, shall we say, in closing down Stansky's operations. That made it impossible for him to bring his account current with us. So, you inherit the account."

Steve continued. "Why'd Tagliani wait more than two years to inquire about his fee, as you call it?"

Joe smiled. It was a smile that failed to soften the menace in his face. "As you know, things got crazy after the power went out. Charlotte was a war zone. The cops were overwhelmed by local gangs and people were starving, attacking one another...it was chaos. Mr. Tagliani had to get things under control."

"Is he head of the police?" Steve asked. He figured he knew the answer but wanted to hear it from Nicoletti.

Now the big guy, Ears, laughed.

"Let's say," Nicoletti replied with his smile still in place, "that he worked closely with the police. After desertions from the ranks and officers getting killed, the police weren't able to deal with the anarchy. Mr. Tagliani couldn't let the local gang bangers just ruin the city, kill anyone in their way. We had to go out there and bust 'em up, put them in their place. Ears here can tell you some stories. We all could. There wasn't no time to worry about Stansky. But after we got things under control Mr. Tagliani decided it was time to call in the debt."

"So, you helped the police get the city under control. Where was the National Guard in all this?"

"They helped, but in the end, they couldn't do what we could."

"They just stepped aside and let you handle things?" Kevin asked.

"They didn't have much choice. So many of their members left and headed home to protect their families, they didn't have the manpower, so we took over."

"That's some story," Steve said. "This guy, Tagliani, runs the city now?"

"We keep things nice and calm," Nicoletti responded.

"You do know Stansky's dead?" Steve asked.

"We heard."

"That means he's not around to pay whatever it is you say he owes you."

"Like I said, you inherit his debt. And we understand Hillsboro has his assets."

"We have the resources that he was stockpiling for the city. They belong to the city."

"But the fee wasn't paid. The fee don't go away, even if Stansky ain't around. It has to be paid."

Steve looked nervous. Kevin could see he was unsure of what direction to take the conversation.

"What was this 'fee' you talk about for? You called it a 'franchise fee'."

"Kind a like that. He paid us a fee for the right to run his operations here in Hillsboro. His nightclubs."

"He was running a criminal enterprise in town," Steve said.

Nicoletti shrugged. "Don't know nothing about that. He was paying us to run his clubs. As far as we were concerned, they were legitimate. If he broke the law here, we weren't part of it."

"Gambling, prostitution, extortion, protection, that's what he was involved in. You'd be familiar with such activities, wouldn't you?" Steve responded.

"We run legitimate businesses. We gave Mr. Stansky a license to operate bars and nightclubs here in town. He made money from them. The city confiscated his assets, so the city needs to pay us the money."

Steve just sat there, staring at Nicoletti who stared right back at him.

Now we have a macho stare-down? Kevin thought.

Finally, Steve rose. He went over to a cabinet behind his desk and took out a bottle of Jack Daniels, along with two glasses. He brought them back to his desk and poured a couple of fingers in each glass.

"I need to discuss a couple of things with my associate here. Please, enjoy some of this increasingly rare bottled whiskey while we talk about this situation. Make yourselves comfortable. We'll be just a few minutes."

He headed for the door with Kevin following.

Chapter 3

W hat the hell do I do?" Steve asked when the two men had left the office.

"This comes from everyone thinking we're resource rich," Kevin said "That's what Knoxville thought when they tried to shake us down. It doesn't surprise me that Charlotte would be aware of that information. Seems as though Stansky paid money to operate in Tagliani's territory. It really is like a franchise fee. And it sounds like we're dealing with the Charlotte mob, the mafia."

"Then their request is illegal. We don't have to consider it," Steve said.

"Of course it's illegal. But that doesn't mean it will go away. Knoxville didn't go away and their request was just as illegitimate. Remember we had to fight them off."

Kevin thought for a moment, then continued. "The question is, does this Tagliani actually run Charlotte? It's a big city. Could he really get it all under his control? Knoxville was dangerous partly because the man we were dealing with ran the whole city and could use all of its assets," Kevin said.

"How could he get control over such a large city?"

"Who knows? We heard there was a lot of chaos down there. If his mob was large enough, organized enough, they could have cornered a lot of weapons and coopted the police while taking down the smaller gangs. A larger version of what Stansky did here. What you need to do is buy us some time until we can figure this out."

Steve opened the door and the two men went back into his office.

"I still have a lot of questions about your request," Steve began. "First does Mr. Tagliani run the city? Is this a request from the Charlotte government or is it an individual request from Tagliani? And I'm still not convinced we're responsible for Stansky's fee as you call it.

"Stansky was a criminal, broke our laws, and tried to take over the town," Steve continued. "He was killed in an operation that removed him from power. If he hadn't been killed, he would have been either imprisoned for a long time or executed. His assets were legitimately forfeited to the government—seized if you will." He smiled, "I'm sure you're familiar with government seizures."

Nicoletti didn't smile. His eyes narrowed. "You got a lot of questions. What you got to understand is that if you don't want trouble with Mr. Tagliani, you need to pay what is owed."

"For the record," Kevin asked, "how much are we talking about?"

"Five hundred grand."

"If it's money you want, I can probably arrange to pull that amount out of the local bank vaults."

"I'm not a fool," Nicoletti said. "Paper money is worthless. We'll need our payment in gold or ammunition or fuel."

Kevin spoke up. "Just so we understand one another, Tagliani is the Charlotte mafia boss, isn't he? I can look it up in our police records and probably confirm the fact. This request is to pay off the mob."

Nicoletti looked at Kevin with a slight smile on his face.

"I'll take that as a 'yes'."

"I can't agree to anything at this point," Steve said. "We have a civilian government, with a city council. Your request has to go before the council to see how they want to respond. I'm going to have to tell them that it's not an official request from the city, but it comes from a mob boss. That probably won't help."

"You can tell them that it comes from the city. Mr. Tagliani is in charge since getting everything under control. He has support from the feds as well."

Steve looked surprised. "You want to clarify?"

"It is what I said. No clarification needed." Nicoletti gave Steve a hard stare.

Kevin could see Steve was taken aback. "I...I can't get you an answer for some time. I'll need to get the council together and they may take days to discuss this. Then, if we agree, it will take some time to put together that kind of payment."

"We could send a message back with our decision," Kevin said.

"You give us some gas to drive back and I'll report to Mr. Tagliani that you'll be in touch with us."

"Give us two weeks," Steve said. "With travel being what it is."

"Two weeks. That's it."

"But we're going to need more time to arrange any payment, if that is what the city agrees to. Plus, there is the issue of figuring out how your demand translates into goods," Steve said.

"We'll work on the rest, just let us know you're gonna pay the fee."

Chapter 4

When dawn came, Jason headed off the interstate and into the woods. He'd been walking all night since turning the boy loose, so he wanted to rest for a few hours before going on. He put an MRE in a pot and activated the flameless heater which he then put in the same pot. After covering it, he waited for ten minutes and the meal was hot and ready.

Once he had eaten, he lay back and closed his eyes. He slept lightly, his ears constantly investigating the sounds of the forest. After a fitful couple of hours, he felt more rested and decided to start walking again. He'd sleep later that night.

He was approaching State Route 74. The road led east, joining Interstate 84 which ran through Gastonia and into Charlotte. He would be approaching the city from the west.

Route 74, also a divided, four-lane roadway, ran just to the north of Columbus. Jason considered checking out the town. It was a county seat and he wondered if it was empty. The range of possibilities intrigued him.

He was two days out from Charlotte. With his aggressive pace, the trip was only going to take a total of four days to complete. After two days of walking, his body had adjusted to life on the move. *Better than sitting at a desk*. He had enough rations, even after giving the young man a meal. He wondered about his generosity. *Trying to make up for all the people you killed?* He rolled that thought around his mind as he strode along. It was fall and the days were cool and crisp. The nights had begun to get colder as well and he was glad he had brought a thermal blanket with him.

Curiosity overcame his caution and Jason decided to check out Columbus. Information about what was going on in smaller towns could be invaluable. *Better to know more than less*. He didn't want to arrive at Charlotte in the daytime, so a short side trip wouldn't really slow him down.

As Jason recalled the town was very small, less than 1500 people, even though it was a county seat. There was a main street with angled parking for the small businesses that had served the community. He wondered if anything survived the breakdown after the EMP attack.

Jason left the highway and walked south towards the main road through town. He'd walk the length of the main street and then swing back up to Route 74 at the other end of the downtown. He switched to high alert as he approached the main road, and, turning left, started down the street. Nothing stirred. As Jason slowly walked along, he scanned the street and buildings, looking for any signs of activity. It was all still.

He went up to the courthouse. The front door was ajar so he stepped inside. The darkness caught him off guard and he stood still waiting for his eyes to adjust. *Used to happen quicker*, he thought. When he could see in the gloom, he started moving around the main floor. There was a lot of paper strewn about underfoot. Opening a few doors revealed offices left in disarray with desks and file cabinets opened, their contents scattered. The court rooms were empty. They showed evidence of people having camped there, but nothing indicated any recent activity.

There seemed to be nothing to be gained by a thorough search so he headed back to the front door and stepped outside. The sun blinded him for a moment after the dark of the courthouse. He switched his M4 carbine from his shoulder to hang it across in front of him. From there he could raise it to fire with a minimal amount of movement.

He started back down the main street. A few cars were sitting abandoned in the street and in the angled parking slots. Small businesses had their doors broken open; their windows shattered. Jason didn't have to look inside. He knew they had been looted clean.

It was beginning to look like a useless side excursion. *At least I can get back to the highway easily*. The emptiness brought back an oppressive feeling, one of loss and destruction. It was so different from the attitude of recovery and hope that pervaded Hillsboro. It reminded Jason of his first walk through Clifton Furnace, seeing the devastation Big Jacks and his formidable outlaw gang had wreaked upon the small town after the EMP attack. *At least there aren't any body parts scattered around*.

Then he saw it. Someone ducking down a side street, momentarily exposed as they ran out from behind an abandoned car. Jason stopped. Two more bodies flitted past the opening, catching his eye. With everything so still, any movement stood out, grabbing the eye's full attention. Jason stopped. Had they seen him? Probably. That's why they were running. He decided to investigate.

He ran towards the intersection. When he got there, no one was in sight. Jason headed down the side street in the direction the figures had gone. He held his carbine at low ready, scanning the sides of the road, checking potential ambush sites. Up ahead there was a patch of woods. A trail disappeared into it. *Probably leads to the highway. A shortcut*.

He entered the woods and started down the trail. Up ahead he could hear branches snapping, the general sounds of someone crashing through brush. Jason quickened his pace. Where the woods ended, there was a low bank, about seven feet high, rising to the highway. Jason scrambled up the bank and carefully looked over the edge. He could see figures to his right, running east.

He started down the road after them. Now he could see there were four in the group, two adults and two children. *A family.*

Chapter 5

The man looked back over his shoulder at Jason as he hurried the female and two children along. The kids were obviously having difficulty in moving quickly, especially the younger one. The woman, Jason could see, was hampered by the large bag she was carrying.

Jason closed the distance between them. Finally, the man halted partly behind an abandoned car and took out a pistol. He pointed it at Jason and called out to him to stop. Jason stepped behind the hood of an abandoned car and held up his hands. The man was far enough away that Jason estimated a shot would miss. He could drop for cover if the situation escalated.

"I mean no harm. I just want to talk to you," Jason called out.

"You chased after us," the man said.

"That's because I want to talk to you. I don't want anything from you."

"What are you doing out here? You're a bandit, aren't you?"

"No. I'm going to Charlotte." Jason thought for a moment. "I'm thinking you are as well. We could walk together."

"We don't need your company. And I'd feel safer without you around."

Jason stood there, trying to not look threatening even with his M4 slung across his chest.

"Well that's a problem since we're going the same way. I'm sure you don't want to keep looking over your shoulder, and *I* certainly don't want to do that." He tried to sound calm. "I'm going to unsling my rifle. I'll do it slowly and with my left hand. Then I'll put it over my shoulder, out of the way. That might help everyone relax a bit."

"Don't try anything tricky," the man said.

Jason slowly moved his M4 and put it over his shoulder, the weapon now behind his left arm.

"I'd like to approach you so we don't have to shout."

"Not too close."

"Just enough that we can talk normally."

When Jason was within twenty paces of the man he said, "That's far enough."

Jason sat down on the ground, slipping off his rifle and backpack. He made sure to sit close to a car in case he needed to duck for cover.

"Why don't you sit down?" he asked.

"I'll stand."

"Suit yourself. My name's Jason Richards. What's yours?"

"Ernie Tillerman. This is Ruth," he said pointing to his wife.

Jason nodded. There was a boy who looked to be about ten, and a girl a couple of years older.

"Where are you coming from?" Jason asked.

"Why do you want to know?"

"Just curious. More information is always better than less."

"We've come from Knoxville if it's so important for you to know."

"Why didn't you stop at Hillsboro? Why head all the way to Charlotte?"

"Hillsboro? They attacked us, almost killed the Chairman. I doubt they'd welcome anyone from Knoxville. We figured they see us as the enemy."

"Are you?"

The man shook his head. "But we're from the town that Hillsboro fought."

The man's wife was standing behind him with the kids tucked under her arms. Their faces were gaunt with tired looking, hollow eyes. The strain of their journey seemed to be showing.

"How long have you been on the road?"

"Ten days."

"You got any food left?"

The man shook his head. "Very little."

"Well you're in luck. I've got some food I can share with you," he paused, then added, "and you're only two days out from Charlotte. But why pick Charlotte?"

"We heard it's under control. The other cities we don't know about."

"But why leave in the first place?"

The man hesitated. His wife put her arm on his shoulder and whispered in his ear.

"Not sure I should tell you."

"You kill someone? Get on the wrong side of the Chairman?"

"Something like that. Not kill anyone, but got in some trouble."

"Stealing?"

"No," the man said, sounding insulted. "I don't do things like that."

"Okay," Jason said. "I don't mean to pry. I'm glad you're not a thief. People are pretty hard on thieves and outlaws these days. That a .38?" he asked looking at the man's revolver.

"It is."

"How many rounds to you have left for it?"

"Enough," came the reply.

"It only takes one to kill a man. I can see from here the chambers are all filled. You have any rounds in reserve?"

"Some. I'm not telling you."

Jason looked at the children. They appeared traumatized as well as fatigued. He felt a twinge of pity for them. "Would you like something to eat? I have a couple of MRE meals I can share since we're almost to Charlotte."

That perked the kids up. Ruth spoke to her husband.

"The kids could use something to eat. We're fine," Ernie said. He paused for moment. Their names are Jennifer and Tommy.

"Great." Jason started to get up. The man's body posture went on full alert. Jason paused. "I hope you're not going to shoot me. I'm going to leave my rifle on the ground here. But I need to get up to get the MREs and heat them." He glanced from Ernie to Ruth. "Do you have any eating utensils?"

Ernie nodded.

Everyone sat at the side of the road. Ernie put his pistol in his belt and when MREs were heated, Jason handed them to the kids. They barely waited for them to cool before they tore into the food, as Jason offered Ernie and Ruth some venison jerky.

"Thank you for the meal. That's going to help them," Ruth said when the kids had finished eating.

"You're welcome," Jason replied. "Do you know what you're heading into in Charlotte?"

Ernie shook his head. "We know it's under control, people can work and eat, survive, get their lives back together."

"It seems to be run by a mafia boss—a gangster."

Concern started to spread over Ruth's face.

"I'm not trying to discourage you. I just want you to know what you're getting into. I'd hide the gun or, if you can't, dump it before you get to town. They probably won't let you in with it." He leaned closer to the parents. "Can I speak to you in private?"

Ruth told the kids to go back to the highway and watch their gear while the grownups talked. They both whined a bit but did as their mother instructed.

"Ernie, you look like you can handle yourself and maybe that's what got you into trouble. I don't want to panic you, but I want to tell you to be careful. Don't let anyone separate your family. And keep you daughter close to you. She's getting to that age where she might attract the attention of grown men."

"Oh no," Ruth said, putting her hand to her mouth. "You aren't suggesting…"

"I'm only saying to be cautious. I've seen some very bad things since the EMP attack. I have no idea how this mob boss might run Charlotte. I'd keep Jennifer as covered up and unkempt as you can. This is not the environment to have her begin showing off her growing femininity. The scruffier the better would be my approach…for both kids."

"We'll be careful," Ernie said in a grave voice. Jason could see this new sense of threat had unnerved both he and his wife.

"I have a little familiarity with Hillsboro, Jason said. "I think they'd welcome you there. From what I hear, they don't hold any grudge against any citizens. They just had a dispute with the Chairman and his men. Sounds like you did as well."

"How far would it be?" Ernie asked. "We're so close to Charlotte and I don't think the kids have the strength for a much longer trek."

"Probably take you four days of hiking. Definitely longer than going to Charlotte. It's just that Charlotte is a greater unknown."

"How do you know so much about Hillsboro? Are you from there?" Ruth asked.

Jason paused for a moment. *Best to not let anyone know.* "No, but I met some people that were."

"And why are you going to Charlotte? You're warning us to not go there, so why are you?"

Jason looked away, across the highway. "Let's just say I have some business in Charlotte."

"Don't want to talk about it?"

"Not important for you to know," Jason thought for a moment. "Probably better for you to not know."

"That sound mysterious...and threatening."

Jason shrugged. "I wouldn't read too much into me being private. It's just how I am."

"But you ask a lot of questions, Ernie said.

"That's for important information, how things are on the road. And remember, I told you something about Charlotte you didn't know, so now you're more informed."

"I appreciate that," Ernie said, "but I think we still have to go there. If it's not a good place, then we'll gather some supplies and strike out again. Maybe Wilmington. I hear there's a military installation there."

Jason sighed. "Just be careful."

After packing up, they started hiking along the highway, together and more relaxed. When Jason inquired about camping Ernie said they just slept in cars.

"That would worry me," Jason said. "I go into the woods where no one can sneak up on me."

"We're worried about the wolves. We've heard them at night. Inside a car it's safer," Ernie said.

"From animal predators, but not from human ones.

That evening, after the family picked out their vehicles for the night, Jason walked off the highway into a patch of woods. It was a small stand, so he wouldn't be making fire. Still, it felt better than sleeping on the highway. He'd reconnect with the family the next morning.

Chapter 6

That night as he lay back under his tarp, Jason thought about his journey and the events that led up to it. He had been happy enough after fending off the Knoxville threat. There was blowback, as he expected, from some elements on the city council, but no one could dispute the fact that Knoxville had presented a significant threat with the weapons they had tried to bring against Hillsboro. Further, no one could dispute the fact that the tactics used by Jason and Kevin had effectively neutralized the threat, sending the Knoxville force back in defeat.

After that struggle, Jason had settled back into a comfortable routine. He had involved himself, not in the politics of the city, but in training people how to shoot. It was a program set up by the mayor and Kevin, as head of the city's defenses. Jason enjoyed training others how to use and care for weapons. He could see the empowering effect it had on people to understand the different arms and how they could be used to defend themselves. Most citizens understood that the world outside their city was still dangerous. But instead of fearing it, they now felt prepared to deal with that danger should it ever threaten them.

Regionally, there was increased cooperation with a few surrounding towns. The story of Knoxville had convinced other municipalities that coordinating their defenses only strengthened them. There was an air of hopefulness in

Hillsboro. A feeling that, even if the country was still in a state of anarchy, they were getting their lives back together. Electricity had returned, however limited. And with electricity, came refrigeration improving food storage. Meats and vegetables could now be more easily preserved for leaner times. The local chemistry teachers were hard at work, making anesthetics which was taking the terror out of certain medical and dental procedures.

Then Joe Nicoletti had shown up.

After Joe's visit Steve had called a special meeting of the town council. He and Kevin related Nicoletti's demands. Jason had attended the meeting along with Charlie Cook, the former Chief of Police, and other town officials.

"Seems like we have another attempt at extortion facing us," Steve said after recounting his meeting with Nicoletti.

There was silence around the dais as the council members digested the news. Jason thought it odd to have politicians struck dumb. They usually weren't at a loss for words. *But these aren't professional politicians, thank God.*

Finally, one of the council members, Bob Jackson, spoke up. "We have to be guided by our previous experience. In that situation, our mayor properly claimed that we needed a treaty with Knoxville before we could consider their arrest warrants. We offered to deal with the city in a proper, legal fashion."

"And that didn't work so well," Raymond Culver said.

Bob looked annoyed but didn't respond.

Les Hammond, the current Chief of Police and council, member spoke up. "That example could be helpful, but this situation is a bit different. They're not presenting us with a legal document, for which we could offer a legal rebuttal or response. We're being told we need to pay a fee that was owed by Stansky. A fee for the right to operate a criminal enterprise." He paused to let the fact sink in. "I don't know how we make a treaty to deal with that."

"Again, why don't we just pay this demand and be done with it?" Raymond asked. "Why do we look to endanger ourselves? Is it worth creating another conflict?"

Steve responded. "The amount of a half million dollars in gold, ammunition and fuel is significant. I'm not sure we have those resources to spare. And who do you think will determine how to work out the conversion?"

"I still want us to consider the payment alternative...this time seriously," Raymond said. "The last time we came up with all sorts of rationalizations as to why we shouldn't pay Knoxville off and just go about our own business. And," he said pointing his finger at Steve, "that decision led to a lot of bloodshed."

"Duly noted," Steve said. He looked around to see if there were other comments, questions or points to be made.

Jason raised his hand. Since he was not on the council, he needed permission to speak. Steve recognized him and he rose.

"We don't know much about what is going on in Charlotte," Jason said. "We don't know if this mafia boss is in charge of the whole town. There's word of a FEMA presence there. Is there a civilian or federal governing force? Maybe this guy, Tagliani, is not the central authority. Steve, you said Nicoletti was a bit evasive when he was asked that question. Maybe there are others in charge and we can appeal to them to intervene."

"What are you suggesting?" Steve asked.

"That we send someone to find out what's going on. We have some time before they expect an answer. More information is always better than less. We preserve all of our options while we gather some intel."

"I'd like to hear what our options are other than paying this demand," Raymond said. "I'm concerned about the alternatives some of us might suggest." He looked pointedly at Jason.

"The floor is open to hear possible options," Steve said.

"I say we tell Nicoletti to pound sand," Bob Jackson said. "What are they going to do? Send tanks? I never heard of the mafia having tanks."

There was the titter of laughter around the room.

"You're suggesting we open ourselves up to some kind of retaliation, even as you make light of it," Raymond said. "But it could come in many forms. The problem is you...we...don't know what form it could take. And I doubt our refusal would be met with acquiescence."

"Let's just get our options on the table for now. We can debate them later," Steve said.

Janet Morgan, who ran the hospital, spoke up. "We have two basic options with numerous variations inside of them. First, we can pay the demand, maybe negotiating the amount, maybe not. Second, we can refuse to pay and risk whatever response might come from that decision. It's a binary situation we face. I have to agree with Jason. We could use more information before we make one of those choices."

"Who would we send?" another council member asked.

"We can't just have someone walk into town asking 'who's in charge?'" Bob Jackson said.

"Send someone undercover?" Les Hammond asked.

"That might be best," Dr. Morgan replied.

"Here we go again," Raymond said. "This will turn into another fiasco with violence following."

"Ray," Steve said, "it doesn't help for you to make dire predictions based on nothing in particular. Let's consider actual steps to deal with this."

"Mr. Mayor," Raymond said, "I just want us to look ahead and not let things get off track and then we're forced into some sort of conflict we could have avoided."

"Let's send someone undercover to find out what the power structure is in Charlotte," Bob said.

"Are you offering that as a proposal to vote on?"

"I am."

"Discussion on the proposal?" Steve asked.

There were a few comments offered after which the proposal passed by a vote of seven to two.

"Now who do we send?" Steve asked.

"I propose that the decision be left to the mayor and our militia commander," Dr. Morgan said. "The mayor can handle an operational detail after we have approved an operation. He and the militia commander can work that out."

There was some argument about that, but no one could challenge the process Dr. Morgan proposed. It fit the structure they had established after the Knoxville incident.

Later that evening, Steve sat in his office with Kevin. Jason had joined them at his own insistence.

"Undercover. That's an interesting idea that Bob Jackson proposed," Steve said. "I wonder if we have any undercover agents in town."

"Probably not like a Serpico," Kevin replied.

Jason sat looking thoughtful.

"What do you think about this?" Steve asked, looking over at Jason.

"Dr. Morgan is correct. We need more information. This probably isn't an empty threat...or demand. But how dangerous it is remains to be seen."

"Any thoughts about who to send?" Kevin asked.

"I do." Jason paused looking at both men. "We need to send someone well versed in dealing with bad people, hard people. The mob is not a band of amateur outlaws generated by the EMP attack. These are professional sociopaths, people who don't have a social conscience. Outside of family or their mob compatriots, anyone is fair game. Someone not familiar with their ruthlessness, their willingness to operate outside the bounds of decency, could be overwhelmed."

"Does someone have to be that familiar with them? Get that close?" Steve asked.

"Possibly. How else can we figure out who has the power? Someone just can't walk in and say they want to observe the power relationships in the city—it's hierarchy of authority and control. Someone has to insinuate themselves into the system and find out from the inside." He looked at both men. "That won't be easy."

"So...who?" Kevin asked.

"Me."

The two men looked at Jason in surprise.

"Why you?" Steve finally asked.

"For the reasons I just mentioned. I'm probably the one that can best understand these men. I'm experienced and tough enough to fit in, to present a narrative that they'll buy." He paused for a moment. "I don't revel in this, but I'm certainly skilled enough at killing to be considered useful to them."

"But you have a two-year old. This is going to be dangerous," Kevin said.

"Yes, and you have a pregnant wife, so you shouldn't go. Most of the possible candidates wouldn't come across as believable bad guys to be considered by the mob. Our local police are not going to be up to the task. It'll be hard for them to disguise their law enforcement background. I don't think we have any real undercover types on our local force."

"And you can come across as a bad guy? You can fit in?" Steve asked.

"When I have to. Let's face it, I've killed a lot of people since the EMP attack. More than I care to dwell on. It has an effect. I also killed people in Iraq as a sniper. Now Gibbs could have done this. He's a hard man. But he's gone and, being a black man, he'd have had trouble being accepted by the mob hierarchy. That's just a fact."

"This isn't going to go over well with Anne," Kevin said.

"You're right. But I don't know who else we can send. For me it's ultimately about defending my family, and my tribe."

Jason broke off his reverie. *Don't get all melancholy, you volunteered for this mission.* He sat up and thought about building a small fire. The night was cold.

The painful part had been talking to Anne. She had not reacted well to the news. She reminded him in strong terms that he had responsibilities: a duty to his son, a duty to his wife, and a duty to his step-daughters. She didn't see his sense of duty to Hillsboro as being on par with those three things. Jason's protestations failed to sway her.

If life became too difficult in Hillsboro, they could always go back to the valley, she pointed out. Just let the world around them go to hell. The valley was well hidden, they could farm it again like they did before they relocated to Hillsboro. It stood as a refuge from the complications that seemed to spring up around them in town.

As to what Catherine, their daughter, and Kevin, her husband, might do if things got worse, Anne didn't have a good answer. In the end she gave in, more in realization that she couldn't dissuade her husband, and, that to insist he not do what he saw as his duty, would only poison him and possibly their relationship.

Let it go, Jason brought himself back to the present. *You're on the quest now. That's what you have to focus on.*

What Jason had not told anyone was that he had brought his M110 sniper rifle along. If the situation called for it, he would use it. *Cut off the head and the body dies.* It's what had worked before in so many encounters he'd experienced. He wanted that option available to him even if it wasn't part of his mandate from the city.

He settled back down in under his tarp and began to relax. He listened to the night sounds, his ears probing, searching for anything unusual. Not too far off he heard coyotes begin to bark and howl. He didn't register them as a threat but guessed Ernie and his family were happy to be crammed into suitable cars. *I'd rather stretch out here.*

The next day Jason and the family walked along, making small conversation in between long silences. Jason gave them some purification tablets so they could refill their water bottles. The boy showed interest in Jason and his rifle. He asked how the weapons worked and if he had killed anyone. The girl kept her distance. She seemed shy, which Jason thought was a good thing considering what they were about to enter into.

That night they sat around a small fire Jason had prepared well away from the road.

"Tomorrow we'll reach Gastonia. It will get more dangerous at that point," Jason said.

"Why is that?" Ruth asked.

"More people. More possibilities to run into bad ones. You've been traveling through countryside with mostly small towns. I'll bet most of them were abandoned and, if not, the people shied away from you. This could be different."

"So how do we navigate through that?"

"If you like, I'll continue with you. I can provide some protection. Just seeing my rifle may dissuade any from trying to rob you...or worse." He looked at Ernie. "But we have to separate sometime before we cross the Catawba River, before we get to whatever barriers Charlotte has set up."

"I thought you were going to Charlotte?" Ernie said.

"I am, but not the way you are." Jason said no more and Ernie didn't ask. Jason continued, "We don't know how far out Charlotte has set up their barriers or checkpoints, but you'll run into them if you travel on the main route. After Gastonia, you should walk along I85. I'm sure they'll have a checkpoint set up there."

"We appreciate your help," Ernie said. "I'm sorry I was so suspicious when we encountered you."

"You did the right thing." Jason looked at the kids who were sitting across from him. Tom was messing about with the fire, poking at it and sticking more wood into it. "Don't make it too large," Jason told him.

The boy looked over at him with a serious expression on his face. "Were you in the Boy Scouts? You know a lot about camping."

Jason smiled. "I was in the army. We did a lot of camping there."

"I'd like to be in the army when I grow up. Camping's fun."

"Well, you may be able to do that. It might be a good profession in the future." Jason felt a surge of enthusiasm at the boy's statement. *We need more of that. There's too much just surviving right now.*

"Are you going to try to keep your revolver?" Jason asked Ernie.

"I'd like to. But I don't want to be caught smuggling it in. If they find it in my pack, they could take it away."

Jason nodded. "It's a big decision, for sure. If you decided to sneak it in, Ruth may be the key. They probably won't search a woman as closely as a man."

"What would you do?" Ruth asked.

"I'm different. I've fought many battles since the EMP attack. Others in the army prior to that, so what I'd do may not be a good plan for you to follow."

Ruth kept looking at him, her face still reflecting her question.

"I'd want to have the gun with me, so I'd find a way to get it in. But I'm not suggesting you do that."

"And you're not going in the normal way because you're bringing your rife, and the pistol you have on your belt in. Are you up to no good?" Ruth asked.

"What I may be up to, why I'm going to Charlotte, are none of your business." Jason leaned forward to focus directly on the two. "You have my offer to help through this last phase of your journey, but there's a tradeoff for that help. You must not mention me to anyone. You came

all this way by yourself. Do you understand? Can you keep
me a secret to yourselves?" He looked from Ruth to Ernie.

Both of them nodded.

"Sure, sure," Ernie said, sounding a bit distressed. "But
that just makes what you're doing seem more suspicious."

"Don't fret about that. We were never together and no
matter what happens, nothing will be connected to you."

Chapter 7

The next day they reached I85 before noon and followed it east towards Gastonia. The interstate ran twelve blocks north of the central downtown. The downtown was populated with local businesses: used car lots, auto repair shops, self-defense studios, restaurants, and a few major banks. They were all closed. Only the town's police department was still functioning.

Jason and the family encountered more people as they walked along the highway. Most gave them careful looks and shied away, seeing that Jason was armed. He thought about Gastonia. What kept it functioning? Was it trading with Charlotte? Did the town provide some service? Perhaps the parks and open areas had been converted to farms in order to provide food, not only for the locals but to sell or trade in Charlotte.

As they passed open areas and athletic fields, Jason's guesses were confirmed. The spaces had been turned into large vegetable plots.

When they were abreast of a giant Walmart fronting the interstate, Jason stopped.

"The bridge is not far ahead and it's a choke point. We're getting too close to possible check points. I'm going to have to leave you here."

"Where're you going?" Ernie asked.

"Not for you to know."

Jason crouched down in front of the kids. "Look, I'm going to leave you now. I need you to both promise me something. I need you to both not talk to anyone about me.

Your parents have agreed to keep me a secret and you need to do that as well. Can you promise?"

Jennifer stared at him wide eyed.

Tom asked him, "Are you on a secret mission?"

Jason nodded. "Yes, in a way. It's very secret."

"For the army?"

"Kind of like that."

"Your secret's safe with me," he declared boldly.

"And you?" Jason asked looking at Jennifer.

She nodded.

"Good. You can talk about it with your mom and dad, but no one else." He got up and turned to Ruth and Ernie. "If you're going to hide that gun, do it now, not after you're in sight of the bridge.

He shook their hands.

"I've got to go."

"Thanks for your help and your advice," Ernie said.

Jason nodded and headed off the interstate and into the woods to the north of the highway.

A sense of relief flowed over him as he entered the woods. He felt more comfortable in the forest than on the highway. The roadways gave him a sense of being exposed which kept him on edge. He worked his way east, following the cover of the trees until he reached the river's edge. With little rain in the last two weeks, the level and flow were down. Thankfully there were woods on the far side that he could disappear into. He'd wait until night to cross. Turning, he went back into the trees. *No fire tonight*.

The evening was dark. Clouds covered the stars. There was a half-moon which gave little light through the thick cover; a perfect night for infiltration. Jason checked his pack to make sure his M110 was secure in its case and sealed. He had used precious plastic to seal his spare clothes and blanket inside his backpack.

With his gear checked, he set out for the river. He would wade as far as possible and then swim, hopefully, only a narrow channel, before returning to wading on the other side. He needed to make sure he didn't get swept down too close to the bridge. At the river's edge, he could see the bridge's outline downstream to his right. A single floodlight shone on the span, powered by a generator he could hear running. As he expected, a checkpoint had been set up there.

The central part of the city, the main downtown, was ringed by an interstate highway. Inside that ring were the high-rise bank buildings competing with one another like grand phallic symbols of corporate pride. There were high-rise, luxury hotels, testimonials to the power and wealth of the city in the pre-EMP days. Also, within the ring were the professional baseball and football stadiums, now probably unused and left to decay.

The city spilled out well beyond that inner ring, but Jason guessed the inner highway acted as another check. One might need a special pass to get inside where he assumed those who ran the city stayed. *First, stash certain gear, then get inside and start the process of gathering intelligence.*

He waded out into the cold water, gasping out loud at the shock of its mid-November temperature. When it reached his chest and the current threaten to pull him off his feet, he began to swim with his pack and M4 carbine strapped to his back. Hard, strong stokes with his feet kicking furiously, slowly pulled him forward. When his boots encountered the bottom, he pushed down, shoving himself along. The intense effort moved him at a snail's pace. He was not very streamlined with his clothes and gear. Soon enough, however, he could walk again without the current pulling him off his feet. He was only a black dot on the black river. Without the moon, there was no chance anyone on the bridge could see him.

As the depth shallowed, Jason crouched and shuffled forward to the bank. On gaining dry land he stayed in a crouch until he reached the cover of the trees. Once inside the woods, he sat down, removed his pack, took off his boots, and emptied them of water. Next, he took off his shirt and pants and squeezed them as dry as he could. He took his jacket out of his backpack and, after getting dressed, put it on to protect from the night's chill.

Jason headed for an industrial warehouse district he knew of northwest of the central downtown. He would set up a hideout there, a place to keep his sniper gear. He moved as quickly as he could, following the patches of woods that interconnected with each other, keeping his exposure minimized. Road crossings were his most exposed moments.

He found a cleared right of way for a pipeline and worked his way along the edge of it. There was a protective buffer of trees that shielded him from the adjacent neighborhood. In spite of the night's cover, he moved quietly, pausing regularly to listen. He had no idea of how many of the nearby houses were occupied, if any, but he wanted to be a ghost, passing through with no notice.

An hour later he reached the interstate that formed the outer ring around Charlotte. It helped define a large urban area that years of development had not completely filled in. Now Jason doubted it would ever be fully developed.

At the edge of the interstate, he sat in the grass to watch and listen. He was shivering from the cold in spite of his coat. His clothes hadn't dried and his feet were going numb. The highway was still; there was no traffic. That was not his worry. His worry was a pair of eyes, to his left or right; eyes he couldn't see, but ones that could see him crossing the open roadway. After waiting five minutes, scanning and listening, Jason moved to his left. Ahead was a tighter cluster of vehicles on the road that had crashed and stalled. A tractor-trailer seemed to have been the genesis of the accident. The vehicles would help cover his movements.

Taking a deep breath, he crouched low and slowly moved to the cars. He threaded his way through them and crossed into the median which was below the level of the roadway to repeat his surveillance of the highway. When he could detect no sound or movement, he crossed the lanes. Upon reaching the far side, he slid down the bank and pushed into the brush and trees.

Once in the trees, he relaxed and picked his way in the dark, using every strip of trees and brush to stay concealed. Shortly, he reached an industrial area. There were multiple warehouses with trucks and trailers parked in rows outside. The stillness of the night gave them a sense of normalcy, as if they were just waiting for the next day's work to begin. Would they would never be started or loaded again? The half-moon now higher in the sky, gave a feeble glow through the cloud cover.

He went into a compound of warehouses. Some of them were large, obviously used as distribution centers. Off to one side were rows of smaller warehouses that had been used for local businesses. Jason prowled through the compound. The doors on all of them were open. They had been well-looted which suited Jason's purpose. He picked an older warehouse. Inside it was ink-black. He felt his way along the walls. Ahead a glimmer of light showed in an inner office. The office had a window which allowed a faint glow of moonlight through the dirty glass. He carefully closed the door, went to the back of the room and sat down against the wall, facing the door and window. He'd rest there until daylight and then hide his gear.

When morning came, Jason stretched his stiff, cold body. He forced himself to move around until he began to feel warmer, ate some of his jerky, and drank some water. Sleeping on concrete floors, even with some worn carpet covering them was not as comfortable as the woods.

He spent twenty minutes exploring the warehouse and finally settled on a mezzanine office with a drop ceiling in place. He pushed aside some tiles and put his two rifles in the ceiling. He would only take his 9mm sidearm into town with him. He was going in cold, with no references established. That meant he had to not only get inside the city, but find a way to get noticed by the mob; to catch their attention in a way that would make them interested in him.

Getting across the next interstate would put him inside that outer perimeter. He'd have to make a connection before he could work his way farther into the inner part of the city, which, he assumed, was where the city's hierarchy was located. Jason put his 9mm in his backpack but kept his knife on his belt. He went back to the office where he'd spent the night and sat back to eat an MRE. It might be the last regular meal he would consume. *Better to cross at night.* He sat back and relaxed. *Rest while you can. There'll soon be more than enough action.*

Chapter 8

That night Jason crossed the interstate and followed a power line south. He could walk along the wooded edge of the cleared right of way, shielded from the streets and buildings. He wanted to get as close to the central city as possible before letting himself get "discovered". Since he had no idea of the power structure of the city, the mob seemed to be the best way in. So, he had to be seen as someone interesting, someone with possibilities they could use.

When he got near a large commercial street, he saw lights. Further in the distance, towards the central downtown he could see the glow of more lights. *They've got power. Enough to light areas at night.* Hillsboro had power from the water mill project, but not enough to squander on lighting up streets at night, allowing businesses and people to continue their activities after the sun went down. Jason stepped out onto the sidewalk and started walking in the direction of downtown.

Even with the lighting, there were few people out on the streets. He stopped at a bar that was open indicating that some form of alcohol was being produced. *Wonder what they use for currency?* He decided to go in and find out. He needed information.

The space was dimly lit with few electric lights. There were a half dozen men sitting at the bar and a few couples at tables. He sat down at the bar.

"What'll you have?" the bartender asked as he came over.

"What do you have?"

"Whiskey, beer and some wine."

"I'm impressed. How long has that been going on?"

"You're new here, aren't you?"

"I guess I can't hide it," Jason said with a smile. "Things have certainly progressed here." He paused for a moment. "How does one pay for all this?"

"We have a local currency, but we also take gold or gems. That's not as easy as just going to a city office to convert what you have into the paper currency."

Jason thought about that for a moment. "So, you have city exchange centers and they set the rates?"

The bartender nodded. "Do you want a drink? And do you have anything to pay for it?"

He seemed to Jason to not be too interested in giving him the background on Charlotte. Jason ordered a beer and a pork sandwich. He pulled some gold pieces from his pocket and laid them on the bar.

"How much of this do you need?"

The bartender hefted the gold, went to an old fashion cash register and grabbed a balance scale from underneath it. He brought it back and weighed some of the pieces and took two of them.

"That'll cover what you ordered." Then he left to pour the beer and pass the sandwich order back to the kitchen.

After getting the beer and sandwich, Jason started eating. The beer was reasonable indicating someone who knew about brewing had produced it. *Electricity and enough grain to make bread and brew beer. Charlotte's doing pretty well.*

As he was eating, one of the men sitting a few places down from him moved up next to Jason. "I think you got ripped off a bit there, friend," he said.

Jason gave him a questioning look.

"Everyone using gold or jewels instead of currency gets taken on the exchange rate. He reached out his hand.

"My name's Harry, what's yours?"

Jason shook his hand. The man looked to be in his late forties or early fifties. He was short and solidly built, with a salt and pepper beard.

"Name's Jason. How bad did I get ripped off?"

"Not too bad. Pete does that with everyone who doesn't have any paper money, especially if you don't know the exchange rate. It's best you get your gold converted."

He pointed to the signboard over the back of the bar.

"The prices are quoted in currency, but Pete can work any exchange to his favor if you don't know what it is."

"Why the focus on paper currency? It's worthless."

"So were dollars actually in the old days...pre-EMP attack. It's just that everyone accepted they had some value. The powers that be want to get us away from barter and back to paper money. It makes trading easier."

"Guess getting ripped off on the exchange is the price I pay for being new. Where do I get this currency?"

"They're called Exchange Stores. You can find them in most neighborhoods. You'll need an ID card to do business with them. You get that when you come into town and register." The man paused. "I take it you haven't registered. How'd you get into town?"

"Just walked in."

"Not through any checkpoint then."

"No. I didn't know I had to use a checkpoint."

"The authorities may not like that. 'Course, if you look like you can pull your weight, contribute, they'll probably overlook that. You got any skills?"

"I'm good at surviving."

Harry smiled. "Where are you from?"

"North of here."

Harry paused to consider Jason's vague response. "What brings you to Charlotte?"

"Survival."

The man nodded.

"You can do that here."

Jason changed the subject. "How does the city generate electricity? They seem to be pretty generous with it."

"We have a coal-fired generation plant that the city brought back on line. It had been offline when the EMP attack occurred, so the generators and transformers weren't damaged. They weren't connected to the grid."

"And there's enough coal?"

"There's enough." Harry frowned. He glanced around him for a moment as if to check on anyone listening in. "All the coal trains stopped running when the EMP attack happened. All those tons of coal are sitting on the tracks. We've been harvesting them."

"But you can't run the town for long on just what's left in the trains."

"Hell if I know. That's above my pay grade." Harry looked around once more. "Whatever you do, be careful of getting on the wrong side of the authorities. You could get sent to a coal gang."

"What's that?"

"Teams that haul the coal to the power plant. It's like a forced labor gang. I've heard a lot of people sent there don't come back."

"So who runs the city?"

Harry shrugged. "I just do my job. I'm not concerned about that."

Jason felt frustrated, but this was a beginning. More information would come.

"What's *your* job?" he asked.

"I've got a garage near here. I work on getting older vehicles running again, trucks and cars. Junkyards are my domain. Old parts are now in demand. The city has taken over the yards. I'm contracted to put parts together to get these old, dead vehicles running. You could say I'm in the resurrection business." He smiled at his well-worn joke.

"Say, where are you staying for the night?" Harry asked.

"Don't know yet. Probably just sleep on the ground."

"I got an extra bed, if you like. I have a house a block from here."

"Thanks for the offer, but I have to ask you, why are you being so nice to me? Most people I've met have been very suspicious of strangers."

The man met Jason's eyes. "You look like an honest guy and I can take care of myself. Besides, what would you steal? I got nothing of value, just a roof over my head and a bed." He thought for a moment and said, "You could steal my extra pair of boots, but you'd risk ending up on the coal gang. I can tell you, that's not worth the risk."

"Sounds like the city's got some law and order established."

"Yeah. It can be pretty harsh, but it works. Most problems are from the few remaining gang members. People who cause trouble get sent away."

"I appreciate your offer for a bed, but I think I'll wander further into town and just sleep outside. I'm used to being under the stars."

Harry shrugged. "Suit yourself. But if you're thinking of going downtown, you can't get into the central city without a special pass."

The man took his beer and moved away. Jason finished his sandwich and beer and left the bar. He'd keep wandering south and see what happened.

In a few blocks he found a secluded place to sleep in a park. Tomorrow he'd try to get closer to the central part of the city. He needed to connect with the authorities, which he guessed were the mafia. And he needed to connect in a way that didn't immediately get him sent to a chain gang which is what the coal gang that Harry mentioned sounded like.

These first steps were tricky to navigate. Catch the eye of the mob, get them interested in him, and then bring him into their structure. This was not going to be easy for an unknown outsider.

Chapter 9

The next evening, when people seemed to be off work, Jason was sitting in a bar close to the central downtown. He put his backpack down at his feet. When his beer came, he paid for it with another of his few remaining pieces of gold. The exchange caught the attention of some of the patrons. It stood out, marking him as a newcomer, and one that might not have arrived in the regular fashion.

There were three men sitting a few seats away from Jason. The largest one watched the exchange with interest. Jason noticed the man and registered him as a possible problem. In a far corner of the bar, he had also noticed a group of four men who seemed to be treated with more deference and attention than the other patrons. *Maybe they're part of the power structure.*

Jason nursed his beer while he thought about how he might approach the men. *Buy them a drink?* That seemed too forward to him.

The man from the first group stepped up close to Jason. The bartender was just putting down another glass of beer in front of him when the man reached over and grabbed it.

"Thanks Ben. Two more for my buddies," he said nodding over to the other two further down the bar.

"That one's for this guy," the bartender said.

"He can wait. You need to take care of your regulars first before you go waiting on strangers. Especially strangers who don't follow the rules."

The bartender, just shrugged and went to pour three more glasses of beer.

"You don't mind waiting a bit, do you?" the man asked leaning close. Jason could smell beer on the man's breath.

He didn't answer and kept looking forward.

"Cat got your tongue? Afraid to talk? We don't like cowards here in town, or people who break the rules. We all got to follow the rules."

"I guess that doesn't include the rules about being polite, especially to strangers." Jason said, still staring straight ahead.

"You trying to be smart with me?" The man's voice started to rise. "How long you been in town? A day? Where the fuck do you come off telling me how to act? This is a neighborhood bar. You don't belong here."

Jason finally turned to the man. He was slouched against the bar. Not the best posture for an attack. Jason set his feet firmly on the floor so he could launch himself forward if he needed to do so.

"The bartender didn't think so."

At that moment Ben came by. He set a glass down in front of Jason and took the other two over to the man's friends. On his way back he told the man, "Leave him alone. I don't want any trouble in here. Just go back to your friends. I got you all your beers."

"Don't tell me what to do. I spend enough of my scrip here. You don't tell me how to behave. If I think this sissy boy should leave, then he should leave."

Jason smiled.

"You think I'm funny? That what you think?"

"It's just that I've been called a lot of things but never that."

"I'll bet you have. But I don't like your attitude. No respect for the citizens of Charlotte. You're an outsider. You want to come in and take someone's job? We got enough mouths to feed. I think you should go."

With that pronouncement he stepped back as if looking to see what effect his words would have. Jason sat there and took a sip of his beer. When he set it down, the man swiped his hand across the bar and flung the glass to the floor behind it.

"Mack," the bartender called out, "get back to your seat. I told you I don't want any trouble in here."

The bar got quiet. Everyone was now looking at Jason and Mack.

"We can settle this outside," Mack said. He turned to Jason. "Can't we? Unless you're too chicken and just want to slink away. You ain't earned the right to sit and drink with the rest of us."

"You're drunk, Mack," the bartender said. "Just leave him alone and go home."

"I'm not ready to go home, but I think this pansy is."

"It's an interesting idea. I have to prove myself by beating you in order to drink in this bar?"

A crooked smile worked its way over Mack's face. Jason studied him. He stood a good three inches taller than Jason and probably outweighed him by thirty pounds. Jason also noted his long reach and meaty hands. *A brawler.* He'd come across them in the army. You didn't want to fight them in any civilized fashion. Certainly not with studio-trained martial arts moves that were only practiced in fake contests, never with full contact. One fought dirty, employing whatever worked with the intent to inflict pain and damage quickly before your opponent could do the same to you.

"I guess we go outside," Jason said.

Mack's smile broadened. He was going to get the fight he was looking for.

Jason hefted his backpack up on the counter. "Will you hold this for me?"

Ben reached over and took the pack.

"I'll be back to claim it, after giving this pussy a beating," Mack said.

Jason stood and motioned for Mack to go ahead. The two other men stood as well and the four of them went outside. A buzz of conversation started around the bar as the men left.

Outside, Jason and Mack squared up. Mack rubbed his hands together and closed them into large fists. Jason did likewise, taking a boxing stance. He had no intention of boxing the man, but wanted him to think so.

Mack advanced, hunched over. Jason let him come. He placed his left foot forward and shifted his weight to his rear foot. Jason knew Mack's longer arms would put him in range before he could land a punch. When he judged Mack was about to punch, Jason swung his right arm forward, twisting his hips and pushing off with his right foot. It was a feint. Mack's left hand went up to block the punch and his torso straightened out.

After pushing off, Jason let his right foot fly, using the push for momentum. The toe of his boot hit Mack between his legs and drove deep into his crotch, crushing one of his testicles. The man screamed and dropped his guard. As he bent over, Jason curled a left into the solar plexus followed by a right to his temple. Mack's head flopped sideways and he dropped to the ground, dazed and in excruciating pain, struggling for breath.

Jason turned in a ready position and looked at Mack's friends. They stared back at him wide-eyed. One of them put his hands up, palms out.

"We don't want any trouble. This is between you and Mack."

"Looks like it's over now. Grab his belt and pull it up. It'll open his diaphragm and help him get his breath back. Then take him home. If any of you come back, I'll break some bones, not just crush your nuts. Got it?"

The men nodded and Jason turned and went back into the bar.

The conversation stopped as he walked in. He went up to the bar and asked Ben for his backpack.

"Where's Mack?" Ben asked.

"His friends are helping him get home. He'll be sore for a few days."

"That was fast," Ben said.

Jason didn't answer. Just then one of the men Jason had noticed sitting in the corner came up.

"Let me buy you a real drink," the man said.

Jason looked at him.

He didn't wait for an answer, but turned to Ben and told him to get out a bottle of Jim Beam. Ben went into a cabinet at the rear of the bar and took out a bottle.

"How do you like it?" the man asked.

"Neat," Jason replied.

"Best way to enjoy it, especially since it's getting so rare. My name's Tony, what's yours?"

"Jason."

"Come on over to my table." Tony nodded towards the corner. All eyes in the bar were watching the exchange.

Jason followed his new acquaintance and sat down after he pulled up an extra chair. He introduced the others sitting at the table.

"This is Rocco, Carlo, and Gino."

Jason nodded to each of the men. They were all dressed in casual dress clothes, not working men's attire. Jason could see they didn't do manual labor. He could also see the bulges of side arms under their jackets. He sat down.

"That was quick," Tony said. "What'd you do out there?"

Jason shrugged. "Took him down. Wanted to do it quick so no one gets too badly hurt."

"He going to be okay?"

"Maybe a crushed nut and a bad headache, but he'll recover. I didn't want to break any bones. That's dangerous in these times."

"Dumbass deserves some broken bones," Carlo said.

Tony eyed Jason. "You know how to take care of yourself. How'd you get into town?"

"I just walked in."

"Didn't go through a checkpoint?"

"That didn't seem like a good idea at the time. Now I find I got to get an ID card in order to use the official exchange."

"Yeah. You probably been getting ripped off giving away gold."

"That's what I've been told."

"What brings you to Charlotte?" Tony asked.

"Looking for work."

"What do you do? You an electrician, mechanic plumber? We don't need sales people, got too many of them. Most of 'em don't know how to do shit and there ain't that much to sell now."

"I'm more in the security field."

"Bouncer or body guard?" Tony asked.

Jason looked directly at him. "Kind of like that. I helped keep things and people in line."

"Oh really." Tony gave Jason a careful look. "Who'd you work for?"

"A guy named the Chairman. He runs Knoxville. You heard of him?"

Tony nodded. "Some. Why'd you leave?"

"He seemed too small time. Plus, he was going to get his ass kicked by Nashville. Hell, Hillsboro embarrassed his general and sent him packing with his tail between his legs."

"So you cut and ran?" Tony arched an eyebrow.

"No. I tried to talk some sense to him. Tell him not to fight with Nashville but instead align with a town that could make a difference, like Charlotte."

"That mean you're here on official business? You represent Knoxville?"

Jason shook his head. "The Chairman didn't want to do that. I think he's afraid of playing second string. When I figured out he wanted to be the big fish in his own little pond, I decided to move on. Since I had talked to him about Charlotte, I figured I'd come and see it for myself."

Tony raised his glass. "Drink up. You deserve it for taking that loudmouth down."

Jason took a sip. It was good whiskey.

Chapter 10

The men talked for another hour, getting something to eat along with more drinks. Jason's altercation had attracted the right attention. Tony and his friends were connected; maybe to the people that made up the real power in Charlotte.

"We might be able to use someone like you," Tony said. "Someone who can handle themselves. 'Course we'll need to know more about you, but right now I want you to meet someone."

"Who would that be?"

"You'll find out when you meet him."

Tony turned to the other three men. "You guys go make your rounds. I'm gonna take Jason to meet Vincent."

Tony and Jason walked through the neighborhood towards the downtown. They were on a main road that ran under the interstate near the football stadium. Before reaching the interstate, Tony led them into an office building along the road.

They stopped at the front door. Tony took Jason's arm. "The man you're gonna meet is my boss. His name is Vincent Bonocchi. Whatever he says goes. If he thinks you're okay, I'll find you some work. If he says no, that's it. You go to an exchange office and get yourself registered. I don't know what they'll want to do about you sneaking in, but you don't get to just wander around town. It don't work like that."

Tony gave Jason a long, hard stare. "You get what I'm saying? You don't act like a wise guy. You don't let Vincent think you cut and run in Knoxville or he won't have anything to do with you."

"You guys are pretty well organized. You run the city?"

"That's the kind of question Vincent don't like. You're an outsider. I wouldn't have said two words to you except you showed you can handle yourself. I figure you might be useful, but it's up to Vincent. This is your one opportunity. Don't fuck it up."

With that he opened the door and headed for the staircase.

They entered an outer office on the third floor. There was a large man sitting at a desk. He was clearly armed with what looked to Jason like a .45 caliber model 1911 pistol.

"Tony, what's up?" the man said.

"Ears." Tony replied. "Got someone here to meet Vincent."

Ears. The man described by Steve and Kevin; the one who came to Hillsboro with Nicoletti. He was as large and solidly built as they had described.

Ears picked up the phone. "Mr. Bonocchi, Tony's here. He's got someone he wants you to meet."

"Go on in," Ears said after hanging up the phone. "Leave the backpack," he said pointing to Jason.

Jason unslung his pack and left it against the wall. Then he followed Tony into the office.

Vincent Bonocchi was dressed in black slacks with a white shirt. His hair was dark, long on the sides and slicked back. He was medium height, about five feet ten and solidly built. His hands were thick and spoke of years of street fights. His face showed the effects of those fights with a large, crooked nose, obviously broken some time ago and thick scarring around his eyes.

He glanced quickly over Jason and then stared at Tony.

"Vincent, I wanted you to meet this guy I ran into earlier today. He might be useful to us."

Bonocchi didn't answer right away but kept looking at Tony.

"This is so important you come over here this evening?" he finally said.

"I knew you'd be in your office, and I figured it best to have you meet him right away."

"What's so special I got to meet someone right away?"

Tony looked a bit uncomfortable, Jason thought. That wasn't going to help.

"I apologize. If this ain't a good time, I can bring him back tomorrow."

Vincent seemed to have accomplished the effect he wanted and eased the pressure. "You already interrupted me, so tell me why I need to meet this guy."

It felt odd to Jason, being spoken about as if he weren't present.

"His name's Jason. Me and my crew were at the Baker Street Bar and this guy was there. One of the regulars, a tough guy who pushes his weight around with the other locals, started in on him. To make a long story short, they went outside and within two minutes, Jason walks back in, untouched, after sending Mack home with his friends."

Vincent just stared at Tony. The whole scenario now seemed a bit ridiculous to Jason as Tony explained it. There was a long uncomfortable silence.

Finally, Vincent spoke. "A guy beats up a local street tough, someone you keep in line by yourself, and you think I should meet him?"

"You make it sound kind of dumb, the way you put it."

"You think so?"

"But the guy can handle himself and he's had experience in keeping people in line. I know we can always use help in that area."

Vincent finally turned to look at Jason. "You're a tough guy?"

Jason paused, wondering how best to answer. Finally, he said, "I can handle myself."

"You new in town. Where are you from?"

"Knoxville."

"What'd you do there?"

Jason gave Vincent a simple story about working for the Chairman. With Tony's advice in the back of his mind, he set it up so that his leaving wouldn't be interpreted as being disloyal.

Vincent listened without interruption.

"What's Knoxville using for power?" he asked after Jason had completed his story.

The question caught him off guard.

"They're using water power to generate electricity. From the Tennessee River."

"Do they know there's a coal mine south of them?"

Jason decided to play dumb. He didn't know how much Vincent knew about the Chairman or what went on in Knoxville. He shrugged. "I never talked about that with anyone. Electricity wasn't my job."

"Your job was just keeping people in line. You bust heads? You kill anyone? How much of a tough guy are you?"

Vincent's face was screwed up in a hard, questioning, almost challenging look.

"I busted a few heads when necessary. I found it better to use persuasion and the threat of a busted head. People's imaginations can come up with more terrifying things than I can threaten them with. I would put out a few suggestions and then let them imagine the rest."

"You're a psychologist, are you?"

Jason shook his head. "Nah. Just someone who figured out a few things about people."

"You go to Hillsboro after you left town?"

Jason thought this might be a point to enhance his desirability. "I stopped there and checked them out, but decided I wanted to get to the big time, here in Charlotte."

"Was Stansky there when you came through?"

Jason played dumb. "Who's that?"

"He ran the town."

"I didn't hear about anyone by that name. The town's run by a city council as far as I can tell."

Vincent told Jason to wait outside. After he left the room, Vincent turned to Tony. "We don't know nothing about this guy. It sounds too pat to me. He comes in the bar where you, conveniently, are sitting. Gets into a fight and impresses you and you fall for it. You decide he's the next great enforcer."

"It ain't like that boss. He is new to town. He's got no ID card, didn't even know about converting gold into to scrip. He had no way of knowing who we were and the other guy was the one who started the fight. It didn't look staged at all."

Vincent sat back. "All right. You can bring him on board, but he's your responsibility. He fucks up, it's on you." He pointed at Tony. "Find a situation that compromises him. Something to test if he really is a tough guy and willing to bust heads. Then maybe you can trust him."

Outside the office, Jason stood in the middle of the reception room.

"Take a seat, Ears said. "You make me nervous just standing there."

Jason sat down across from the desk where Ears sat.

"You box?" Jason asked.

Ears gave him a long look before answering.

"Used to."

"You must have done well, you're a big guy. You fight as a heavyweight?"

"Yeah. I did okay."

"How high did you rank?"

"Never got to any title bouts, if that's what you're asking."

"Still, I'm guessing you did all right. You join this group after the EMP attack?"

Ears looked at Jason for a long moment. "You got a lot of questions."

"Just trying to make conversation."

"Well, don't."

He turned back to an old magazine that was on the desk.

Tony came out of the office and motioned for Jason to come with him.

"You're in luck. Vincent says you can join my crew. You work for me now. I'll get you an ID card in the morning and some scrip. I'll set you up in a hotel room. Ain't fancy but it'll do."

"What will I be doing?"

"What I tell you to do. We make sure people have paid their taxes. We also collect vagrants, slackers, and trouble makers. We're peace keepers." He smiled at what seemed to be an inside joke.

"Guys like Mack?"

"No. Mack's an asshole but he works hard, so we give him some slack."

"Well, thanks for giving me a chance, Tony."

"Just don't make me regret it. Vincent's not so sure about you."

"Okay. I have to tell you one thing, I got a gun in my backpack, a 9mm. It's one of the reasons why I didn't want to go through the checkpoints."

Tony gave him a long look. "That's a surprise I wouldn't have wanted. You keep it, but don't go flashing it around. Makes civilians nervous."

He took Jason to a local hotel that rented rooms by the hour, day, week or month.

"Meet me at Vincent's office tomorrow. You wait outside until I get there."

After Tony left, Jason sat in his room and thought about his next move. *They're going to test me, set me up to beat someone. I'll have to figure out how to do it without inflicting too much damage.* Getting the information he needed might take some time, but he now had identified the street boss of a crew and his boss, a capo in the hierarchy. This was the mob and they seemed to be running a large part of the city. But was there another power structure above them, using the mob as an enforcement tool? Hopefully he could find out.

Chapter 11

The next day Jason accompanied Tony to a small store. It sold meats. Cured hams and venison and sausages made from a combination of pork and venison.

"This guy's got some great tasting sausages. When pasta is available, we can make some tasty meals. The wine still ain't so good, but it's getting better."

"Why are we here?" Jason asked.

"He keeps coming up short on his weekly payments. He's got records to prove he ain't making much money, but I don't buy it. The food's too good."

"You post anyone to watch and see how many customers come in the store?"

"Yeah, but I don't get an accurate count. Anyway, I'm not letting him give me any more excuses. Vincent says we got to get tough. No one gets to slide." Tony turned to Jason as they approached the store. "That's where you come in. Time to show me how you get people in line."

"You want the money, the payment? Or just a busted head."

"The money. But he's got to understand to not try to scam us again. Word of that can't get around."

They entered the store. Tony leaned close to Jason. "His daughter works with him. She could be leverage. Probably wouldn't want to see her old man get beaten. Let's see what you can do."

"Mr. Lucho, what brings you in today, some fresh sausage?"

"Frank it's time for you to get current. I'm here to collect."

"I told you, business is slow. I got a supply problem and my customers aren't coming by like before. If I can't make the sausages, they stop coming. I'll be able to pay you something next week. And hopefully I'll get some meat soon and can get my volume back up again." The man shook his head and looked sad. "Right now it's tough."

Just then an attractive woman came out of the back room, wiping her hands on an apron. She stepped behind the counter to stand next to the man. She had dark, shoulder length hair that framed a pale face. Her eyes were dark and penetrating, her lips full. The effect was a slightly sultry look layered over an innocence of youth.

"Good to see you, Ramona," Tony said.

She nodded without answering.

"Frank, this is Jason. He's helping me collect. He's not a very patient man, and you're going to have to deal with him."

Jason looked around the shop. It looked to be in good shape, better than most in these post-EMP times. Maybe the man's business was down, but if not, why would he try to scam the mob? That could be dangerous. Tony expected to see Jason take some action right in front of the daughter.

"Frank, is it?" Jason said.

The man nodded.

"Frank, show me the back room. I'm interested in how you make your sausage."

He motioned for the man to come out from behind the counter. Jason noticed that Frank motioned for his daughter to stay. *Enough customer traffic so he doesn't want the counter unattended?* They walked into the back room.

There was a large assembly table in the middle with racks for drying and curing hams along one wall. One the other wall was a commercial stove and a large walk-in cooler stood in the back. Two meat grinders were attached to the counter along with a stuffing machine.

"Bet that cooler takes a lot of energy to run."

"That's the problem. Even if business is down, I got to pay for the electricity, that's what Tony collects. And if I don't have any business, it's hard to pay. I still need to buy meat."

"You seem to be doing pretty well. Your store's neat and clean." Jason poked around, looking into a side room, opening the cooler, which held a good supply of ingredients for making the sausage.

He turned to the man. "Frank, I'd have to say, it looks like you're holding back from Tony. And that doesn't seem to be very smart, or healthy on your part."

"But I'm not, business—"

Jason grabbed the man by his collar. He hoped he could impress him without resorting to violence. "Don't give me that crap," he said, his voice low and threatening. "You already went through that song and dance out front. You're not being smart. First, what you're doing is going to get you physically hurt. Second, you have a beautiful daughter and you're putting her in danger."

"Don't you touch Ramona."

"I won't, but others might. Don't be a fool. Pay the man what he's owed. Tony can't have you stiff him and he'll target Ramona next."

"But I need some time."

Jason had seen enough. He turned and went back out front. Tony stood at the counter. He gave Jason a questioning look. Jason stood looking around. *If he's holding out, where's he putting the scrip?* He didn't think there were any banks operating yet. Frank followed Jason out from the back room.

"Frank," Jason said without looking at him, "maybe we visit your home, where you live. Maybe we go through it and find the money you're holding out. That work for you?" He kept his eyes on Ramona.

The girl's face didn't register any sudden look of anxiety.

Frank's voice was calm. "You can do that. You won't find anything there. Just don't break things needlessly."

Jason stepped behind the counter. He scanned the details, looking for something out of place. Ramona was standing at the cash register, an old mechanical one. On the floor next to her was a small, padded rug. Something wasn't right. She wasn't standing on the rug. *It should be at the register, to pad your feet when you're standing there.*

"Ramona, come out from there," Jason told her.

She looked at him, now with more concern in her face.

"Get out and stand by your dad," Jason said.

She came over to her father. Jason walked to the register. He stooped down and pulled the rug away. The girl tried to stifle a small gasp, but Jason heard it.

Jason knelt down and took out his 9mm. He gently tapped the butt of the handle on the floor, starting from under the cash register. The sound was solid. As he moved towards where the rug had been, the sound went hollow. Jason stopped and looked up. Tony was leaning over the counter.

"What's up with that?" Tony asked.

"Sounds loose," Jason replied. "And it was covered by the rug. Better keep an eye on the two of them."

Jason felt around for a loose board. He couldn't find anything and stood up.

"There's nothing there," Frank said. "I've been telling the truth."

Without answering, Jason walked into the back room and grabbed a large knife. Going back behind the counter, he began to pry at the boards with the knife. Finally, he got one to lift and quickly pulled it and the others out. Underneath was a small cavity between the floor joists and inside it was a metal cash box. Jason pulled it out and put it on the counter.

"That's my savings." Frank said.

"That's not yours," Ramona added.

Tony glared at the two of them. He held out his hand for the kitchen knife. Jason handed it to him and Tony pried the lid open. Inside was a large stack of the local scrip along with a pile of gold jewelry.

"Frank, you've been lying to me," Tony said in a dangerous voice.

"No, I haven't, I—"

"Shut up," Tony said.

"That should cover his missing payments," Jason said. "Let me talk to him again."

Tony nodded as he started counting the money.

Jason went over to Frank and grabbed him by the arm.

"You leave him alone," Ramona shouted. She grabbed Jason's arm.

Jason released her father and turned to her. He put his hand around her wrist and squeezed tight. Her eyes widened at the pressure he exerted but her face remained defiant.

He leaned towards her. "If you have any sense, you'll stop and shut up. Things could go very bad right now if you don't." Jason's look left no doubt. She released his arm. He turned and pushed Frank into the back room.

"Now I don't have a lot of time. I'm trying to save you from a serious beating, or worse. Tony has to save face. You've embarrassed him. Luckily it wasn't in front of the rest of his crew or you would be a bloody mess on the floor."

"But that's all my savings."

"Shut up and listen. Ramona is in danger now. You're going to lose all that's in the box. Tony isn't going to negotiate with you at this point. You tried to stiff him."

"But they always take more than they should."

"That's the way it is. You're stuck with them in charge. If you don't like it, tell the city council to stop them." Jason went on without waiting for a reply. "Here's what you're going to do. You pay Tony, or whoever he sends every week. You don't give them any trouble. The next step is they take Ramona. They might put her in a brothel or worse. In any case you lose your daughter."

Jason put his face up close to Frank. "Do you understand me?"

The man nodded. He had no more words.

"Good. Now I'm going to hit you a couple of times. It'll hurt, but it will keep Tony from doing worse. You just pay up each week and don't give anyone any trouble. You got it?"

Frank nodded.

Before he could think about what was coming next, Jason hit the man in his stomach and then lightly in the face, enough to cause a bloody nose without breaking it.

With a suitably bloodied face, he walked Frank back out.

"No!" shouted Ramona as she went over to her father who was bent over and wiping blood from his face. "You bastard," she said. Her face was full of anger. Her father put his hand on her arm to restrain her.

"Looks like we're even now," Tony said.

"But you try to hold out again, I'll take Ramona for payment." He grinned at the two of them and turned to leave.

Jason nodded to Frank and followed Tony out the door.

"How'd you know the money there?" Tony asked when they were on the street.

"They got to put the money somewhere. They didn't react when I suggested we toss their home, so I guessed it might be at the shop.

"But behind the counter?"

"The rug looked wrong. It should have been under the register, to cushion someone who would stand there for a long time. It made no sense to be where it was...unless—"

"Unless it was hiding something. Very clever of you."

"I try to be observant. Notice things that are out of place."

Chapter 12

Jason spent the week with Tony and his crew. Their work consisted of collecting what they called taxes from the businesses that had sprung up since the EMP attack. People who worked for the city in some capacity had these taxes deducted from their pay so collections weren't needed.

At the end of the week, Tony reported back to his boss, Vincent.

"This guy Jason's working out. We've increased our collections by thirty percent. He's definitely convincing some of our tougher customers to pay up."

"He's busting some heads, is he?" Vincent asked.

"That's just it. He's not having to do much of that. He's like the horse whisperer or something. He takes them aside and talks quietly to them, maybe along with some arm twisting, but they seem to come around. All in all, it makes for easier collecting and everyone's calmer."

"A regular magician." Vincent didn't sound convinced. "You hear what he's telling them?"

"Not really. He takes 'em aside, like he's giving them word in private. But whatever he says it seems to work."

"Maybe you want to listen in sometime. Find out what he's saying."

"You sound like you still don't trust him. Things are settling down, collections are going well, what's not to like?"

"I don't trust anyone I don't know." Vincent leaned forward over his desk. "And I don't know this guy. He's a little too pat, too perfect for me."

"I don't know boss."

"Look, Tony, if something seems too good to be true it probably is. This guy comes out of nowhere, seems to have all these persuasion skills. You say he can handle himself and now he's the world's greatest collector, without any beatings."

"But boss—"

"I'll tell you what," Vincent went on, "he's vague about his history, who he is, where he's from. All we know is that he worked for the Chairman, but we can't verify that. He spent some time in Hillsboro and what you don't know is that we're trying to collect a debt from them. And he never heard of Stansky? I'm not sure I buy that."

Vincent waved his hand to dismiss Tony.

"Just keep your eyes open. That's all I'm saying."

"Okay boss. I'll keep a watch on him."

He turned and left the office.

Once Jason had been around with Tony and one of his other crew for a week, he was sent out on his own. Collections were done weekly, so there was a steady list of people to visit. This day his route took him to visit Harry, the mechanic, who had first talked to him after Jason got into the city.

Jason walked into Harry's garage. It was a large place that had once housed taxis. There were twenty repair bays. Half of them were filled with old cars and a few trucks. The building had a tall, metal ceiling with dirty skylights that struggled to relieve the gloom. Harry didn't seem to want to use much electricity to light the shop during the day.

"Hello Harry," Jason said to the man who came over after he walked into the shop. Harry looked at him, trying to place him.

"I look different without my backpack and jeans. I met you about ten days ago at the bar down the street. You clued me in to the Exchange Centers and let me know the bartender had ripped me off."

Harry's face lit up. "Oh yeah, your name is..."

"Jason."

"Right. What are you doing? You're better dressed than when I saw you last."

"I'm working for Tony Lucho."

Harry's face took on a guarded look. "Tony? What do you do for him?"

"I'm one of his collectors."

"Oh hell. Why do you want to go and do that? I thought you wanted to settle down and do some honest work."

"I did, I mean I do. This just came along and it seems like I'm pretty good at it."

"I thought you were a straight up guy. Not one to go around harassing people, beating them up when they can't pay what they owe."

"I don't beat people up."

"No?" Harry's voice was filled with disbelief. "Just how do you do that?"

Jason shrugged. "I guess I'm gently persuasive. Tony likes what I do. Says it fits in with the plan to have things to run more smoothly, without so much muscle."

"You carry a gun?"

Jason nodded. "Always have, even when I met you. I'm told to keep it out of sight which I'm happy to do."

"So, you're here for some money?"

"You're on my list." Jason looked around the shop. "Why do you keep the lights off?"

"I negotiated a lower payment for that. I use enough electricity just to keep my compressors running. Can't fix these old wrecks without air impact drivers. So many frozen bolts to get loose. I always pay the fee, don't want any trouble."

"That's what Tony said."

Harry just stood there looking at Jason. He finally shook his head and turned to the office. Jason followed.

"I never took you for a hood, no offense." He said as he walked.

"None taken. It's not my calling, but I've had experience with work like this before, keeping people in line. I've learned to apply a soft touch when I can. Of course, there's some hard asses, cheats who need a wake-up call. Why they want to take on the mob is beyond me."

Harry turned to Jason after they got into the office. "I wouldn't use that word around them if I were you."

"I know. But it's what they are. Doesn't take a genius to figure that out even if they're trying to become more respectable."

Harry went to his desk and took out an envelope and handed it to Jason. "Here's my weekly payment. Dues I call it. Count it if you like."

Jason gave Harry a serious look. "I trust you. And I want to thank you for talking with me that night."

"I didn't do anything. You still wound up sleeping under the stars."

"Yeah, but you were helpful...and honest. That's rare nowadays."

Harry shrugged.

"Can I ask you something?" Jason asked.

"Sure."

"Does the mob run the whole city?"

Harry gave him a sharp look. "Yeah, but why do you want to know?"

"I like to understand the lay of the land. Where the power lies."

"Well it doesn't lie with our mayor, or the FEMA guy in town. They're both under the thumb of guys like Tony and his boss."

"Vincent?"

Harry nodded.

"And who does Vincent report to?"

"There's two guys, Joe Nicoletti and the big boss, Albert Tagliani, those who know him call him Big Al. I don't know anything about them and wouldn't tell you if I did. You nose around, ask too many questions about guys at that level, you're going to get yourself into big trouble. I suggest you go about your humane money collecting and keep out of the politics. "

"Like I said, I try to understand whatever situation I find myself in."

"Well just watch out. And if you know how to work on cars and need a job, come see me."

"I'll keep that in mind." Jason started for the door then stopped. "And Harry, he said, turning, "don't mention our conversation with anyone, okay?"

"I guess I can keep a secret, but I might need a favor in return someday."

"You get in touch. I'll do what I can."

Chapter 13

That evening, Jason left the bar where Tony sat receiving the day's money. As he started down the street, Gino, another of Tony's crew, came up to him.

"I've got my eye on you," Gino said. His tone was unfriendly, aggressive.

"What are you talking about?" Jason responded.

"You may have Tony fooled, thinking you're some kind of collection genius, but you don't fool me."

Jason smiled at Gino. The man was shorter than him but thick, with solid arms. He didn't move fast. He seemed to Jason to be more tank-like in action, but Jason guessed he could take some punishment and then dish out more in response. The man could hurt you if he got you cornered or pinned down.

"Gino, I'm not trying to fool you, or anyone."

"There's something not right about you. I can sense it. I can smell a rat a mile away. You don't talk about where you came from. It's like you're hiding something. I'm telling you that I'm watching you. You'll fuck up at some point and I'll be all over you."

Jason didn't answer and Gino pointed to his eyes and then at Jason. He didn't wait for a reply and turned to leave.

Jason continued walking, thinking about the exchange. He went over his own actions since joining Tony's crew. He couldn't come up with anything that might have set off alarm bells. Was he not playing the bad guy well enough?

Giving some civilian a serious beating would help, but Jason couldn't bring himself to do it. He had made do with having serious talks with the slow payers, letting them know he was their buffer against serious injury and making them realize how dangerous injury was in the post-EMP world.

It generally worked except for some harder cases that were just as corrupt as the mob that was collecting from them. Jason used more force then. Still something had triggered Gino's suspicions. He began to feel more and more that he was on borrowed time. *Better stay tight with Tony.*

A meeting of all the mob bosses had been scheduled for downtown. Vincent had been called in. He told Tony to come along and Tony told Jason to come with him. They would both be backing up Vincent, showing off his muscle to the other capos. Gino was furious as were the others in Tony's crew. Gino was staring daggers at Jason when Tony said he was going.

"Why the new guy?" Rocco asked.

"'Cause he's earned it. He's the biggest producer in the crew. You guys should take a lesson."

Jason knew that comment was not going to help him with the others. But this was the chance he had been looking for, moving up in the ranks.

"Boss, something just ain't right with Jason," Gino said. "He ain't really part of us."

"He's doing what I tell him to do and getting results. That's what counts. Now shut up about it."

The next day they drove into the inner part of the city in a 1963 Oldsmobile. Ears, Vincent's bodyguard, drove, Jason sat up front with him, while Vincent and Tony sat in the back. They were passed through a checkpoint. Jason tried not to crane his head around too much in checking out how the inner perimeter was protected. It looked like a concrete wall had been poured in places. He caught a glimpse of some buildings that had been bricked shut to provide barriers. Across secondary roads, barriers of abandoned busses or trucks had been set up.

"Looks like it's hard for anyone to get inside without going through a checkpoint," Jason remarked to Ears.

"That's the idea. Can't have the everyday punks coming and going," Ears said.

"Hey Jason," Vincent called out from the back seat. "You said you spent time in Hillsboro. I may want you to tell Mr. Nicoletti, about it. He also visited the town. Maybe you two can compare notes."

"I doubt I can add anything to what Mr. Nicoletti knows," Jason responded.

"You never know." Vincent's voice sounded cold.

They drove on in silence. Ears pulled in at the Omni Hotel in the center of the city. It was surrounded by high-rises that had been banks in the pre-EMP days. Jason could only guess what those monsters were used for now.

They stopped at the front door. Ears got out and opened the rear door for Vincent while Jason did the same for Tony. The two went inside leaving Ears and Jason to park the car.

Jason stood looking up at the impressive height of the buildings.

"You never been to Charlotte before?" Ears asked.

"I have, before the attack. But I didn't have business downtown. Never saw these close up. They sure liked to go high." After parking, they started walking back to the hotel. "Are they used for anything now?"

"Not sure if there's much use for 'em now. A lot of people died after the attack. You know, old folks, the sick. A lot died that winter too. The gangs added to the mess. There was a lot of killing. We had to get pretty brutal to put 'em down, get the city under some kind of control. Now there ain't as many people around."

"And you run the city now?" Jason askes.

Ears looked over at him.

"I mean Mr. Tagliani and the bosses."

"Ain't no other boss besides Mr. Tagliani, Ears replied. "But yeah, you could say that. We still got a mayor, but he works for Mr. Tagliani. Most everyone realizes that we got the city under control." Ears paused for a moment. "I heard it's kind of like the old days, in the twenties. The organization keeps order and city hall leaves us alone. Only now we're the ones bringing in the money, so we get to call the shots."

"What's the end game? I mean what happens when the feds show up?"

Ears gave him a sharp look. "I don't know anything about that."

They got to the front door. "Now keep your mouth shut. Stay with me when the bosses go into their meeting. Got it?"

Jason nodded.

They met up with Tony and Vincent and followed them into a ballroom. There was a band playing music at one end. Food was set out on a long, center table. Jason marveled at the selection. Shrimp, cuts of beef, pork and venison, pasta, salads. He'd hadn't seen that much food in one place in years. Scantily clad women moved through the men with trays of wine and snacks of cheese, vegetables and small breads along with various sauces to dip.

Ears headed for the side of the room and Jason followed. Other bodyguards were standing around the perimeter. Ears greeted some of them. He didn't introduce Jason, but when asked, told the others who he was. On the other side of the room was a long bar. Many of the mob men were getting something stronger than wine to drink.

"This happen often?" Jason asked to one of the bodyguards standing near him after Ears had wandered off.

"Twice a year. They like to put on a show. It's good for us. We get to eat pretty well when the bosses go into their meeting."

"There's some good-looking women circulating. They part of the meetings?"

The man looked at Jason with a smile. "You're kidding me, right? Ears said you were new, but you can't be that dumb. They're professionals. They'll be providing the late-night entertainment, after the meeting and the show." He turned to look across the room. "Not that it'll do us any good. But who knows, maybe you'll get lucky." He laughed and turned away to talk to someone else.

Jason watched the scene. Vincent's suggestion that he talk with Nicoletti worried him, but it was also a way to connect upward. It was looking more and more like the mob really was in control. But what did they want with little Hillsboro? The scene he was witnessing was outlandish in the extreme. Hillsboro seemed a small side issue in comparison.

There had to be an end game to all of this theater. Some direction this was going. He sensed the mob wasn't just enjoying having power without interference from authorities, either federal, state or local. They must be planning for the future. Jason kept trying to work out how all that he was seeing could be perpetuated.

A smaller set of side tables had been set up for all the bodyguards. The "unranked", Jason thought. He kept working, talking to members of the different crews. From conversations he confirmed that the electricity came from the Riverbend Steam Station north of Charlotte. No one Jason talked with knew what would happen after the coal trains had been drained of their contents. Teams were being sent increasingly far afield to find this important resource.

After an hour, the capos disappeared into a smaller room. Someone explained they would have their meal and a meeting in the room. The crews were free to hang out, enjoy and free drinks and food until they returned.

"When the bosses get done with eating and business, we all move to the nightclub. That's where the fun starts," Ears said.

Jason gave him a confused look.

"Strippers and more drinking. You got any scrip on you, you can get a lap dance or more." Ears winked at him. Jason could tell Ears was looking forward to that part of the night.

"That's the highlight of the evening?"

Ears gave him a condescending look. "What else?"

They walked over to the food table.

"Ears, how long did you compete?" Jason asked, wanting to deepen his relationship with the man.

"I started when I was a teenager, amateur bouts. Did some Golden Gloves. I was pretty good, won a lot of fights, so I moved to the pros."

"That go well?"

"At first. My manager kept pushing me forward, more fights with better and better boxers."

"Why'd you quit?"

Ears looked contemplative. His eyes wandered across the room as if recalling some past scenes. "I got to a level where the guys I fought moved too fast."

He turned back to Jason.

"I'm a brawler." He made a fist and put it in Jason's face. It was huge.

"I got a big fist and hit hard. But I reached a point where the heavyweights moved too fast. They had good footwork, something I never quite got right. It made it hard for me to land punches and they'd keep peppering me with jabs and counter punches."

He shook his head.

"Takes a toll after a while."

"So you figured better to get out and try another career? That what brought you to the organization?"

Ears shook his head.

"My manager started putting me up against the up and coming stars. I realized I was being used as a punching bag...and not getting paid enough."

"That brought you to the mob."

Ears gave him a sharp look.

"Don't use that word. The bosses don't like it. And, yes, I quit and wound up here. The pay's better and the punks I have to deal with don't stand a chance with me."

"Hey Ears," someone called over to him. "Who's the punk with you? Ain't seen him around before."

Ears turned to the man.

"He works for Vincent and he's with me. He ain't no punk and if you think so, I'll let him kick your ass."

The man came up to them with a lopsided grin on his face. He appeared to Jason have had too many drinks. He stared at Jason.

"He don't look so tough."

"Luca, you dumb shit. You're so drunk I could take you with one hand tied behind my back," Ears said with a grin.

"Think so?" Luca swayed on his feet. Why don't we go outside now and find out? Better yet, let's find out how tough this new guy is. He looks like a pussy to me."

Ears looked around at a couple of men who had joined them. He shoved Luca into one of the men.

"Get him out of here. He ain't worth me spoiling my evening teaching him a lesson."

They hustled Luca across the room with the man still loudly proclaiming how he was going to mop the floor with both of them.

"Don't worry about him. He's generally okay when he's not drunk."

Ears gave Jason an appraising look.

"You probably could handle him just fine without my help."

"I appreciate the vote of confidence...and thanks for covering for me."

"Don't mention it."

Ears winked at him.

"You probably don't want to drink too much. You may have to drive back."

Chapter 14

Three hours later the meeting broke up. It was now 10:30 in the evening. The bosses filed out of the meeting room and the crews connected up with them. Jason followed Ears as he homed in on Vincent and Tony. Together the four of them walked along with the crowd of men to the nightclub which was located off the lobby of the hotel.

Once settled at a table, drinks were ordered. The girls came onto the stage to do their acrobatic pole dance routines. Jason marveled at the atmosphere that had been established. If one didn't go outside, this evening would seem to be set in the pre-attack days. It was as though the mob was reinforcing the idea that they were the ones able to recreate the world like it was before.

It was an illusion, made possible by spending an enormous amount of resources, food, booze, energy in the form of electricity, and assembling a large group of men and women to play their parts. He doubted all of the strippers and wait staff could support themselves doing only what they were doing this night. Still, the effect was powerful.

Vincent looked over at Jason. "Come with me. We'll go talk to Mr. Nicoletti." He stood up. Jason nodded and followed him. They maneuvered through the tables until they came to a large one with six men seated at it. Vincent approached the group.

"Mr. Nicoletti, this is the guy I told you about. He's spent some time in Hillsboro. I thought you might want to talk with him."

Joe Nicoletti was in the middle of telling a joke. He finished his story and then turned to Vincent. His gaze swept over to Jason standing next to him. He gave him an appraising once over and nodded.

"Pull up a couple of chairs," he said to Vincent.

When the two men were seated, Joe turned to Jason.

"You come from Hillsboro?"

"No sir," Jason replied. "But I did spend a little time there recently."

"You got a last name?"

Jason hesitated. Giving him his last name exposed him just that much more to the risk of being discovered. He wanted to be cautious even if he didn't expect anyone in Charlotte to know of him.

"My last name's Rich. I ain't, so I stopped using it and just go by Jason."

Joe smiled. "One name, like Madonna or, what's that guy's name who plays that schmaltzy music?"

"Yanni," someone at the table said. "He's Greek, I think."

"Seemed like a fag to me. My wife used to love it. Put me to sleep."

The men chuckled.

"Okay Jason Rich, tell me about Hillsboro."

Jason paused for a moment. "I'm not sure what I can tell you. I didn't stay long."

"Tell me what you know, what you saw. For example, how is the city defended?"

"They have a rubble wall surrounding the town. Not as secure as what I saw protecting the downtown here. There's a couple of manned entry points but I'm not sure how many."

"The wall go all the way around?"

"There's a river passing south of the town, so it stops there."

"They got a military?"

"I saw men in uniforms, so I assume they do."

Jason could see Nicoletti getting a bit impatient with the sparse information he was giving out. He'd have to divulge more if he was going to keep this conversation going and possibly learn more.

"You don't seem to be know much. What were you doing in Hillsboro?"

Jason went into the story he had told Tony and then Vincent about Knoxville and moving on.

"You didn't join the militia?"

"No. I got enough of that in the army. Plus, I was looking for an organization that could use my skills as a persuader."

"Like what you're doing now?"

"Yeah. Hillsboro is run by a civilian government. They're pretty well organized from what I could tell."

Joe seemed to be pondering what Jason had said.

"What do they use for power?"

"They have limited electricity. It's generated by a water mill. I don't think they get enough power out of it to run the whole town. Nothing like here. I heard you got a coal-fired plant going?"

"You heard right. Makes local water mill projects look puny by comparison."

"Where do you get the coal?"

Joe ran his gaze over Jason, sizing him up again. "That interest you?"

"I'm just interested in understanding how things work."

"You a fucking engineer or an enforcer?"

Jason chuckled and shook his head. "Not an engineer. But it *is* impressive what you've accomplished here compared to other cities."

"And what do you know of other cities besides Knoxville and Hillsboro?"

"Not much but I passed through some other towns in southern Virginia before I wound up in Knoxville."

"Speaking of Knoxville, how do they generate electricity?"

"They're also using water power."

"Don't they know they've got a coal mine not far to the south of them?"

Jason shrugged. "Mr. Bonocchi asked me that question. I told him I didn't know. Didn't hear anyone talk about it."

"The Chairman's a dumbass if he don't know that," Nicoletti muttered.

"Someone told me you get the coal from stalled trains. What will you do when that runs out?"

"You *are* inquisitive, aren't you?" Nicoletti said. His eyes narrowed as he stared at Jason.

"We have plans, options."

Jason decided to risk another question. "Can I ask why you're interested in Hillsboro? I mean enough to talk to me about it?"

Nicoletti seemed to think for a moment. "Let's just say Hillsboro owes us something and we may need to go there to collect it."

There it was. More confirmation. But what were their capabilities? He needed more. He considered another question, but Joe had already turned back to the others at the table. One of the pole dancers had approached the table and was tempting the men into going to the back of the room for some lap dances.

"Thanks for your time, Mr. Nicoletti," Vincent said. He got up and motioned Jason to follow.

"You weren't much help," he said as they walked back to their table.

"I told him what I knew. I didn't want to make anything up just to impress him."

"Don't get smart. There's still some odd parts to your story. I like to know more about the people that work for me. We'll have to talk more."

When they got back to the table, Vincent turned his attention to the dancers on the stage and called out for a round of drinks.

As the evening went on, the men got louder and raunchier; the liquor flowed freely. Even though it was hard to keep his attention, Jason started to work on Tony for information.

"Are we going to go to Hillsboro and try to take them over?"

Tony looked at Jason with a boozy stare.

"Hell no. We ain't the military. We got a militia to do that for us. We stay here and keep the town quiet and under control. Let those army types march off." He leaned towards Jason, "Tell you what, though. If Mr. Tagliani decides to send them, they'll kick Hillsboro's ass."

"Why the interest in Hillsboro?"

"They owe us some money. A shit load from what I hear." Tony turned towards the girl on a pole nearest them. "Man, she's hot. I want a piece of that. How 'bout you?" He turned back to Jason.

"I'm okay. Never did get into that lap dance thing. It's just a tease."

"You're a strange one for sure. Maybe Vincent's right about you."

Jason felt his stomach turn. *What did Tony mean by that?*

"'Course it's a tease," Tony said as he turned back to the stage. "That's the point. Get the real thing later if you're lucky...and got enough money." He called out some encouragement and got a smile from the dancer. Ears whistled through his teeth.

When Jason noticed Joe Nicoletti leaving for the restroom, he got up. "I gotta take a piss," he said, his voice purposely slurred, and headed off with a slight stagger.

Inside the bathroom, he took a urinal a few places down from Joe. "Nice party you're putting on. I never saw anything like this since the EMP attack."

Joe looked over at Jason as if trying to place him. Jason could see recognition appear in his face.

"We're getting things back to normal. This is just the start."

"Anything I can do to help, Mr. Nicoletti. I appreciate being given the opportunity."

Joe nodded. "I'm told you can handle yourself, that you're a serious guy with good people skills. We'll see as things progress."

"I appreciate it," Jason said looking at his urinal. Then he turned back to Joe. "I gotta ask, Charlotte seems so advanced, why go after Hillsboro? I mean I understand they owe us, you, something but they're a pretty small town."

"Vincent was right, you do have a lot of questions. And some of them aren't your business." He paused for a moment. "Let's say, just to satisfy you curiosity, they're important in ways you might not realize."

Joe finished and zipped up his fly. When he reached the door, he turned back towards Jason.

"Remember that saying about curiosity and the cat." And he walked through the door.

The drive home was uneventful. As Ears had predicted, Tony told Jason to drive and started to fall asleep. He and Vincent sat comfortably in the back as Ears quietly gave Jason directions when he was not sure of the way to go.

Chapter 15

J ason needed more information. It had been a week since the party. None of the crew members knew much and Gino was openly hostile. He was working alone now, as were the others. Spreading the men out enabled Tony to cover more territory in a shorter amount of time, giving everyone some extra time off.

This day he went down to Frank Russo's meat shop. Ramona glared at him from the counter when he entered. She still had not forgiven him for hitting her father.

"Hi Ramona, is you father around?"

"It's not payday, if you're looking for money."

"No, I stopped by to talk with him."

Just then Frank came out from the back room.

"What do you want to talk about?"

Jason pointed to the back. "Can we go back there?"

Frank shrugged and turned back the way he had come. Jason followed.

"Frank, I've apologized for hitting you a couple of weeks ago. But you know that was for your own good."

"It still hurt."

"I'm sure it did. And Ramona is still mad at me for it." Jason paused for a moment. "You know I'm not really a part of the mob. I've sort of been grafted on to them."

"You've been polite since that confrontation. I'll give you that. And you don't seem like the others that work for Tony."

"I'll take that as a compliment. I run interference for you with Tony and the other crew members. You're getting along since that day, aren't you?"

"Yeah. But I'm not saving much since I got to pay up in full each week."

"What you did was dangerous. What are you trying to save for that's so important to risk getting Tony mad at you?"

"I want to get out of here. Take Ramona somewhere that's not controlled by the mob, somewhere with real civilian control. You see how beautiful she is. It's only a matter of time before someone goes after her."

Jason shook his head. "That's a hard situation."

Frank continued. "They don't have any morals, inhibitions. It's only family for them. Everyone outside of their group can be used by them, for money, power, sex, whatever."

"Frank, I think I can help you. I don't want to see anything happen to Ramona either. But to help both of you, I need you to keep whatever I tell you a secret. I can be your ally, but only if we work together."

Frank gave Jason a wary look. "What are you saying?"

"Just that you can help me to help you. First by keeping what we talk about secret, even from Ramona and, secondly, giving me information."

Frank continued to look wary but agreed. "All right."

"Good. Now tell me what you know about the civilian leadership in town."

"There's not much to tell. The mayor is a figure head. There's no town council. He comes out and gives speeches when there's a big meeting or rally. He'll write something in the newsletter that's sent out. I'm guessing it's just what that guy, Big Al, tells him to write. Big Al s the boss."

"Do you know anything about the FEMA guy in town?"

Frank shook his head. "He also writes something for the newsletter, but I've never seen him. Why the questions? What do you plan to do?"

"That's not for you to know. It wouldn't be safe for you. But I think it will help you in the end."

"Nothing much will help me except enough money to get some supplies and get out of here."

"Where will you go?"

"I'm still working on that. I ask around about what nearby towns are like and where the federal government is in charge, but there's not much good news. Most of the nearby towns are under Charlotte's thumb. The feds are in Wilmington, but word is they've closed it off in order to maintain control over the port. It's just used to try to get relief supplies into the country."

"There's a city north of here, Hillsboro. It has a civilian government and you and Ramona could find a place to fit in. You should consider it."

Jason turned to go.

"Thanks for the tip," Frank called after him.

The conversation didn't add much information to what Jason already knew. He needed to work higher up the chain, even if that meant increased danger. He started working on Tony.

"I heard there's a FEMA guy in town. Does he run anything?"

"Not really. He's a wimpy little guy.

"What's his name?"

"Michael Daniels"

"Did he get sent here after the attack?"

"No. I think he was here all along. Probably worked a desk before the attack, directing resources around the state after floods and things like that. When the attack happened, he was out of his element."

"So, what did he do?"

"That's just it. Nothing."

"Joe and Big Al had a talk with him and told him the role he was to play. He turned the city's resources over to us and now just sits around. If we get any visitors, we haul him out to let them know he's got everything under control."

"He just hangs out downtown?"

"That's about it. City hall."

Later Jason got out a map of Charlotte and found city hall. He'd have to pay the FEMA guy a visit sometime soon if he was going to find out more. He had to assume the man was uncomfortable being used as a puppet for the mob, but would he have the nerve to tell Jason anything? And could he trust the man not to blow his cover?

A week later Jason left his apartment by the back door.

He had told Tony he was taking a few days off to explore the world outside of the city.

"You were so rushed to get into Charlotte, now you want to leave?"

"Not leave, just going to take a hike around the area. I'm used to hiking and camping. That's what I had to do when on the road."

Tony shook his head. "Never understood people who wanted to sleep in tents. That's not civilized. Why you want to be uncomfortable on purpose?"

"Hell, I don't know how to explain it. Maybe being a bit uncomfortable makes things in the city seem better. I know it clears my head."

"I don't get it. You are one strange character. Maybe we should call you 'Camper', or 'Mr. Natural', make that your nickname."

Jason gave a short laugh. "Most people wouldn't get it. Not like 'Ears'."

"Yeah. That one's easy to understand."

That night Jason went down a side street towards the central part of the city, keeping to the shadows. It was well after midnight and no one was about. When he got close to the barriers, he headed away from a checkpoint to an unused minor street. *They'll be a way through here.* He inspected the vehicles that were jammed in the street along with a rough concrete wall. The barrier was not manned. It took only a few minutes for Jason to climb over the vehicles and then he was on the inside.

He made his way to city hall and found a place to hide for the remainder of the night. He was in an overgrown park, nearly a block in size, surrounding a municipal building that looked unused now. The park provided good cover, having returned to its natural state. He nestled down in the underbrush and tried to get some sleep. The night was cold, winter was coming, but at least it wasn't raining.

He was across from the city-county government building. When morning came, Jason unpacked his clean clothes and put them on. He wore slacks and a suit jacket that Tony had arranged to have made for him by a tailor. The man was skilled and cut down a suit that had been saved after the attack. The mob not only had collected the immediately necessary items of food, fuel, ammunition, and medicine, they had also locked down clothing and other goods stored in various warehouses around the city.

Jason was on edge. The meeting could be dangerous. He'd have to assess whether Daniels was a willing participant in the mob's activities or a reluctant hostage and front man. How courageous was he? Would he use Jason's visit to score some points with the mob leadership? If the man reported Jason's visit, he'd have a hard time explaining his action.

When people started entering the building, Jason emerged from his hiding spot and casually walked over to the entrance. He had left his 9mm behind, hidden in the bushes with a bedroll he had brought with him. He hoped he could pass for just another post-EMP bureaucrat going to work.

He entered the building without incident There was no security other than a metal detector at the door. Once inside, he headed for an escalator in the lobby, now inoperable and functioning as a staircase. Once on the mezzanine, he asked a worker where Daniel's office was.

The man gave him a questioning look.

"I've been asked to bring him a message. It's from an assistant to Mr. Nicoletti."

The mention of Joe's name triggered immediate helpfulness.

"He's on the sixth floor, room 635." The man pointed to the far end of the mezzanine. "Take the stairs over there."

Jason smiled and headed off.

Once on the sixth floor, he quickly found the office. There was a receptionist inside.

"I need to speak with Mr. Daniels this morning. I have some information for him. My boss, who works for Mr. Nicoletti, asked me to come here and deliver it."

Again, Nicoletti's name seemed to work.

"Wait here a moment," she said.

The woman got up and went into an inner office. In a few minutes she came out.

"Mr. Daniels can see you." She said, pointing to the inner office door.

Jason took a deep breath and went in.

Chapter 16

The man behind the desk stared at Jason with a bespectacled, near-sighted look. His face was screwed up into a question mark. Jason walked in and took a seat across the desk from him without it being offered.

"Do I know you?"

"No," Jason said. "But I've learned a bit about you and wanted to meet you."

"You said Joe sent you." This came out almost as a question.

"Not exactly. I'm more here on my own. I'm new to Charlotte and work for people who work under Mr. Nicoletti. I'm new to the town so my visit today is to better understand the power structure and where you fit into it."

"So, Joe didn't send you."

"I told you, no."

"I'm not sure I should be talking to you if Joe didn't send you."

"You can talk to me. I work for Vincent Bonocchi and, like I said, I'm new to the job. I want to learn more about how things run here in Charlotte. Don't worry, Vincent knows I'm curious. Let's say, he indulges me because I'm good at what I do."

"And what is it you do?"

"I'm part of the collections crew."

At that Daniels flinched.

"I'm good enough at it that I can be persuasive without using much force. Vincent sees the advantage of a softer touch."

"I don't know what I can tell you that you haven't already been told."

"My visit is to fill in the gaps. First of all, how is the city organized? I understand the group I'm with," Jason avoided using the word 'mob', "does the collecting of taxes, but who makes the rules? Who decides what the city is doing or going to do next?"

Daniels was silent, as if considering his answer.

Jason continued, "Do you or the mayor have any say in what the city does? I'm sure there are a lot of rebuilding projects going on. You've gone beyond what most of cities have done in getting a power plant back online."

"Yeah, that's quite an accomplishment isn't it?"

"Did you do that?"

Daniels shook his head. "No, I made a few suggestions but that was Albert Tagliani's idea. The mayor and I helped round up some of the technical people to make that happen."

"I imaging they were pretty special, with skills like that. They must have been heroes to the town."

Daniels smirked. "You'd think that wouldn't you?"

Jason paused to stare at the man. "That wasn't the case?"

"Let's just say, they did their job and were happy to be done with it. Others are now used to keep things going."

"So, what do you do? Are you in touch with other FEMA offices?"

"Not really. You know there's no communication over any distances now. I don't do much of anything. I wasn't trained for anything like this." He turned to look out of his window at the overgrown park across the street. "We can barely hold off the chaos of nature, let alone that of humans."

"What's the plan for Charlotte? What's Mr. Tagliani trying to accomplish?"

Michael Daniels turned back to Jason. "They don't tell me much. So far, it's just to bring more order to the city. They've done a lot to pacify it and restore services."

"That's it? Just maintain order? Doesn't seem like much of a goal for the group."

"There are rumors," Michael almost muttered to himself.

"Tell me."

"You should wait to hear it from your boss."

"That's just it. I don't get to talk to my boss that often, just my crew boss, Tony, and he doesn't know much."

"Then why should you know more?"

"It's in my nature for one thing. For another it's for my safety. I'm new here, remember. Also, I can keep secrets. That's one of the ways I've made it so far."

Daniels seemed to be thinking about Jason's words. "It's just a rumor. I don't know how true it is, but I've heard some discussion of the families joining together to organize the whole east coast, Boston to Charlotte."

"That's impossible. How could they do that?"

Daniels shrugged. "Who knows? The government stood by and allowed them to pacify Charlotte and now they're in power. Maybe like that?"

"It seems a bit fantastic."

Daniels nodded. "Ambitious isn't it? Charlotte is sort of the southern anchor. The group in Atlanta doesn't have much power. It's a FEMA regional center. They have a lot of assets and so civic order didn't break down as much there. Anyway, the way I understand it, the plan is to connect the cities and create a unified control structure under the organization from here up to Boston."

Jason sat there stunned. "But how? From what I've seen, the crew I work with wouldn't be much good at conquest and control. Collecting payments, yes, busting heads, yes, intimidating, but not taking over other cities and territory."

"That's what a militia's for. We're building a large one here. Organized, well trained. They got some military guy to run it and he's doing a good job."

"And then they'll send it out? What about the army, our own military? This sounds crazy."

"It's only a rumor as far as I know. Maybe just a dream. Maybe the families think this is the best way to preserve their organization. Who knows? The feds may be aiding them, or at least not standing in their way, figuring this is a good way to restore order. Remember, the government has worked with the mafia in the past. Think about Cuba for instance."

"And that didn't go well from what I read."

Daniels held up his hands. "I'm just an observer and as far as I know it's only a rumor. But I do hear that the other families are busy working to gain control in a number of cities. Charlotte is pretty far along compared to the others. I heard Joe talking about New York. He said it was still chaotic with different gangs fighting each other. You have the Mexicans, the Columbians, the Russians, the black gangs. The mafia families there are trying to align with the Feds who are struggling to create some order. Together they may be able to stamp out the other gangs, or at least tamp them down. That might put them in charge in the end."

He got up and walked to the window.

"All I know is I'm glad I'm not in New York or Boston."

"In the meantime, you don't really do anything?"

"Nope. Just write up an article now and then about rebuilding projects. All aimed at keeping people encouraged and happy with things as they are."

"And the mayor?"

"The same."

His voice sounded sad, defeated. There seemed to be little else Daniels could tell Jason. He stood up.

"I appreciate your candor, filling me in."

"Not sure what you do with the information." Michael gave Jason a discerning look. "You're not a member of the gang, are you? Not one of them?"

Jason shook his head. "It shows? No, I'm not. I doubt I'll ever be."

"Not cut from the same cloth. There's something different about you. I can't imagine you beating up innocent people."

"You mean 'civilians'? That's the word the mafia uses."

Daniels winced and nodded. "You have another purpose for being here? You're not just an itinerant gun for hire, are you?"

Jason smiled. "Let's just say, I'm someone who might be of some help to you down the road, if you help me."

"And how do I do that?"

"Let me know what you hear. If important things are going to happen, I'd like to know about them early on."

"That could get me in trouble."

Jason gave him a stern look. "Mr. Daniels, if things progress as you outlined to me, how long do you think it will be before someone wonders what use you are to them? I suppose they pay you pretty well for your PR work, but what about when they don't need it?"

Daniels face clouded over.

"What I'm saying," Jason continued, "is I may be of help to you when that time comes."

"If we're going to help each other, how will we keep in touch? I assume you didn't just wander through a checkpoint. Most people at your level need permission to get in."

"I'll find a go-between. Someone who can navigate back and forth. I'll have them get in touch." Jason reached out and shook Michael Daniels' hand. "Thanks for your help and thanks for keeping this meeting off record. Is your receptionist okay about this? Can she keep a secret?"

"She'll be fine." He smiled. "This has been an interesting morning."

Jason turned and left.

Chapter 17

The next day Jason asked Tony if he could meet with Vincent.

"What do you want to bother Vincent for?"

"You know Frank Russo, the meat guy?"

"Yeah, what about him?"

"Well you know how good his product is. I was thinking if Vincent could get him a pass into the inner part of town, he could go once a week, maybe, and set up a street stand. Sell more product, make more money."

"What good does that do us? We only get to collect a certain amount each week."

"Maybe we take a cut off of his extra earnings. He'll still net more after he pays his taxes. It's a win-win, for him and for us."

"You talking about skimming from Vincent? Pocketing the extra take?"

Jason shook his head vigorously. "No, no. I get that's a bad idea. It's extra kicked up to Vincent. He may give us, you, some of that, but he can do with it what he wants. In any case it makes our crew look good because we increase his earnings."

They were in a bar having a beer. Tony smiled and looked out the window to the street as he thought about it.

"Whether Vincent wants to kick the money up is his call. We don't want to get involved with that."

"Damn right we don't," Tony said.

"I'm also guessing this is something Vincent would have to do. Hell, Tony, I don't know who issues those kinds of passes. I'm still trying to figure things out."

"I think you've got a lot of things figured out." He took a swig of his beer. "It's a clever idea. I'll take it to Vincent."

"You want me to come along?"

"No, I'll do it. You keep doing what you're doing. I like the idea, but don't get thinking you're a mastermind. Vincent won't appreciate it."

Jason lifted his glass to clink against Tony's. "Well, let me be the one to work it out with Frank. I haven't told him yet. I wanted to see if it could fly first."

"Jesus, Jason. Get your ass over there and get Frank on it. If Vincent gives it his okay, Frank's gotta do it. Otherwise we'll look like idiots. If Vincent says he likes the idea, Frank ain't got a choice. You let him know."

He waved his hand to indicate Jason should leave and get on with setting things up.

Jason sat down with Frank and his daughter in the back room of their shop. Ramona kept an eye on the front door in case a customer came in. After explaining the idea to both of them he sat back with a smile on his face, thinking he had scored a victory.

"I don't know," Frank said after listening to Jason. "I make more, I just have to pay Tony more."

"You do pay him some more, but it's a cut off of the extra you make. Your weekly taxes don't change, so you're money ahead, even after giving Tony a cut. You said you needed to save up money to fund an escape for you and Ramona. Here's your chance without risking getting beat up. Hell, they'll be protecting you if your adding to their income."

"How do we know they won't change their mind and just take all the extra we make?" Ramona asked. "They're not very trustworthy."

She seemed to have finally gotten over Jason's treatment of her father. All his subsequent visits had proven peaceful. She also seemed happy because Jason's visiting meant the other members of Tony's crew didn't come around as much. They always were hitting on her. Gino in particular seemed to be the creepiest. She was afraid of him.

"I can't guarantee anything with the mob, but it's not in their interests to make this deal not be economically viable for you."

"You realize I have to purchase more to do this?"

"I do. But you're a businessman. You invest in the materials, make a product, sell it for more than your cost, and take home your profit. Increase your sell-through and you increase your profits."

"The initial step forward to higher volumes is the hard part. It's front-loaded with costs before I sell the first sausage. And the hams are a longer-term investment when you consider the curing time."

Jason smiled at Frank. "I get all of that. But in the end, it works." He leaned forward. "Look, things may get crazy around here in the near future. Don't ask me how, but you need to maximize your income now. An upheaval may be coming."

"What do you know?" Ramona asked.

Jason just shook his head.

"I'd start with the sausages. They're special. And raise the price. The people in the inner city have more money. They can afford it. That should help cover you upfront costs."

The conversation went on into the evening with Frank and his daughter finally coming around.

"Why do you want to help us so much?" Ramona asked.

"First of all, you're good people. That's reason enough. Second, I need something in return from your father."

"Here it comes," Ramona said with a harsh tone in her voice. "I knew there'd be a price to pay."

"It's pretty straightforward," Jason said. He looked at Frank. "I need you to connect with the FEMA guy once a week. I'll get word to him that you're the go-between for us. If he has any information, he'll give it to you and you'll pass it on to me."

"He can't do that," Ramona said. "If my father gets caught sneaking notes back and forth, the mob will beat him, or worse."

"No notes. It'll be verbal communications only. There'll be nothing to discover. The FEMA guy stops at your stand, buys a sausage, talks to you, gives you some information, you pass it on to me when I come by to collect. Nothing out of the ordinary."

The two finally agreed and Jason left the shop.

It was dark as he turned down a side street. Suddenly he was struck by a blow to the back of his head. Darkness closed in as he began to fall to the ground. Strong arms grabbed him and dragged him into an ally.

Jason's head was swimming. He wanted to shake it to clear his vision, but his head exploded in pain when he tried. His arms were pinned back by one man. The other stood in front of him. In the faint light, Jason could make out it was Gino. He bent his angry face close to Jason.

"Don't pass out golden boy. I got some questions for you. I saw you sneaking through the streets last week. You said you were going camping. But you weren't. You were doing something in town. I want to know what it was."

"Gino, you dumbass, I was coming back from camping."

Gino hit him in the stomach. Jason grunted as the air went out of him and he bent over. Gino grabbed his hair and pulled his head up.

"Don't get cute with me. I'll bust you up some more. You're up to something and I want to know what it is. What were you doing at Russo's shop for so long this night? You two planning something? Gonna rip Tony off? Maybe he'd like to know about that."

Jason smiled as he caught his breath. "You tell Tony. Tell him you mugged me 'cause I went to talk with Russo. He told me to talk with him, you dumb shit. How do you think that will go over?"

Doubt clouded over Gino's face.

"Maybe this ain't a good idea Gino," Carlo said.

"Damn right it ain't," Jason said.

"That still don't explain why you were sneaking around town," Gino said. His confidence now returning.

"I guess I, or Tony, could ask you the same question. I didn't advertise where I'd be. You must have been doing a lot of sneaking around to find me, if you even did. For all I know you might be making that up."

Gino grabbed Jason's collar. "You just admitted you were sneaking around."

"Walking around, coming back from the countryside."

"There ain't no record of you going in or out of the city. We keep logs."

"If you had been paying attention, you'd know that I don't use checkpoints. I like the sport of going around them. Don't like the hassles." Jason pushed back a bit against Carlo, giving himself just enough separation from Gino. "Now let me go before I hurt both of you and Tony finds out about this. You're interfering with his plans to make more money."

He felt Carlo's grip loosen. "That's enough, Gino. We don't want to piss Tony off."

"What plans are you talking about?" Gino asked.

"If Tony wants you to know, he'll tell you. Meanwhile fuck off and if you ever jump me again, I'll break both of your arms." He twisted his body and shoved Carlo off of him. "That goes for you as well. Now get the hell out of here."

Both men backed away.

"This ain't over," Gino said. "I know you're up to something and I'm going to find out what it is."

Jason watched the two men as they backed up, out of range. He thought with some concern that Gino was more right than he imagined.

Later that week, Tony and Gino were sitting in Tony's favorite hangout, the Baker Street Bar. He met with his crew and neighborhood people at his "reserved" table in the back.

"Gino, you got a problem with Jason, you come to me. I didn't make you my enforcer."

"Boss, something's not right with him. He ain't one of us."

Tony gave him a disdainful look. "He's new. We got to give him a chance."

"He'll never be one of us."

"Maybe, maybe not. We got a lot of use for guys that ain't made. And right now, he's earning good money and looking for ways to make more. Something you should be doing."

Gino shook his head.

Tony leaned over the table to put his face closer to Gino's. "You do what I say, you got it?"

Gino leaned away in his seat and nodded.

"Just like Vincent," Tony muttered, sitting back. "You'd think we didn't need the extra help," he said louder. "If we're gonna control other towns, we'll need more guys in our crew to run things and still cover Charlotte. We need all the help we can get." Tony waved his hand at Gino. "Now get out of here and do your job."

Gino left the meeting angry and determined to expose Jason. Something was up and he'd find out what it was.

Joe sat in Big Al's office. Big Al was pacing.

"We got to do something about the coal problem. Nino's not getting the job done."

"Yeah, I know."

"So? You can't let that go on. We need the power. Generating electricity on a city-wide scale separates us from most of the other cities. It's key to our success."

Big Al kept up his pacing. Joe always worried when Big Al paced. Bad things could happen.

"I'm not going to put up with it. Something has to change. You got any ideas?"

Al stopped across the desk from Joe.

"Maybe," Joe said.

Big Al waited for him to continue.

"There's this new guy, an associate with Vincent's crews. He's been pretty impressive so far. According to Vincent, he's increased their collections and gotten a new scam going that will improve earnings. Seems smart and ambitious."

"New guy? Maybe you should meet with him, check him out."

Joe nodded, happy to offer a solution and calm Al down.

Chapter 18

"Get over to Vincent's office right away."

Tony was sitting at his table in the bar. Jason had just walked in.

"What's up?"

"I don't know. When Vincent says come, you come. Now get your ass over there."

Jason turned to go.

"And after you meet with him, you come back here. I want to know what's going on. Got it?"

Jason turned and nodded, before going out the door.

Was his cover blown? There was no way. Jason hadn't been going into the downtown since he'd set up the communication system using Frank and Michael. Nothing much had come of that. Jason still kept asking questions of everyone he ran into but he was getting very little additional information. The coal plant was working. It had its hiccups, but was delivering more electricity than any water mill system. He'd heard that the method for retrieving the coal was essentially a chain gang and the weak sometimes died from their labors. He'd also heard about efforts to reopen a coal mine in the Greensboro area, the Deep River mine. North Carolina was, unfortunately, not blessed with much in the way of coal deposits. *Not like West Virginia, Kentucky or Tennessee,* he thought.

He tried to relax as he walked to Vincent's office. He'd just play things out as they came to him. Hopefully Vincent's suspicious mind hadn't found something of substance to latch onto.

Ears smiled at him when he entered the office.

"Go on in, Vincent's waiting for you."

Ears' smile gave Jason some encouragement. He opened the door.

Vincent pointed to a chair in front of his desk without speaking. Jason sat down and waited. Vincent looked at him for a long moment, his gaze neither friendly nor unfriendly. Jason couldn't read it. He sat still. Vincent would decide when to break the silence.

Finally, he spoke. "Joe Nicoletti wants to talk to you. Why, I don't know."

He stood up and went over to a side cabinet, poured two glasses of whiskey, and turned back to Jason.

"I still don't get you. You keep this fog over your past, like a veil I can't see through. What're you hiding? Crimes? You know that don't mean anything to me. Something you're not proud of? Hell, join the club." He handed Jason his glass and took a sip. "Or is it something we shouldn't know. Like maybe you're working for the feds. They want to infiltrate us, find out our weaknesses. Is that it?"

Jason returned Vincent's gaze. He couldn't let the man see any hint of agitation or panic.

"Well?" Vincent asked.

Jason shook his head. "I didn't do much of anything important before the power went out. None of it's relevant." He shifted in his chair. "As far as the feds go, I heard they're happy to have us pacify Charlotte. I hear we're pretty well off compared to some of the other bigger cities."

"Where'd you hear that?"

"Just the scuttlebutt going around. We talk with one another. I mostly listen since I'm so new."

"You are new, but there's something that don't feel right about you."

"I'm sorry you feel that way. Tony seems to like what I'm doing. I set up that sausage maker, Russo, so he could earn more money, I hope you like that. I'm trying. And I think Tony sees that. I can't help I'm new, just like I can't help I'm not Italian. Maybe that's what doesn't feel right to you."

Vincent shook his head. "We got room for non-Italians. Lots of work to do. That ain't it."

He went back to his desk as if he had put the issue aside.

"Tomorrow you go downtown to meet with Mr. Nicoletti." Vincent gave him two pieces of paper. "This is the address of his office. And you'll need this note to get you through the checkpoint. Be at his office at 10:00 am."

Jason stood up.

"Don't be late. When you're done, report back to me." Jason turned to go. "And don't embarrass me," Vincent called out.

Jason left the office.

"Going to see the big man?" Ears asked.

"I guess it's the assistant big man," Jason relied.

"Yeah. You don't want to see Big Al. Not people like us. That usually means a major screw up and something nasty coming your way."

"Well I hope Big Al doesn't join the meeting." Jason grinned at Ears and left the office. It was helpful to have a few of the crew friendly to him.

On the way back to Tony's bar, he went over the development. Vincent was still suspicious and maybe a little put off by Joe wanting to meet with him. No one knew why, especially Jason. Joe's interest could mean there was a high-level focus on Hillsboro. The situation felt more dangerous, but it was a good step forward.

When he sat down and related the conversation to Tony, the man was impressed.

"Joe wants to talk with you. Damn, I never had a conversation with him directly. Not so's he'd call me into his office. Looks like you're getting popular."

"Shit, Tony, I'm just trying to do my job and help out...make you look good."

"You keep doing that.

"I figure if I make you look good it'll be good for the whole crew. Make you more important."

"It's all about the Benjamins. Things didn't change all that much after the power went out. We're more in charge, don't have to worry about the cops any more, but we still got to earn. It's easier now in some ways since we got the other gangs under control—the local gang bangers and drug dealers." He took a swig of coffee. "So, keep figuring out how we do that, increase our earning power, and we'll do fine."

"Yeah, but Vincent still doesn't seem to like me."

"Vincent don't like strangers and you're still one to him. He doesn't see how you work, carry yourself, get things done. If he did, he'd like you better. Don't worry about him. If we keep our earnings up, he'll be happy enough."

Jason left. Tony would provide a buffer for him with Vincent, but rank would prevail and Vincent was Tony's boss. If things got ugly, Tony would pull the trigger if Vincent told him to. Jason had no illusions about the extent of his friendships with the mob figures.

He'd try to stop in and see Michael Daniels if the opportunity presented itself after meeting with Joe. First, he had to get through that and harvest as much information as he could. That was his mission. Perhaps after the meeting he could go home. Jason smiled to himself. *Wishful thinking?*

The next day, after shaving as best he could with a dull razor, Jason dressed in his dress slacks and suit jacket. He looked in the mirror. *Not too bad*. He kept up his self-examination. *I can see what triggers Vincent's concern.* He didn't have the look of a street hood. He could act the part, but he didn't have that "look".

Maybe that comes from deep inside. In any case, he had to accept the fact that he wasn't a great actor. Being undercover was hard and if you got too far into your role, you could become someone you didn't want to be. Jason had killed enough men to be hardened. He sometimes worried that he may have crossed the line that scarred one's conscience. Too much violence against one's nature kills something inside. Jason didn't want to explore that dark area more than he had to. It held too much danger.

Best I can do. I don't quite look the part, but I'm sure Joe's heard about my contributions. And actions speak louder than looks. He hoped.

He headed down the stairs and into the street.

Chapter 19

Jason was not surprised to find Joe's office in the city government building, the same one where Daniels had his office. Joe was up higher, on the tenth floor. It was a suite of rooms with a receptionist area and a conference room off to one side.

He was kept waiting for fifteen minutes after arriving promptly at 10:00 am. *Probably for effect*, he told himself. The receptionist, after asking him if he'd like something to drink, ignored him. She was a dark-haired beauty, well-endowed with a tight, revealing dress. She sat there reading some old magazines from the pre-attack days. He wondered how many times it had been read. *Some good books at the library*. He resisted the urge to suggest any further reading opportunities to her.

The phone rang. She picked it up and, after listening, motioned for Jason to go in.

He opened the door. Joe was sitting behind a huge desk that seemed to dwarf him. As Kevin had described the man, he was slim and only about five feet nine inches tall. Even though not large, Jason could see that he was solidly built. His hair was dark and slicked back. The scar down the side of his face completed his underworld look. He wore a dark suit and dress shirt with a bright, bold colored tie, a classic mob look; a link to their past.

In the old days, the mob ran certain neighborhoods in the large metropolitan cities. Ran them so completely that the cops held no sway amongst the civilians. Indeed, if there were disputes or transgressions, people went to the mob boss for rectification. Maybe the mob saw this post-EMP world as a way to reinstate that dominance. One where the cops were again subordinate to the gang and the politicians who worked for them.

"Jason Rich," Joe said, standing up.

Jason nodded. Joe reached out his hand and Jason took it.

"I remember we talked at the meeting." His voice held a slight east coast accent with just a hint of New York City. "Bet you're wondering why I called you in." Joe smiled but it didn't relieve the sinister look that resided in his face.

Jason just smiled back.

"I want to talk more. I heard some things about you."

"Good I hope."

"So far." He paused for a moment. "Seems you've got a good head on your shoulders and know how to handle yourself. Those abilities are useful to me."

Jason didn't answer, just stood there.

"Sit down," Joe said. He took his seat behind the large desk. "You want something to drink?"

"If it's okay with you, I'll pass. It's a bit early for me."

Joe laughed. "How about some good coffee?"

Jason looked at him. He'd had coffee a few times with Tony, but it was a bad tasting brew, old and stale, and made weak. Brown water was the term generally applied.

Joe smiled as Jason's face evidenced his interest. He picked up his phone and told the receptionist to bring them two cups of coffee.

Within a minute she entered the office. The aroma floated before her from the steaming cups as she strutted in with her high heels. Jason inhaled the delicious scent that enveloped him.

"How...?"

"Some deals with traders. There's people working the highways, taking goods down south, trading for goods from south of the border. It's like the old days again in many ways. It's one of the things we're going to get involved in.

Not the trading, but controlling the routes, taking our cut from the deals."

He took a sip. Jason was holding the cup under his nose, enjoying the smell rising from the hot liquid, before indulging himself in a first sip.

The two were silent for a moment. Jason wondered if he should probe or wait to see where Joe led the conversation.

"Is control over the trading part of the overall plan?"

Joe looked up at Jason. His eyes were baleful and cold. "What overall plan?"

"I heard that the families were working to connect into a regional organization all up the east coast."

"Where did you hear that?"

Jason shrugged. "Talk among the crews. You know how it goes. Some of it seems preposterous. But control over trading is a good tactic for regional control, so I wondered."

Joe seemed to study him. Finally, he smiled. "That's an interesting conclusion. Most of the crew I know wouldn't have made that connection. You're smart."

He went on. "You've managed to survive okay on your own. Vincent says you're pretty vague about your past, but you've managed things it seems. And you slipped into town without any problem, wound up coming to our attention and getting yourself hooked into the organization. Now you've got a good situation for yourself. You don't have to be an outlaw or road bandit. That's a hard life."

Jason nodded. "I've encountered some of them along my travels."

"And just where have your travels taken you? Where did you come from?"

"Further north, in Virginia. I headed south to get away from the feds—the army, mostly. They wanted people in relocation camps. Control the chaos with regimentation."

Joe nodded and waited.

"So, I eventually wound up in Knoxville and then here."

"With a stop in Hillsboro."

"A short one."

"Let's talk more about that."

Jason repeated what he had said before. Joe listened without interrupting.

When Jason had finished, he leaned forward; his eyes bright with enthusiasm. "Seems as though there's a lot of talk going around about what we're up to. In our crews and probably among the civilians. I'll tell you what it's all about, if you haven't already figured it out."

He pointed his finger at Jason. "It's about power. Always has been, always will be." He leaned back. "And power now days comes from resources and one of those is energy, along with the obvious ones, guns, ammo, food, fuel..." He ticked them off on his fingers.

"That's why the interest in the power plant and the coal?"

Joe nodded. "Feeding that damn monster is the problem. The engineers got it up and running, but we need to increase our coal supply."

"Beyond the abandoned trains?"

"Beyond them. I need new leadership for the project. We got a guy who's out of his depth."

"You thinking about me?"

Joe stood up. "Let's go for a drive. I want to show you something."

He picked up his phone and told the receptionist to get his car sent around. Jason thought the mob was wasteful of precious gasoline. Maybe they had more reserves than he imagined.

"Where are we going?" Jason asked when they were in the car. Up front was a driver and a large man who held an M16 carbine in his lap. *The bodyguard.*

"Out to visit the coal operation. It's about energy, I told you. Energy leads to chemistry and medicines, however that works. Energy also gives us mobility and the ability to extract more resources. We gotta provide services in order to maintain control. And with control comes wealth."

He looked at Jason. "You understand, first the power then the wealth."

"Which leads to more power and then more wealth."
"You got it." Joe smiled.

Chapter 20

West of Charlotte, they came to the stalled coal train. There was a camp set up in a field along the side of the tracks. A barricade had been set up on the road fifty yards before the rail crossing. A fence separating the pasture from the tracks had been removed. In the field, there was a large tent with smaller ones set up in multiple rows next to it.

Workers were busy with hand tools at several of the coal cars. One of the hoppers on a car had been opened, dumping some of its coal underneath. Jason could see a line of men, all covered in coal dust, shuttling wheel barrows of the coal that was being shoveled from under the cars. They dumped their loads into a pile where a front-end loader could get to it and put it in a dump truck. It looked like close to a hundred men working at the site.

"Each car holds a hundred tons of coal," Joe said. "We have the crews working twenty-four hours a day, seven days a week and we still can't keep up. That's why we don't have the whole city electrified."

"How many cars are in the train?"

"A hundred."

Jason did the math in his head, one hundred cars times one hundred tons. It was a staggering amount of coal—ten thousand tons of it. And still not enough. The energy demands of a city were staggering when he considered how hard it was now to find the fuel.

"If we could get the natural gas pipelines back working, it would be easier to get power plants on line," Joe said.

Jason just stared, taking in the scene. There were boys and men in the work crew. They looked tired and were covered in coal dust. There was no sound except for the noise of the tools; no talk, no banter, no calling out. The silence gave the scene an eerie, hellish quality.

"How do you get people to volunteer for this?"

Joe's smile was sinister. "We don't. These are the ones who broke laws. If we don't have enough from that group, we just take who we need off the streets. No one gets to say no if they're picked."

"And you work all one hundred cars from this camp?"

"It's worked in sections. When the cars you see here are emptied, the men move down the train and work the next section of cars. They return here at the end of each shift."

"How long is the train?"

"About a mile in length. When the trek gets to be too far, we move the camp."

The two men walked towards the work area. From what Jason could tell, the method was to open one hopper at a time on each car and let the coal spill out. Everyone got out of the way when that happened. Then the men with the shovels moved in and started shoveling it into the wheel barrows, which moved it to a pile accessible to the front-end loader.

Once the majority of the coal was cleared from the car and off the tracks the crew would move to the next one. A second crew, mostly boys, moved in to glean the remains from under the just-emptied car.

"Impressive sight, isn't it?" Joe asked.

"How long does it take to empty one car?"

"With ten men on a car, they're doing one car in about ten hours. You can see the more men we can set on the train the more cars can be emptied in that ten hours. Right now, a one hundred car train will take over ten days."

"Looks like tough work."

"It is. That's why we use prisoners."

Jason could see the armed guards standing around. They weren't there to protect the resource from theft.

"You can look around some more. I got to meet with the camp bosses." Joe pointed to the large tent in the pasture. "Meet me at the mess tent in an hour."

Jason started walking around the site. He got surly looks from some of the men in the shovel and wheelbarrow crews. The work area was full of dust and dirt—and quiet, except for the sound of the shovels and the engine of the front loader. It felt odd to be dressed for the city, so obviously out of place in this rough, dirty environment.

As he was walking around, one man stood up after dumping his wheelbarrow and stared at him. Jason looked back. Most of the workers only gave him a surly glance and then turned away, back to their work, as if not wanting to attract undo attention to themselves. This man was staring directly at him.

Suddenly he walked up to Jason. "You're Jason Richards, aren't you?"

Jason stared back. There was only one person he had told his real name, the father of the family he had met on the road before getting to Charlotte.

"Ernie? Is that you?"

The man nodded. "You remember."

"What happened?"

"No time for that," Ernie said. "We're not supposed to talk to anyone, not even other prisoners."

One of the guards yelled out for him to shut up and get back to work. A few other workers looked over as if interested in what might happen to the man.

"Please check on my wife and family. They're at an apartment building on Grove Street, 4256."

Now the guard was headed towards him. "I told you to shut up!" he shouted. He had a night stick in his hand along with a revolver on his belt.

"I asked him a question. It's not his fault," Jason said, stepping in front of the man before he could strike Ernie.

"Who the hell are you?"

"I'm here with Mr. Nicoletti. He told me to look around. You want to argue with him?"

The man's aggressive demeanor softened. "Well, he ain't supposed to talk…to anyone."

"I didn't know that and I asked him a question. He felt he needed to answer me. No harm done. He's back to work."

Jason gestured to Ernie who had shuffled off with his wheelbarrow.

"Just look," the guard said. "Don't talk to the prisoners."

Jason nodded and the man strode off.

After Joe had finished his discussions, he and Jason drove back to the city. Joe spoke about a scouting party that had visited the Cliffside Steam Station far west of Charlotte. The power plant was unusable since the EMP attack, but there was a mountain of coal and a partially unloaded coal train there. All of which was waiting to be harvested. Joe wanted men transferred to this location as soon as possible.

The never-ending search for coal to run the greedy furnace to produce the steam that ran the turbines weighed on Joe. He didn't want the job, but Al Tagliani, his boss, insisted he do it. Joe wondered as they drove along if Jason could take over some of this burden. He was new and Joe felt some of the caution Vincent had expressed to him, but he could discern no hidden agenda with the man. Jason's arrival and coming to the mob's attention still seemed coincidental enough. There was no way anyone could have discovered all the players in order to set up such a sequence of events. Still Big Al would have final say. The thought provided him some comfort.

"Joe, you've got so many huge projects, why are you concerned about Hillsboro? They seem small time compared to what's going on here," Jason asked as they drove along.

"Good question. They're small but their reputation is much larger."

Jason gave him a questioning look.

"They have a big reputation in the other smaller towns. They're an example of government run by civilians, democracy, when what is needed is top-down authority, something we can provide. We can give the populations security, safe travel, and safe trade in a chaotic world. We can suppress the gangs and outlaws."

"Kind of like Rome?"

Joe looked at Jason. He didn't understand the reference.

"Not modern Rome, but ancient Rome...the empire. It provided what was called *Pax Romana*, peace under the roman dominance."

"Yeah. Something like that. And Hillsboro and any other towns like them stand in our way. They have to be brought under our control."

Jason didn't say more. He sat in silence as the car made its way into Charlotte. Jason's mind was swirling as he said goodbye to Joe and started walking off down the street.

Chapter 21

Jason made his way to the address Ernie had given him. He knocked on the door. No one answered. He knocked, louder this time—more insistently. Finally, he heard footsteps.

"Who's there?" a woman's voice called out.

"Jason. I met you on the road. I've seen Ernie."

A latch turned and the door opened. Ruth stood there. Her hair was disheveled and her face drawn. She had on a pair of loose jeans and a shirt. She stepped back from the door and Jason entered.

He told her about his visit to the coal train.

"You've seen Ernie? How is he? Is he coming back?" The fatigue in her face was replaced with an eager look. Her eyes lit up.

"Let's sit down," Jason said.

"Oh God. Is he hurt?"

"No, but we have much to talk about."

Out of the corner of his eye, Jason saw the two children standing near the front room. Ruth went over to a couch and motioned for Jason to sit next to her.

"First of all," Jason said, "Ernie's okay. He's not injured as far as I could tell."

"Will he come back? They took him away without telling me anything."

"I don't know. The men live in a camp out there. It looks like they could be there for a while. Now tell me what happened."

Ruth took a deep breath. "We got into town. There was a checkpoint at the bridge. Ernie decided to bring the gun in, to have it with us, wherever we wound up living...to protect us if necessary. I hid the gun under my clothes. They searched the packs like you said they would."

"Did they find the gun?"

She shook her head.

"After we were assigned an apartment, some people, they looked like gangsters, came in and searched the rooms. There were some uniformed police, but the gangster guys were in charge. That's when they found the gun." She looked at Jason. "You're dressed like one of them. Are you one of the gangsters?"

Jason shook his head. "I'm working with them for the moment, but I have another plan, another purpose."

"What's that?"

Jason shook his head and didn't respond.

"Can you free Ernie? If you're one of them, you can put in a word, get someone to let him go. We can't survive without him."

She gripped her hands tightly together in her lap. "We get a ration card, but it's only for one meal a day. The kids are always hungry. I was so scared after they took Ernie, I took the kids out of school. They have schools set up. I was afraid someone would take them. I don't go out except to get food to bring back here. The children don't go out at all. I'm afraid for Jennifer. The men were looking at her..." She shuddered visibly. "I don't think she'd be safe outside."

"You're doing the right thing." He put his hand on her arm. "It's hard, I understand. But you're being careful and that's good."

"But...we can't live this way. And when will they let Ernie go? He didn't do anything. He just had a gun. They could have just taken it. They didn't have to take him."

"The mob that rules Charlotte doesn't want citizens armed. They want everyone to be defenseless and compliant. And Jennifer may not be safe now. She might have been, but these people are predators. Since Ernie was taken, you're a marked family and who knows what that allows. You could be culled from the herd so to speak."

Ruth put her hands to her face and started to cry. Both children came over to her and put their arms around their mother.

"Don't make her cry," Jennifer said. Her voice was angry, defiant.

"I'm not trying to be mean, but you need the truth. Ruth, look at me."

Ruth lifted her head and turned to Jason.

"Things are going to change around here. I'm going to see what I can do to get Ernie freed. You do what you've been doing. Keep yourself and your kids out of sight as much as possible. But if I come to you and tell you to go, to leave town, you go without hesitation. Your life may depend on it."

"I can't go without Ernie."

"You may not connect with Ernie until you're out of the city. In any case, you need to do what you can to save your kids."

"You're scaring me. Even more than I've been scared."

"Your situation is serious. You know that. I'm just confirming it and telling you that it may get worse. On the plus side, you have me as an ally. I'll be trying to do what I can for Ernie. That's better than it was before...right?"

He paused to get a reaction from Ruth. She managed a hint of a smile but tears still shone on her face.

"I guess so." She bowed her head for a moment. Then lifted it and looked directly at Jason. "We can't live here, can we? If you get Ernie free, we'll have to leave."

"Yes. This place isn't for you. I still think you should go to Hillsboro. This city is run by the mob, the mafia. That means civil rights are subject to their whim, not the rule of law."

She put her hand over his. "Thank you. We've just been surviving with no hope. Now you've given us some hope.

It's painful, but you've made me think there may be a way out of this nightmare."

"Nothing's guaranteed. But I'll try." He stood up. "I'll bring some extra food around when I can. You stay close to one another."

"Can we go out? The children need to get outside."

"Pick a time when the mob isn't around. Or a time when other civilians are out in large numbers. Go out and blend in. There's safety in blending in."

Ruth nodded and Jason turned to go.

"Thank you," she said as he left the apartment.

Chapter 22

Albert Tagliani, Big Al, was a large man. He was over six feet tall and weighed in at two hundred and forty pounds. He could bench press more than three hundred pounds. He had a massive chest to go with his thick torso and large arms. His face was usually florid, heightened by his explosive temper. No one wanted to be on the receiving end of his temper.

The plans for the mafia's consolidation of power in the east presented an opportunity for him to move up. His Charlotte organization was small-time compared to the more prominent families in the larger northeast cities. This was his chance to gain power and stature. Charlotte was the southern anchor for now. Big Al wanted to make sure it played a key role in the success of the overall plans.

To do that, he needed power, and right now, energy meant power. He had enough weapons and was building a sizable militia. A good energy source would enable those under him, those with the knowledge, to rebuild the capability to produce some of the vital resources like fuel, medicine and ammunition. That would be a huge step forward. The city would not just be consuming left-over resources. But the effort was going too slowly.

The meeting was attended by Joe, his underboss, all the capos, including Nino Vitale, the man assigned to deliver the coal. Everyone was on edge. They sat around a table with Big Al at the head and Joe sitting next to him.

Big Al started talking about the need for more coal to expand the hours of operation of the power plant.

"We ain't getting enough from the coal trains and we're running out of them. Now I had some people scout around and we found a plant west of here, the Cliffside Steam Station. It's ruined from the EMP attack, but there's a lot of coal there."

"That's good boss," one of the bolder capos said.

Big Al eyed him with a dark look on his face. "Yeah, that's good. But I had to find it by myself. Nino here, who I put in charge, didn't find it." His voice was beginning to raise in volume. "He's focused on the trains and didn't think to send scouts out."

He turned directly to Nino. "Did you know where you were going next after you stripped the last train? There ain't an unlimited number of trains sitting around."

Nino didn't answer; just stared back at his boss.

"I put you in charge of the whole operation. All you focused on was stripping trains. That won't get the job done." His voice grew more menacing.

Big Al's fist slammed on the table. Glasses jumped and rattled. He stood up, his face now even more red. Everyone in the room was silent. Nino now didn't dare look at his boss. He knew he was in for a bad time. He'd known it since told of the meeting. Everyone could see he was out of his league and not able to get a handle on the full scope of the project. But Big Al wanted results when he assigned you a job, not excuses.

He started pacing.

"Maybe you didn't understand the importance of energy, what it means to us. Maybe I didn't explain it properly to you. Did I miss something in my explanation?"

He had stopped across the conference table from Nino.

Nino shook his head.

"What'd you say?"

"No," Nino said in a whisper.

Big Al started pacing again.

"So, you understood how important energy is. How important it is to this family, to us gaining more power with the other families. And yet, you didn't get the job done. And we're struggling to feed the one power plant we got running.

"Do you know how much coal that son-of-a-bitch eats? Tons of it, and we still aren't running it at full capacity."

He stopped behind Nino.

"You know how much coal is needed each day?"

Nino only looked at the table as Big Al shouted behind him.

"Answer me!"

"A lot," Nino said, his voice soft.

"A lot of coal. Do you provide it a lot of coal?"

Nino shook his head.

"And you don't look for other sources, dead coal plants, abandoned coal mines. Did you look around?"

Big Al's voice was loud and sounded dangerous.

"You were told to get me more energy, enough to feed that power plant. You knew that was necessary to getting things back to normal. You let me down. You didn't come to me for help. You just kept shuffling along."

He put a large hand on Nino's shoulder, pinning him down in his chair.

"Did you think I would accept that? Did you think I'd be happy? That I'd let you get away with stumbling around? Not getting the job done? Answer me!"

Nino shook his head.

"No one gets away with fucking around. No one gets away with not getting their job done!"

His right hand, balled into a face-sized fist, swung down with ferocious energy and crashed into Nino's right ear. His head snapped sideways. Big Al held him in the chair with his left hand as he rained repeated blows to his neck and head. "You didn't show respect. You didn't do what I told you to do." Big Al spoke through panted breaths.

He swung him around, the man barely conscious, and began to hit him in the face with both fists, left, right, left, right. Finally, he grabbed Nino by the collar and threw him to the floor. Nino's face was a bloody mess, unrecognizable

"Get him out of here," he said to his bodyguard.

The man dragged Nino out through the door. He was not alive.

No one at the table moved. No one looked at Big Al as he went back to his seat. He was breathing hard as he sat down. The red in his face began to recede slightly.

"No one." He looked around at his capos. "No one gets away with not doing their job."

He took a drink from his water glass.

"Joe and I are going to appoint someone to be in charge of finding and getting the coal we need to run that damn power plant. Run it full time. I expect whoever we pick to get the job done. Find the people to help, find the resources, but Get. The. Job. Done. All of you are to help him. Now get out of here."

After the meeting Joe sat down with Big Al. They shared a whiskey and talked about their plans.

"Did you really need to do what you did?"

Big Al took a sip of whiskey. "I made an impression. No one wants to come up short now."

"And no one wants the job. Hell, I wouldn't."

Big Al looked at his Underboss. "I *made* an impression. That's important. Just like I'm going to make an impression on the towns around us, starting with Hillsboro."

"We're going to collect what they owe us—"

Al shook his head. "I ain't worried about that. We'll get what's owed us. But I want to make an example of them."

He leaned forward in his chair, a wild look into his eyes. "When we send the militia there, we wipe them all out, every single one of them."

Joe stared back at his boss.

"Just like Genghis Khan."

"I don't get it."

"He'd wipe out a city. Leave one survivor to pass the word to other cities and they'd surrender the moment he showed up. No more fighting. We don't want to waste resources fighting to get all these small towns under control. We make an example of one of them, like Hillsboro, since it's got such a reputation. After we take everyone down, the others will fall in line without a fight." He leaned back.

Joe smiled. "Brutal, but effective."

Big Al changed the subject. "We need to talk about Roper."

"What's to talk about?"

"He's doing a good job. The militia is getting pretty professional. My worry is that he controls a serious amount of muscle."

"You worried about him turning? He give you any reason to worry about that?"

Big Al shook his head. "No. I think he still wants to retire in luxury in South America. But people's plans change when they see other opportunities. A large military can control a city...or more."

"What's he going to do? The other families will never agree to support him. He'd be all alone."

"Agreed. It would be a stupid move on his part, but if he tried, it could mean big trouble for us. We don't need that."

Joe thought for a moment. "Whaddaya want to do?"

"Let's hedge our bets. I want you to identify his senior officers. We'll get pictures of their families. Then you visit each one, show 'em the photos. Let them know we can reach their family members if they step out of line."

"Threaten them?"

"Not directly. It's insurance to make sure they do what we want in the end. They'll be taking orders from Roper, but they'll know the safety of their families is in our hands. If Roper starts turning on us, we want them to let us know and not follow him."

"If there's a split and they side with Roper—"

"Right. We whack the families. It'll be the first thing we do."

"Gotta hand it to you, boss. You cover all the bases."

"We can even let them know there's money in it for them, besides the safety of their families. In the end it's all about the money."

"But what about the coal project?" Joes asked. "You need someone to run it."

"I need someone smart. Someone that can tap into the brains that are here in the city. Hell, I don't expect our guys to know about this crap. But we want someone smart enough to find the people who do…and to convince them to work for us."

"Does it have to be one of our guys?"

"You got someone in mind?"

"I'm thinking, we got a guy, an associate. He works for Vincent. He's smart and productive. He'd find the experts. He's that kind of a guy—resourceful."

"I'm not putting an associate in charge. One of our guys has to oversee it. Is this guy a possible crew member? The books ain't open now, but I could make an exception."

"No. He's not Italian. At best he's a good associate. He can help a lot, though. Seems to want to be useful."

"If I give the okay, who runs him?"

"His boss, Vincent."

"Or you, maybe?" Big Al gave Joe a dangerous look.

"To hell with that. I got enough crap to take care of. Got to take care of Hillsboro."

"You do what I told you with them."

"Still, it's gonna be some work. The guy I'm thinking about for the coal project came from Hillsboro. I want him to talk with Roper. He'll be ready to attack soon."

"Set it up when he gets back from training. What's this guy's name?"

"Jason Rich."

Chapter 23

Joe and Vincent met at a bar located in the downtown area.

"Vincent, you know I got to pick someone to head up the coal production."

Vincent felt a chill come over him. After discussing the problem with the other capos, no one could come up with a possible choice. Now he was afraid he was going to be tapped by Joe for the job.

"I got an idea," Joe continued. "I ran it by Al and he's willing to give it a try."

Vincent looked warily across the table at Joe.

"I want to use that new guy, Jason. I met with him the other day. He's smart. He don't know about coal or power plants, but he's resourceful. He'll figure things out and get the problem solved."

Vincent felt a wave of relief spread over him.

"Just one thing," Joe said. "You'll need to watch over him, supervise him. Big Al doesn't want an associate running the operation without one of us looking over his shoulder."

Now Vincent's dread returned.

"Joe, I don't have time for that. What the hell happens if he fucks up?"

Joe didn't answer but just stared at him.

"Look if my ass is gonna be on the line, I got to work at that full time. Look what happened to Nino. How'm I gonna let some associate run things without me being there every day?"

Joe shrugged. "You figure it out. At least I got one guy in between you and the problem."

"And further," Vincent said as if he didn't hear Joe, "what happens to my collections? I can't let them go to hell while messing around with coal trains."

"Put someone in charge."

Vincent was thinking as fast as he could. He had to side step this job. It smelled like a death trap.

"How about I put Tony on it? He gets along with Jason. Thinks he's the greatest thing to come along. He can monitor him and report back to you. I can easily get someone to cover his crew so my earnings won't take a hit."

dumbass, Nino.

"Okay. I can sell that to Big Al. Joe looked thoughtful. Vincent knew he saw through his offer. But Vincent knew Joe understood. Hell, he wouldn't want the job after what happened to that But he reports to you, not me."

"You're trying to keep clear of this ain't you?"

"Vincent, watch what you say. You gotta be a part or Al won't buy it. I can always put you directly in charge. You got a buffer. Now just make sure the job gets done."

Vincent sighed. It was the best he could do. Maybe it was enough to keep him from Nino's fate. Vincent didn't have much hope that the gang would find the coal needed to keep the plant going for long. They were going to have to mine coal and no one knew how to do that. Hell, no one knew if there were any miners in the city.

"There's just one thing we got to do first," Joe said. "I want Jason to talk with Roper. Set it up for next week. The militia'll be back. Then you put him on the coal job."

"Can I tell him and Tony about it?"

"Sure. But don't tell Jason about Nino until they start." Joe smiled. "What happened to Nino shouldn't go to waste. Use it to motivate the next in line. It'll help them take the job more seriously."

The next week, Jason, Vincent and Joe were sitting at the restaurant in the Omni Hotel, the hotel where the meeting of all the capos had taken place. Jason was on edge, but also excited. Things were moving fast but the ground underneath him might get unstable *Price to pay for moving up. The higher I go, the more dangerous it gets.*

"We got a new job for you, but before you do it, I want you to meet with the militia commander and talk about Hillsboro with him."

Jason nodded. Here was a chance to find out first-hand how prepared the militia was. He could get some information on their capabilities and plans before he dropped out of sight.

"The militia's back this weekend. You come to my office next Wednesday," Joe said. "You can meet the commander and tell him what you know. I know you were there only a little while, but you're the best source we got right now."

"You still got a thing about Hillsboro? You going to try to take them over?"

"We got plans. They want to be independent and we can't allow that."

"What about this other job?"

Joe glanced at Vincent. "You impressed me. I'm gonna put you in charge of supplying the power plant with coal."

"What? I don't know anything about coal or power plants. The only thing I know is what I saw when you took me out there."

Joe cracked a smile. If he was trying to make it a warm one, it didn't work.

"No one in the organization knows much about it. You find people who do. You'll have Tony working with you, he can help."

"With all due respect. I doubt if Tony knows any more than I do. How much coal does a power plant use each day? Anybody know?"

"See," said Joe. "That's the kind of question that needs to be asked. We need to get some planning into this. The previous guy didn't think it through. He just went after stalled coal trains and never looked beyond that source. You need to find the guys who know about these things. The guys who helped get the power plant back on line. They'll help you out."

"I thought Nino had already done that."

Joe looked over at Vincent. "I told you. He'll know what to do. Even if he don't know about coal plants." He turned back to Jason. "Mr. Tagliani is looking forward to your success. He's anxious to generate more power, show everyone how well Charlotte is working since we've taken over. Stansky had the same idea, but he didn't understand how to manage the population. He couldn't get the services back soon enough, so people revolted."

Jason knew there were other reasons, but kept his mouth shut. The mob here in Charlotte must have known what Stansky was doing. Maybe that's why they were trying to operate with a softer touch. Not the brutal terror that Stansky brought to Hillsboro's citizens, especially through his lieutenant, Leo.

"When do I start?"

"Right after your meeting with the militia. Pack your bags when you come. I'll drive you and Tony out to the site and you can meet with the crew bosses. They got the manual part of the job down. You need to move forward to find other resources and plan how we'll make the plant work long-term."

"You expect Tony to be able to do this?"

Now Vincent spoke up. He had been sitting quietly during the conversation. Jason wasn't sure if he was in favor of this move or not. Joe's decision would prevail in any case.

"Tony won't be much help in that. He'll work with the crew bosses and check on your progress. Tony'll report back to me so I'll know what's going on. I want to see progress on our current work and on finding new resources."

The discussion went on through dinner. After, Ears drove Vincent and Jason back to their neighborhood.

"Are you okay with this?" Jason asked Vincent. "You've been worried about me since I came aboard."

"Not worried. Suspicious. I don't know you that well. Maybe things will change later. You do a good job with this and it will go a long way to staking your place in the organization."

"What happened to the last guy?"

Vincent paused for a moment. "He was out of his league. The job was too big for him, so Big Al had to retire him."

"And he thinks I can do this?"

"Joe thinks you can do this. And Big Al is going along." They were both sitting in the back seat. He turned to Jason, "If you fuck up it goes back on Joe…and me. You don't want that to happen."

Jason could guess what the word, "retired" meant. The stakes had just escalated with such a high-profile assignment.

"Besides giving me this job, why is Joe so focused on Hillsboro? He wants me to talk with the militia commander? I already told Joe as much as I know."

"It don't matter. You tell it to the commander if that's what Joe wants."

Jason shook his head. "It doesn't make a lot of sense. This coal project is a huge challenge. Messing with Hillsboro seems like a side issue."

"It ain't a side issue. Big Al wants to make an example of the town."

"What do you mean?"

"He's going to send the militia to wipe everyone out."

"Kill everyone? Why?" Jason felt a cold shiver run through him.

"Says it's like Genghis Khan. Kill everyone in one town, the other towns hear about it and they'll all give up without a fight." Vincent looked over at Jason. "He figures that will save time and resources. The commander seems to be enthused by the idea."

Jason worked to keep the dread he felt out of his voice. "Who is this militia commander?"

"He's ex-Army. A guy named Roper. He was a captain before he retired out. We made him a better offer, better pay. He's whipping the militia into shape and is excited about the mission, especially making an example of Hillsboro."

Jason's stomach clenched. Another cold chill ran up his neck. Captain Larry Roper, the disgraced officer that Kevin had run out of Hillsboro. Of course, he'd want revenge. He had the men to get it and now had been given permission to annihilate the whole town. There was no possibility of paying off the mob. Big Al had decided everyone had to die to advance his plans.

Roper would recognize him. He might put it all together just from his undercover name. Jason knew he couldn't meet with him. He might even be uncovered as soon as Roper got back from training.

He faced a frightening situation. An existential threat to Hillsboro and his unmasking. He had to drop out of sight and take action. Hillsboro's survival depended on him finding a way to disrupt the planned holocaust.

Chapter 24

When Roper got back to Charlotte, he met with Joe. Joe wanted to go over plans to pacify the smaller towns and set up the meeting with Jason.

"How did things go?" Joe asked when they sat down in his office.

"The men are ready. They're disciplined, know the weapons, and are good with the mission. They know that we're bringing stability to the region and they understand some will resist and we'll have to deal with them."

"What about the heavy weapons?"

"We have four 105mm howitzers, two M60 tanks and a dozen APCs. We're in good shape. Of course, we don't want to use them unless we have to. You don't want the towns reduced to rubble. But they'll provide a strong incentive for towns to give in without a fight."

"That's the idea."

Roper looked over at Joe. He liked the thin, swarthy man. He was cunning, not like Leo, Stansky's henchman. When their paths had crossed, Roper realized that Joe and Big Al could provide his way back to riches and the good life in South America. That dream had been taken away from him by his previous lieutenant, Kevin Cameron. He was forced out of Hillsboro with only the barest of provisions.

Once on the road, the men who had elected to depart Hillsboro with Roper, began to complain. Disputes had broken out ending with the group splitting up. Of the dozen men who had departed, five remained with Roper and the rest left to find their way back to their families as best they could; done with military life.

Roper and his remaining cohorts headed south, hoping to reconnect with Colonel Stillman. Roper had worked out a tale of mutiny and treason on the part of Lieutenant Cameron. The men with him joined the story. However, before connecting with Stillman, they arrived at Charlotte and Roper met Joe.

As the two men engaged with each other, they discovered a mutual desire for wealth and control along with a willingness to do what was necessary to achieve their goals. This new order imposed by the EMP attack called for new responses and Joe and Larry Roper found theirs to be in synch.

In Roper, Joe got someone to develop his growing militia into a formidable fighting force. In Joe and Big Al, Roper got a group that had the same goals as Stansky, but knew how to accomplish them.

Roper was set up as commander and given a steady supply of resources, including the local scrip, as payment. Within a year or two at the most, ex-Captain Roper would be back on his way to his luxury retirement abroad while the U.S. muddled along in a state of semi-anarchy.

"Al has escalated the mission," Joe said. "He wants you to wipe out Hillsboro."

"Level the town? What good does that do?"

"Not necessarily level it but kill everyone."

Roper stared at Joe in disbelief.

"You got a problem with that?" Joe asked.

"Not necessarily, but why? It seems unnecessary. I can overcome them with my firepower. They'll capitulate."

"Al wants them all killed. I know it sounds harsh, but when the other towns hear about it, you'll have no trouble with them. We don't want to take time fighting each town."

Roper shook his head. "I don't know…"

Joe leaned close to him. "All you got to know is that you do what Al says." He leaned back, with his eyes on Roper. "Got it?"

Larry looked at Joe. The man's face was set hard. If Al decreed it, he had to do it. He sighed. "I still think it's unnecessary."

"Your job is not to second guess Al. Your job is to do what he says. You want to go tell him he's wrong? Tell him you think you know better?"

Joe's voice dripped disdain.

"No."

"All right. That issue is settled. Don't let me hear about it again. Now, I got someone you need to talk to before you go out," Joe said. "He's from Hillsboro, recently passed through there. He's got the latest info on the town. It might be helpful to you."

"Did he live there?" Roper wasn't sure he wanted to meet a citizen. Who knows what had happened after he had left? The only thing he knew was that Stansky had, against all odds, been overthrown. He could hardly believe it when he had heard. The results proved Stansky and Leo were not up to their vision and had been doomed to fail.

"No. He's been traveling from town to town, looking for a group to hook up with. He's joined our organization, an associate. Shown himself to be smart and resourceful. He could have useful insights."

"Okay, I'll meet with him. What's his name?"

"Jason Rich."

Roper eyebrows went up. He stared at Joe.

"You know him?" Joe asked.

"Jason Rich. That's what you said, right?"

Joe nodded, "Yeah."

"And he comes from Hillsboro?"

"He spent a short amount of time there. He came from Knoxville and, before that, from up in Virginia."

Roper described Jason as six feet tall, solidly muscled, brown hair with dark, piercing eyes.

"He looks kind of like that, but so do a lot of people. What's up? You know him?"

"Is he doing anything important for you?"

"Big Al is putting him in charge of energy resources. We had to retire the previous guy. Jason seems like the kind of guy who can figure things out, look beyond the obvious solutions and get us a steady supply of fuel for the power plant."

Roper kept his gaze on Joe. *Were all criminals stupid?* "If this is who I think it is, you've got a problem on your hands. This guy may not be someone who wants to be a part of your organization. He may be an undercover operator, planning to dismantle or cripple your group."

Now Joe's eyes darkened. "You know who this is?"

"Maybe. The names similar. I knew a Jason Richards. He was the leader of the revolt against Stansky. If this is the same guy, he's not from Virginia, he's from a valley north of Hillsboro. The town thought of him as some kind of hero. He defeated a gang led by Big Jacks, someone you may have heard of."

Joe nodded.

"The Jason I know shot up the gang and personally killed Big Jacks. He's not someone to take lightly." Roper paused for effect. "And I certainly wouldn't put him in charge of anything important."

Joe sat quiet for a moment. "You'd be able to identify him?"

"Maybe. I saw him only once."

"But you could ask some questions. Get down to details about his past?"

"I could do that."

"Great. Meet here, in my office, on Wednesday. I've got a meeting set up with the two of you. If he's who you say he is, he won't leave the meeting. If he isn't, you get what information you can and we'll both get on with our plans.

"Do you really think all this will work? Getting a power plant going again, pacifying the surrounding towns?"

"What do you mean? We're doing it."

"Yeah, I see you got it started, but you still got the U.S. Army to deal with as well as the feds."

"Larry, I explained this before. The families up and down the east coast are united in this. The New York families are already working with the government to get the city under control."

"Yeah, but after they do, will the government be happy with them running things?"

"The government has more to worry about. They need an end to anarchy. There's challenges from the outside, the rest of the world, you know that."

"I know there's a world-wide recession, some are calling it a depression. The Islamists certainly won a victory with that EMP attack.

"Fuck the Islamists. They're stuck in the same mess they created."

"Yeah, but they probably aren't unhappy about that."

"It don't matter. We got an opportunity and we're taking it. As for getting power back up, it may be localized, but there's enough coal in the east to run all the power plants we need to get running."

He stood up and went to the bar along the side wall. "Once we're in control, the feds won't be able to get us out of the picture. We'll be partners with them, even if they aren't completely comfortable. By then, we'll have bought off most of the officials who'll keep us in power."

Roper shook his head. "It sounds great, but I don't know. The army still has its loyalties and traditions. They're not necessarily going to be on your side."

"They may not like it, but they have this tradition of bowing to civilian authority. You pointed that out to me. They'll go along with the elected officials, even if we're the ones electing them."

Joe poured two whiskeys and sat back down at his desk. He leaned across it to give one to Roper.

"And the military has its hands full with the Mexican and Columbian drug cartels in Florida and the border states. Then there's the so-called help from China. They're taking over the west coast. We may wind up with a smaller United States when this is over."

"And that doesn't bother you?"

"Does it bother you?" Joe responded. "I know you're planning to head to South America when you get enough loot together."

A look of concern came over Larry's face.

"Don't worry," Joe continued. "It doesn't matter to me. Long as you do the job we hired you for and train your replacement, you can do what the hell you like." Joe finished his whiskey and stood up. "For now, let's find out who this Jason really is."

Chapter 25

J ason lay on his bed. He couldn't sleep. *If Roper even hears my name associated with Hillsboro, he'll be suspicious. Joe would tell him about me and he would tell Joe about his suspicions. I may be compromised even before the meeting.* He might have to drop out of sight over the weekend. Joe might set someone up to keep an eye on him until Wednesday. He certainly was not going to go to the meeting.

Better to disappear now.

It was clear to Jason that with ex-Captain Roper leading the militia, Big Al's plans would be fully supported by Roper. And who knew what heavy weapons Roper had at his disposal. Jason guessed he might not be reluctant to use them against his town.

Time for counter measures. Have to neutralize any pending attack. But what to do about Ernie and his family? Ernie was in a bad spot. Jason hadn't any idea how long he would be kept. From what Joe had said, they desperately needed coal; Jason couldn't see the gang releasing anyone from the work crews. If anything, they would be worked harder no matter what the cost in lives. No one wanted to fail Big Al the second time. Ernie wasn't going to be freed any time soon.

When he disappeared, Jason needed to take Ernie's family with him. Hide them until he could free Ernie. Then what? Help them leave.

Jason thought about the next moves. He had to give Ruth a heads up and make sure she was in the apartment with her kids when Jason came to take them. He'd go there first thing tomorrow. With the first steps of a plan in mind, he tried to sleep but sleep wouldn't come.

The next morning Jason left his apartment to meet with Ruth and the kids. He hoped Joe had not yet connected with Roper. Jason wasn't sure when Roper would be back, but guessed he had one more day at least before he might be uncovered.

Gino started early. Since Jason had been to some high-level meetings indicating that he was going to be given greater stature, Gino decided to put all his energy into exposing him. The man was a fraud, or worse. And Gino was not going to let him fool the others like he seemed to have fooled Tony. He was waiting down the street when he saw Jason leave his apartment.

From his path, Gino could tell he was not headed for his regular routes or the crew's bar. His interest perked up. He'd follow and see what Jason was up to. It wasn't hard to tail someone, there were fewer people about since the EMP attack. That fact also made it harder to not be noticed, so Gino kept back a good distance.

A half-hour later Jason disappeared into an innocuous apartment building. Gino stopped at the entrance. *Who could he be visiting?* The only way to find out was to go inside and see which apartment he entered. There were too many to search after Jason had left. He opened the door.

Once inside, Gino heard Jason's steps on the stairs. He quietly followed, trying to close the distance so he could see on what floor Jason exited. He heard a door open and ran up the remaining stairs just as he saw the fifth-floor door close. He slowly opened it and peeked around the opening to see Jason knock on an apartment door. It opened and he went inside. Gino marked the location and went back down the stairs.

Jason entered the apartment after Ruth opened the door. He sat with her in the kitchen. The children stood at the doorway.

"I told you I would do what I can to get Ernie freed."

Ruth nodded.

"How I was going to do that has changed. I can't do this as part of the mob. I'm going to be exposed soon and then I won't be a help to anyone."

"What does that mean?"

"It means that I have to act right away and if you want me to help Ernie, you have to act right away."

"You're scaring me."

"I don't mean to, but what I'm going to tell you is quite serious." Jason took a breath. "I'm going to drop out of sight tonight. You and the kids have to come with me. Once you do that, you can never go back. Charlotte is over for you."

"There's no other way?"

"I can't get Ernie free in a way that lets him come back here and all of you lead a normal life. You can't do that in a city run by the mob. It isn't going to happen. And if I don't free Ernie, I'm not sure he'll ever be let go."

"But why? He didn't do anything bad with the gun, just brought it in."

"I understand, but the mob needs workers to recover coal. They can't lose a single one so I don't think anyone is going to be let go. Meantime, you run the risk of getting grabbed by someone, or worse, Jennifer getting grabbed."

Ruth sucked in her breath. Jason could see panic rise in her face. "They can and will do that but I can get you out. You'll have to be brave. Your kids will have to be brave. And if I'm lucky, you'll all be reunited. But you'll have to go on the road again. This time to Hillsboro."

"What do we have to do?" Ruth asked in a timorous voice.

"Gather your things today, get food if you have any ration cards. I'll come for you after midnight. Everyone should be ready to depart, jeans, good shoes. Wear dark clothing and put everything into one pack each. You still have your packs?"

Ruth nodded.

"Good. Pack them with one change of clothes, any medical supplies you might have, some blankets, and any food you can fit. Remember only one pack per person." He turned to the kids. "You can both pack yourselves? Did you hear what I told you mom?"

They nodded; their faces solemn.

"How will we find Ernie?" Ruth asked.

"I'll find a place for you to hide and then I'll get Ernie. That may take a few days so you'll have to remain hidden. Can you do that?" He looked at each person. They all nodded their heads.

"Good. I'll be back tonight."

Jason got up and left. His days of being undercover were going to be over. He felt a new energy flow through him. He would reunite this family *and* complete his mission. When he left, he didn't notice Gino hiding behind a dumpster in an ally across the street.

After Jason had disappeared, Gino went over to the apartment and climbed the stairs. Did Jason have a woman on the side? He didn't seem the type.

He knocked on the door. Ruth opened it. She looked like she was expecting a familiar person and, seeing Gino, her face clouded in suspicion.

"Yes?" she said.

Gino pushed past her.

"Jason was just here. I work with him. I need to know what's your relationship to him. You his woman?"

Ruth gasped. "No." After a moment's hesitation, she added, "He's a friend."

"How'd you meet? He don't get out much."

'We met on the way to Charlotte. My husband and I were coming here to find some work, some stability."

Just then Tom and Jennifer peeked around the corner of the living room.

"Your husband, you and your kids, eh?"

Ruth nodded.

Gino smiled. "Come on in, kids. I got to talk to all of you."

"You can just talk with me," Ruth said.

Gino turned to her, the smile slid off his face, replaced by a hard look. "No, I need to talk to everyone." He turned back to the boy and girl. "It's okay, he said with his smile back in place. You come over here and sit down. We all need to talk."

The kids hesitated, they looked from Gino to their mother and back to Gino.

"Tell them to come over here. We'll all go into the kitchen and sit at the table." Gino's voice was now darker, more threatening.

Ruth nodded to the children and they went and sat down in the kitchen.

"Why did Jason come over today? You see he's a part of our organization and we need to know who he meets with, who he sees."

"Like I said, we met on the way here. He just visited to check up on us, to see how we're getting along."

"And how are you getting along?"

"Okay."

"Where's your husband. You said you got one."

Ruth hesitated again. "He's...he's away right now."

Gino leaned towards her. "Away, where?"

"I...I...don't know. He said he had to go do something special for the city."

"Who'd he talk to? Where does he work?"

"I don't know. I don't understand how things work here. It's all so crazy!" she burst into tears. Jennifer and Tom got up and put their arms around their mother.

"Don't make her cry," Tom said.

Gino smiled, but it didn't have any warmth. "Pretty tough, ain't you? You gonna beat me up?"

"Just leave us alone, we haven't done anything to you," Jennifer said. "If you want to know more, ask Jason."

"I will smart girl. But right now, I'm asking your mother." He looked at Ruth. "What's your name?"

She looked up. "Ruth."

"Okay Ruth. Now tell me again, where your husband went. I can always take Jennifer outside and ask her personally."

He could see Ruth shudder.

"You leave her alone," Tom said. His voice quivered as he spoke.

"Ernie's been taken away. Jason comes by to see how he can help us. He's being nice. Is that a crime now?"

"While the cat's away, the mouse comes over to play, that it?"

Ruth shook her head. "That's not it at all. Maybe you don't know what it's like to be nice to someone."

"What did you talk about that was so important he came here before checking in with his crew?"

"I told you he was just checking up on us."

"I'm not buying that."

He grabbed Jennifer by the arm. She screamed. Tom jumped up and ran at him, but Gino flung his arm out and smacked him, knocking him to the floor.

"Stop, don't hurt my family!" Ruth shouted.

Gino stood up, dragging Jennifer with him. Tom got up off the floor, glaring at Gino.

"Don't come at me again, boy, or I'll hit you with my fist and break your jaw."

"Let her go!" Ruth demanded.

"I'm taking her with me and we're gonna talk about what went on here unless you tell me."

"No, don't. I'll tell you," Ruth said.

Gino stood there with Jennifer. "I'm waiting."

"Jason came by to warn us that people, people like you might come around and try to harm us, separate us. He said he'd take us somewhere safe and then try to get Ernie released. Then we could all leave town together. He said, with Ernie in trouble, I wasn't safe and there was no future for us in Charlotte."

"What a crock. And you believed him?"

"Why wouldn't we? He's helped us and now you've come around. Seems like that proves what he said."

"He's trying to get you alone, for himself. Not sure I understand why he'd want a built-in family, but he's weird."

Ruth kept her mouth shut.

"When's he coming to take you away and rescue you like some hero?"

"Tomorrow night."

"Maybe I'll take the girl downstairs and ask her the same question. I can be pretty persuasive. If don't like her answer, you might not see her again." Gino paused as he watched Ruth tremble. "You want to change your answer or should I check it out with the girl here?"

"He's coming tonight," Ruth said in a whisper. "Now please leave us alone."

Gino let Jennifer go and she ran to the other side of the table.

"I'll leave you alone...for now. You've been very helpful."

He turned and left the apartment.

Chapter 26

Gino returned to the bar where Tony had his table. He sat down with a thud.

"I found out something about Jason today."

Tony looked at him with an exasperated expression.

"You still going on about that? I told you to knock it off and concentrate on collecting."

"I'm doing that. But I followed him today. Saw him heading to another part of town. Turns out he's meeting with a woman and her two kids. She says he's coming back tonight to help her hide or get out of town. The woman's got a husband that must have been arrested. He's working on the coal gang."

"Jason's about to be put in charge of the coal gang. So what if he wants to help her out? Maybe her husband can help *us* out. You know Jason tries the soft approach with people. It's what Joe and Big Al want as well."

"I can do soft, but most of the people I collect from understand hard better. They don't fool around and they don't give me any trouble."

Tony sighed. "Gino, let it go. Jesus, you're like a dog gnawing on a dry bone."

"I don't mean no disrespect, but I think you're being blind to Jason. He's conned you into thinking he's so great, you don't see how things don't add up with him."

Tony stood up. Gino looked at him.

"Stand up," Tony said.

When Gino was standing, Tony poked a finger in his chest. "Don't ever accuse me of being blind. I'll take you out. I've covered for you in the past and will in the future when you fuck up, but you don't accuse me of that. You understand? You work for me and I expect you to do what I say. You start undermining me and you'll have a short life."

His finger punctuated each sentence.

Gino put up his hands and stepped back.

"Okay, okay, boss. I didn't mean anything by it. I'm just concerned that's all."

"Gino, you meant something by it. I'm not stupid. And if you ever talk like that again…" He left the rest of his sentence unfinished.

"I'm sorry, boss. I won't talk about him anymore. But the woman said he was going to take them away, somewhere safe, tonight."

"If it makes you feel better, follow them and report back to me. After that I don't want to hear another thing about your suspicions. Got it?"

Gino nodded and left the bar.

The same afternoon Jason went over to visit Frank Russo. He handed him all the scrip currency he had accumulated working for the mob.

"Frank, load me up with as much ham and sausages as this will purchase. I want the sausage that has been cooked. Not the ones that need cooking."

Frank looked at the pile of money. "What's going on? This is a lot of money. It'll buy a lot of meat."

"Stocking up. You put the meat aside, in a sack for me."

"You're not going to take it with you?"

"No. I need to pick it up tonight, after you close. I'll be by late in the evening."

Frank thought for a moment. "For you, I can leave it in the back room. I'll leave one of the windows unlocked. You can open it and climb in to get your sack. But you know this is a very odd request. What're you up to?"

Jason shook his head. "No need for you to know. But if this is enough money, with what you already saved, you should consider leaving right away."

"What's going to happen? My business is going well, especially the cart sales in the downtown area, thanks to you. Is all this going to come to an end?"

"I don't know. But it's going to get unsettled soon. That's as much as I'm sure of."

Frank shook his head. "I don't understand, but I'll have the sack ready for you."

"Thanks. And if I don't see you again, good luck and be careful."

Jason left before Frank could ask any more questions.

That night he finished his own packing. He hung his working suit neatly in the closet. An ironic gesture to his undercover work. He was now dressed in his travel gear. Jeans, dark shirt, sweater, and water proof jacket along with sturdy hiking boots. He took out his 9mm and checked the gun carefully. It was clean and oiled. He loaded two extra magazines and put them in his jacket pocket. Then he screwed a suppressor onto his pistol. The extra length made the gun awkward. It was a necessary price to pay but a stealthy weapon was what he needed tonight. He pushed the gun into his jacket. It rested uncomfortably there. *Can't stuff it in my pack, though. I might need it.*

It was midnight when Jason descended the stairs. He opened the front door and went out into the night. He was changing from undercover sleuth to, what, assassin? He had been called to fight and kill before in defense of himself, his family and his town. Now events seemed to be forcing him to do it again. The realization weighed heavily on him. There seemed to be no way out of the cycle of violence he found himself in.

It would be complicated. The mob would soon be looking for him. Still he wished there was another way to neutralize the threats that arose besides killing. In the end, it didn't matter. If this was the field of action, Jason knew it well, probably better than his opponents.

Gino crouched in the shadows. He was cold, stiff, and angry. Tony's dressing down hadn't helped. Now it looked like Jason was leaving. To meet the woman? He'd find out and he'd show Tony that he wasn't wrong. Then there'd be a reckoning. Vincent would see Gino's instincts were right. Maybe he'd make Gino the head of the crew.

He carefully followed Jason. When they came to Frank Russo's store, Jason went around to the back. Gino took up a position a half-block away and watched. Jason tested a couple of windows and found one unlocked. He opened it. After putting his backpack down, he climbed through the window and disappeared. *What the fuck? Robbing the sausage maker?* That didn't make sense. Gino kept watching.

In a moment a sack was tossed out of the window and Jason quickly followed. He looked around and after putting on his pack, he picked up the sack and headed down the alley. Gino stood up and followed.

Jason knocked softly at the apartment door.
"Who's there?" a voice asked.
"Jason."
The door swung open and he stepped in.
"Everyone ready to go?"
Ruth and the kids nodded. They were all dressed as Jason had instructed. Their faces reflected a mixture of anxiety and hope. Tom looked excited. *Maybe he thinks this is a big adventure*. It was, but one far more dangerous than the boy could imagine.

"I'm going to take you to a hiding place where you can be safe. It may take me a couple of days to get Ernie free. You'll have to be patient and wait there."
Ruth held out her hand to stop him. "Someone came here today. After you left. He asked why you were here. He

made me tell him that you were coming to take us to a safe place tonight."

Jason stared at her. "You told him that?"

Ruth shrank back. "I had to. He threatened Jennifer."

"Damn." Jason's face darkened. "He'll try to follow us." He thought for a moment, then shook his head. "Doesn't matter. We still have to go. We'll try to lose whoever it is on the way."

He led them out of the door and down the stairs.

Gino watched. As he expected, Jason emerged with the woman and kids. *Where's he going with them?* Tony's idea that Jason could be just helping the family, didn't fit well with him taking them off in the middle of the night. *Hiding them? Why?*

He began to follow as Jason led the family though the streets. They went past a burned-out transformer station and then followed the edge of the power lines north, heading out of the city. They crossed a freeway and started up the green area surrounding Stewart Creek. The riparian green space made a convenient pathway with screening from the nearby streets.

Gino was uncomfortable. He was dressed for the city, slacks, dress shirt and shoes with a long overcoat to protect against the night.

His shoes quickly got wet and his feet cold. *Fucking Boy Scout. Where the hell's he taking them?* In spite of his discomfort, Gino resolved to carry on. He had his .45 caliber handgun. He needed to get something solid on Jason so he could take him down. If he got cold, it would be worth it to nail the SOB.

They trudged on until they came to I85. After a few minutes of scanning the area, Jason led the family across the road. When they had disappeared into the woods Gino ran across the highway. Now he needed to catch up with them.

Gino ran through the woods until he came to a warehouse compound. It was old. The broken windows and grass growing through the blacktop spoke of years of neglect and disuse. He could see no figures moving beyond the compound. *He's hiding them in one of the warehouses.* He moved forward, stopping at each row of buildings to listen and look. At the third row, he saw the figures enter one of the buildings. It would be pitch-black inside. Gino headed towards the door. A flash of a light confirmed that they went inside.

If he wanted to get closer, he'd have to go inside and navigate his way in the dark. There were few clouds scudding past in the cold wind. The moon was on the horizon. In a half-hour it might give him enough light to keep him from stumbling and giving himself away. He'd wait and watch. If Jason left, he would follow him. That seemed to be the best play. Whatever Jason had planned for the rest of the evening, Gino didn't think it was to go back to his apartment. Something else was up, and it involved this family and the husband in the coal gang.

During the hike, Jason could see that Tom was excited with the adventure of it all. Unlike his sister and mother, he seemed to be enjoying the experience. The boy probably assumed Jason would rescue his father without any trouble and they would all go on another adventure together. Things were going to be more difficult than that, however.

Jason breathed a sigh of relief when they arrived at the warehouse with no one having seen them. They would be safe there. They had shelter from the wind and rain and enough clothes to make it through the cold nights in late November. He'd find a corner with no windows, most of which were broken, and have them make camp. They had water, food and shelter. Tomorrow he would head out to the coal gang to try to find their dad. After taking care of the family, he would go back to his original mission.

They'll notice me missing tomorrow. By tomorrow night they'll assume something is wrong. That's when my cover gets blown. Jason went over the timeline of events in his mind. *They'll assume that I split and am heading back to Hillsboro. Roper might not be worried. He's probably thinking he has overwhelming firepower. Hopefully it won't cause him to accelerate his plans.* He needed Roper to remain in the city for a few more days. *It should take a week to get everyone organized.*

Jason risked letting a thin shaft of light escape from his flashlight. He led the family up a set of stairs to a mezzanine. In one of the office sections he found a place at the far corner of the room. There were no windows, just the walls making a right angle. Jason pulled some desks over to keep out the drafts.

"This is where you'll stay for a few more days while I go to get Ernie."

"We just stay here?" Ruth asked.

"That's right. You can't go out. Go down to the main floor and go to the other side of the warehouse to do your business. But you can't be seen so you must stay inside."

"How long will it take to get Ernie? Is it far?"

"We're halfway there now, so it won't take me too long. Getting him freed is another story. That will be a challenge."

"Can I help?" Tom asked.

Jason smiled in the dark.

"Yes, you stay here and keep a lookout for anyone. Freeing your dad is a job best done alone."

Jason stopped talking. There was a scraping sound on the floor. Just for a moment. He shushed everyone and they listened. Jason's ears tried to penetrate the surrounding dark, but no other sound came to him. After a few moments he spoke in a whisper.

"I thought I heard something, a scraping on the floor."

"I heard it too," Tom said.

"Me also," his mother said.

Chapter 27

Gino froze. He had almost stumbled and fallen. Now he stood still; no more sounds coming from him. He heard murmuring start up again. It came from above, on the mezzanine. Now footsteps sounded out. Someone was coming. There was no time to get back to the entrance. He was stuck in the building. The woman wouldn't be coming, it had to be Jason. If he was discovered he'd have to get the jump on him. The man had already warned him to not mess around in his business. He'd have to try to take him down; there'd be no discussions.

If Jason was on the up and up, he'd welcome help in getting the husband freed to work with him. But why sneak around? Just tell Vincent or whoever that he needed this guy. No, Jason was up to no good and Gino had to stop him. He slipped his .45 out of its holster.

When he heard the footfalls on the stairs, Gino moved just behind where they joined the main floor. Between the faint moonlight and his eyes growing accustomed to the dark, he could see shadows now.

Jason reach the floor and started for the door. He'd gone two steps when he heard the click of a safety lever. He stopped.

"Just stand still," Gino said. "I can see you well enough to kill you."

"Gino. You followed me all the way out here?"

"I wanted to see what you're up to. It sounds like it's no good."

"I'm just trying to help this family out."

"Cut the crap. I talked to them earlier. If you're helping them, helping to get the woman's husband free, why not go to Vincent or Joe? You're a big man now, got Joe's ear. Going to run things for Joe. I'm sure he'd help you. Why sneak around?"

"Gino, you don't know what you're talking about."

"Don't try to play me. I'm not an idiot. You can fool Tony, but not me. You're gonna break this guy out. Why, I don't know, but that ain't something Joe would want to hear about, is it?"

"Gino, I swear you've got this all wrong."

"Have I? Let's go back upstairs and sit down with the rest of the family. We can talk about it. Then we'll all go back to see Vincent tomorrow and you can explain everything to him."

Jason turned back to the stairs.

"Stop," Gino said. "I know you've got a gun on you. Take it out slowly and set it on the ground."

"It's in my coat pocket," Jason said. He reached in, took the 9mm out, and laid it down.

"Put your hands on your head and let's go."

Gino picked up Jason's gun and put it in his pocket. The two men went back to the mezzanine. Pale light came through the warehouse windows, casting faint shadows on the empty floor. Enough light made its way through the mezzanine windows to make out the family huddled in the corner.

They gasped when Jason appeared with his hands on his head and Gino behind him holding a large gun.

"This is nice and cozy. A family camping trip? Now Jason just has to go find the old man to make it complete. Sit down," he told Jason.

"What are you going to do?" Jason asked.

"Wait 'til morning. Then we're all going to visit Vincent. He can decide what will happen next."

"He's not going to like your messing around, neither is Joe."

"I'll take that chance. Somehow I think he'll like you sneaking around even less."

"What's going to happen to us?" Ruth asked.

Gino looked over at her. He gave her a crooked smile. "That'll be up to Vincent. If it was me, I'd put you to work with the whores. The ones who take care of the members. You still got some looks on you."

"No!" Ruth said. Her response was almost involuntary.

"The boy," Gino continued, "I'd put him on the coal gang, getting water for the men. When he gets a bit bigger, he can start wielding a shovel like the others. As for the girl...she's a bit young, but she'll be ready in a couple of years. I'd put her in training, if you know what I mean."

Jennifer started to cry.

"You're a mean man," Ruth exclaimed "How can you be so cruel?"

"You don't mean anything to me. You're just something to use. If we can use you, fine. If not, I get rid of you. You crossed the line when you went off with wonder boy here. Now you got to pay the price."

He turned to Jason. "Of course, if Vincent or your new best friend, Joe, think you're just fine then all is forgiven. No problem. We'll find out everything tomorrow."

"You better leave my mother and sister alone," Tom said from the corner.

"Well ain't you a feisty one? What're you gonna do, beat me up?"

Now Jennifer spoke up. "You're just a big bully. No one ever taught you manners."

"You better shut your mouth or I won't wait to let Vincent decide what to do with you."

Jason let his arm slowly move to his side as Gino focused on the children. At that moment Tom sprang up and started for the door. Gino lunged after him.

"No you don't you little punk." He grabbed at the kid.

Jason leapt to his feet and launched himself at Gino. He slammed into him and both men fell heavily to the floor. Jason scrambled desperately for the gun in Gino's right hand. His hand closed over it and a deadly wrestling match ensued, both men grunting in an effort to control the weapon. Gino rolled over onto Jason who wrenched his torso in a violent twist, throwing his legs to one side, in an attempt to right himself.

At that moment, Tom jumped on Gino's back. The boy had a pocket knife in his hand. He plunged the blade into Gino's right arm. Gino screamed and Jason tore the gun from his hand. Gino flung the boy off his back; he landed on the floor, slamming up against a desk. Jason turned the gun on Gino and pulled the trigger, hitting him in the chest.

The gun's explosion was loud, accompanied by a flash and screams from all three of the family. Then it was silent except for a few gasps from Gino as his life slipped away. Jason stood up.

"Tom, are you alright?"

The boy looked up from the floor and nodded.

Ruth and Jennifer were holding one another. Tom was staring at Jason, almost in shock.

"Thanks," Jason said. "You saved my life and the lives of your mother and sister. That was a brave thing you did."

The boy looked at him and then crawled back to his mother, who wrapped her arms around him.

Jason picked up the knife, wiped the blade on the man's shirt, and folded it back into its handle. He stepped over to the family and gave it back to Tom. The boy hesitated but took it and put it back in his pocket.

The three of them were softly crying, huddled in each other's arms. Jason put the .45 in his waist band. He reached into the dead man's coat pocket and retrieved his 9mm, then grabbed Gino by the arms. He dragged the body out of the office and down the stairs. After pulling

Gino across the warehouse floor, he left him in a far corner and went back upstairs.

Ruth looked at Jason with fear in her eyes.

"You killed him," she said.

Jason didn't answer her.

"Did you have to kill him?"

Jason gave her a long look. "Yes."

"What happens now?"

"You wait here and I try to free Ernie. Same as before."

"But what about him?" Ruth nodded in the general direction of the stairs.

"Nothing. He stays where I put him."

"Won't others be looking for him?"

"They will...and me as well. But they won't know where to look and they won't be looking for you and the kids. No one can connect us. It will take some time for anyone to figure out what's going on. Hopefully, by then, I'll have freed Ernie and you can all escape together."

"When they find Ernie missing, they'll come looking for us. They have a record of where we lived."

"But you'll be long gone."

"Will they come after us?"

"Probably not. I'm going to disrupt things even more. I doubt they'll be concerned about you or Ernie."

Ruth still looked fearful. "What are you going to do?"

Jason shook his head. "You just keep the kids together and quiet until I return with Ernie."

Ruth nodded. She looked at her children and then back at Jason. "But what if you don't come back? What do we do?"

Jason squatted down and put his face in front of hers. "You wait two days. If Ernie or I don't show up, you take the kids and leave. Walk north, the direction we headed to get here. Do not go back into town."

"Without Ernie?"

"Without Ernie."

Chapter 28

A fter making sure Ruth and the kids understood the need to stay put, Jason left. It was still dark with about five hours to go before the sun came up. He took his backpack, with some food and water, his 9mm with its suppressor and the extra magazines. He left his M110 and his M4 behind along with most of his camping gear. He was thankful that the train being unloaded was not a full day's walk away; there was no car to speed him along.

Outside of the building the air was sharp and cold. The moon, now higher, gave its pale light to the stillness that reigned in the abandoned warehouse district. He didn't expect to find anyone here with the major businesses now out of operation.

Jason breathed in a lungful of the cold air and started jogging north along the road. If he could keep to a good pace, he'd get to the camp that morning. With some scouting, using his binoculars, he hoped he'd be able to identify Ernie and then locate where he would sleep. He'd have to go into the compound that night to free him. The danger would be not only the guards, but the other men in the tent.

An hour later he stopped for five minutes, drank some water and stretched. Then he started again. Muscles not having been called on to run for hours for some time, protested, but Jason kept going. His body would adjust, although he noticed that it took longer as the years went by. *You can't stave off the effects of age forever*. He had a flash of insight into the challenges facing older people in this more dangerous age. He was in a race in some sense to achieve a level of stability in a chaotic world before he got too old. It was a worthwhile goal, for him, his family, and others around him. *Four years into the post-EMP world and this is still my goal. Will we ever get there?* He had no answer to his question. He just kept running. What he would do next was set by the commitment he had made to Ruth and her kids.

The Catawba River loomed ahead. He'd have to wade and swim across like before. The cold night would not make it easier. He paused at the shore, still in the cover of the bushes that grew thick beside the river. He took off his coat, boots, and socks and put them inside the plastic in his backpack. He was farther north with the I85 bridge downstream but nowhere in sight. After scanning up and down the river, Jason waded into the water. The shock made him gasp. He waded as fast as he could and when the water got chest deep, he broke into an awkward swim. Once his feet hit the bottom again, he started pushing for the shore.

On the other side, after getting into the cover of the trees, Jason took off his shirt and pants and squeezed the water out of them as best he could. He put them back on, along with his dry socks, boots, and coat and started jogging again. He worked his way through the woods until he found a road. When he came out on pavement, he followed it northeast, not the direction he wanted to go, but he set out on it anyway. *Faster to run on the road than to stumble in the dark of the woods.* A mile up the road he came to an intersection. Jason turned left and kept going. He was headed west now, a direction that would lead him to the rail line. Once he found that, he'd just run along it until he reached the abandoned train. An hour later he was running down the tracks.

His body ached from the cold and damp of his clothes. His coat, even though dry, failed to fully stem the chill that pressed in on him. The running, however fatiguing, helped, causing his body to generate more heat from the exertion. But it was taxing; he had to resist the urge to slow down and walk or stop and sleep.

Dawn saw Jason still jogging along. His body had loosened up and settled into a rhythm. He was tired, but felt he could maintain his pace. The key was to not go too fast and to take a short break every hour. The day grew warmer. Jason could feel the late fall sun on his back. The extra warmth felt good. He would soon be at the camp.

Later that morning, Tony sat down at his table in his favorite bar. Rocco came by and talked with him for a few minutes, drinking some bad coffee. Carlo came in a few minutes later.

"Anyone seen Gino?" Tony asked. "He's usually here first thing."

Both men shook their heads.

Tony thought about that for a moment. He'd given Gino permission to follow Jason and settle his suspicions once and for all. Tony found it tiring. If Gino couldn't get past it, he wasn't going to pick him to run the crew when he went off to work with Jason on the coal project.

Jason hadn't shown up either and, after an hour of sitting around, Tony got up. He'd go on some of the rounds himself. He wasn't worried. Whatever was going on, it seemed to have held up both Jason and Gino. When they got back, they'd report to him and he'd settle things once and for all between them.

"You see either of them, tell 'em to come see me."

The men nodded and left.

Jason saw the locomotive ahead and immediately turned off the tracks and into the woods. He was reasonably dry now after some hours of running through the cool air. He made his way through the trees, being careful to not snap branches lying on the ground. He was not wearing any camouflage gear but his dark pants and jacket helped. *Find a place to scan the work crews. I need to find Ernie and keep track of him throughout the day.* He didn't expect to get any sleep and there had been none last night. Fatigue was going to become a problem soon.

As he got closer, he heard the clank of metal on metal and the noise of an old diesel engine, probably the front-end loader. Jason crawled to the edge of the woods. He was on the opposite side of the tracks from the work camp. His vision was limited. He took out his binoculars and studied the area. After scanning the scene, he couldn't locate Ernie, so he backed up and moved forward in the woods. Thankfully the crews were working only a small section of the one hundred car, mile-long train. Crawling forward to a new vantage point produced the same results. No Ernie in sight.

I'll never be able to pick him out from watching with the binoculars. Got to get into the camp. Jason retraced his steps until he was far enough down the track to cross it without being seen. Now on the same side as the work camp, he moved forward through the woods. When he got closer, he stopped. He took off his backpack and straightened his clothes. He slipped his 9mm into his coat and stepped out onto the road leading up to the camp.

He walked with a confident stride as if he belonged. At the entrance, a guard braced him and asked him what he was doing.

"I'm taking charge of the coal project next week so I'm here to check out the operation, get a head start. Big Al and Joe Nicoletti assigned me to the project."

The man looked confused.

"We didn't hear anything about that."

"I doubt you would. First it hasn't officially happened yet and second, you're not someone who'd get notified."

"How'd you get here? You walk?"

"What difference does that make to you?" Jason acted as if the question was an affront to him. "I was dropped off down the road. I'll be going back there later today to meet my ride back to town."

Jason stepped up to the man.

"Now let's not waste more of my time. I have a lot to see. If you got any questions, get your supervisor here and I'll explain to him how you weren't helpful."

"No need to do that. Just give me your name so I can tell my supervisor."

"It's Jason Rich. Now do you give me a pass? I don't want to have to go around explaining myself to every guard."

The man gave Jason a badge that he pinned on his jacket. With that Jason walked into the camp. As he was walking around a man approached him. He wore a police uniform.

"I understand you're going to be in charge of the project," the man said when he came up to Jason. "The entrance guard told me."

"That's right. Jason Rich is my name, what's yours?"

"Todd Waymire. I'm the boss of the work camp. No one told me about you."

"It's not official until next week." Jason looked the man over, noting his uniform. "Are you in the police department?"

The man smiled. "Kind of. The department's been joined with the militia. We're all under the new structure."

"And what's the new structure?"

"You don't know?" Todd now gave Jason a questioning look.

"I'm new. Recently brought in to straighten things out. Joe and Big Al need to increase coal production."

"Well we're under the organization's command structure."

"The family."

Todd nodded. "Nino was fired?"

Jason looked at Todd with a blank face.

"Nino Vitale. He was in charge. We didn't see much of him."

"Yeah, he was fired. I'm replacing him. We need to do more than just strip coal trains. Of course, you should know that we need to up the level of production here. That's important because we have to put men to work on other sources."

"That's a tall order." Todd looked concerned. "More production with fewer men?"

"That's my orders. I'll work with you and we'll figure it out. For now, I don't need you to walk around with me. I want to do it alone and talk with everyone. Nothing personal, but I get better information that way."

Todd reluctantly withdrew and let Jason go on alone.

For an hour Jason listened to crew bosses talking about their work, which was essentially the equivalent of chain gang slaves, in a cold, clinical manner. Then he spied Ernie. Jason caught his eye and walked up to him. Ernie looked at him but didn't say anything. There were other workers in earshot, so Jason asked him some general questions.

"What do you do here?"

Ernie followed Jason's lead, answering as if he didn't know who he was.

After a few more questions, the other workers moved on.

Jason whispered to him. "Tell me which tent you're in, row and number."

The sleeping tents were in three rows, with five tents to a row. They were set up beside the mess tent and the rows went back from there into the field. Fencing has been set up around the perimeter to keep the men inside.

Ernie thought for a moment, glanced at the row of tents and replied, "Second row, fourth tent."

"Get outside tonight, late, after midnight. Can you go to the latrines?"

The latrines were set up away from the tents in the far corner of the field.

Ernie nodded.

"Are guards posted at night?"

Ernie nodded again.

"I'll meet you at the latrines. I'm getting you out. Your family's waiting. What time is the shift change?"

"We work 8 am to 4 pm. Then we're off to 8 pm. Then it's back to work till 4 am, then off from 4 am to 8am. Eight on, four off, round the clock."

Jason thought for a moment. "Meet me at the latrines at 5 am."

He moved on before Ernie could ask any questions and continued his inspection.

When Jason had completed what he thought looked like a thorough inspection, he went back to see Todd.

"I got a good idea of how things are going. I'll be seeing you next week when I officially take over."

"I hope you saw that we're working as fast as we can. With no way to unload the cars directly into trucks, or even the loader, we're stuck with the slow, manual transfer."

"We'll work on that. You're right, the key is to try to eliminate the manual parts of the process."

"Just so you understand, no one's slacking. We're doing the best that we can."

"Don't worry. I won't throw you under the bus with Joe. My ass is on the line as well."

Jason smiled, shook his hand, and left. He'd go back to his gear and wait for dark. The guards posted overnight would present a problem. He wasn't sure he could get Ernie out without dealing with them. *Got to do what's necessary.*

He settled down to wait. *Always the waiting.* Jason closed his eyes and listened to the clink of tools accompanied by the eerie silence of no voices.

Chapter 29

By evening Tony had moved from annoyed to concerned. Neither Jason nor Gino had shown up. No one had seen or heard from them. None of the civilians they would have dealt with during the day had seen them. Something was up. Something not good. Something he didn't relish telling Vincent about. *Give it some time.*

"What do you think, boss?" Rocco asked. They were sitting in the back of Tony's favorite bar. "Where could those guys be?"

Tony didn't tell Rocco that Gino had planned to follow Jason the night before, to see what he was up to.

"Hell if I know," Tony said. "Maybe they decided to go to the beach together."

Rocco let out a short laugh. "Not likely. Gino don't like beaches and he don't like Jason. He wouldn't go anywhere with him."

"I was joking, dumbass."

"Sorry boss." Rocco looked chagrined.

Tony got up. "I'm gonna visit some of Jason's customers. You can wait here, but I doubt I'll be back."

"Gino and I were going to go over to that club on Summerset. Have few drinks, get a lap dance." He shook his head. "Can't believe he'd miss that. I'll be over there. He might show up."

"You do that."

Tony left the bar. He headed over to Frank Russo's sausage shop. If he hurried, he could catch him before he went home. Frank had been friendly to Jason ever since he had gotten Frank the opportunity to sell in the downtown area and increase his income. Maybe Frank had heard from him.

Tony arrived just as Frank was locking up for the night.

"Frank, take a minute. I need to talk with you."

Frank looked at Tony, then back at Ramona. "You go on ahead. I'll be along in a few minutes."

Ramona gave Tony a sour look and walked off. Frank opened his shop door and he and Tony went inside.

"What do you want?" Frank asked after they sat down in the back room.

"You seen Jason today?"

Frank shook his head.

"When's the last time you saw him?"

"What's up?"

"Just answer me." Tony's voice showed his irritation.

Frank thought for a moment. He came by here yesterday, in the afternoon."

"Did he say or do anything unusual?"

Frank hesitated. Tony noticed the pause. "Don't hold back on me, Frank. I helped with the plan for you to sell downtown. You owe me on that. You get to keep a pretty good part of the extra income. Don't make me regret helping you out."

Frank sighed. "He didn't say anything but he bought me out of sausage. All the smoked and pre-cooked ones. Some ham's too."

"Why would he do that?"

"He didn't say. He just bought them all. It was a nice bump in income for this week, but now I've got a shortage of product."

Tony sat there. What the hell would Jason want all that meat for? Was he feeding a family? People Tony didn't know about? Jason didn't seem to be one to keep a family on the side, hidden like that.

"Did Gino come by as well?"

Frank shook his head. "No, I haven't seen him for a week." He looked at Tony. "You know Ramona doesn't like Gino. He gives her the creeps."

Tony gave Frank a hard look, his eyes cold and unfriendly. "Frank, I don't give a crap what Ramona thinks. You keep her in line. She goes around bad-talking me, Gino, or anyone else in my crew, she's going to have problems. You got that?"

Frank nodded.

"I didn't hear you," Tony said, his voice cold.

"I got it. Don't worry about Ramona. She keeps her opinions to herself...except for me."

Tony got up.

"You hear from Jason. He gets a message to you or comes by, you come and tell me. You know where to find me."

"Okay. But I doubt I'll see him again."

Tony stopped. "What makes you say that?"

"I don't know. Just his tone and attitude."

"What'd he say?"

"Nothing in particular. It was just like I said. Something in his tone. He told me to not mess around with you, play it straight. It was like giving me a last piece of advice."

Tony looked long and hard at Frank.

"And that's it?"

Frank held up his hands and nodded.

"Well, if he shows up you tell me, right?"

Frank nodded his head.

Tony left the store. Did Jason just stock up for a long trip? Was he bugging out? Hell, he'd just gotten a big promotion. It had pissed Gino off and was going to put pressure on Tony and the rest of his crew. Did Jason find out what had happened to Nino and decided he didn't want any part of that? If he didn't show by tomorrow, Tony was going to have to go to Vincent who'd have to go to Joe. Better to let his boss know. He didn't want to keep him in the dark if something was wrong. Gino was another issue, but Tony had the feeling that both of them being missing was somehow related.

After Jason had left the camp, Todd wrote a short note and handed it to one of the young men in the tent.

"Get on your bicycle and take this to Joe Nicoletti." He gave the messenger another note. "This will get you into the inner city. Go to the city-county office building and tell them you have a message for Joe.

The boy nodded and ran out to his bike. He liked the opportunity to get away from the depressing atmosphere of the camp. He didn't find riding his bike fifteen or twenty miles a hardship. He bicycled before the EMP attack as a little kid and, now four years later, was even more skilled at it, having grown strong with the steady routine of exercise.

He got to the office building while it was still daylight but he'd be riding back to the camp at night, in the cold. It wasn't the most comfortable thing to do, but then he could take his time. And maybe Joe, the boy knew he was an important boss, would offer him a meal, or give him some money to buy one.

He was frisked by a guard and allowed to enter. After telling the person manning a counter on the main floor his instructions, he was directed to the top floor. The courier grew more nervous with each floor he climbed. When he got to the office, his voice was shaking when he told the receptionist why he was there.

She picked up her phone and spoke into it. Then she ushered the boy into Joe's office after knocking on the door.

"You got a note for me?" Joe said looking up from his desk.

The boy nodded, afraid to speak. He held out the note and Joe took it from him. After reading it he jotted down a response and handed it back to the boy.

"Don't lose it. Get this back to Todd tonight."

"Yes sir."

Joe waved him out of the office. The boy left, disappointed that he wouldn't be getting a free meal. As he passed the receptionist, she called out to him to stop.

"Did you get anything to eat?"

The boy shook his head.

She reached into her drawer, took out some bills, and gave the boy a small wad.

"Get something to eat before you head back to the camp. That's a long trip. Did you walk?"

"No ma'am. I rode my bike."

"Good for you." She smiled. "Anyway, treat yourself before you go back. You look like you could use a good meal." She smiled at him and he turned to go.

Night fell. Jason felt more energized after having some rest. He ate some food and drank some of his water. *Ernie won't have a way to tell time. I'll have to get closer and watch for the shift to end.* Ernie's work shift was now in action. He would be at it, under lights, for eight hours. Around four in the morning, he'd go back to his tent to sleep. Jason couldn't act until then.

He wrapped himself in his jacket and curled up. The night was getting colder. Sleep wouldn't come, but he continued to rest and conserve his strength.

After the messenger had gone, Joe sighed and got up. He went out to the receptionist.

"Call the car around. I got to go see Vincent."

She nodded and Joe headed downstairs. He'd let Vincent know Jason had gone to the camp, getting a head start on his job. Vincent probably wondered where he'd been all day. It showed initiative, even if it was odd that he'd told no one.

Joe and Vincent were eating dinner in one of the hotels in the central downtown. There were four that survived with limited menus. They worked because of the introduction of the scrip money. The chefs, happy to not be reassigned to some other tasks, worked hard to prepare tasty dishes from the variety of meats available to them, rabbit, chicken, venison, wild boar, duck and geese, with the occasional pheasant or quail thrown in. The fact that these establishments served the power elite ensured they had a good supply of food even if the rest of the civilians got by on a more limited fare available to them.

"That explains why I haven't seen him all day. But why the hell not tell anyone?" Vincent asked after Joe told him where Jason showed up.

"Maybe he figured you wouldn't give him permission," Joe replied.

"Maybe."

"It shows initiative. He wants to make this work. Good for him, good for you as well."

"You think he heard what happened to Nino?"

Joe shrugged his shoulders. "Hell if I know. It doesn't matter in the end. He's the one now has to do the job."

"I was beginning to think he'd disappeared, left town. That maybe he'd heard the story and didn't want any part of that."

"Why would you think that?"

Vincent related what he'd been told about Jason's visit to Frank Russo.

"And Gino's missing as well. Haven't seen him all day."

"What the hell does that have to do with Jason?"

"He said he was going to follow Jason. Told me yesterday. He was sure Jason was up to something. The man had visited a woman and her kids. She said he was going to help her get her husband back. He's in the coal camp."

"Maybe he had two reasons for going out there. But I still don't see what Gino has to do with all this."

"I don't either. But something in my gut says they're related. And that may not be good. If Jason whacks a made man, that changes everything."

"You telling me you think that's what happened?" Joe asked.

"Anything's possible. They didn't like each other."

Chapter 30

Around 2 am Jason headed for the camp. He worked his way through the trees next to the road. He'd wait near the latrines. From there he'd be able to see when the shift changed. There had to be men going to the latrines all through the night which would give Ernie an excuse.

As he got closer, the smell wafted over Jason when the breeze shifted. He was glad of the cold; it helped to tamp down the noxious odor. *Waited in worse places, but not by much.* Again, he huddled under his jacket.

The latrines consisted of a series of long tarps arranged as canopies over pits dug into the ground. They were in four parallel rows that stretched away from the housing tents. They had a look that indicated they could be uprooted and moved to a new location easily. *Probably do that every once in a while. Bury the crap and start all over again.*

There was a guard posted at the latrines. He walked around the entrances for each of the four rows. No one could get past without him seeing. At the far end of each latrine, a tarp was staked down. It kept the men from leaving at the rear without having to do something overt, like cutting the tarp. Such an act would be seen as the equivalent of trying to escape which Jason figured would have severe consequences.

Ernie's going to have to slip under the back flap or else I'll have to deal with the guard. He had no desire to kill the guard who was likely someone culled off the street and probably didn't want to be there any more than the workers. But whatever it would take. The guard might suffer from being on the wrong side of things before the night was over.

An hour after the change in shift, the camp had settled down, deep into the late fall night. Aside from the muted noise of the never-ending work, everything was dark and silent. As Jason watched a figure emerged from one of the tents. A moment later two smaller figures emerged from an adjacent tent and joined the first. *What the hell?*

Now Jason was unsure if the first figure was Ernie. He'd have to wait until they got closer.

When they approached the latrines the three were stopped by the guard. Jason could only hear murmurs of the resulting conversation. Then the three figures entered one of the latrine rows. The guard watched and then walked off to place himself at the path leading back to the tents. A few minutes later, when no one emerged, the guard walked back and peered into the dark latrine row.

Probably can't see inside much. Jason watched and then saw the three figures emerge from the back of the latrine. At the same time the guard, either seeing the three go under the flap, or suspecting that had occurred, ran around to the back and confronted them.

He had his rifle up and aimed. Jason crept through the trees and emerged into the tall grass behind the latrines. He crept closer. The guard's attention was focused on the three. Jason could now see that it was Ernie and two boys. He crept closer to get within striking range.

"What are you up to?" the guard asked in a surly voice.

Ernie didn't answer. Neither did the two boys.

"You thinking about escaping?"

"No," Ernie said.

"Then why crawl out through the back?"

"I just wanted to see what was back here."

The guard gave a short laugh. "I doubt that." He shifted his rifle to point directly at Ernie. "I'm going to walk you three to the guard's quarters. You can explain yourself to my boss. I don't know what you're up to, but it don't look good. In fact, it looks pretty stupid. You think I wouldn't notice you going out the back?" He shook his head. "Pretty dumb."

"Please don't take us to the guard's quarters," the taller boy said.

The guard ignored him, keeping his focus on Ernie. "And what's up with the boys? You trying to do something with them? That'll get you into more trouble. Nobody gets to do that."

"I wasn't trying to do anything with the boys. I've taken care of them. I don't let the other workers harm them and I keep them away from the guards who might abuse them. I've got a son of my own."

"Tell it to my boss. But from what I see, you're going to get time in the box. Now let's get going."

Jason had been inching closer during the conversation. Now he sprang from behind. He slammed into the guard's back grabbing the man's trigger hand, blocking any pull. They fell to the ground; the guard's face pressed into the dirt. He gave out a grunt as the wind was partially knocked out of him. Jason flung the carbine aside. The man squirmed and Jason punched him in the kidney.

He took out his sheath knife and put it to the man's neck. With his knee in the guard's lower back, he leaned close to him.

"One sound out of you and I'll cut your neck open, he whispered. "Grab his rifle," Jason said to Ernie.

When the rifle was in Ernie's hands, Jason turned back to the guard.

"I've got two choices. The safe one is to kill you now and dump you in the woods. The less safe one is to tie you up and leave you to be found in the morning. If you make any noise or cause me any trouble, I'll take the first option. Got it?"

The man nodded.

"Jason—"

"No names," Jason said in a sharp voice.

"Sorry. Please don't kill him."

"If he cooperates, he'll be fine. He won't be found until his shift changes. Help me take off his jacket and we'll use the sleeves of his shirt for a gag." Jason leaned down again from behind the guard and spoke to him. "Don't do anything foolish. You make a sound and I'll take the easy way out of this and kill you on the spot. I'm going to take the knife from your throat, but I can slice you open in an instant if you try to call out. Stay quiet and you'll live."

Ernie and Jason wrestled the guard out of his coat while the two boys looked on. When they had it off, Jason cut one of the sleeves into strips. One he bunched up and jammed into the guard's mouth. With another he tied the gag in place.

"Now for his arms," Jason said. "Take off his belt."

Ernie removed the guard's belt. Jason pulled the man's arms behind his back and tied them with the belt.

"Pull his cap over his eyes," Jason said. The man was wearing a wool watch cap. Next he had Ernie remove the man's boot laces.

"We'll use them to tie his ankles and then pull them up to his arms in a hog tie. That will keep him secure until he's found."

The guard mumbled something in protest.

"Don't worry. You'll be found. They'll do a search and you're in the woods close to the fence. You'll be uncomfortable and cold, but that's all."

Jason looked around. The camp was silent. If there were sentries posted along the fences, or in the corners of the fields, they couldn't have seen what had taken place. Being behind the latrine, they were effectively screened. Now, crouched in the grass, they were even less visible.

"Let's get him back into the woods," Jason said.

They all crawled forward on hands and knees with Jason leading. Ernie held the guard to keep him from falling over. After they got in the strip of trees, Jason tied the guard's ankles and pulled them up to his back. The man could only squirm on the ground. He couldn't move and couldn't make a sound heard more than ten feet away.

"Time to go," Jason said, standing up. He led the three to the fence. After scanning the road in both directions, they climbed over and ran across it. Jason led them to his pack and put it on.

"Now, before we go, who are these kids?"

Even in the dim light, Jason could see the concern in Ernie's face. "This is Jack," he pointed to the older, larger boy. "And this is Bobby," he said gesturing to the younger one. "I've been keeping an eye out on them."

"So, you thought you had to bring them along?"

"I'm sorry. I didn't have time to tell you when you were at the camp. Jack gets beat up a lot, protecting Bobby. Some of the older men and guards want to take Bobby, probably to abuse him. Jack's pretty fearless which gets him in trouble. I've been helping to keep things from getting out of hand. If I disappear, I don't know what would happen."

"Where are you planning to go now that you're out?" Jason asked.

Jack shook his head. "We don't know. Anywhere's better than here."

"They'll come with me and my family. I'll be responsible for them."

"That might slow you down."

Ernie nodded. "It might, but I'll risk that. I couldn't leave them here."

"Okay." Jason bent down to the boys. "We're going to move fast. There'll be people after us in four hours or less. Can you keep up?"

Both boys nodded. Their eyes wide.

"If they have dogs to track us, we've got a big problem and the only solution is speed." He stood up. "Everyone understand that?"

Everyone nodded.

"Grab the rifle and follow me," Jason said. He headed off at a trot through the dark woods.

Chapter 31

That morning a search went out for the missing guard. It wasn't long before someone found him in the woods. He was brought in to see Todd Waymire, the camp commander. Todd sat in his chair as the guard stood and nervously told his story.

"So, you don't know who ran from the camp—the man and the two kids."

The guard shook his head.

"Did you see the face of the man who attacked you?"

"No, but the worker called out a name, 'Jason', and the guy told him, 'No names'."

"Jason?"

"That's right. I heard it clear. After that they didn't talk much."

Todd dismissed the man. He'd be punished later. Todd went over recent events in his mind. A Jason Rich had visited the camp the day before. He said he was taking over next week. He went around to inspect what was going on. Todd remembered that Jason had specifically told him that he wanted to do his inspection alone.

Was this the same Jason? The coincidence was too strong. But why break a prisoner out? And threaten to kill the guard? Todd had a feeling this guy was not going to show up next week to take charge. And what about the kids? He didn't have a clue. He needed to talk with someone right away.

Todd grabbed his coat and told his guard to bring the car around. He'd go to the city and talk with Joe. Before he left, he had his assistant go get the man who owned some tracking dogs.

After talking with Todd, Joe went to see Vincent.

"We got a problem," he told Vincent. "It seems Jason slipped into the work camp last night and freed one of the workers along with a couple of kids."

"Why the hell would he do that?"

Joe shook his head. "Beats me. But I don't see him taking over next week if he did that."

"Anyone see him?"

"No, but the guy he freed said his name before he was told to shut up...the dumbass."

"On my end, neither him or Gino have shown up."

"You got your crew looking for them?"

Vincent nodded.

"I'll tell the other capos to search as well. I want them found, even if I have to turn this city inside out."

"Big Al isn't going to be happy about this."

"You let me worry about Big Al." Joe's face was full of anger. "And don't forget who hired Jason. If something has gone sideways, you'll be responsible."

"I was always worried about him."

"But you hired him. I don't give a crap who encouraged you. It didn't get done without your approval. Now get the fuck out of here and find him *and* Gino."

Vincent got up and hurried out. He'd have a few words with Tony when he got back to the neighborhood. His next thought was to find out where that woman lived. The one Gino talked about. Maybe Gino told one of the others.

Carlo gave Tony the location for the woman's apartment. Tony went there and found the block warden. The man accompanied him to the apartment and let Tony in. He looked at the clothes strewn around the rooms.

"Looks like they left in a hurry," Tony said.

"Yeah," the warden replied. "Her husband was taken away. Some issue about a gun he was hiding in the apartment."

"You have any idea where they might have gone?"

The man shook his head. "After her husband left, the woman didn't go out much, and her kids less. She would show up and pick up meals at one of the food centers with her ration card. She'd say her kid was sick and get a meal for them that way."

Vincent headed back to his neighborhood. The family disappeared after Jason visited them, but also after Gino talked to them. Did Gino spook them or did Jason plan something with them? "Need to find one of the two," he mumbled to himself as he walked through the streets.

Back at the work camp, the dogs were waiting. Todd grabbed his rifle and four other men and they set out. The dogs quickly picked up the trail and the pursuit began. The trail took them through the woods and then out onto the railroad tracks. *We'll find them.* Todd had faith in the dogs and if the escapees didn't know about them, they'd catch up before the day was out.

A pale dawn was breaking over the city when Jason and the others arrived at the warehouse. They had jogged most of the way, Jason forcing the pace. The boys had kept up pretty well, but Ernie lagged behind. His fatigue from being overworked and underfed was evident.

"Ernie!" shrieked Ruth when she saw her husband.

She ran to him and jumped into his arms, almost throwing him to the ground. Jennifer and Tom followed and Ernie was engulfed in a family huddle of hugs and crying. The two boys stood apart. Bobby had a sad look in his eyes; Jack's face was impassive. Jason couldn't see any emotions showing.

Ruth broke away from her husband to look at Jack and Bobby. "Who are these boys?"

Ernie introduced them to his wife and kids "I was helping protect them at the camp and I couldn't leave them behind. They don't have any parents to help. They're coming with us."

"Speaking of that," Jason said. "You can't wait. You have to get moving right away."

"They're coming after Ernie?" Ruth asked.

Jason nodded. "We have to assume they'll have dogs and be able to track us, so there's no time to waste. Pack up your gear."

"Do it," Ernie said.

Everyone gathered their belongings. Jason took out a map of Charlotte and showed it to Ernie.

"I suggest you try to get to Hillsboro. You can't go direct as that takes you back past the coal train project. There's too much of a chance to run into the men who will be looking for you." He pointed to the map. "Head north, past Lake Norman, towards Hickory. Part of the way there, you'll see a sign for a monastery. Stop there. They'll give you sanctuary. It should be a safe space. Push until you get there. Keep moving day and night. If they use dogs, they'll be on your trail."

"Do you think they'll chase us that far?"

Jason looked at Ernie. "You willing to bet your life they won't? The lives of your family and those boys?"

Ernie was caught by his stare. "I guess not."

Jason turned back to the map. "You head up I77. You see how to get to the interstate?"

"Head northeast from here?"

"Right. That's away from the coal train camp. Then follow Route 16. Keep moving day and night. It'll be hard on the kids, but they'll survive it. You can rest when you get to the monastery. Don't assume you're safe 'til you get there."

Jason went over to a corner of the office. He came back with Gino's .45 pistol and an extra magazine.

"You take this along with the guard's carbine. And don't be afraid to use them if threatened."

He showed Ernie how to operate the both weapons. Ernie went to put the pistol in the pack that his wife had brought over.

"No," Jason said.

Ernie stopped and looked at him.

"It won't do any good in the pack. Keep it in your coat pocket. Put the spare magazine in the other pocket. Keep the carbine over your shoulder."

Jason hurried everyone along until they were ready to go. Then he walked them downstairs to the door. At the door, Ruth reached up and gave Jason a big hug.

"Thank you for getting Ernie free. You've brought new life back to our family. I know this is going to get you in some kind of trouble. You sacrificed a lot for us. We'll always be in your debt."

"Are you going to be okay?" Ernie asked.

"I'll be fine. I'm not going to be in trouble so much as cause trouble. Things may get so chaotic no one will want to keep pursuing you."

"Thanks for getting us out of that camp," Jack said. "I'll help Ernie defend everyone."

"So will I," Tom said.

The two boys looked serious about adopting the role of protector.

"I'll help as well," Jennifer said. "We don't have any weapons, but we'll help however we can."

"Sounds like you've got some fighters to go with you. For now, just do what Ernie says and help each other keep up. Can you do that?"

The children nodded, their faces all solemn, grasping the seriousness of the moment.

"Off you go, then," Jason said.

Ernie shook his hand and gave him a hug. "Thanks. I hope to see you again. Are you going to Hillsboro?"

"When I'm done here."

The family left and Jason turned back to the mezzanine. A darkness began to envelop him. It wasn't oppressive. But it scattered all thoughts of home, of peace, of comfort, from his mind. Reservations about killing, the weariness he felt at needing to use violence, dissipated like a morning mist. He was going to become an assassin now. He was going to bring terror to the mob. They had brought some form of stability to Charlotte but the price was terror and servitude of the population; the price they paid for their peace.

That was going to change. How would the citizens respond? Would they take advantage of the turmoil Jason was going to create? Would they shake off the oppression the mob brought? He didn't know. That wasn't his concern. He was the agent of disruption. That, hopefully, would be enough to protect his community, his tribe.

Chapter 32

As soon as the Ernie and family departed, Jason went up to the mezzanine. He took a chair and reached up into the ceiling, pulling down his sniper rifle and M4. After strapping the sniper rifle to his backpack, he left the building and headed towards the Catawba River. He was going to cross in the daylight, something he didn't want to do, but if there were dogs on his tail, he couldn't wait until dark.

At the river's edge, Jason took time to watch and wait. He was out of sight of any bridge and, after not observing any activity along the river's edge, he waded out and began the awkward swim to the other side. Once he was back in wading depth, Jason turned up stream and pushed through the water. He wanted to go as far as he dared before heading to shore in order to throw off any following dogs if they crossed the river. If they didn't find his scent on the other side, Jason hoped his pursuers would assume he had floated downstream and search in that direction. He needed to generate as much confusion and doubt as he could.

When he had gotten a hundred yards upstream, he bolted to the shore. Once hidden in the trees, Jason went through the now familiar routine of stripping and wringing out his clothes. The day was cold and continuing with fully wet clothing only invited problems.

Two more hours of walking, being careful to not be observed, brought him further into the city. Along the way,

Jason had purposely soaked his boots in some motor oil he found spilled on a garage floor. He hoped it would kill his scent. After wiping the excess off, he worked his way to an abandoned golf course on the southeast side of the city, outside of the inner downtown. The grounds were covered by tall grasses and sprouting trees. The fairways looked like fields and even the greens had become overgrown with only the sand traps indicating their presence. The wooded areas had grown denser and provided Jason with good cover for camping and planning his next move.

He set up camp in a large section of trees. He put trip wires around the camp area to alert him to any intruders and then started a small fire. He wanted a fire while there was daylight left, making it less likely to be noticed. Then he dried his clothes and heated some of the sausage on a stick. Before night fell, Jason killed the fire. He'd sleep without one. It was the price to pay for stealth. Who knew how far and wide the search for him would be? If his pursuers thought he had run off with the family, they might not search for him in town. But if they thought he might return their search would intensify.

He hunkered down under his tarp and wrapped up in his thermal blanket. It was a cold night but he'd experienced worse. He felt a sense of freedom, being released from the role he had played with the mob. Now he could operate in his own style. He could be the deadly aggressor, wreaking havoc and sowing fear in his enemies. Tomorrow he would find a spot from which he could target the mob leadership. He was going to take his battle directly to Big Al and Joe.

Jason slept only a few hours. While it was still deep in the night, he packed up his camp and started for the downtown area. He'd need a place to hide, while he scouted for a shooting position. Maneuvering in the daylight was out of the question with the larger number of people and activity in the inner part of the city.

He also needed more information. Where was the militia housed? Where did their commander, Roper, stay? There were blind spots in his knowledge that could be dangerous to him.

Jason worked his way east from the golf course. He wanted to get into the inner city perimeter and find a hide before daylight. After passing a school he came to a complex freeway interchange that marked the I277 road which formed the inner perimeter. The trees had multiplied and the grasses grew high with bushes and other volunteer plants working to turn the once well-trimmed areas into a tangle of brush and woods.

Jason's tactic was always to use the now overgrown green space corridors to conceal his movements. The problem was inside the downtown, there were fewer of these areas and they didn't connect into any continuous passageways.

Most of the streets running under I277 were blocked off. The few that remained open were manned as secured entry points. Jason picked a dark underpass, not a road, but a ramp to the freeway from the downtown.

He watched the underpass from the concealment of some trees. Caution dictated patience. The underpass was blocked with a rubble wall almost to the height of the upper roadway. Jason scanned the barrier. There had to be a chink in it somewhere. Along the edge, where the slope climbed to the upper road, Jason could see the attempts to seal the gap were incomplete. He'd have to remove some of the block. *That's the best way through, after I do a bit of work.*

After assuring himself he was alone and unobserved, Jason went to the barrier and crawled up the slope. He put is gear down and began to remove the concrete blocks that had been stuffed into the gap of the barrier. In a few minutes he had a man-sized hole that he could crawl through. He peered into the greater darkness under the highway. He could see no one.

He stuffed his pack and rifle through the opening and then crawled after them. Small blocks of concrete from the wall pulled loose and rolled down the inside slope which was fully paved up to the overpass. The noise made Jason freeze. When the silence returned, he grabbed his gear and slid as quietly as he could down to the roadway.

Now under the highway, there was no place to hide. He brought his M4 up to the ready position. *If I have to use this I'm probably toast.* The shots would be heard at the checkpoints and he would be on the run with a hot pursuit. If discovered, there was no way to retreat except for a scramble back up the concrete slope to crawl through the gap he had made. That didn't make for an attractive option either.

Jason stepped onto the road and walked forward. He carefully placed his steps to avoid the scattered branches that littered the pavement. A snap from them would sound like a rifle shot in the quiet of the night. The underpass was about seventy yards long, but it seemed to go on and on.

He was a third of the way through when he heard footsteps. He ducked behind one of the columns holding up the overpass. He was not sure he could remain undetected if anyone walked the length of the underpass.

There were indistinct voices. It sounded like two men. They were headed into the underpass; Jason could now make out their conversation.

"Damn sergeant, makes us walk around checking out every sound."

"He's a pisser ain't he?"

"Probably some animal knocked something loose. It's all it ever is."

The men came forward. Jason laid his carbine down and took out his knife. He'd try to take them out without a shot. It was more dangerous, but he had the element of surprise on his side. *Better than shooting. If the loose concrete was heard, a shot will bring more for sure.*

"Do we have to bother?" one of the men said.

"Can you see what's down there? It's too damn dark. So, we got to go and inspect it. If there's a big hole the sergeant will have our asses if we didn't see and report it."

"How big a hole can there be? I didn't hear much."

"Don't be so damn lazy. It's only fifty yards extra to walk. What the hell else are you gonna do? It ain't like you can go back and go to sleep."

The men started forward again. Jason shifted his knife in his hand. He had to strike hard and fast. Slash one, stab the other and then finish them off before they even think to shout for help. *Aim for the neck.* The men came closer. They were only one column away now.

"That's enough," the lazy one said. You can see the barrier's not broken."

"Can you see up the sides? You can't. you go climb up and check it out. Something came loose."

"I ain't doing that. If you want it checked, do it yourself," the first one said.

"You lazy son-of-a-bitch." It sounded like the man gave the first speaker a shove.

"Fuck off, or I'll deck you," the first one said. His voice now threatening.

"Yeah?" There was another shove.

"Bastard." the first man said.

As he swung at his partner, Jason sprang from behind the column. He slammed into the first man, shoving them both against the second sentry. At the same time Jason's knife slashed across the neck of the second man. The three fell heavily to the road. Jason landed on top of the first man when they hit the pavement and thrust his knife into the man's neck. He then slashed the neck of the second man again, from his artery across his throat.

"Oh God!" the first man exclaimed as he tried to staunch the flow of blood out of his neck. The second man was gurgling, unable to speak and beginning to choke on his own blood. Jason held his hand over the first man's mouth. Their eyes met, victor and vanquished, predator and prey, as the man's life seeped away and he fell unconscious.

Jason stood up, his chest heaving. He wiped his hands on the clothes of the dead sentry. He stood still, looking at the two men, both now dead. A wave of what...remorse? Began to arise from within and overcome him. He tamped it down. *No time for that. This is the enemy.*

Without further hesitation, he grabbed the legs of the first man and dragged him to the base of the barricade. Then he dragged the second man next to him. From the entrance to the underpass, they could not be seen. *But someone'll come looking for them, even before dawn. I've got to get under cover right away.*

He grabbed his gear and headed towards the exit. At the end of the underpass, Jason paused. The checkpoint was to his left, the direction he needed to go. He'd have to move deeper into the downtown before heading west. His goal was to get to an unoccupied high-rise building and set up on the roof. He moved forward, using the few trees or bushes for cover.

Chapter 33

It was still dark as Jason made his way through the downtown. Once past the barriers there were fewer sentries about. He found only an occasional guard at a building that was being used during the day. Few street lights were lit in an attempt to save energy, giving Jason more cover as he snuck through the city. He soon heard a commotion from behind. *They must have found the bodies.*

He gave a wide berth to the city government center. There were numerous sentries posted around the building complex. A couple of them were heading south to check out what had happened at the checkpoint. Jason kept going north into the high-rise area. The major hotels were out of consideration. He knew some were occupied and used for various events. He needed a general office building that was now surplus, that had no use anymore in the post-EMP world.

Five blocks from the city center compound he approached a glass high-rise. It looked unused as nearly as Jason could tell in the dark. He hiked around the building, almost a city block, trying all the doors, none of which opened. Parts of the street level held small shops and restaurants which had been abandoned. They were open and had long since been stripped, but they didn't offer any access into the main building. On the north side of the building an enclosed second floor walkway led across the street to connect to another building.

Jason tried the entrances to that building. After ten minutes he found an unlocked door and entered. He searched for a stairway and got to the second floor. From there he found his way to the connecting walkway and soon was inside his target building. More searching brought him to a stairwell. Now he had forty or more flights to climb to get to the top floor. An hour later, out of breath, he staggered into a hallway.

Dawn was beginning to break over the city. The gray light seeped into the hallway from windows at each end. *Now to find the roof entrance.* He walked the length of the hallway until he came to another set of stairs. It was still dark inside the stairwell. He propped the door open to allow the dim light inside. There he saw another door labeled ROOF ACCESS. It was locked.

The door didn't have a dead bolt, just a door knob lock. Jason went back out into the hallway. He opened an office door. Inside was a spacious reception area with an expensive desk made of exotic wood and comfortable chairs for the visitors to wait. He walked on a cushion of plush beige carpet.

Two doors headed off from the area. Jason opened one to reveal a large conference room with a massive table, the sides shaped in a long arc. At one end were multiple screens that could be pulled down. The table seemed to be wired and had connectors for various electronic equipment at each seating location. A projector was attached to the ceiling to direct visuals onto the screens. A bar was inset along one wall with a sink and refrigerator built in.

The other door opened to a massive office with large windows looking to the south. Another, larger, polished hardwood desk in a modern design with intricate inlays of contrasting wood formed the anchor point to the room. It had a commanding executive chair behind it and four lesser, but comfortable looking, seats on the other side. Again, a bar graced one wall with a couch and stuffed chairs stationed along the other wall.

The place reeked of corporate opulence which seemed out of place now. Jason went back out of the suite. What he needed was something he could use as a bludgeon on the roof doorknob. Farther down the hallway was a cabinet inset into the wall. It contained a fire extinguisher. Jason grabbed it and quickly returned to the stairwell. He swung the extinguisher against the knob. It took three blows and the doorknob fell off. Jason inserted his knife and unlatched the door.

After opening it, he stood still and listened. If someone was in the building, nearby or in the stairwell, they might have heard the blows and might come looking. He would have to intercept that person if they came up the stairs.

Within a minute he heard someone on the steps far below. Jason stood back from the rail and waited. The steps came closer.

He readied his carbine. He didn't want to shoot, but had to be ready to take command of the encounter and control it. As the footsteps slowly came closer, Jason opened the door to the hallway, being careful to not make a sound. He stepped back so he couldn't be seen by the approaching climber. He didn't want them to see him and have a chance to flee down the stairs.

He could hear the puffing now as the climber came closer. Finally, the figure turned the corner and approached the landing. Jason stepped out with his carbine pointed at him.

"Stop right there. Run and I'll shoot."

The man was dressed in oversized jeans that had been cinched tight to his waist with a leather belt. He wore a plaid flannel shirt, two of them it seemed as Jason looked closely at him. He had long, unkempt hair and a full beard. He looked up at Jason staring at his carbine with wild eyes.

"Whoa pardner. I'm not a threat to you. Don't shoot me."

"I won't if you don't try to run."

The man raised his hands.

"Come on up and let's go into one of these offices and talk," Jason said.

"I'm comfortable here if it's all the same to you."

"It wasn't a suggestion," Jason told him, in a stern voice.

"Okay, okay. Don't get testy."

He climbed the last few steps and entered the hall as Jason backed up out of the man's reach.

"Head down there," Jason nodded in the direction he had explored. He directed the man into the luxury suite. They went into the main office. Jason pointed to one of the chairs in front of the desk. He pulled another one away from the row and sat in it with his carbine on his lap.

"You mind putting that away? It makes me nervous. I ain't armed. Don't believe in violence myself, but it seems like you might."

"What's your name?" Jason asked.

"Luke. Luke the Duke, my friends used to call me. Best card player on the east side of town. Friend to everyone and foe to none. Iff'n you don't like me, that's fine, but I like everyone. Everybody represents an opportunity. That's my motto."

He smiled showing a large mouth full of now stained teeth.

"Well Luke, what are you doing here?"

"I could ask you the same question. Being's you're the stranger." He paused as if sizing Jason up. "If you must know, I live here."

"On this floor?"

"Heavens no. This is too damn hard a climb. I couldn't manage that each day. I live tens of floors down, where the air ain't so thin and the climbing ain't so hard. What brings you all the way up to this rarified elevation? You looking for a place to hide?"

"Why do you say that?"

The man grinned at him and nodded towards Jason's carbine. "That ain't something you put on the welcome wagon...or take around with you on charitable outings."

Jason allowed himself to crack a smile. "You might have a point there. Still in these times one can't be too careful."

"Indeed. That's why I climbed those stairs after hearing the banging. Not sure that was a good idea now."

"I'd have run into you sooner or later."

"You think?" Luke smiled again at Jason. Iff'n I didn't want you to see me, you never would. I been living here for two years. I know every inch of this building." He looked around. "Course I never spent much time up here except to scavenge the high-priced liquor that was stocked in these offices." He leaned forward towards Jason. "You'd think the captains of our industries," he swept his hand around the office, "the ones who ran things and made a gazillion dollars, who inhabited these rarified heights, would have been less involved in drinking."

He shook his head. "No. From what I could tell, they liked their expensive booze." He poked his chest with his thumbs. "And now I get to like it. How about them apples?"

Luke sat back enjoying his sense of victory over the elite. "I camp in their offices, sleep on their couches, drink their booze. And, where are they? Probably dead and gone. They didn't know how to survive when deprived of their protection and insulation."

"So, you live here? All alone?" Jason cut into the soliloquy to try to get some useful information.

"There's a few others live in the building. We see each other once in a while, leave messages for one another if necessary, but we mostly stay to ourselves. I guess that's why we chose to live here."

"And the authorities leave you alone?"

"Why would they waste time looking for us or trying to root us out? We don't bother them and they don't bother us." He thought for a moment. "I guess if they needed the building, they'd come and evict us, but they don't need it. Too many empty buildings as it is. They got all the offices they need."

"The authorities know people are here and don't bother with you?"

"That's what I said. What does the mob need offices for anyway? It seems like a violation of natural law or something to have a mobster sitting in a plush CEO office. Don't you picture them in the back rooms of bars and restaurants? A good Italian restaurant, that's the natural habitat."

Suddenly Luke looked concerned.

"I'm sorry. You're not Italian are you? I didn't mean to offend you. It's just the everyone equates the mob with Italians."

"But not all Italians with the mob," Jason replied.

Luke laughed and smacked his hands together. "That's it...in a nut shell. You got a quick mind."

In spite of himself, Jason couldn't help but smile.

Luke's face now turned serious. "But why are you here? I see a pistol at your side and the rifle in your hand. You're like a law man or an outlaw. You ain't dressed like a mob-type."

"I need a place to lie low for a while."

"Ahhh, you're on the run, are you? Cross the mob bosses? They don't like being crossed here in Charlotte. We're all pretty careful about that around here."

Luke crossed his legs and tried to slouch more comfortably in his chair. Jason could see his boots were pretty worn. It didn't look like he had any socks on inside of them.

"I need to decide what to do with you."

"Hey, boss. You don't need to do anything with me. I'm no snitch. Like I said. The few of us in here just want to stay off the radar from those mob types. Next thing you know, they'll be puttin' us to work." He shook his head. "Sweatin' ain't my thing, if you know what I mean.

Fighting and working never sat well with me. I'm a lover. That's my style."

"You mean you're lazy, right?"

"I wouldn't say that." Luke sat up straight with an indignant tone in his voice. "It takes being clever and slick to get by without doing a lot of manual work." He tapped his head with his finger. "I like to use my brain instead of my brawn. Save my body for the ladies." He grinned broadly.

"Well if you don't have much to do with the mob, how do you eat?"

Luke looked serious again. "That's always a bit of a challenge. "I scavenge things of value from the building. Little things that were overlooked during the initial days. Gold plated letter openers, key rings, some crystal or jewelry missed in those rounds of looting. We can trade it for food. Certain establishments like our trade. Some of us will scavenge from other empty office buildings but the pickings get scarcer all the time."

"I've still got to figure out what to do."

"Boss. I can help you. Whatever you're up to, I know the local territory. I can be your guide. I'd rather help you than get shot. That won't do either of us much good...especially me."

"How can you help?"

"Keep anyone from finding you, for one thing. Keep you from running into the others." He pointed his finger at Jason. "And, if the mob comes calling, I can say no one's been in here. They don't want to search all forty floors, believe me, so if I tell them that I ain't seen or heard anything out of the ordinary, they'll be happy to go on their way and check this building off their list."

He leaned forward. "This is your lucky day, running into Luke the Duke."

Jason held himself back.

"They might offer you a reward."

Luke snorted. "What are they going to offer me? A few meals? They'll also want to put me to work. The more I interact with those types the less they'll want to leave me alone." He shook his head and looked sad. "No, there's not much call for a card-playing man these days."

Chapter 34

The conversation went on for some time. Luke was an engaging fellow for sure, but Jason figured him for a trickster.

"I'd like to trust you. But you understand if I can't leave you alone, especially at night."

"Hmm. I see your problem. We have to figure a way around it. I'm guessing you're here, not just in this building, but in town, for some larger purpose. You look too serious to be a run-of-the-mill bandit or highwayman. Besides, if you were, why would you be here in town instead of out on the highways? The mob crushed the gangs a year ago. There's not much space for other outlaws here anymore. They like a monopoly on that action."

Jason tried a new tack.

"You're smart so you must realize that your lifestyle exists on borrowed time. You said yourself, the pickings from scavenging are getting slimmer and there's no place for a card playing man in this new world. And even if you cleaned up and put on some sharp duds, there's not much call for a gigolo either."

Luke looked at Jason. His face mirrored his confusion about how to take his comments.

"Living off the ladies was something men did before the power went out. You seem like you had the skills for that, if you're the lover you claim to be. But that time is gone."

"What's your point?" Luke voice now was filled with caution.

"I'm going to insert some chaos into things around here soon. Chaos provides opportunity and you seem like a man that can exploit opportunity. You help me and you get to make what you can of things when I break them apart."

"What are you going to do?"

Jason shook his head. "Not for you to know. What I need to know is if you're in. If you'd like to see what you could make of a fresh set of conditions."

Luke looked thoughtful. "One doesn't want to think about things like that...living on borrowed time, it brings you down. But it has sat in the back of my mind for a while. I'll be needing a new plan. I don't know if the others in this building think about that. When they can't make it anymore, they'll probably just go to the mob and get themselves assigned to anything the mob wants them to do. Become slaves to the system."

He shook his head. "That's not for me. I'll need a better plan."

"I don't have a plan for you. I can just break the system and let you make what you can out of the ensuing confusion. The power structure is going to change. Maybe you can help make that happen."

Luke looked up at Jason with a serious face. "Me? I'm not part of the power structure."

"Not the current one. But you could find a role in the next one. You've got the makings of a politician."

Luke smiled at him. "You think so?"

Jason nodded. "You're quick on your feet, verbally speaking. You're bright. If you've got any vision, you could help others chart a different course for Charlotte. It's worth a try isn't it?"

Luke looked thoughtful, then slapped his knee. "By George! I'm in. That's the new game. I been waiting for inspiration to hit me, and the inspiration was you. Fate brought us together. I guess it was worth climbing all those stairs after all."

He stood up. Jason stood with him, not entirely letting his guard down. Luke reached out his hand and Jason took it.

"I'm your man. After you trigger the chaos, I'll come in to help restore a new civic order." He paused and looked down at his feet. "But I don't know how to do that. Hell, I don't know anyone in power. I've got no connections." He looked back at Jason, now with a lost look in his eyes.

"Luke, I need to find someone and talk with him. You help me do that and I'll get you set up with him. He's got some power but he's not with the mob. Maybe the two of you can work together. You could have a chance to prove your worth to him. How's that sound?"

"Wow, you are the man. Luke the Duke salutes you." He raised his hand in a close facsimile of a real salute.

Jason explained who Michael Daniels, the FEMA agent, was and where he had his office. Luke agreed to get dressed as presentable as he could and give Daniels a message to meet Jason in the building where he was hiding. Luke would bring him to the meeting.

"Now go trim your beard and hair."

With that, Luke left and Jason went back to the roof access door. He climbed the steep steps to a small landing. From there he opened a door onto the roof. There was an eight-foot high metal partition that screened the multitude of air conditioning units from sight. The partition consisted of metal slates with gaps to let the wind through. The arrangement was ideal for Jason. He had cover and he could shoot through the openings. He could build a shooting rest and fire without exposing himself or his rifle. When he took a shot, the suppressor would mask the source and all anyone would hear would be the bullet's sonic crack which would not be directional. He went back down to the suites and, in multiple trips, carried up a table, chair and some cushions to build a shooting platform.

When he was done, Jason covered it with some curtain material torn free from some windows. If there were any surveillance from the sky, which he doubted, it would look like debris, perhaps from prior looting. He had heard no planes for years, but there were old planes around, like old cars. At some point, someone would get them back in the air. For now, no one saw any utility in either expending the effort or the fuel.

Luke showed up part of the way through Jason's preparations. He had put on a pair of slacks that were closer in fit and found a pair of dress shoes. He now wore only one flannel shirt, neatly tucked into his pants. He had a jacket with him, the day was cold. His hair was combed and his beard trimmed.

"How do I look, Boss?" Luke smiled proudly.

"You look great, like a real player. You should have no trouble getting into the building. Just remember to ask for Mr. Daniels and tell him you have some information from the FEMA office in Atlanta. Can you sound like you come from Atlanta?

"Yessir, I can." Luke drawled out his reply. "Ah been on the road for a week just to talk with Mister Daniels and I'm damn near wore out."

Jason smiled. "Don't overdo it. Just enough to get past the guard on the main floor."

He gave Luke the office number for Daniels and sent him on his way.

Twenty minutes later Luke was at the city government building. He didn't let himself gawk. He'd seen it before, of course, but never with the intention of entering or interacting with people in power.

You're playing in the big leagues now, Luke. Make like a duke. Make like you belong. If you were playing cards with 'em, you'd not be timid. You'd hustle them like the marks you know they are.

He finished his internal pep talk and stepped through the doors.

Luke's story got him past the guard with a minimum of conversation. He climbed the stairs and walked down the hall. After knocking on the door number Jason had given him, he walked in.

"May I help you?" the receptionist said.

Luke gave her his brightest smile.

"Yes, you can, darling. I'm here to talk with Mr. Daniels. The Atlanta office sent me. I've been on the road for a week and I'm plum worn out. I never figured to have to go on such a journey." He beamed at the woman. "But if I had known there was such a beauty at the end of my trek, I wouldn't have protested a bit." He winked at her.

"Well," the woman looked slightly flustered as well as flattered. "What's your name?"

"Luke. Luke Duke" He continued to smile at her. "It seems my parents had a misplaced sense of humor...at my expense."

"Well, Mr. Duke, I'm glad you made it here safely. I understand it's dangerous out there on the road."

Luke leaned over the desk. "You don't know the half of it. I could tell you stories." He paused for a moment. "In fact, I could tell you some over dinner. What do you say?"

"Well, I have to get home tonight—"

"That's okay. I'm going to be busy with Mr. Daniels tonight. How about tomorrow night? You can show a weary traveler your fine city and a good restaurant. It'll be like a celebration of the completion of my mission."

"Ahh...okay." She said with some hesitation.

"What's your name, darling?"

"My name's Suzy."

"Suzy," Luke bowed slightly. "I'm pleased to make your acquaintance and I look forward to tomorrow evening. I'll meet you here, will that work?"

"Yes, that will work fine." She smiled, then turned to her phone. "Let me announce you."

Chapter 35

Luke took a breath and entered Daniels' office.

"You're from the Atlanta office?" Daniels asked as he stood to greet his visitor.

"Kind of," Luke replied. "I'm Luke Duke...my parent's misplaced sense of humor on display."

"Who in Atlanta sent you?"

"No one, really."

"Really? You're here on your own? How did you know who I was?"

"Can we sit down? I have a short tale to tell you and my shoes are killing me."

Daniels waved towards a chair in front of his desk and both men took their seats. Daniels sat back with his fingers entwined and waited.

"I'm not really from Atlanta, but I was instructed to seek you out and give you a message."

"I'm listening. Who and what?"

"The message is from a Jason. He didn't give me his last name, so I assume you know who I'm talking about."

A look of concern spread over Daniels' face.

"He wants to meet with you," Luke continued. "Tonight. He says it's important."

"Jesus," whispered Daniels.

"What's up? I get a sense from you that something is very wrong here."

Daniels shook his head, looking at his desk. "There's been some commotion this morning. Some people think it may involve this Jason. I never thought he'd be coming around again." He looked up and met Luke's eyes. "Where is he?"

"I'm not really at liberty to say at this point in time. But I'm to escort you to meet with him. It's a secure location. He was very clear that no one else should know of this meeting. He thinks you're the only one he can trust...except for me." This last Luke said with some pride in his voice.

"And I'm supposed to take your word? That this isn't a set up?"

Luke pushed himself up straight in the chair.

"I assure you sir," his voice rang with authority. "I can be trusted. I give my word and the word of Luke Duke is something people have always been able to rely on. Men believe in me because I keep my word and women admire me for it as well."

Daniels studied him for a moment.

"How did you meet Jason?"

"Our paths collided. Some might say by chance. I see it as a twist of fate, a once in a lifetime of two lives coming together to make momentous things happen. You, apparently, are going to be brought into this great adventure that is just beginning. I urge you not to shrink from the moment but embrace it as I have done."

"That's a lot to read into his request to meet with me. It could be just that he's in trouble and on the run and needs my help. Help that could land me in some serious difficulties.

"Mr. Daniels, what do you do here all day in this office...if I might be so bold as to ask?"

Daniels put his hands back on his desk and pushed around some papers.

"Not much, really. I write up speeches and some encouraging articles for the newsletter that goes out to the community. But not a whole lot more."

"But you get paid pretty well for that, I'm guessing. At least in today's terms."

"I don't know what that has to do with what we're discussing."

"Let me connect it for you. I've been a man who lived by my wits all my life. Luke the Duke I'm called, or used to be. Over on the east side I was known as the Duke of East End. I didn't run anything but was sort of a goodwill ambassador for my neighborhood."

He leaned forward now, warming to his theme.

"I'm a card playing man. I can read people. I played cards with all the power people, the rich people who wanted to sample a bit of the low life action on the East End. It didn't bother me. I took their money. It was the price they paid to live on the wild side for a night. I had to work with the mob. Not higher-ups like Joe Nicoletti—"

"You know Joe?"

"Only by reputation. I had to deal with the lower levels of the mob. I managed it well, if I do say so myself. My point is that I understand the mentality of those now running our fair city. You may not have grown up here, but I'm sure you can see what this city used to be. Our nickname was the 'Queen City'. It's not only for being named after Princess Charlotte, but because we are, were, is maybe the better word now, a classy place.

"Now here's the thing. I'd like to have a job such as yours, in fact, in other circumstances, I could see myself lobbying you to be your assistant. Not that you're busy enough to need one, but I could make myself useful...and entertaining.

"But things have changed. My intersection with Jason has opened my eyes to new possibilities. You need to open your eyes as well, since he seems to think you are part of the change that's coming."

"You're not making a lot of sense, you realize that, don't you?"

"Background material, I'm preparing the soil for you to understand things." Now Luke stood up and began to pace around the office.

"Do you realize you're on borrowed time? Jason opened my eyes to the fact that I was. Now I see you're in the same situation in some sense as me. The mob won't need you soon, once their control over the region is complete. I don't know what they have planned, maybe you do, but I do know they don't carry around much extra baggage. Down on the streets, if you didn't perform, didn't earn well, you were disciplined or eliminated.

"I made it because I was entertaining enough to bring marks for the card games, so the mob put up with me. The civilians loved playing at my games. I was...colorful. That produced more income for the mob. Everyone was happy. But you're expendable. When they don't need you, they won't keep you around."

"Jason implied much the same thing."

Luke sniffed. "I don't doubt it. He's very perceptive."

He went back to his chair and sat down.

"He's also a serious man. A hard man. I've seen them and he fits the type."

"So, again, what does this all have to do with me meeting Jason."

Luke threw up his hands.

"Everything! He's going to disrupt things. He's offering us the opportunity to make the most of the chaos. Out of chaos comes new order. Those who are ready, reap the rewards."

"I don't know. What you're talking about sounds dangerous."

"It is. But, Mr. Daniels, may I call you Michael?" He didn't wait for a reply. "Michael, change is coming whether you're ready for it or not. And I'm the one you need to partner with. I can help you navigate through the chaos. Together we'll come out ahead and with the power to change this city. I'm born for this. I've lived at the edge of chaos my whole life."

Luke now sat back and grinned.

"It's fate that brought us all together. You and me connecting through Jason, the agent of destruction. I'm not sure what he'll reap from this, but we'll redefine ourselves and our future. One without a drop-dead date."

"Sooo—"

"Meet with Jason tonight. That's all. Then you can decide."

Chapter 36

When the pursuers from the coal train camp reached the warehouse, they found Gino's body. The trail split into two. Todd had the men split up with the two dogs and sent them off to follow both trails. He hurried back to camp and got in his car to head for the city.

Once downtown, he went straight to Joe's office.

"Mr. Nicoletti, we found a body. It's probably Gino. He was in a warehouse north of the city. He was shot and dragged into a corner. We pursued the escapees to that warehouse. The trail split from there. One leads south towards the river and the city, the other heads northeast, away from town."

"Jason." Joe said. His voice hard and angry. "He freed that guy from the camp and now he's heading back to town."

"You think he'll come back? After what has happened?"

"I know he's come back. Two sentries were killed last night. He's slipped back in and is here, downtown."

Todd looked shocked. "Why would he come back here? This would be the worst place for him."

"Yeah. I don't know what he's up to and I don't know how the camp worker fits into this, but I got the militia out looking for him."

"I think the camp worker may be long gone. He may not fit into whatever Jason's planning."

Joe looked at Todd. "So you're the expert now? You got the answers? He sprang someone from your work camp, remember. Seems to me your guards should have caught him."

Now Todd looked scared. "He's very good at what he does. We were surprised."

"Well, I'm not going to be surprised. When Mr. Tagliani hears about this, there'll be hell to pay. We not only lost someone to take over the coal project, he killed a made man, one of our own. That can't stand."

Joe waved his hand towards the door.

"Get the hell back to camp. Find the worker and track Jason's movements. I want to follow where he went. It'll confirm if he's the one who killed my sentries."

Todd left quickly and headed back to camp. He already had his pursuit team on both trails. Hopefully they would catch someone. He felt on shaky ground. Jason was going to become his problem if he wasn't careful and that wouldn't have a good outcome for him. He wasn't a part of the mob, just someone hired to do a job. It wouldn't take much for the mob to dispense with him and he knew that could be fatal.

Luke told Michael where to meet him and, after a few flirtatious comments to Suzy, he left the building. He positioned himself near the basketball stadium. There was no one about, the day had been cold and the night was going to be colder. The commotion that had occurred during the day on the south side of the downtown area had settled down. He saw small groups of militia checking buildings. They were coming closer and Luke sensed he didn't want to be caught out by them.

Before the search crews reached the stadium, Daniels showed up. Luke grabbed him and they walked casually, but quickly off in a circuitous route, finally arriving at the building across the street from where Jason was waiting.

"We go in here. I've got the other building locked up." Luke produced a set of keys. "The keys to my kingdom."

They entered the building. Once inside, Luke locked the door.

"Make the search groups think no one is in these buildings."

They climbed the stairs to the second floor. After entering the walkway connecting the two buildings, Luke motioned for Michael to crouch down. He studied the street in both directions. After making sure there was no one about, Luke locked the doors leading into the walkway.

"Let's go," he said.

The two ran in a crouch across to the other building. Once inside, Luke locked those doors as well, sealing the walkway off on both ends.

"Make it harder to get into my territory."

He led Michael to the stairs and they began the laborious climb to the top floor.

They entered the suite where Jason was waiting.

"Hello Michael," Jason said. I'm glad you came."

"Do you know they're looking for someone, probably you, everywhere? What did you do?"

"You don't need to know."

"I heard some sentries were killed. Did you do that?"

"No comment."

"What do you want? What's going on and why am I here? I could get into serious trouble for this. Joe will expect me to tell him where you are."

Michael looked panicked.

Jason answered. "But you won't. No one will know you've been here."

"What do you want from me?"

"Do you remember that I told you your position was not secure for the long run?"

Michael nodded. "This guy said the same thing. Did you coach him?"

"Actually no. We both seemed to have come to the same conclusion. Luke is very perceptive, if a bit unusual."

"Go on," Michael said.

"Well, I need just a little help from you and I'm going to break this organization down. There'll be chaos. Luke sees the possibilities of making use of that confusion to change things. You can as well."

"What are you going to do?"

"You've heard the saying, 'cut off the head, the body dies'? That's what I'm going to do. I need to know how to reach Joe, Big Al and the head of the militia, Larry Roper."

Michael just stared at Jason; his eyes wide.

"You're not serious? You're going to take them out? Kill them?"

"These are hard times. These are men who will kill you without a second thought when they don't need you, or think you crossed them. They're planning to wipe out my town, Hillsboro. I can't let that happen. Taking them out of the picture should stop that. Helps Charlotte as well."

"I can't have anything to do with that. I'm with FEMA."

"Does FEMA deal with gangsters now? And how much support do you get?"

Michael was quiet.

"Everything's in the hands of the mob. Therefore, your future and maybe your life is in their hands." He gestured to the luxurious couch. "Come over here and sit down."

"I'll get us all a drink," Luke said and disappeared through door. He came back a few minutes later with a bottle and three glasses. "Got a stash set aside even here on the top floor...or especially on the top floor. Impress the ladies with it."

After the drinks were poured, Jason spoke up again.

"You said it yourself. The mob is going to try to run the east coast from Boston to Charlotte. You'll be a lacky for them at best. FEMA is going to stand by if that's what the feds want in order to gain control. What they don't understand is they're making a bargain with the devil. The mob will corrupt everyone and soon they'll be unchallenged, with a lot of federal officers and bureaucrats working for them."

"Why are you so against that?" Michael asked.

"For one thing, I don't want to see my country run by the mob, any part of it. That happened in the large cities at the beginning of the twentieth century up until the seventies, from what I've read. If the whole east coast comes under their influence and control, honest people might never get us out from under them.

"For another thing, they're planning to wipe out my whole town just to get others under their thumb. They're the modern equivalent of barbarians."

"And you think you can keep this from happening? A few assassinations and everything will be fine?"

Jason shook his head. "No. It may take more than that, but it's a start and it could save a lot of lives in Hillsboro." He took a sip of his whiskey.

"And here's the opportunity it creates. You have the connections to other civic leaders who have been put on the sidelines. Luke, in spite of his eccentricities, has a fresh imagination and could provide you and the others with a vision of how to reinvigorate the population into demanding better. While there's disarray, you can grab the reins of power."

"'Power comes from the barrel of a gun', didn't Mao say that?" Michael asked.

"Something like that. You've got a militia. You can get some of them, maybe most, on your side."

Michael shook his head. "I don't know. It seems so risky. The mob isn't going to just roll over and give us control."

"I can handle them," Luke said. "I told you I dealt with them my whole life."

"Then you know how ruthless they are," Michael said.

"You'll only have the Charlotte mob to deal with. The other cities won't be able to come here. And this group will be in chaos," Jason said.

"There's gonna be power plays," Luke said. "Those under Al and Joe will be more worried about maneuvering for their own advantage to be too worried about what we might be doing. You can trust me on that."

"Look, all I need is some information. I'll do the rest. You stay in touch with Luke. The two of you make whatever plans you want. I'll be going my own way. You'll have no further connection with me."

"We don't meet again?"

"Not after tonight if you give me what I need."

Michael turned to Luke. "And I can't be connected to this building? I never came here?"

"Never," Luke said. "I'll lead you back and you'll just head home like you usually do." He paused for a moment. "Of course, I'll stop in once in a while. Maybe you could make a position for me? Community outreach or something like that."

"I guess I can do that," Michael said.

"And I've got a date tomorrow with Suzy. I hope that's okay with you."

Michael just stared at Luke and shook his head. Jason couldn't tell if it was in disgust or wonder.

Chapter 37

Michael told Jason where Big Al and Joe lived and where their offices in the city government building were located. He said that Roper stayed out at the airport with the main body of militia, but he had an office in the city building. Michael guessed he might be there to help direct the search for Jason. He said he'd find out more and pass it on to Luke. Michael seemed more comfortable having Luke as the go-between, keeping himself separated from Jason who he now considered a dangerous person.

After the two men left, Jason sat back. His thoughts went to Anne and his family back in Hillsboro. They seemed to be a world apart from his situation. Would it be enough? Just to take out one or two leaders? Could he then leave and head back to the life he wanted to live? The assassin role weighed heavily on him.

He shook his head. *No time for that. Concentrate on the mission. If you don't, you'll get yourself killed.*

He went over his next moves. He was secure enough in the building. Luke would run interference for him here, and there were many places to hide if a search occurred. His concern was that he had to figure out how to strike quickly and lethally and then get out of town. Once he took one of this three targets out, the others would harden up. They would make themselves less visible and have more security around them.

If he took out the first one with a sniper rifle, the others would avoid putting themselves in a target situation and their increased protective measures would make it harder to execute a close-up assault. He concluded that his first target would have to be attacked up close. The others would then protect against that situation leaving him the option of a sniper attack.

Joe would be the first. Big Al might think he was more protected. He might feel less of a target. Now he had to figure out how to get close to Joe. With everyone on the lookout for him in the downtown, moving around was not going to be easy. He'd go to Joe's residence and ambush him there. Joe lived on the south side of the downtown area. It was once an expensive neighborhood, heavily wooded with large homes on secluded lots.

The next night he made his way out of the high-rise. He wore dark jeans and coat over a thick sweater. There was a hood on the jacket that he pulled up over his head. He had to be careful getting out of the downtown. He would have to find a place on the perimeter less patrolled.

It was cold. The cloud cover increased the darkness of the night. There was no moonlight to relieve the black. He started walking east. He came to a set of railroad tracks, now unused. Jason moved slowly using every bit of screening he could find. Thankfully there had been no attempts to stem the return to nature in the landscaped areas. Their unchecked growth offered points of concealment along his route. He saw militia patrols along the way. They were still searching through buildings for him. It was not a large geographic area, but was dense with large buildings that proved troublesome to search and check off a list. He easily avoided the patrols by keeping to the overgrown areas.

The tracks went under the interstate that ringed the inner downtown. They were blocked off just before going under the highway, but it was an imperfect seal. It was enough to disincline the opportunists, but not enough to withstand a serious effort. Jason watched the barrier for a long five minutes before approaching it. He was in an undeveloped area, one of the few inside the ring road. The ground had been cleared for probably another high-rise, but the EMP attack had intervened.

At the edges of the train right of way, where the ground sloped up to the overpass, the barrier offered gaps. Jason wedged his way through one of them and continued under the highway. Once on the other side, he quickly sought the cover of the brush and made his way further from the road. With far less scrutiny outside of the downtown, he would have the night and the streets to himself.

On the other side of the perimeter road, nestled nearly up to the overpassing highway, was a parking garage. Like the others, it was now one of the more useless structures in the city. There might have been homeless people at one time living in the lower levels, the upper floors were too open to the wind and cold, but with the drop in population, there was no shortage of houses to occupy.

He had a long walk ahead of him. Once to the south of the downtown area it took a good hour of navigating through neighborhoods to find Joe's house. The area was filled with shrubs and trees, now overgrown. They offered good cover, shielding him from the houses, which were set well back from the streets.

When he got to the address, Jason entered a thick stand of trees between the mansion and the street. He crept through the dense foliage to get a view the building. Joe's home had a large, four-car garage set off from the main house. The house had two wings coming off the main section forming a semi-courtyard which contained a patio and large pool. The drive and turning area in front of the garage and house was laid with paving stones in an elaborate pattern. A black Ford Galaxy from the sixties was parked near the front door, facing out to the street.

Jason assumed it was Joe's ride back downtown in the morning. For now, he'd have to wait. There was always the waiting.

He hunkered down in the underbrush and tried to keep warm. He had no idea when Joe would leave the house. If he was not an early riser, it raised the risk of Jason being discovered. An attack early in the morning, in the dim winter light, would be best.

Sleep came fitfully with confusing dreams of the mob descending on Hillsboro, the Hillsboro council embracing them. Jason being told to follow Joe's orders. Through it all Jason fidgeted. The dream morphed into the whole east coast being under Joe's control and the president standing behind him with a smile on his face. Could it come to that? Jason doubted it. Dreams often amplified the deeper emotional content of one's mind, throwing rationality aside to make a point.

As the grey of dawn dissolved the dark of night, he got up and began to stretch. He drank some water and chewed on a piece of venison jerky that he had brought with him. Then he crept closer to the driveway. The house, now seen in more light, was huge. It had a long, three-story front wing facing the road but screened by the trees. It looked like the front made a left turn towards the rear. Along the driveway was an irregular shaped façade that held the formal front doors. The garage sat at the end of the drive, facing the road. With hired drivers, none of the house residents would have to walk to their car in inclement weather. *Ah the joys of being rich.* Jason smiled. *And with it a complicated life.*

He positioned himself so it was a short dash across the driveway to the car. He wanted to be on the house side, so no one could use the vehicle for a shield. The key was surprise and speed. When he was satisfied with his position, Jason took out his 9mm with its suppressor and checked the weapon thoroughly. Thirteen rounds in the magazine, one in the chamber, safety on, ready to switch off and go into action.

He waited, cold but patient, as the daylight increased. He kept still and only rubbed his hands occasionally to keep them from going stiff in the cold. It was a cloudy November day with a hint of rain. He hoped it would hold off until he got back to the high-rise. *Such mundane thoughts at a moment like this.* Maybe that was compartmentalization at work. He'd experienced that effect in the army and since the EMP attack.

Suddenly the front door opened. Two men stepped out in coats and ties. They looked around, then one of them called back to the doorway and Joe emerged. He kissed a woman goodbye at the door and stepped out on the driveway. The men turned. One went to open the back door and the other looked like he was going to get into the driver's seat.

Jason broke from the bushes and ran towards the car. The two men stopped for an instant before reacting. That hesitation proved fatal. While running forward, Jason leveled his 9mm and with two quick shots, hit both men in the chest. The sound the gun made was a muffled "thwack". The men went down. Joe saw it was Jason.

He put his hands up and shouted, "Jason! What are you doing? You don't want to kill me."

Jason stopped about ten paces from Joe. He knew he should just pull the trigger and leave, but something held him back. Joe was on the wrong side, but Joe had believed in him. At least the undercover version of him.

"Don't hurt my family, please. We can work this out." Joe said. "I gave you an opportunity. We're growing, making things better for everyone. Why not be a part of it? You afraid of Big Al? I can protect you from him." His words tumbled out of him, seemingly desperate to stave off Jason's intent.

"It isn't that. I'm from Hillsboro."

He let that sink in for a moment. Joe's eyes widened as he digested all that statement meant.

"Look, I don't have anything against Hillsboro. It's not personal, it's just business. If they pay and knuckle under, we'll leave them alone."

Jason shook his head. *Get this done!* His inner voiced shouted to him.

"That's not what you said."

"I can change that. It was Big Al's idea. You can take one of my cars and head home now if you want. I'll make sure no one stops you. I'll work something out for Hillsboro's benefit."

Jason shook his head again. "Too late for that, Joe. You said it yourself, 'It's not personal, it's just business.'"

"No!" Joe shouted. Jason pulled the trigger and shot him in the chest. With Joe's shout the door opened and the woman reappeared. She screamed as she saw Joe on the driveway along with the other two men. She started out of the door but Jason glared at her and she retreated inside.

Jason stepped forward and put a shot through the head of each of the guards. He went over to Joe and hesitated. Then he shot him through the heart. He'd keep his face unmarked. Next, he reached into the driver's pocket and found the keys. He got into the Ford and drove off. As he pulled out, he saw the woman running out to the fallen bodies.

It would take some time for the word to spread and when it did, everyone would feel more exposed at their homes than at their work. Just what Jason wanted. He drove at a steady pace to the parking garage near the train tunnel. He'd park the car there for possible use later to escape.

Chapter 38

Back in the high-rise office, Jason was thankful find himself alone. He clamped down on his thoughts, not allowing them to run into dangerous areas. He was in attack mode. He had a job to do to protect his family, protect Hillsboro. These men had chosen their path and so had Jason. But they didn't realize how good he was at what he was about to do. He stopped his mind from ruminating on the morality of his task, and concentrated on the logistics of it. He had to stay focused to pull off what he was attempting. He'd deal with any conscience issues later.

After eating something and taking a large, stiff drink of the whiskey Luke had provided, Jason headed to the roof. Once up there, he took his spotting scope and scanned the city building. He had a sight line to Big Al's office. But he wasn't sure he could make a shot through the glass, especially since it wasn't straight in. Hitting the glass at an angle could disrupt the trajectory enough to cause him to miss.

He turned his attention to the entrance. Some cars drove up to drop off their passengers, the higher-ups in the mob and some of the city big-wigs as well. Daniels didn't have a car which put his status down on the pecking order; something Daniels was probably well aware of.

After an hour of watching, the traffic pretty much ended. Only pedestrians were entering the building, and not too many of them. They'd be looking for Joe soon. Maybe his wife would drive herself downtown to report his killing. Jason didn't know if she had access to a car, but Joe's death would certainly be discovered today.

That would increase the tension. Could he count on Big Al leaving the building at the end of the day? Would he forgo going home to throw off an assassin? Jason only needed Big Al to exit the building; go somewhere. It didn't matter where as long as Jason got the opportunity when he went out the front door.

Things settled down and Jason let out a yawn. Maybe he should grab a few hours of sleep and take up watch in the afternoon. If he got his shot, he'd be busy tonight without much chance of rest. He got up, stretched, and went back downstairs.

Luke was sitting in the office suite.

"When did you get back?" Luke asked as Jason entered.

"You sound like a parent."

"Yeah. Guess I do. You didn't come home last night. I sat up and worried myself sick about you." Luke mimicked a worried mom's voice.

"It's okay, I was out with the boys."

"It's always the boys. I told you not to hang around with that crowd. You'll get into trouble."

Jason allowed a thin smile on his face.

"You don't know the half of it."

Luke changed back to his normal voice. "And I don't want to know. Are you planning some action?"

"It's already started. I'm planning the next steps. I need to rest now. I'm going back on the roof later this afternoon." Jason looked around. "Can you rustle up something to eat? I'm starving."

"So now I'm supposed to feed you? You're talking to the Duke of East End, remember."

"*Mr. Duke*, can you please gather up something to eat? Seeing as how you know where everything is in this building?"

"That's more like it." Luke grinned at him. I can certainly do that." He got up. "I spent some time with Michael this morning. Got me an official pass into the building. Things are going well. I think I'm going to be a big help to him."

"He say anything about Roper, the militia commander?"

"Said he would find out if he's here, downtown, and get back to us this afternoon if he can. He'll probably leave his office early. I'll be going back there to pick up Suzy for our date."

"We may need to talk about that."

Luke looked at Jason with concern. "You planning on doing something tonight?"

"I thought you didn't want to know."

"I don't unless it involves me or makes things dangerous for me."

"We'll talk about it later, maybe when Daniels gets here."

Jason walked over to the large couch and lay down. He took a deep breath, stretched his legs out and let the tension flow out of his body.

"After I eat, I'm going to take a rest. Wake me in a couple of hours, okay?"

"Sure boss, anything you say boss."

Jason gave Luke a dismissive look but didn't answer.

It was early afternoon when Jason awoke. Luke had just come back into the office with Daniels.

"I left early today. Wanted to give you the latest news," Daniels said as the two sat down with Jason.

"I thought you wanted to stay clear of here, use Luke as an intermediary," Jason said.

"I did. But things are different today. All hell has broken loose. Nicoletti's wife showed up. She told Big Al that someone ambushed Joe this morning and killed him along with his two body guards. Right in front of their home. She saw the man from her front door."

"She get a good look at him?" Jason asked. He kept his voice calm.

"Not really, just that he was about your height and build. She knows enough about guns to know the shooter used a silencer."

"What did Big Al do?"

"He called Roper, me and some other mob bosses in, along with our mayor. Said we have to be 'all hands on deck' and find the killer. He's convinced it's you."

"But he isn't sure."

"He doesn't have to be sure. It all fits. You disappear, free someone from the coal camp, kill Gino, head back to town—they followed a trail to the Catawba River before they lost it. Then two sentries guarding the downtown get killed. Then Joe gets killed at his home."

"Quite a list of events," Jason said.

"That's an understatement if I ever heard one. All this is being ascribed to you. Now everyone, and I mean *everyone*, including the militia, is out looking for you. Big Al figures you've got all the bosses home addresses. He's told them to not go home tonight. Stay here in one of the hotels or stay at their offices. Everyone's on high alert."

"Did you whack Joe?" Luke asked.

"Does it make a difference whether or not I did?"

"Mmm, probably not. But you said you were going to sow chaos and that seems to be what is taking place."

"And you and Michael should get ready to take advantage of that fact."

"Hell, we haven't had time to even begin to think about things. This is happening too fast," Michael said.

"Then move fast." Jason stood up and began pacing. "Find allies. Go to the mayor. He may be powerless right now but he has connections, all politicians have connections. Sound him out if you need to. I'm guessing he's frustrated at being put aside. Get him to work with you, at least to give you access to connections. He's got to have some support from the remnants of the police. How about the militia? They can't all be completely loyal to Roper. He was a corrupt captain in the army. Now he's leapfrogged all the chain of command to become the head of the militia? He's got to have some enemies there."

"You know Roper?" Daniels asked.

"Yeah. He was driven out of Hillsboro. He's a failed con man, basically." Jason looked at both Michael and Luke. "You understand what I'm saying? Make connections. You don't need commitments right now. You need to get people thinking about possibilities. Things are going to get more chaotic which will help your position."

"How do we not get caught?" Luke asked.

Jason turned to him, his eyes flashing in anger. "Damned if I know. Where's the Duke? Where's this man of action and influence? Michael's going to be doing most of the leg work on this. He can run under the guise of doing what Big Al instructed, corralling all the resources to find me." Jason thought for a moment. "Maybe you should go out to your old neighborhoods. You're the Duke of East End. Prove it. Get some people to support change when you trigger it."

He turned back to Daniels, "You two work on multiple fronts."

The men thought for a long moment. For once Luke didn't have a flippant reply.

"You might have to cancel your date for tonight," Jason told him.

Luke looked over at him. "I guess you're right." He took a breath. "I'm in. Are you?" He turned to Michael. "Remember we're living on borrowed time."

"I'm in, Michael said. "I can use that point with some of my connections."

"Good," Jason said. "That's your plan,".

Michael and Luke stood up.

"Before you go. Is Big Al staying downtown tonight?"

"I don't think he's going home," Michael said. "He'll be at his office late, but probably go over to the Omni for a meal. After he'll probably come back to his office. He'll be heavily guarded each way."

"But they think I'm outside the inner city, right?"

Michael nodded his head.

"And what about Roper?"

"He was at the meeting. He's working with his officers. I don't know if he'll be downtown all night or not."

"Okay, thanks. You guys get going."

"You going to stay here?" Luke asked. "Even if the search is working outside the downtown, there's still a lot of militia on the streets here. It could be dangerous for you out there."

"I may not be here when you get back. But you should plan on working most of the afternoon and night. Remember, you've got to get things set up fast to take advantage of what's happening and what's coming. The time to sleep is later."

Chapter 39

After Luke and Michael had left, Jason took out his M110 and spotting scope. After checking the rifle over, he went up to the roof. It might be a long wait, but from what Michael had said, he was confident his target would show. He made himself as comfortable as he could and settled down to wait for either of the two men to emerge from the building.

Two hours went by. Jason drank some water, ate some sausage, but stayed at his position. The day progressed into afternoon. He was aiming south, and the winter sun would be setting in the southwest; not quite in his eyes. There'd be no reflection from his scope to worry about.

The entrance to the building was swarming with soldiers. Lower level workers started exiting, walking home for the evening. They either didn't know of the threat or felt they had nothing to fear. Whoever killed Joe Nicoletti was hunting for bigger, more important targets than they presented.

I'll take whoever comes out first. Jason figured there'd only be one chance. And when the search outside of the inner city didn't turn up any results, the troops might begin a more thorough search of the downtown. There were enough militia to do both, if Roper decided the threat might still be downtown. Jason couldn't assume he was safe in the high-rise for any length of time. *Act on the first opportunity, then get the hell out.* He'd figure out his next move after that. Improvising was always called for. With so many variables, he couldn't pre-set his next steps.

Another hour passed. He still had good light and hoped Big Al was not going to work late or, worse, stay in the office for the night.

Then an older sedan drove up. Three men got out. It was followed by another one, a Ford as near as Jason could guess. Five men got out of that one. Jason switched from the spotting scope to his rifle and watched, now on high alert.

The entrance to the city building opened and a dozen militia members with what looked like M16s emerged and fanned out, rifles ready. The men waited outside the door with the militia forming an outer perimeter spreading out from the doorway. Everyone was scanning the area in front of them. *Checking by sectors. Each one responsible for spotting threats in an assigned field of view.* This went on for a full two long minutes. *They think the threat still might be near-by. They're focused on a close-up attack. Big mistake.*

Then one of the civilian men, inside the circle of militia, pulled open the front door. Jason swung his scope to the door. He could clearly see Big Al emerge, flanked by some of his capos.

There was little hesitation. As soon as Big Al came out, the men formed a protective shield around him and began to move to the waiting vehicles. Fortunately for Jason, Big Al came by his nickname for a reason. He was a good head taller than the men around him. Jason slowed his breathing, his heart rate. He was the hunter. He locked down the deadly link to his prey.

When they started down to the street, Big Al was more exposed as the men in front began to step down. Jason paused his breathing mid-exhale, and squeezed off a shot. The M110 gave a muffled bark along with a solid kick to his shoulder. Big Al's head exploded in a burst of blood and brains at the same time the supersonic crack of the bullet rang out at the building entrance. He collapsed to the concrete. The men and militia around him brought up their weapons and looked around. The civilians all dropped to the ground or started running back towards the building to get inside.

Jason sat back from the M110. The bodyguards and capos around Big Al were good targets, but there was no sense telegraphing his position further by taking more shots. The militia could be at the building in a minute if he gave them an opportunity to pinpoint his location. He began to dismantle the rifle and pack it away. Before leaving the roof, he took a look through the spotting scope. Big Al lay in a heap, hardly recognizable from the head shot. He saw Michael appear at the top of the steps and look down. When he saw the body, Michael looked in Jason's direction and then went back inside.

After throwing the table and chair into a corner of the roof, Jason hurried down to the office suite. It wouldn't take someone familiar with ballistics long to figure out the general direction of the shot. Then a massive hunt would begin. They had their killer, here in the downtown area, possibly trapped. They wouldn't let him escape easily. He had to move now.

He packed up his gear. Exchanging the M110 for his M4. He went around the suite and cleaned up any evidence of his presence. *Don't want to get Luke into trouble.* Then he shouldered his pack and stepped out into the hall. He walked briskly to the stairs and started down the forty flights. He let gravity propel him at a run, being careful not to trip, but moving as fast as he could go. Getting caught in the building would be certain death. Once on the streets he had the possibility of fight and retreat. He hadn't seen Roper, but he knew the man would be on the scene and probably direct the search himself, even if from the safety of the building.

Michael was coming down the stairs in the city-county building when he heard the sound of the shot. He stepped out of the door and saw Big Al lying on the sidewalk. Everyone was shouting and looking around. Michael looked down the blocks to the high-rise. The roof could be seen clearly from where he stood but he could see nothing through the metal curtain on the top of the building. He turned his gaze away and stepped back inside.

He was pushed aside by Larry Roper who stopped at the door. Someone opened it and he peered out to look at the body but didn't step outside. *Must be worried about being a target himself.* Michael stayed back and watched the action.

Roper said something to a man next to him. The man ran out to the body and kept anyone from moving it. He shouted some orders and the militia fanned out to secure the full plaza in front of the building. When that was done, Roper came out. He bent down to the body and examined the entry point of the bullet. It was at the left temple between the ear and eye. The lower right backside of the man's skull was blown out in a bloody mess with the neck damaged as well.

He stood up faced forward, as he guessed Big Al had been doing. He put his finger up to his head at the same point of entry, then turned to an officer near him.

"The shot came from up the block." He pointed north along the street. "Can't tell how far away. I want a hundred men assembled here. You check every building along this block. I can't tell the height, but all we need is the direction."

He pointed up the street. "The killer is up there somewhere. Get the men together to search every building and get more troops to seal off six blocks in that direction." He turned and started back inside.

One of the mob associates stepped in front of him.

"You was supposed to protect him. And Joe." The man looked aggressive. "What kind of protection is that?"

The other mobsters assembled around him. Some of Roper's militia saw the confrontation and shouldered their way next to their commander.

Michael watched. The chaos was beginning to happen. *Is this the start? A split between the militia and the mob?*

"You find your next-in-command and send them to me. I've figured out where the shot came from. Have you?"

The man didn't respond.

"I didn't think so. Now get out of my face. This isn't the time for any of that crap. This is the time to catch the shooter. We know approximately where he is, so don't get in my way while I'm trying to catch him."

With that, Roper pushed the man aside and stepped back into the building.

"What are you looking at?" Roper said to Michael. "Don't you have anything useful to do?"

Instead of cowering, Michael responded. "I wish I did."

"Go talk to the fucking mayor. Find out if there are any keys to the buildings along this street. We need to check them all out." He pushed past Michael and started up the stairs.

Roper's command sounded like a good opportunity to begin what Jason had talked about; Michael headed off to talk with the mayor. There might be keys, maybe with the fire department. If not, the militia could just smash doors. But he'd take his time finding out. He had more important things to discuss with the mayor.

Michael was getting a sense of how unstable the situation could become. Roper might use his militia to try to take control of the city. That would exchange one dictator for another. Now was the time to get the mayor moving. Maybe he'd had enough of the results of his decision, two years ago, to turn control over to the mob.

Chapter 40

Jason emerged from the high rise on a side street. He was shielded from any visibility to the city building. His immediate problem was that he had to cross the street that went straight past the city government center, which would expose him. It was only four blocks away. But he had to get east in order to get to Joe's car.

He turned north and ran down an alley. *Put more distance between me and the shooting, then cross and head east.* He went west a half-block and turned north, moving at a fast jog. The dense, high-rises petered out after two more blocks. There were a few civilians about but they only cast furtive glances at Jason as he ran by. After covering four more blocks he turned back east.

Now he was far enough away to be hardly visible. There were a few pedestrians on the streets. He hoped he would look like one of them from the greater distance. As he crossed the street he looked to his right and saw the troops coming north. They were jogging forward, passing all the buildings along the way.

They figured out where the shot came from. Going to set up a perimeter, then hunt through each building. Jason gave a sigh of relief. He had a chance to stay outside the cordoned-off area. He allowed himself to slow to a quick walk. *Try not to attract too much attention.* There were other militia around as well as city cops. Not being noticed would be hard. He had the M110 in its padded pack strapped to his backpack; all making a large load on his back. His 5.56 rifle was slung over his shoulder His

9mm was in his coat pocket. He looked odd and out of place.

Everyone in the downtown area dressed in a style more like one saw before the attack, as if the city was trying to recreate a normal, pre-EMP look. He stood a good chance of being stopped by a patrol even if they hadn't heard of the shooting. *Can't pretend to be a hunter for the city. They don't show up downtown.*

While he was thinking about his appearance, two policemen crossed the street to intercept him. The police had been partially merged with the militia, in that Roper had ultimate authority over them. Below Roper, they got their orders from a police chief who was controlled by the mob. In that sense the mob ran the police department. While the militia did city patrols, as they got ready to go through the countryside to pacify the smaller towns, the police were left alone more and more to deal with city issues.

"Hold up there," one of the officers said as they approached Jason. "Who are you and what are you doing downtown?"

"You don't look like a hunter. And anyway, hunters aren't allowed here," the other said.

Jason stopped. He sized up the two men. They weren't in full alert mode, so an attack on them had a chance due to the surprise factor. Still, he'd try to talk his way out of the situation.

"I got my card in my coat pocket," Jason said. He pointed to his right-hand pocket. The officers tensed. He pulled out his mob ID card, the one that let him into the downtown area, and handed it to the first man.

They both looked at it carefully and then Jason. "It's got a name on it, but no picture. How do we know this belongs to you?"

"Are you nuts? How many IDs have you seen with pictures? You can't get one of these unless one of the bosses assigns it to you. Joe Nicoletti authorized this. I used to report to Vincent Bonocchi, but now I work directly under Joe." He reached out his hand for the card. "Now stop trying to bust my balls and give me my ID back so I can get going."

The officer handed the card back to Jason. "I gotta ask, why are you dressed that way? Nobody I know works for Mr. Nicoletti looks like that. You look like a militia fighter or some kind of highway bandit...well-armed I would say."

Jason gave him a withering look. "I could say the same about you. You've got a half uniform on at best."

"That doesn't answer my question."

"No, it doesn't. And I don't have to answer it. This ID says I can come and go as I please. And there aren't any rules about uniforms. Sometimes my work calls for rougher clothes, sometimes for suits and dress shirts. Why and when isn't your concern."

With that Jason strode off before the officers could come up with any other objections. As soon as they heard about the shooting, he had no doubt they'd think of him. It was best to put distance between himself and them as quickly as possible. He could sense the cops watching his back as he walked down the block. He forced himself to walk deliberately, not appear to be in a hurry or nervous.

When he turned the corner, he quickened his pace. As he approached the railroad tracks, a group of three militia men came towards him. When they were within fifty feet, they aimed their rifles at him and ordered him to stop.

"Put down your rifle," one of them ordered.

Jason slipped his 5.56 off his shoulder and laid it on the ground. He stood facing them.

"What's up? I'm on an assignment for Joe Nicoletti."

"Mr. Nicoletti's dead. Killed this morning. And Mr. Tagliani's dead as well. He's just been shot by a sniper. Now we got to search you."

"Joe's dead? How can that be? I talked to him just yesterday."

Jason pretended surprise and shock. It didn't seem to faze the men.

"I've still got to do what Mr. Nicoletti told me to do. We need this information I'm out to collect."

"That can wait," the leader of the three said as they approached.

"Can you lower your weapons? It makes me nervous. I can show you my ID. Mr. Nicoletti signed it himself."

The leader motioned for the men to lower their rifles.

"We'll still have to check your pack before we can let you go. Where are you headed anyway?"

"East. Joe wanted me to canvas the East End to see if there are any groups fomenting dissent. He heard some things and I'm going to check them out."

"Why the backpack and gear? You look like you're on a shooting mission."

"Can't be too careful. Besides I have some other work to do, it's confidential."

He knew his justifications sounded weak. The men approached. If they looked into his packs, his ruse would be exposed. The M110 was enough to convict him.

"Let me get my ID out," Jason said. "It's in my coat pocket." He pointed to his right-hand pocket which also held his 9mm.

"Slowly," the leader said.

"I'll slip off my pack so you can check it."

Jason slipped off his pack and bent over to set it on the ground. As he straightened up, he reached into his pocket and pulled out his pistol. In one quick move, he flicked the safety off and fired.

Thwack, thwack, thwack. Three quick muffled shots rang out. The bullets hitting the men in their chests before they had a chance to react. They fell to the ground. Two were dead when they hit the pavement, the other one looked at Jason in surprise.

"Sorry about that, but you found the sniper. I can't get caught so I can't stay to help you. Maybe someone'll come along, but I've got to go."

He scattered the weapons away from the wounded man. Jason guessed he had only minutes left to live, but he didn't want to chance the man shooting at him as he walked away. He re-shouldered his pack and rifle and headed off towards the tracks and his waiting car.

Chapter 41

When he reached the tracks, Jason turned east and walked along the side of the right of way. He had four long blocks to go before he could get through the barrier and reach the car. Running didn't seem prudent; he could see groups of men blocks away. He needed to look like another member of the militia when seen from afar. Running would attract too much attention.

The rail line was for commuter trains taking people in and out of the city. They had stopped working along with other trains after the EMP attack. Jason's path took him past a station two blocks from his goal. He heard footsteps coming from a parking lot to his right. The lot was shielded from view by a building. The footsteps were coming closer.

Jason unslung his rifle. He wouldn't survive a close inspection from a larger group. He stopped at a shelter for the commuters next to the tracks. From there he would be able to see the approaching patrol.

The first of the men came out from the side of the building. There was a dozen of them, headed towards him. He began firing. The first three went down before anyone could react. The rest of the men ran back to the cover of the building. Quickly shots came from the corner, but the shooters were firing blind. Two men sprinted across the opening to get a flanking position. Jason dropped one of them, but the other reached cover. Soon more accurate shots were coming from his direction.

Jason loosed ten shots in quick succession, both at the corner of the building and at the flanker, then he got up and ran towards the barrier two blocks away. Within a moment he heard shots ring out. There was yelling and Jason guessed the men pinned behind the building were now moving out onto the platform.

Beyond the station platform there was a construction site. It took up most of the block. It consisted of sections of poured concrete foundation with holes dug for more forms and now left empty. Jason ducked behind one of the concrete pieces. He put in a fresh magazine and turned to return fire.

Bullets clanged along the tracks and some thumped against the concrete, chipping chunks of it away. Jason lay in the prone position and fired around the edge of the concrete. He was systematic, not shooing without a target, but taking quick shots at any bodies that presented themselves. His accurate fire sent the patrol diving for cover. The return fire was now slower indicating the men were keeping their heads down.

Jason noted where some of the patrol had ducked and watched them. Unfortunately, he couldn't see them all, nor could he cover them all. Soon the shots from the patrol made it too dangerous to peek around the edge. He crawled to the other side and found a gap in the concrete. He slipped his M4 through and started firing. Again, his accurate shots shut down the return fire.

Go now. Jason got up and ran towards the barrier. He kept the concrete wall between him and the patrol as much as he could. His goal was escape, not a prolonged firefight.

He hadn't covered a full block when shots started hitting close. He dove into a hole as bullets screamed over his head. He turned and raised his rifle over the lip and loosed a half-dozen rounds at the figures he saw coming forward. That emptied his magazine. Jason pulled back into the hole, ejected the empty mag, and snapped in a fresh one. Shots were now zinging over the hole he was in with their deadly whistle. Others peppered the dirt around him. It was lethal to stick his head up.

He slipped his rifle over the rim of the hole without raising his head and fired some rounds in the general direction. His earlier accuracy demanded respect and the return fire from the patrol stopped for a moment. Jason took that instant to now aim properly and send more deadly rounds in the patrol's direction. Then he jumped up and ran again, zig zagging away from the station.

The tracks crossed a road at street level just before the barrier. There was an overgrown planting area along side of the road. The brush and trees offered concealment. Jason ran into the brush at speed with bullets zinging past him.

In the brush were some trees large enough to conceal and protect him. Better still, he could not be easily be seen inside the cover. There was only a half a block to go to the barrier. That stretch was, however, open and dangerous. He had to pin the patrol down and keep them far away when he made his final sprint.

He started sending deadly shots downrange. Every third or fourth shot was hitting a target. As Jason was working his rifle to good effect, he saw some men break off and head to the south, his left. *Gonna to try to flank me again.* That would reduce the number of shooters with a direct line of fire to him when he made his run for the barrier.

He emptied his third magazine and inserted a fourth. He sent more shots at the pinned-down patrol and stood up. *Time to go.*

He broke from the cover, partially protected from sight and ran for the barrier. Fifty yards out from his position he could now be seen and shots started coming. Jason ran in an erratic pattern but always towards the barrier. He reached it with shots hitting the wall and ground around him. He didn't pause. While at a full run, he slipped his pack off and dove through the opening he had made the night before.

Once on the other side of the barrier, he started to return fire. As his shots suppressed incoming rounds, he half crawled back through the gap and reached for his pack. He pulled it back through the small opening. His arms and back were scrapped and bleeding from his dive.

Suddenly a new burst of shots began to hit around the opening. *The flankers.* Jason got up and ran for the parking garage. He hoped he had enough time to get to the car and drive off. The patrol might have sent a runner back to report the engagement. If that was the case, reinforcements would be coming soon and overwhelm him. He didn't have the luxury of fighting from a sniper's distance. This was a close-up fire fight and he would be overwhelmed, or run out of ammunition.

He had parked the car on the second floor in the middle of the garage. He threw his pack with the M110 strapped to it in the passenger seat and jumped in. He squealed down the ramp. There was a rumble coming from the freeway above. Jason could hear it over the roar of his engine. *Diesel engines.* That meant military vehicles. The rest of the militia had been alerted and was arriving.

Jason swung out into the street and headed north parallel to the higher interstate. *Got to put some blocks between me and that road. I'm a sitting duck for them up there.* Shots rang out. They were shooting at him on the run. It sounded like an M60 machine gun. Jason swung the steering wheel to the right and the car slewed into a parking lot with a partially built structure giving him some cover. There were trees near the exit.

The machine gun paused as the operator lost his target. Jason knew he couldn't stay and accelerated. *Have to move faster than they anticipate. That'll give me a second or two.* The car burst out from the cover of the abandoned building. Jason heard the chatter of the M60 start again, and, as he hoped, the shots hit behind him. The gunner didn't waste much time in sweeping forward and bullets raked through the sedan as Jason slid into the road, turning right. The car went wide, and, with a bang, bounced off the curb.

He floored the accelerator and the sedan shot down the road, away from the higher freeway. There was a moment of silence as the Humvee had to stop and back up. The deadly staccato of the machine gun began again. Jason lowered himself in the seat until he could barely see over the dashboard. The rear window burst out and the shots carried through to the windshield. *The seat won't stop those rounds.*

Jason yanked the wheel to the left and slid around a corner, again bouncing off the curb. He nearly collided with an abandoned car that was parked. He pulled his car to the right, up on the sidewalk to miss the obstruction and then lurched back into the street. No bullets chased him. He was blocked by buildings.

An intersection approached. He'd be open to the machine gun as he crossed. Jason accelerated the abused sedan forward. He hit the intersection at seventy miles an hour. The car leapt off the ground as he crossed the crown of the intersecting road. He heard the machine gun but it was behind his path. The shooter hadn't been ready for him.

Jason kept up his speed and at the next intersection he turned right in a more controlled slide to gain more distance between himself and the Humvee. As he raced down the road, he heard the machine gun start up. He put the car into random swerves across the street, using abandoned cars as picks to give him a moment of cover. After two more blocks, Jason turned right this time and accelerated. That move would require the Humvee to turn around and give him more time to escape.

Chapter 42

Luke came back to his high-rise in time to see the militia breaking down a street level door. He walked up to one of the men to find out what was going on. "Where you been?" the man asked.

"I been out in the city, visiting my old neighborhood," Luke replied.

"Someone shot Al Tagliani. A sniper. Our commander figures the shot came from one of these buildings along the street. You live here?"

Luke shook his head. "No, no. I live outside of the inner city. I work for Michael Daniels, the FEMA rep. I was just headed back to the city building to report to him when I saw you guys breaking in. Thought I'd see what's going on."

"All hell's broken loose, that's what's going on." The man turned and went through the door.

Luke headed towards the city building. He did need to report back to Michael. He also needed a place to stay. There was no way Luke was going back to that high-rise. He was sure the militia would find some evidence of a shooter's set up on the roof. Anyone connected to the building would be locked up and submitted to intense interrogation. Someone had to pay for Big Al's killing.

Michael was frustrated. While he knew that he had not defended FEMA's role in how things had developed in Charlotte, it was Martin Chambers, the mayor, primarily, and the city council, secondarily, that had allowed the mafia to gain control over the city's operations. The mayor was weak, unfortunately. Now Michael had to buck him up so he could help, or at least not get in the way.

He had just finished going over Jason's theory in detail with Chambers.

"So, you see, we're on borrowed time, you and me. The city council's been dissolved, the mob controls all the public functions, the police, the militia. They make the rules, we just put a civic face on it to the public. They soon won't need us."

He hoped the argument would move Chambers out of his position of submissive acceptance of his figurehead role into one of more action.

"I don't know Michael. It seems a bit melodramatic to me. Won't the organization always want a spokesperson? Someone like me?"

"What's the saying? Tits on a boar hog? You really think they'll put up with you after they don't need you? If they do, it won't involve a luxurious lifestyle, whatever that means these days. The mob," he saw Martin wince at the word, "doesn't like to share. Haven't you noticed that?"

"If they found out we were plotting against them, they'd kill us...and probably not too pleasantly."

Michael leaned forward to close the distance between him and Martin. "Didn't you hear me? Nicoletti's dead. Tagliani's dead. Who takes over? There's going to be a struggle between the capos. They all act like family, but when power is up for grabs, they will kill their own."

He pointed his finger at Martin.

"Now if they'll kill their own, why wouldn't they kill us? We're going to be told which side to get on before too long. The problem is we don't know which side will be the winning one and if we're wrong, we're dead."

He leaned back. "Better to plot our own path." He could still see doubt on Martin's face. "Besides, aren't you the least bit remorseful about letting them take over? Now's the time to take back control."

"How would we go about that?"

"Martin, you're a politician. You should have the answer to that." Using Jason's comments, he pressed on. "Use your connections. First the police, then the militia, then the civilians that have been pressed into service, the ones who actually run the city's infrastructure. They've got to be unhappy being under the mob's thumb. We find out who we can rely on, who's on our side. That's how we start."

"Then what?"

"Shit, I don't know. But it's a start. I'll find someone to head to Atlanta to get some support from FEMA. We'll see what's happening with the capos, who's going to emerge from the fight. They'll all be wounded by the struggle. You know these guys get bloody. But this time it will be to our advantage.

Michael took a deep breath. "My point is we'll see what our moves are as things develop."

"Well...maybe I can reach out, see what others are thinking, reactivate old alliances..."

"You do that. And get the police on our side along with some of the militia officers. Some of them came from our National Guard and police department."

Michael sighed after leaving Martin's office. The meeting went well. The mayor was more than cautious. He was frightened. He wouldn't stick his neck out, but he would make the connections, sound out others. Maybe Michael could do the rest. Suddenly he felt the weight of stepping out of his passivity and his comfort zone. He didn't like it.

Heading back to his office, Michael ran into Luke who looked panicked.

"They found out where the shot came from. From the roof." His voice was hushed in a hoarse whisper.

"Let's go to my office," Michael said. He pushed Luke down the hall and through his office door. Suzy smiled at seeing Luke. Michael kept pushing him along, not allowing him to stop and talk with Suzy.

"Sit down and tell me what you found out," Michael said.

Luke took a seat in front of his desk. "I was heading back to the high-rise and ran into a large patrol. They were smashing down the door and told me the shot must have come from one of the tall buildings in the area. They'll go up to the roof and find Jason's set up. I can't go back there. I can't let anyone know I've ever lived there."

"No you can't. But don't panic. There's no way for anyone to connect you to the shooting." Michael paused for a moment. "You're sure they'll find the spot?"

"Can't miss it. They'll go right to the roof. Jason set something up there. Snipers don't shoot standing up and holding their rifles, I don't know what you call it, free-hand or something."

"Off-hand, I think it's called."

"In the end it doesn't matter. They're already convinced it's Jason. Where he took the shot is not important. What's important is that he's sown the chaos he talked about."

Michael paused for a moment to think.

"Did you do any good over in East End?"

"A little. I've got some men, tough guys who worked the bars and games. They're under the mob's control even more now and they don't like it. They could be helpful if we need them."

"Can we rely on them?"

Luke shook his head. "Not sure you can rely on anyone. Everyone's going to be hedging their bets now. Not sticking their necks out and trying to play all sides as things get crazy."

"I wonder how long you can do that? Play all sides."

"Not too long," Luke said. "You get caught out and then no one trusts you. Not a good position to find yourself in."

"Okay. Let me know how to get in touch with these guys. I've got the mayor going to work his old connections to see what he can come up with."

"Why do you need these contacts of mine? They don't know you. Better to let me work this side of the street."

"I agree, but I need you to do something for me...for us."

Luke looked at Michael, one eyebrow raised in suspicion.

"I need to send you to Atlanta with a message. Maybe we can get some help from FEMA down there. They've got things pretty well under control, from what I last heard."

"Me? Go on the road? It's dangerous out there."

"You told Suzy you came from Atlanta. Everyone thinks so. So now you get the chance to live the story."

Luke was shaking his head. "No, no. Don't need to do that." He looked up at Michael. "I could get killed."

Michael sat back and thought about the situation. He couldn't really order Luke to go, but he had some leverage. Luke needed Michael for his cushy job and cover. Maybe he could set up some security for him and mislead the capos as well, getting cover for himself along the way.

"Here's what we'll do. I'll get in touch with one of the capos. I'll tell them that I'm sending you back to Atlanta to tell them things are under control here. The mob won't want FEMA coming around. They've stayed away because I tell them things are good here. If they heard about this, they might be worried and send people."

"That's nice, but it won't help me out on the road."

"It gets better." Michael smiled. His brain was now humming with schemes and connections. "I'll get you some help...maybe a vehicle, a Humvee. You recruit a couple of your bouncer friends from the neighborhood to go along as protection. We'll make sure they're well-armed and you'll be sent out with the mob's blessings."

Michael now beamed. "What the mob won't know is that you'll be giving FEMA my message and getting them to come here."

"What happens if they do come?"

"Doesn't change what we've said to the mob capos. We'll just tell them FEMA didn't believe us. By then things will have changed dramatically here anyway."

He leaned back and crossed his hands in his lap with a satisfied look on his face.

Chapter 43

Jason needed to get out of the city. As he drove through the streets, the car began to splutter and misfire. He looked down at the gas gauge. It read empty. *Shots must have hit the tank.* Now he had a big problem. The car was not going to be his ticket out of town and the militia was coming. They would fan out in the last direction they had seen him go. They'd stop everyone they saw; people will have seen him pass and could easily describe the car he was driving. Not many cars drove on the streets these days. However imprecise, his pursuers would close in on his direction of travel and set up a new perimeter to close him in. The attempts to cordon off the downtown blocks would have been abandoned by now. They'd be in full pursuit.

He passed close to Frank's store but didn't stop. He didn't want to catch Frank and Ramona up in his trouble. He headed to Vincent's office. Vincent had a car and it would probably be there. Ears would have the keys. But Ears was not going to be easily intimidated. He and Vincent might not even be there, but it was worth a try.

The car gave out three blocks from Vincent's office. Jason pulled into an alley as the car gasped for the last of the fuel. He grabbed his M4, shouldered his backpack, and started down the street. He was on high alert even though there were only a few people out. Jason watched them as they passed by, looking for any signs of recognition. Nothing. Most looked away, averting their eyes.

When he got to Vincent's building, he took a breath and stepped inside. At the top of the stairs, he pulled out his 9mm and opened the outer office door.

Ears was behind his desk, reading an old magazine. He looked up. There was confusion in his face. Then he saw Jason's semi-automatic. His eyes went cold and hard. Jason swung the pistol up to cover Ears.

"Just stay seated. I need the car. Give me the keys and tell me where it is."

Ears just stared at him.

"Come on, Ears. Give me the car and I'll be on my way. I don't want to shoot you."

"What the fuck are you up to? Did you whack Joe? He just put you in charge of a big deal. What the hell you go and do that for?"

"I don't have time to explain things to you. And keep your voice down. If Vincent comes running out of that office, someone's going to get killed. No need for that."

Ears shook his head. "I ain't giving you any keys. You'll have to take them from me."

His face was set in a hard expression. Jason locked onto his eyes. They were cold.

"Ears, I like you. But you gotta know I have my reasons for what I did. And now I got to leave."

"Rat fuck. That's what you are. Double crosser. I take guys like you and get rid of 'em, slow and painful."

"Not a rat. Just on a different side."

"You pretended to be one of us. That makes you a rat."

"I never was one of you. You forget. Your club's pretty exclusive. If you aren't family all you can be is an associate. Second-class member. So, to hell with that bullshit. I'm defending my family and town against whoever threatens it."

Just then Vincent opened the door.

"What the hell?"

"Don't move or both of you get killed."

Jason swung the gun over to Vincent and then back to Ears as the man reached behind his back. Jason fired and hit Ears in the arm.

"Fuck! Son of a bitch!" he shouted.

His gun dropped to the floor.

Jason swung back to Vincent.

"Don't reach for anything. Next shot will be to your chest."

"What the hell are you doing here? You the one who shot Joe? Why the fuck do that?"

It seemed to Jason that Vincent hadn't yet heard about Big Al.

"Just give me the keys to your car and I'll be on my way."

"I told you no way you bastard," Ears said. His voice was filled with pain and anger. "I helped you out. Defended you when some of the boys ragged on you, called you a pansy for not being tougher. I'm gonna kill you."

"Sorry Ears. We're on different teams."

"Ears," Vincent said. His eyes didn't waver from Jason. "Give him the keys. We'll get him later."

"Boss?"

"The keys. I don't want you shot again."

Ears cursed half under his breath and took out the car keys with his good hand and threw them at Jason.

"It's around back," Vincent said. "And I'll see you later."

"Maybe, maybe not."

Jason stooped down to pick up the keys, not taking his eyes off Ears. He motioned for him to stand up. Then he picked up Ears' .45 and slipped it into his belt. He pointed to the inner room.

"I hear you come out before I've left, I'll shoot you through the door."

He closed the door, then backed out of the office and ran to the stairs. He heard a flurry of sounds coming from the office as he flew down the stairs and ran to the back of the building.

The car was sitting alone in a small parking lot. Jason jumped in and turned the key. The engine turned over. *Come on, come on.* He glanced at the back door. In a moment the two men would come out guns blazing. Just then the engine caught. Jason pulled the shift lever into drive and stomped on the throttle He was exiting the lot when Vincent and Ears burst through the door. Shots were fired and a rear passenger window shattered as he drove down the alley and back onto the street.

He drove as fast as he could, heading north. He'd go up the west side of Lake Norman. It was less crowded and offered more options if pursuit caught him. Even though his pursuers were not going to be organized, he had no idea how large the group might be. It would include militia vehicles and some heavier weapons. A stand-off fight was not possible.

He rolled his window down in spite of the cold day. He could hear the rumble of diesel engines somewhere behind him but couldn't tell if they were closing in on him.

When Jason disappeared, Vincent stopped shooting. He turned to Ears and checked out his arm.

"Looks like the bullet went through cleanly. Let's get something to wrap over the wound."

"Let's go after that son of a bitch. I want to kill him."

"You'll get your chance."

After binding Ears' arm, they went back out on the street. Vincent could hear engines some blocks away. He fired his pistol in the air twice, waited a minute and then did it again. Within a few more minutes, a couple of Humvees came down the street.

The vehicles pulled up; a door opened; and Roper got out.

"Did you see anything?" he shouted.

"Jason. He stole my car and headed north."

"Which street?"

"I'm going with you. I'll show you."

Roper motioned for Vincent to get in.

"You get over to the hospital," he said to Ears "Get that arm bandaged properly,".

"I want to go."

"Don't be stupid. An infection'll kill you. If we capture him, I'll make sure you get a chance to interrogate him."

Vincent jumped into the Humvee and they roared off in pursuit.

Jason found Route16 which went north and west of the lake. He drove as fast as he could. The road was clear in sections and he floored Vincent's old sedan, pushing it to eighty or ninety miles an hour. Some sections were more congested and he had to slowly weave his way around abandoned cars and trucks. Here he could go only twenty miles an hour or less. *The Humvees won't fare any better.* He began to hope he could outdistance them.

He had no idea how many were in hot pursuit. Certainly, a larger force had been assembled. The assassinations had sewn some discord; maybe it was enough to cripple any serious, large-scale pursuit. If the capos descended into fighting one another for power, they might enmesh the militia and the chaos would spread.

At one point, the route looked completely blocked. Jason stopped. He shut the engine off and got out to survey the jam. The shoulder was steeply sloped and he ran the danger of slipping off it and getting stuck in the ditch. He had no chains or straps to pull the vehicles apart. As he was pondering his situation the breeze brought the faint sounds of engines from behind. *They're coming!*

There was no time to speculate. He needed to make a path quickly and get moving. He picked a spot where he could push and wedge open a gap. He gently brought his car up to one of the vehicles. It was a smaller car, so he had chance to move it. He got out and put the stalled car in neutral.

His older car's bumper nudged up against the rear quarter panel of the newer car. With the angle, his radiator was not involved in the contact. After inspecting the connection, Jason got in, put his car in drive, and pushed down on the accelerator. The older car's rear wheel started to spin but the other car began to move sideways. Ever so slowly, the gap opened. After a minute of pushing with his engine racing, wheels spinning, the gap was wide enough. Jason backed up and straightened his car out. He drove through with both front doors screeching as they scrapped along the sides of the blocking cars. His outside mirrors tore off. It didn't matter, he was through.

He realized that what slowed him down only helped his pursuers. It didn't matter. He had to push on.

Chapter 44

The light was beginning to fade. Jason switched on the headlights. There were no lights when in his mirror which was a good sign. As the dark grew Jason knew it would make getting through tight spots even harder which would play into the hands of his pursuers. Still he had no choice. *There's always the woods.* If they got too close, he might have to abandon the car and go on foot, but there were mostly fields along the highway, with only smaller patches of woods. He would go as far as he could on the road.

Up ahead, in the dark, Jason thought he saw a flash of light. He'd seen no one on the highway since he got out of town. He slowed slightly and kept looking in the direction of where he had seen the light as he navigated through the stalled vehicles. Then he saw it again. *Not my imagination.* It couldn't be bandits. They wouldn't be so careless. It had to be refugees on the road. Unusual this many years after the attack, but that was the only explanation he could think of.

There was a clear section and Jason floored the abused sedan and roared ahead. Now he saw the light clearly. It flashed on some figures, people trying to get off the road and hide in the ditch.

He pulled up just before the point where he'd seen the figures disappear and stopped the car. He got out with his M4 in his hands. The road congested here and he would have to move through it slowly. He didn't want someone shooting at him as he worked his way around the stalled vehicles.

He moved to the edge of the road, keeping a stalled car between him and where he'd last seen the figures.

"Who's there?" he called out. "I'm not going to hurt you. I'm just passing by, but I don't want you to shoot at me when I go past. I have no interest in you."

"Jason?" a man's voice called out from the ditch.

"Who's that?"

"It's me. Ernie. I'm here with my family. We heard you coming and then you got here so fast we were caught off guard and couldn't get to the woods."

"My God. Is this all the farther you've come?"

"Ruth sprained her ankle. It's been slow going. You've got a car. Can you help?"

"Get up here right away. There are people coming after me."

The group emerged from the tall brush in the ditch along the road. Jack and Ernie helped Ruth and the others followed.

"Thank God you came along. We're not making much progress and Ruth could use some time off her feet."

Jason took Ernie aside as the kids helped Ruth sit down on the pavement.

"The militia is pursuing me. They'll kill anyone they find with me. You sure you want a ride?"

"What choice do we have? We're going too slow. Our food and water will run out before we get to safety. We'll be prey to any bandits out here. The farther away from the city we go, the more dangerous it'll be. With six of us, it's hard to move quick."

"True enough. Just so you know the dangers."

"I'd rather we go with you. At least for a while."

Jason looked over at the group.

"Everyone, get in," he shouted. "Ernie, you and Jennifer sit up front and keep your pistol out. The rest of you cram in the back but leave room for Ruth. She should sit sideways and put her leg across your laps."

The boys, especially Jack and Bobby, looked shocked.

"It may be uncomfortable, but it's best for Ruth. Don't complain."

Everyone piled in the car which settled low on its springs. Jason started off. He could hear the engines behind them, not too far away.

He had to drive without the headlights now. The pursuers wouldn't hear his engine, they were making too much noise. But if they saw his lights, they'd know they were closing in and increase their pace. It was slower going, which frustrated Jason.

"They're going to catch us before too long," he said to Ernie.

"How long?"

"We've got an hour, maybe a little longer."

"What do we do then?"

"Abandon the car and get in some woods. I can hold them off as you move on."

"We'll be going so slow. They'll catch us for sure."

"Maybe. I can do a lot of damage. It's what I was trained for. I may even stop them. Make them wait for reinforcements. In any case it's the only chance you've got. Unless you want to bail out now and hide. Let them go past you."

Ernie thought about this offer.

"We'd still run into them somewhere up ahead as we go north. Remember I'm an escaped prisoner in their eyes, so are the boys." He shook his head. "We'll stick with you."

"Not many good options. They find our tracks, they'll put dogs on our trail and we'll be caught for sure. I can hold them off, but if they send a sizeable force, they'll overwhelm me."

Jason's mind went through all possible options as he swerved his way through abandoned cars and trucks. He relished the open spaces where he could accelerate and try to maintain the distance between him and the pursuers.

Then the car misfired. It was only one miss, a hiccup that might not be noticed by anyone else. But it made Jason's hair stand on end.

"You got a flashlight," he said to Ernie. "Cover it with most of your hand and let a sliver of light shine on the gauges."

Ernie did as Jason told him. The gas gauge was reading empty. They were going to splutter to a halt in a few more miles.

"We've got no more than five or ten miles left in the tank. We're going to be on foot soon."

"Oh my God," Ruth said.

They were on a part of Route 16 that angled west away from Lake Norman. The area consisted of abandoned farms and crossroad communities of six to ten houses. Many of the fields had overgrown with volunteer plants, all hardier than the hybrid crops that had been left on their own. The open ground was slowly turning back into woodland.

The surrounding land didn't offer the same possibilities for defense as did the more mountainous terrain to the west. It would be easier to move large numbers of men, even the Humvees and any other vehicles the militia might bring, through the fields in a chase.

"Last chance to bail," Jason said. "You can stay off the road and out of sight and keep going no matter what happens to me."

Before Ernie could answer, Jack spoke up from the back seat. "I'm sticking with you,"

"Me too," said Bobby.

"You should help Ernie and Ruth. Ernie helped you escape," Jason said.

"We should all stick with you," Jack said.

"We'll go with you," Ernie said. "I think it's our best chance. We're crippled and can't move or defend ourselves much." He paused. "But do you want the burden of us? You could get away if you were alone."

"Maybe. But I won't abandon you if you want to come with me."

"We're coming with you," Ernie said.

"You're going to have to move fast, even with Ruth." He looked over his shoulder at Ernie's wife. "You're going to have to push yourself hard. It'll be painful, even with help."

"I'll do what's necessary. I don't want to hold anyone up."

"It's settled then," Jason said. He wracked his mind to think of how to find an advantage in this easier terrain. He couldn't see any strong defensive positions to take. And to dig in would only mean getting surrounded. That would lead to starving the group out, or overwhelming them if their pursuers had little patience to wait.

"There *is* one thing," Jason said. "Somewhere along this road is the monastery I told you about."

"I saw the sign for it back a ways," Ernie said. "At least I think it was. Couldn't see that well in the dark."

"We'll head there. It's our best option for now."

A few more miles and the car began to stutter and misfire more frequently.

"Ride's over," Jason said.

He slowed the car and nudged it against another stalled one as if it were part of a pile-up.

"This might throw them off, if they don't recognize the car at night."

Everyone climbed out. Jack helped Ernie with Ruth. Tom put on a backpack, along with Jennifer. Jason shouldered his pack with the M110 strapped to it. The group pushed through the overgrown field towards a line of trees. Jason stopped just inside their cover.

"The monastery is to the northwest." Jason pointed in a direction parallel to the road. He took Ernie's flashlight and shone it in the sky aiming at the north star.

"That's your guide. The north star. Keep heading just left of it and you'll be going in the right direction."

"You're not coming?" Ernie asked.

"I'm going to wait for the militia. If they pass by, we're pretty safe. If they stop where we did, I'll try to pin them down from the cover of the woods. In any case I'll be able to catch up with you. I want to give you a head start."

"Do you want help?" Jack asked.

"No. you help Ruth. It's important for the group to keep moving. No more talk now. Get going."

The group set out in the direction Jason had pointed. They disappeared into the dark. Jason could hear their crashing through the underbrush.

He took off his backpack, assembled his M110, and settled down to wait.

Chapter 45

Vincent was sitting in the lead Humvee along with Roper. He had seen some other mob members going with the militia. They were in three Humvees. It was their fight after all. Jason had killed some of their own.

"I want him taken alive," Vincent said to Roper.

"If we can, but we get him, dead *or* alive," Roper responded.

Vincent turned to the man that the mob had put into power. He could barely see his face in the dark cabin of the vehicle.

"He belongs to us, to the organization. He killed three of our men."

"Yeah, but he helped drive me out of Hillsboro, so I owe him a big payback."

"You don't get a choice on this. He's ours to do with as we want. You can be sure it won't be pleasant."

Roper stared at Vincent who didn't flinch. "I'll do my best."

"Just remember who you work for, who put you in power. We take him alive."

They drove along, headlights illuminating the stalled vehicles on the highway. Progress was made easier by the fact that Jason had opened the blockages to get his car through. That allowed the Humvees to push through with little loss of time.

"We'll catch him," Roper said. "He's got to open the areas that are blocked. Even though we're wider, we can push through them faster."

"When we get within range, just shoot at the car. Aim for the tires."

The lead Humvee had a .50 caliber machine gun on its top that could obliterate the car and its occupants. Vincent wanted to be sure Jason would not be killed. They had enough men to overpower him and take him alive. Bringing the man back, could elevate his status enough to make him the new Don of the family.

The engines came closer. Jason adjusted his position. He held his M110 with the M4 nearby. The distance was no more than a hundred yards but he would need the larger caliber M110 to stop the Humvees if they came into the field. Now headlights flashed from farther back on the road. The three Humvees came past without stopping. *They didn't notice the car*.

His enthusiasm was short lived, however. Fifty yards up the road the group stopped. The lead Humvee turned around and drove back. Some figures got out and went over to the car Jason had abandoned. He could hear voices and shortly the other two vehicles turned around.

The lead Humvee turned pointed its headlights off the highway. They illuminated the ditch and field. *They'll see where we walked. The tramped down grass*. Within a moment it started forward and drove through the ditch along the edge of the road. The other two followed. If they were up-armored, they would be hard to stop. Jason aimed for the grill of the lead machine and fired three shots. It swerved but kept coming. He then shot at the windshield. The vehicle still kept coming. *Got to be hard to see, even if I'm not penetrating the glass*.

After six rounds aimed at the windshield, the Humvee slowed to almost a stop. Jason turned his attention to the other two. He emptied his magazine into their windshields which stopped them. Jason ejected the mag and shoved another one into the rifle.

Men scrambled out of the stalled vehicles. They spread out taking cover in the field. Jason was able to hit two of the men before they could disappear in the overgrown brush.

Now it'll be a slow advance. If they're organized. He expected rounds of intense fire followed by the men running forward to drop out of sight again in the tall growth of the pasture. The problem for the militia was that they would have trouble pinpointing him. His suppressor also hid most of his muzzle flash. Even if they located him, he could slide to one side or another and start again.

The field erupted in a flurry of shooting, most of it scattered across a wide swath of woods. Jason watched and waited. When it was over, the men got up and started forward. Jason returned fire, taking down three who charged before the shooting from the field shut him down. *They'll get to me eventually, even if it costs them a lot of casualties.* He knew he would have to retreat before they got too close.

After the next charge and Jason's returned fire, he backed away and, grabbing his pack and two rifles, started running through the woods in the direction of the others. He stopped when he reached a slight rise, giving him ten feet of elevation. *Not high enough, but I'll take what I can get.* He lay down behind a fallen oak and watched.

In the dark of the woods, Jason could only see vague shapes as they began to close in. He was using his M4 now, lighter and more agile. He fired some rounds at the shapes and saw them drop to the ground. Almost at once, shots were returned zinging overhead with that deadly snapping whistle sound. Some rounds thudded into the trunk of the fallen tree. Jason sent a few more rounds at the muzzle flashes he saw and then slid back. When he had more trees between him and the militia, he got up and began jogging through the woods.

In the dark, he almost ran into a barbed wire fence at the edge of a field. He climbed over it and sprinted across the open ground. He set up in the cover of the trees on the other side of the field.

He could hear his pursuers approaching. They stopped at the fence, seemingly unsure whether or not to go out into the field. *They all won't come straight forward. They may try to flank me.* He scanned left and right, searching for a flanking move.

He could hear the rustle of brush across the field, but saw no bodies. To his left he saw some shadows, crouching and moving through the tall grass. Jason got off two shots and the figures dropped out of sight. He didn't think he had hit them but couldn't be sure. The ones directly in front now opened fire, having seen his muzzle flash. Jason hunkered down as the bullets flew past.

If they keep crawling, I can't see them in the dark. They'll be on me before I can take them out. He got up and started through the woods away from the field. Crawling through the field, slowed them down and allowed Jason to extend his separation. When he had retreated twenty yards into the woods, he began to run.

After crossing a small creek, Jason took up a position on the far side. Something like a creek would slow the advance of those chasing him and allow him to get off some lethal shots. The stream lay in a shallow depression with trees close to its sides. Jason lay thirty yards away and about twenty feet higher. He could see the shadows of his pursuers on the far side. They were moving carefully now, after experiencing Jason's ambushes. His effective shooting had forced them to move more carefully, lessening the possibility of catching and overrunning him.

They stopped short of the creek. Jason couldn't get a firm count of his pursuers but it looked like the number of militia had increased. *Called in more to join the hunt?* The number didn't matter. His actions were providing Ernie and the others the space they needed to reach the monastery.

Suddenly the woods erupted in intense shooting. Jason could only stay behind cover while bullets screamed past or slammed into trees with a muffled *thunk*. They were shooting at the slight ridge where he was positioned. *They'll cross under this cover fire.* There was no way he could hold them off. Just raising his head to shoot could be fatal with so many rounds flying through the air.

He crawled back from his position and turned to run again. It was beginning to get light. The cold night would soon give way to a cold, grey day. Jason flew through the woods, the added light helping him move faster, hopefully faster than the group chasing him.

After a half hour of running he came to a fence and a field. This one was different. It had the look of being tilled. Crops had been harvested and the field now seemed to be waiting, idle through the winter, for spring and the planting of new crops. The ground sloped upwards and beyond the field, and beyond the woods on the far side, he saw smoke rising in the cold air. *The monastery?* It must be. Behind him he heard the pursuit, the crashing through the woods. The sound of engines to his right, far away on the road he had abandoned, indicated that the pursuit had grown.

He took off, running as fast as he could over the half-frozen ground. If they cut him off from the monastery, he would have nowhere to go. There were no mountains where he would have the upper hand and could have held off the militia as long as his ammunition held out. Or simply disappeared. He knew the forest after having absorbed many painful lessons. He was a man of the woods as much as anything now. When he reached the trees on the far side, he didn't stop. This time he kept running, slightly up slope towards the smoke he'd seen.

With his lungs searing from the cold air, he came out of the woods onto the grounds of the monastery. There was a solid, ten-foot high wall of brick and block. A long gravel drive led to a heavy iron gate which was closed. He could see the roofs of different buildings inside showing over the wall. The surrounding grounds were arranged in garden plots. There were a couple of outbuildings, greenhouses for wintering plants. In between the gardens and buildings, the grass grew high. There were paths worn from people going back and forth between the interior of the compound and the gardens and outbuildings. Behind the walls, he could see tall conifers reaching up higher than all the structures.

Jason ran up to the gate, both rifles in his hands. He shouted through the bars for someone to let him in. Nothing stirred inside. He put the weapons on the ground and shouted out again.

A man came out of a nearby building and approached him. He wore a cloak over rough pants and shoes with a watch cap on to protect his shaven head from the cold. He stared at Jason with a wary look.

"What do you want? This is a private space."

"People are chasing me, trying to kill me, let me in."

"We have nothing to do with the outside world, this is a monastery. You need to go on your way."

Jason paused for a moment.

"I'm asking for sanctuary. Let me in before I'm killed at your door." He looked around, now more frantic. The pursuers would be emerging from the woods very soon. He hadn't expected to be turned away.

Chapter 46

Did you let in a man and woman and four kids? I rescued them, and those pursuing me want to kill me and them. Let me in before they get here."

Another monk came up, dressed as the first. They huddled in conversation which Jason couldn't hear. When they were done, the first one unlocked the smaller man-door built into the large gate and swung it open. Jason stepped through it.

"You better lock it behind me. The ones coming won't be so polite."

"You can't be armed in here," the second monk said. "I have to take your weapons."

Jason hesitated. This was the price to pay; he didn't have any options now. He handed over both rifles and his handgun.

"Come with me," the man said. He walked into the compound. In the middle was a large, but simple church with a cross on top. Two buildings were attached to either side of the church. Separated from this center structure were two other buildings. The larger one looked like a dormitory and the other looked like it held offices. To one side of the office building was a large dining room with a kitchen attached. This was where the smoke came from that Jason had observed. Behind these buildings were other structures, one of which looked like a barn.

The monk led Jason into the office building. He carried Jason's weapons with him. They came to a door with a cross on it. The monk knocked quietly and waited until the voice inside said to enter. He opened the door and indicated for Jason to go inside.

A tall monk with white hair sat at a solid, simple wooden desk. He was dressed the same as the other two Jason had seen, a brown cassock and rough pants. Hung around his neck and centered over his chest was a large, ornate cross. This object seemed to be the only differentiation from the dress of the other monks.

"Father, this man came to our gate asking for sanctuary. He says he freed the people we took in a short while ago."

"What are you doing with those weapons?" the Abbot asked.

"He was carrying them. I took them from him before bringing him to see you."

"Put them in the corner." He pointed to the far corner of the room.

"What is your name, son?"

"Jason. Jason Richards."

"And you freed the people who just came to us?"

"Yes sir."

"How are you connected to them?"

"I met them on the road. They were...are, refugees. They're a family, but they have two boys, in addition to their own children, that were part of a prison gang scavenging coal near Charlotte. The father of the family, Ernie, wanted me to help them as well when I came to free him from the camp."

The Abbot had bright, blue eyes that burned into you when they centered on you. He was of an indeterminate age, not young but with that mid-life strength that some men possess. Jason began to tell his story but caught himself.

"Before I go into the whole story, you should know that there's a group after me, and possibly the family. They're from Charlotte and are made up of militia members—military types—and mafia gang members."

"They are coming here to our monastery?"

Jason nodded his head. "And they won't be very polite about protocol."

"So, you've put the monastery in danger?" The Abbot's eyebrows rose.

"Not intentionally. I directed the family to head here because the woman was injured. They were moving too slow and would be caught. I delayed the pursuers and then had to seek my own shelter."

The Abbot turned to the waiting monk.

"Brother Thomas, go assemble the brothers in the courtyard immediately. Don't ring the alarm bell, but just spread the word. And tell them to bring their staffs."

The monk nodded and rushed out of the door.

The Abbot stood up. He was over six feet tall and his movements supported Jason's impression of strength.

"Come with me," he instructed.

Jason glanced at the corner with the weapons. The Abbot caught his glance.

"We leave them here. We will deal with this without guns."

Outside at least thirty monks had assembled with more gathering. Jason didn't see Ernie and the kids. They must have been told to stay inside. At the door to the offices, the Abbot stopped.

"You wait here, inside. You can watch from the window, but under no circumstances do you show yourself." He stood close to Jason. "Do you understand?"

"Yes sir."

Jason turned back inside. The monks gathered around their Abbot. When they had assembled, he began to speak.

"Brothers, we have given sanctuary to a family and some orphan children and just now, to the man who freed them from their captivity." He gazed over the assembled group, now about fifty strong. "You understand the custom of sanctuary. It still is operative for us. Since I have granted sanctuary, we must now defend it."

Jason listened at the window. Looking over the monks, he noticed there were no obese ones among them. All the men, from the oldest to the youngest looked hard and fit.

"There is a group following these people, possibly violent. You will follow my lead when they arrive. Now spread out around me, not too close, but not too far away."

Quickly the monks assembled as directed.

"They're coming," a lookout shouted.

Some fifteen men came marching up to the gate. Jason could see Vincent in the group, along with Larry Roper. Roper stepped forward.

"From the way you're all assembled, I think you know why we're here."

The Abbot stepped forward a couple of paces.

"Perhaps you will be specific and explain your presence on our property."

"We're chasing a fugitive. Someone who's killed three of our men, and more during this chase."

The Abbot didn't reply.

"We think he's come here. You are to turn him over to us."

"On what authority do you make that demand?"

His eyes bore into Roper's. Vincent was now standing next to Roper and felt the weight of the Abbot's gaze as well.

"On the authority of the City of Charlotte."

"We are not under the authority of Charlotte, nor of any city. We are under authority of the Pope, and of God." He cocked his head towards Roper. "Do you have an edict from the Pope?"

"Don't play games with me," Roper said. "You don't have the right to protect him."

"Ah but I do. And I have almost two millennia of tradition to support my right."

Before Roper could answer, the Abbot turned to Vincent.

"What part do you play in this? You are obviously not part of a military unit."

"I represent the civilian authorities in Charlotte and I stand behind the commander here."

"What's your name?"

In spite of himself, Vincent answered.

"Vincent Bonocchi."

"So, Vincent Bonocchi, I take it from your name that you are Italian." The Abbot stepped forward another couple of paces. "Are you a Catholic?"

Vincent nodded.

"Good. I assume this man isn't, since he seems ignorant of how this works. When was the last time you went to confession?"

Vincent paused. The power of the authority figures of his faith rose up from deep inside him. He hadn't confessed in decades. But he regularly went to church to light candles for friends and family members who had died.

"It's been a long time."

"This is bullshit," Roper said. "I'm in charge here and you need to release this man to us. He's broken our laws and killed people. He needs to pay for what he's done."

"We'll all pay for what we've done, sooner or later," the Abbot said. "By the way, what is your name?"

"Roper, Commander Roper of the Charlotte Militia."

"Well Mr. Roper according to the long-standing tradition of sanctuary, I can't release anyone into your hands just because you demand it. You are free to wait outside the monastery and can arrest anyone leaving who's not a monk. But," he stepped forward again and now was at the gate nearly face to face with Vincent and Larry, "you do not interfere or harm any of my monks."

"That's your final word, is it?"

"I'm happy to have more words with you and perhaps enlighten your mind and soul, but on this subject that is the final word."

Roper now raised his rifle. "Perhaps you should open the gate and let us in. I haven't had my final word yet."

The Abbot looked calmly into Roper's eyes. Roper's carbine was now centered on his chest. The monks stood still but were now clearly tensed. Finally, the Abbot nodded to the gate keeper.

"Open the man-door and let these men in. We can offer them our hospitality and maybe improve their thinking."

He then backed up into the courtyard as the monk did as he was told. Roper and Vincent went through the door followed by the rest of the men, a mixture of militia and mafia. Once inside, Vincent and Roper walked up to the Abbot with their men behind them. The monks quietly shuffled aside and, in the process, surrounded the intruders.

"I think we'll just search the compound. If no one's here, we'll be on our way and no harm done. But if the guy we're chasing is here, we'll take him with us. You won't have to give him up, we'll just take him." Roper smiled. "Then you won't be breaking your century's old tradition, we'll break it for you. You can't really stop us so your conscience can be clear. No one will fault you for avoiding any bloodshed."

"And are you an expert on conscience? I'm surprised."

"You know what I mean. Let's not waste any more time," Roper said, turning to the men behind him. "Fan out—"

"I wouldn't do that if I were you."

Roper turned back to the Abbot. "You're not giving orders here anymore. I'm in charge and we're going to find our fugitive."

"Your men will not leave this assemblage."

"How are you gonna stop us?" Roper pointed his rifle at the Abbot. The barrel almost touching his chest.

The Abbot calmly looked over the barrel, down at Roper.

"You see the brothers assembled around you? If you initiate violence, they will defend their Abbot, their monastery, and themselves. With their lives."

Roper laughed, but it sounded nervous.

"Sticks against guns? You don't stand a chance."

"You won't kill us all. We'll have enough left to stop you."

"But your men will die, needlessly."

"Not needlessly. In defense of a long-standing tradition. Also, we know where we're going after we die. Do you?"

The Abbot now raised his face to the rest of the pursuers. "Do you know where you're going after you die?"

His voice now boomed out, a deep baritone. "Do any of you know what you face after killing a man of God? After violating a sacred place? One set aside for contemplation of God and His works?"

The men looked at him with growing concern in their faces. Vincent stepped up to Larry.

"This has gone far enough," he said.

"You want to back down? This is just theatrics."

Vincent shook his head. "It's not. This man means what he says."

"There gonna commit suicide to stop us? To save Jason? Someone they don't even know?"

Vincent held Roper's gaze. "They will."

Roper now looked around. Most of the gang members looked like they wanted nothing more than to leave. The militia members just looked confused and concerned.

"We go outside. Then we can talk about what to do next," Vincent said.

"We're not leaving, we—"

"Now. We leave now." Vincent's voice was hard and unyielding.

Larry looked at him, his gang members, and the rest of his men, and cursed under his breath.

He turned back to the Abbot. "You haven't heard the last from me."

The Abbot said nothing as the men shuffled back out through the gate which was then locked shut.

Chapter 47

Once outside, Larry turned to Vincent. "What the hell was that? Giving in to an unarmed man?"

"He's a priest. We don't kill priests."

"He's a monk. He sits in this place, cut off from the world. What good is he?"

Vincent shook his head. "We don't kill priests. As the Abbot, he's the priest for this monastery. He can perform the sacraments, marry, bury the dead. He can do all the things a priest in a church can do."

"So what? You kill people when they get in your way or cross you. How the hell is this any different? He's blocking us."

"It's different because he's a priest. I may kill people but there's a code. Loyalty to the organization, family, the church. Something you don't know about."

"The guy's in our way."

Vincent turned to look back at the gate. "True. But he's in a different category. He's not taking sides against us, but following his faith and tradition." He turned back to Roper. "We can wait him out. He has to come out sooner or later."

Roper looked at Vincent in disgust and stomped off.

"Get the Humvees up here," he shouted to one of his militia officers. "The ones that work. If any don't, strip their fuel cans and bring them with the other vehicles."

Turning back to Vincent, he said, "I'll wait for now, but I won't promise to wait forever. If this drags on too long I'm going back in with my men. With or without you."

Back inside the monastery, the Abbot entered the office building.

"Follow me," he said to Jason.

With another monk in tow, he led him through some corridors, through the church and into the building attached to the other side. He stopped at a door at the end of a long hall and knocked. Someone said "come in" and he opened the door.

Inside were Ernie, Ruth, and all the children. They were sitting or lying on the cots distributed around the room.

"Jason!" Ernie shouted as he followed the Abbot into the room. "You made it. Thank God."

The kids jumped up and ran to him, putting their arms around him. Ruth smiled from a cot where she lay.

"We could hear the gunfire as we moved through the woods. You were right. We followed the directions you gave us and made it. If you hadn't slowed them down, we never would have gotten here."

"You didn't make it by much it seems...but it was enough," Jason said.

"We did. The Abbot granted us asylum. We can stay until Ruth's ankle is healed, then go on our way."

"Ernie and the children will help by working here while they stay," the Abbot said. "I want to talk with both of you men. We can talk in my office over breakfast." He turned to the monk. "Arrange for food to be brought to the family. They will stay here while I meet with the men."

With that, they headed back through the building to the Abbot's office.

"My name is Father Gregory," the Abbot said when they were seated in his office. "As you can see, I'm in charge of this monastery. He leaned forward. "Now tell me, what have you embroiled me in? You can start by telling me where you're from."

"My family and I are from Knoxville. We were headed to Charlotte because we heard that things were under control, that life was returning to normal. I don't know where the two boys are from."

"And you?"

"I'm from a number of places, it's not really important—

The Abbot held up his hand.

"If I ask the question it is important. I expect a clear, honest answer. If you can't provide that, I'll turn you out now."

The Abbot's intense eyes bore into Jason.

"Can I trust you?" Jason asked.

"You saw me put my life, the lives of my fellow monks on the line for you. And you ask that question?"

"You're right. It's just hard to let my guard down, I've had it up for so long."

"I can hear all about that later. If you need to confess, I can hear that as well. Right now, I want to understand the situation I find my monastery in and that starts with understanding both of you."

Jason took a deep breath. "I'm from Hillsboro. Members of the gang, the mafia that runs Charlotte, showed up one day and told the town leaders that we owed the gang a half a million dollars."

"Why would they do that? What did they say to justify such a demand?"

Jason told Father Gregory the story of Joe Nicoletti's visit.

"So, we decided that someone should go see what was going on here and how much of a threat Charlotte posed to our town. I volunteered to go undercover, ingratiate myself into the mob and find out what we were facing."

Jason continued with his story, explaining how Larry Roper was the corrupt Captain that Hillsboro had driven out of town and how he had a motive for revenge.

"I was about to be put in charge of coal collection for the power plant. I also learned that the mob boss was planning on wiping out everyone in my town. The mob wanted me to meet with Roper to tell him what I knew about Hillsboro. I couldn't do that, he'd recognize me, so I had to go underground. I also had to find a way to disrupt the mob's plans and save my town.

"Before I disappeared, I was taken out to see the coal collection efforts. That's where I came across Ernie. He had been put on the coal crew as punishment for having a gun in his apartment. He gave me his family's address and I looked them up. They were pretty destitute and so when I decided I had to disappear, I also decided to get them out of the city and try to free Ernie.

"Is this true," the Abbot said to Ernie.

He nodded. "Every word. These are not upright people running the city. They're thugs and they act like it."

"While you were working for the gang, did you kill anyone?" The Abbot asked, turning back to Jason.

"No sir. In fact, I figured out how to collect the money they took from the local businesses and citizens without violence. It made some of the members suspicious of me."

While they were talking, a monk came into the room carrying a large wooden tray. On it was a bowl of scrambled eggs, bacon, bread and butter, along with cups and a pot of tea. He set the food down on a side table along with three wooden plates and without a word departed.

Father Gregory gestured to the food. "Please, help yourselves. We have plenty to eat here. We are a self-sustaining community."

Jason felt his hunger wake. His stomach gave out a growl. Both he and Ernie went over and filled plates of food and then sat back down. The Abbot poured himself a cup of tea and returned to his desk.

"You stayed undercover until the pending meeting with this Roper fellow came on the horizon. And then you left." The Abbot took a sip of his tea. "I don't understand why you're leaving would generate such a pursuit. And what is

Roper talking about, saying you killed three people before you departed?"

Jason knew the worst was going to come out now. He decided that he had to be completely honest with the Abbot or else he might risk, not only his sanctuary, but that of Ernie and his family.

"My purpose in Charlotte was to assess the level of their threat to Hillsboro. When I learned of their plan to wipe out all the citizens, to make them an example to other towns, I decided I had to do whatever I could to disrupt those plans. There was no way we could withstand any major assault from them. They would crush us.

"I decided that I had to take out their leadership and sow seeds of chaos, disruption, so that Charlotte would have to look inward and forget about Hillsboro."

"And you did that?" Father Gregory asked.

"I think so."

The Abbot's eyes stayed on Jason.

"You cut off the head, the snake dies."

Father Gregory looked at Jason, waiting for him to continue.

"What I mean is that I had to eliminate the leadership in Charlotte, the gang leaders running the town. If I could do that, it could throw them into internal fighting which would take their eyes off of us."

"You killed the leader."

Jason nodded. "The boss and the underboss. The two top men in the mob family. Before that I killed a man named Gino in self-defense. He was trying to expose me and had threatened Ernie's family."

Father Gregory leaned back in his chair. His eyes never left Jason.

"You are a murderer then?"

Jason shook his head. "I was a sniper in the army. I killed some men while on duty, men who were trying to kill my fellow soldiers. I see this as no different. I'm a soldier fighting for Hillsboro and my family against this gang."

Father Gregory gave a thin smile. "You may be making too fine a distinction. How many men have you killed?"

"Ironically, only a few while in the army. After the EMP attack, more than twenty. All in defense of myself or my family."

Father Gregory turned to Ernie. "Tell me your story."

After Ernie had finished Father Gregory told him he could stay as long as he wanted except the females would be sequestered apart from the men.

"I understand this may be a hardship, but we are an all-male community, and we work hard." Father Gregory smiled at what seemed like a sudden memory. "We have an old story, it may be apocryphal. To ease crowding in the jails, some criminals in Sicily were transferred to one of our monasteries. After some weeks, they asked the authorities to put them back in prison where life had been easier."

He glanced over at Ernie. "I doubt you will want to stay too long under our conditions. Certainly, you should stay until the men outside have tired of this game and gone away. But it is up to you. I don't think they are looking for you. Jason seems to be the issue here."

He dismissed Ernie, who left to follow a brother back to the room where his family was waiting.

"Jason, you present me quite a challenge," Father Gregory said when Ernie had left the room. "I can understand vigorous defense. You saw me ready to do that in the courtyard. But killing, assassination, is different. You sacrificed at least two lives for the possibility that your action would disrupt a *potential* attack on your town. There are two hypotheticals that would have to be met in order for such an attack to happen, yet you took action."

"In my mind it wasn't hypothetical. I was convinced that such action would occur, especially with Roper leading the militia. He wants to get back to Hillsboro. And if we were to wait for the potential to turn into reality, it would be too late. I had to stop the possibility from happening."

"You're comfortable with your decision? No second thoughts? Those men may have had wives, children."

"I thought about that. So do the citizens of Hillsboro. I wasn't going to stand by and let them be murdered." Jason looked at a cross on the wall, turning his thoughts inward for a moment. Father Gregory waited.

"It might be a rationalization, but I felt these men chose their path. They lived by violence. It's one of their tools, and they died by it. They died as they lived."

He looked back at the Abbot. "The mob will kill anyone, even their own, if they think some part of their twisted code is violated. It sounds all honorable when they talk about it, but they have no mercy on wives or families, even their own." He leaned forward. "They were willing to kill a whole town to further their aims."

"So, you have become a man of violence. Somewhat like them it seems."

"I didn't set out to be one. I left Hillsboro after the EMP attack to live on my own, away from the chaos and corruption I saw developing. The violence followed me and I had to fight fire with fire, so to speak, in order to save not only myself, but those I had come to love. That loyalty has now grown to a whole town."

Father Gregory didn't answer.

"Do you know what it's like out there?" Jason asked.

The Abbot just stared at Jason.

"Chaos rose up almost immediately. After the power went out there was looting and starvation. Violence became the appropriate course of action. It seems those who live outside the law are best equipped to deal with chaos and embrace it's opportunities."

"We are the antidote to chaos," the Abbot said.

Jason gave him a confused look.

"I can explain that later. Right now, I see you are very tired. You were probably up all last night."

"The last two nights."

"Brother Thomas," the Abbot called out.

The monk came into the office.

"Take our guest to a spare room, show him where to wash up so he can get some rest." Turning to Jason, he said, "We can talk more later. I still haven't made a decision."

Chapter 48

That evening, Jason was awakened by the faint sounds of chanting, men's voices in unison, singing ancient Latin words with rhythmic interplay. The sound drifted through the dormitory building. He stretched and let his body relax and sink back on the cot where he lay. It was not soft, but much better than the hard, frozen ground outside. The sound soothed him like a balm spread over his sore body and he drifted back into sleep.

Later there was a knock on his door.

"Come in," Jason called out.

The door opened and a monk said he should get up. The Abbot wanted to meet with him. Jason quickly put on his boots and followed the monk through the dark corridors, across the church, and into the office building. He gently knocked on the Abbot's door and then opened it for Jason.

"Jason. I hope you got some rest. I could see your fatigue when we talked earlier."

"I did. Thank you."

"I've had Brother Thomas bring some food from our kitchen, It's there on the side table. Please eat. I have already partaken of the evening meal."

There was a steaming bowl of stew along with a large chunk of bread. Jason's hunger again asserted itself and he went to work on the food. The Abbot sat quietly as Jason wolfed down the meal.

"This is delicious," he said after mopping up the last of the stew with a piece of bread.

"We eat simple but wholesome food. Many would find it boring, but we are happy with it."

"This would never be considered boring in my opinion. Especially these days, after the attack."

"Yes, the attack. With our lifestyle, we were hardly affected. Of course, we noticed the lack of planes in the sky and the missing sounds of distant trains or trucks on the highways. We sent out scouts who came back with the story, somewhat confused and unclear, of how our country experienced an EMP attack and what that meant."

He got up and poured two glasses of wine and offered one to Jason.

"We have a small vineyard and make our own wine."

"After the attack we had to deal with the large number of refugees that came to our gates. Obviously, we couldn't take them all in or the monastery would have been overrun. We gave them food, short term shelter for the most desperate, medical assistance if someone needed it, and then sent them on their way."

"Did you experience bandits? They quickly became a major threat, not only to refugees, but smaller towns as well."

"Some did come by."

"How did you keep them out? I don't think they would be so considerate of your faith as Vincent was earlier."

"No, they weren't. We kept our gates closed to those who came with evil intent. We have no guns so we used what we had to defend ourselves. Some of the techniques were medieval in style. We could repulse them from the walls. They're high enough one needs a ladder or platform to get over them. The brothers would push them off. Many got hurt by their fall, so that would put them out of commission. Another effective technique was to throw boiling oil on the ones who tried to climb the front gate."

"That does sound medieval."

"We suffered casualties and some deaths but the attacks lessened as the gangs lost their momentum."

"So here you are. You live as you always have, life goes on the same for you." Jason shrugged in his chair. "I have to ask, at the risk of sounding impolite, what good are you doing cloistered away like this?"

"Do you remember I said earlier that we were an antidote to chaos?"

Jason nodded. "I don't understand what you mean by that."

"We preserve. The faith, and with it, our history as a people. We keep order." He took a sip of wine. "The world is in tension, a battle between order and chaos. It's been that way since Adam and Eve."

"You believe that story?"

"That story may not be literally true but it is foundational."

"What do you mean by that?" Jason asked.

"It's a tale of lost innocence." Father Gregory hunched forward. "What if we were created in the image of God as the Bible says? What if we were created in innocence and then lost it?"

"The apple?"

"Precisely." He sat back in his seat now with a hint of a smile on his face. "We chose at that moment to become self-aware. To know the difference between good and evil, to become like gods. And when that happened, we were thrown into struggle between order and chaos."

"Good and evil."

"Right. Ejected from the garden, and history began at that moment." Father Gregory folded his hands in front of his face. "The odd thing to me is that we seem to need both order and chaos. I think, and this is my opinion, not the church's, that too much of one or the other is not good for us. Not, at least, in our fallen state."

"So, we need some evil along with the good?"

"This where the equivalency breaks down. Good is not identical to order and evil is not quite the same as chaos. Think about it. If we have only chaos, it's hard to survive.

Structure, civilization break down. Humanity can go nowhere. It can't build on chaos. But," he pressed his hands down on his desk, "if we have only order, we become petrified into structure, nothing new breaks in and order can easily become tyrannical."

"Now you've got me really confused," Jason said as he sipped his wine.

"New things come out of chaos, but order is needed to develop them. Chaos will tear the new apart before it can be developed. The best of us, the creative ones, have to inhabit the border between order and chaos."

Jason followed the Abbot's point but didn't understand how it related to the situation in which they found themselves.

"So, me stirring things up is good? Like bringing in some chaos to help create new things?"

The Abbot shook his head. "You are an agent of chaos. That is what you sow, you even said it yourself."

"Then what's this story about?"

"Our role, the monastery's role, is to maintain the order. But too much of us would petrify humanity's progress. As I said, we seem to need both in our fallen state. Utopias always go bad in the end. You can't create them in our fallen world. We were banished from the garden eons ago and we haven't found our way back."

He pointed to Jason. "You've seen attempts to build utopias I'm sure. At least someone's personal idea of what one should be. They wind up being tyrannical, don't they?"

Jason nodded. "I've had to fight against a number of them. Charlotte is the latest."

"My point is that I'm on the side of order while you inhabit the world of chaos...or maybe that border region I talked about. Even though I think you are a man of violence and I should send you away from here immediately, I recognize that we need some of you, humanity needs some of you. You step out of the ordered parts of existence to slay the dragons, the dragons of chaos if you will." He paused. "Dragons have been a symbol of chaos since humans first began telling stories."

He now stood up and started towards the small window looking out at the back part of the courtyard.

"If we could create the perfect utopia, someone would come along to tear it down. Humanity would do that, because we seem to need some chaos in our lives, even if we don't recognize it. We are still rebels, even as we strive to find our way back to God." He turned to Jason. "You are one of those."

The Abbot went back to his seat. "Are you married? Do you have a partner?"

"Yes. I have a wonderful wife and a son, now three. And I have two beautiful step-daughters, both now married."

"I am sorry for your wife."

"Why do you say that?"

"Because you are destined to not sit at hearth and home, in the midst of order. You thrive on stepping into chaos and engaging the dragons. She will never have you to herself."

"You don't know me or my personal life," Jason said. His voice had an edge to it.

The Abbot smiled and stood up again.

"It's getting late. I have to make my rounds and then I have much to pray about. You should sleep. Who knows what tomorrow will bring for either of us?

Chapter 49

Jason awoke to the sound of men's voices in the church sanctuary. It was still dark. He lit a candle and, in the flickering light, could see his breath in the air. He quickly put on his boots and pulled his watch cap over his head. After slipping on his coat, he opened his door and started through the hallways. He found himself outside. Looking through the front gate he could see the shadows of the military vehicles arrayed in front of the monastery. There was no movement from the camp.

Father Gregory is going to wait them out. They didn't come prepared for a siege. He knew his pursuers would need shelter and more food in order to wait. But would they? Roper hadn't shown any inclination to respect the Abbot and his monks. It seemed he would be willing to gun them down and when he'd killed enough, crash through the gates, kill him, and raid the supplies. Jason wondered if Father Gregory understood what the man was capable of doing.

Maybe I better slip out and give Roper a moving target so he'll leave the monastery alone? The thought stuck in his mind. He didn't relish being on the run, so far from what he considered to be the sanctuary of the mountains.

He was deep into thinking about his next move when the morning service broke up and the monks streamed out to head for the dining room. Father Gregory came up to him and grabbed him by the arm.

"Come along. We'll eat and then we have more to discuss," he said.

Jason went with him into the dining hall. The warmth of it, fueled by the meal preparation and the assembled bodies was a welcome relief from the cold outside. There were steaming bowls of what looked like oatmeal to Jason. Slices of cured ham were loaded on plates along with loaves of dark bread. There were also pitchers of beer to pour into one's cup.

Jason was directed to sit next to Father Gregory. No one moved until all were seated. They bowed their heads and Father Gregory gave a blessing in Latin. At the "amen", the monks eagerly dished out the food. Jason noted that there was no rush and no one stuffed too much into their bowls. The beer had a strong malt taste.

"Beer so early in the morning?" he said to the Abbot.

"You've tasted it, you know it has very little alcohol in it. We drink water, beer, and wine. Not so different from most people except for the lack of processed sodas. Of course, no one gets to drink those now."

After the morning meal, Father Gregory led Jason back to his office. On the way they looked out at the vehicles spread in front of the gate. Men were just getting up and gathering wood to start fires. They looked cold and damp.

"We are far more comfortable than those poor fellows outside," the Abbot said.

"That worries me a bit," Jason replied.

The Abbot looked at him as they walked to the office building.

"I don't think Roper has any inhibitions about attacking you. Not like the other man, Vincent. Roper could unleash a massive amount of destruction. Far more than the unorganized bandits you encountered after the EMP burst."

"Yes, I'm aware of that fact and that Vincent's ability to hold him back is uncertain."

"I think I should leave before they do you any damage."

"We'll see. Let them be uncomfortable a little longer."

Roper got out of the Humvee he had slept in. He had to sleep sitting up and was quite stiff. He was not in a good mood. He saw Vincent getting out of another vehicle and started towards him.

"Vincent, I want to talk with you," he called out.

The two of them walked away from the others.

"You undermined me yesterday. Do you have a plan or are you going to cave in to this monk?" Roper asked.

Vincent gave him a long look. "You act so outraged. That man killed members of my family. I don't take that lightly, but we don't do it by wiping out a monastery."

"I'm not looking to wipe it out. Hell, I don't give a crap about these monks. They can sit here and garden all they want. But I want that son of a bitch and I won't let anyone stop me."

"So, you're ready to invade the compound? Kill monks?"

"You got a better plan? Any plan at all?"

"It might help if I talk with the Abbot. I could get a sense of what he's thinking. And I have you as a threat in the background. That could put pressure on him."

"You're okay with pressuring the Abbot?"

Vincent nodded. "Just not killing him...or his monks."

Roper looked around the collection of vehicles and men.

"We're not set up for a lengthy stay. I'm going to have some of my men go return in one of the Humvees and bring back food and shelter."

"If the Abbot sees that, he'll know we're here to stay. That could be good." Vincent paused for a moment. "I want one of my men to go back with you."

Roper gave him a sharp look. "You don't trust me?"

"I want to find out what's going on back in the city. The other capos will be jockeying for taking over since Al and

Joe were shot. I'm not about to be caught off guard while sitting out here."

"You're at each other's throats already?"

Roper started thinking about possibilities for him. Forget South America. If the mob started fighting one another, he could play power broker and put his forces behind a winner who'd owe him. It could be a chance to become the real boss of Charlotte.

Vincent stopped walking and stared at Roper. "I know what you're thinking. You think we're stupid enough to give you all that power without some control on our part?"

Roper stared at Vincent, giving him an innocent look. "What do you mean by that? We're on the same team."

"We are. But just to be sure, the family has visited your top officers and showed them the pictures we have of their wives, families, and girlfriends. If you're stupid enough to make a play, and they support you, we'll be paying them a visit."

Roper stepped up to Vincent. "You threatening me?" His voice was sharp with anger.

"Don't get all worked up, Larry. You didn't think we wouldn't look out for ourselves? You and your men have nothing to worry about if you do your job and remember who's running the show. I'm doing you a favor by letting you know, so you don't make a big mistake and find you're out on a limb all by yourself."

"You sons of bitches," Roper swore.

"Just looking out for our interests. It's all about leverage, Larry." Vincent stuck a finger in Roper's chest. "Something you need to remember."

Roper studied the man for a long moment. He'd figure out if Vincent was bluffing later. For now, he'd have to go along.

"Pick one of your guys. I'm sending my men out now. I'll give this monk two days and then we act."

He turned and walked back to the vehicles, shouting to one of his lieutenants.

"I've decided to leave."

Jason had walked into the Abbot's office unannounced. Father Gregory looked up. He studied Jason.

"You want to control your decision, is that it? Not have me order you to leave?"

"Maybe. But there's no good in me staying here. I've done what I came to do and Ernie and those with him are safe for now. I should go."

"How will you get out without them seeing you?"

Jason stepped further into the office.

"I haven't figured that out yet."

"I may be able to help in that matter. Sit down."

Jason took a seat and waited.

"There is a tunnel that leads out to the stand of pines behind the monastery. You can elude any sentries they put out and be well on your way before they find out you're missing."

"What will you do? They may storm the place before too long."

"When you're gone, I'll say I've reconsidered and invite them in to search for you."

"What about Ernie? If they find him, they'll take him away along with the rest of his family."

"Don't worry about Ernie. I can hide them where they won't be found."

Jason paused to think for a moment.

"If you can hide all those people, Roper may think you're hiding me. He's sure I came here. That could lead to violence to get the truth out. The mob is good at that."

"The solution is to show them the tunnel."

Jason shook his head. "Now I'm worried. They may take some revenge on you for aiding my escape."

The Abbot shrugged. "I can live with that. I'm not without cards to play."

"You know where you're going...?"

Father Gregory smiled. "That's part of it. It gives one a certain amount of leverage as well as freedom from fear. But don't do anything right away. One of the vehicles just left. Let's see what develops over the next day."

Chapter 50

That night Jason checked the perimeter walls of the monastery. He took a wooden ladder with him and climbed up as he worked his way around the enclosure. As he expected, the militia had placed sentries out to make sure their prey didn't escape. He made note of where each sentry was stationed.

After midnight, he put on his dark pants, sweater, jacket and watch cap. Then he made his way to the Abbot's office. Thankfully the Abbot didn't lock it. Jason retrieved his 9mm with its suppressor from a cabinet where the Abbot put the weapons. He also had his sheath knife, which the Abbot had not confiscated, on his belt.

On his earlier reconnoiter, he had found a gap in the visual coverage of the sentries. If he could get over the wall undetected, there was some tall grass and thick plants in a garden bed on the other side that would shield him until he could crawl behind the surveillance perimeter. From there he could get to the militia camp undetected.

He made his way over to one of the barns where he got a coil of rope. There was no watch put on by the monks except for the main gate. Father Gregory had explained that the sheep dogs they kept, ones Jason had purposely gotten familiar with, would sound an alarm if any stranger made their way over the wall.

One of the dogs woke as Jason walked back to the wall. He came up sniffing around him and wagging his tail. Jason petted him and scratched his ears while whispering to him. After checking him out, the dog went back to the barn, not that interested in Jason's midnight excursion.

He found a large, rounded rock which he rolled to the base of the wall where he wanted to climb. He laid the rope on the ground and rolled the heavy stone over it. Then he tied the rope tight around the rock. The stone weighed over a hundred pounds. Jason figured the stone, with the friction of the rope going over the wall, would hold his weight when he had to climb back inside.

He placed the ladder against the wall and climbed up to locate the sentries. They were in the same spot as before. From the top of the wall, he eased the rope down to the ground. Then he crawled over the top and, grabbing the rope, slid down as if in slow motion.

Crouching in the tall grass next to the wall, he could barely make out the rope. *The sentries won't see it*. After checking their location, one to his right and one, farther away, to his left, he began to crawl away from the wall.

A half hour later, Jason was behind the lookouts. He was still in the cleared ground surrounding the monastery. There were fewer garden plots this far outside of the walls. He was crawling through an old hay field that had been mowed to provide feed for the livestock. Thankfully, it had regrown to some extent providing Jason with a small amount of cover as he crawled towards the parked vehicles.

Earlier in the day he had located the Humvees that both Vincent and Roper were sleeping in. The two men had displaced the other passengers, leaving them alone in the vehicles to try to sleep for the night. The men had to fend for themselves with tarps out on the cold November ground. Their campfires were now well burned down, providing little heat and almost no light. *Hope I don't run into someone getting up looking for wood.*

He moved slowly and quietly. There were no heavy sleepers outside when there wasn't enough shelter to get comfortable.

It took another half hour to reach Roper's Humvee. There was no one outside of it, the displaced men having moved to huddle themselves against the other Humvees that housed more fortunate militia members. Gathering *en masse* to conserve heat seemed to be their response to the cold.

When Jason reached the Humvee, he unsheathed his knife and carefully opened the rear door. The gentle click didn't disturb the peace of the night. Jason reached in and clamped his hand over Roper's mouth as he put his knife to the man's neck.

Roper lurched out of sleep and his eyes opened to see Jason's face close to his. Jason pressed his body down on him so he couldn't move.

"Don't struggle. Don't try to call out or I'll slit your throat." He said in a harsh whisper.

Roper's eyes opened wide as he finally realized what was going on.

"You understand?"

He nodded.

"We're going to have a talk. We can do it quietly here in the Humvee if you cooperate, or I can knock you out and drag your ass back to the woods. You'll be more comfortable here, believe me. Want to do it the comfortable way?"

Roper nodded.

"Good. Now sit up slowly and put your hands under your butt. I want you to sit on them."

Roper began to adjust his position as directed while Jason kept the knife blade pressed against his throat.

"One false move, I slice across your throat and through your carotid artery. It'll be a race between drowning in your blood or bleeding out from the artery. Not sure which will happen first."

When Roper was sitting up, Jason moved the knife to the side of his neck and relaxed his hand from his mouth.

"What do you want?" Roper's voice was shaky with fear and fatigue.

"We're going to talk. You know you must live under a lucky star."

"What do you mean by that? I don't feel so lucky right now."

"Maybe not but consider. Cameron and Gibbs let you live when I probably would have killed you. Now I'm in a position to end your life and I'm considering letting you live."

Roper tried to look over at Jason.

"Just sit still. I'll explain."

"I hope you know you're in a box," Roper said. "You can't get away and the mob guys really want to make an example of you. I can save you from that. I can arrest you and hold you, keep the mob away from you, since I'm the commander of the militia."

"You can't do a thing for me. If I were in a box, how did I get out to sit here with your life in my hands? Think about that."

Jason shifted his position so he could look directly at Roper.

"I know what your end game was going to be when you were back in Hillsboro, collect enough loot to make it to South America and live like a king. It made sense. I guess you didn't have faith the country would recover and your career could get back on track.

"It seems like you still think that way since you resigned from the army to pursue another attempt through the Charlotte militia. I don't know what you said to convince Big Al or Joe, but they bit on it. Your problem is that I've thrown your set-up into chaos.

"But here's where you get lucky," Jason continued. "I'm going to give you the chance to go back to Charlotte, collect your winnings, and take off. You must have amassed enough by now to live pretty well. Maybe you can even get work helping to run things down south if you get bored.

Jason could see Roper, now fully awake, was getting himself more under control.

"You think you're invincible?" Roper asked. "You can just run around the countryside killing whoever you want, whenever you want?"

Jason stared at him. "That's just what I've been doing. But if you think you're safe from me and don't have to do what I say, maybe I should kill you right now and be done with it."

"No, no. Let's talk." Roper's face showed a hint of panic.

Jason allowed himself a thin smile. "Let me lay it out for you. The mob didn't put you in power without setting up some leverage over you. Some way to control you."

Jason could see on Roper's face that he had hit on the truth.

"You're just a tool for them, like everyone else in their world who isn't family. Right now I've thrown all that out of balance. What you don't know is who in the mob will wind up in power and will they want to keep their arrangement with you? You could be out in the cold. I guarantee they've got the leverage to throw you out if they want.

"It doesn't serve my purposes to kill you now. I'd rather have you leave and try your luck somewhere else. Doing that creates more disruption than me just killing you. You wind up being more useful to me alive than dead. Like I said, you must live under a lucky star."

"So, you'll just let me leave?"

"I will. But I'll be around to make sure of it. If you don't, if you try something cute, something you think will turn the tables on me, I'll just kill you."

He leaned close to Roper now, almost nose to nose. His knife pressed harder against Roper's neck; his voice now cold and deadly.

"I can snatch the life right out of you any time I choose. From a thousand yards away. One minute you're standing around, the next your body is in a crumpled heap on the ground, your brains spattered on the pavement. I can kill you up close, like right now. Slit your throat and let you bleed out. You will not survive trying to be clever with me. You only survive by moving on, leaving, and forgetting about Hillsboro."

There was a long silence as Roper stared into Jason's cold eyes.

"What do you want me to do?" Roper asked.

"What have you arranged with Vincent?"

"I told him I was sending some men back to get supplies and camp gear so we can wait you out. He had one of his men along."

"That should tell you something. They'll be back tomorrow?"

Roper nodded.

"Wait for your men to return. Vincent doesn't want you to attack the monastery. Use that. Tomorrow night, when they're back, tell him you're taking your men back to Charlotte. Since its personal with him and he doesn't want you to attack, you're leaving the situation in his hands. Got it?"

Roper nodded.

"He'll be suspicious but you'll be doing the logical thing. Tell him you want to get ready for Hillsboro."

Jason leaned in close again.

"When you get back, you pack up and go while your men are distracted with preparations."

"They may still attack Hillsboro, even if I'm gone and have nothing to do with it."

"Maybe, maybe not. The mob's in disarray. Things are going to get messier, not cleaner. You head south. Where, I don't care, but don't come close to Hillsboro.

"Do we have a deal? I let you live. You leave the area and forget all about Hillsboro."

"We got a deal."

"Good. Now remember, I'm not the trusting type so I'll be watching. If you try to double cross me, you'll die without warning, never know it's coming."

Roper nodded again.

"I'm going to leave now."

Jason took his suppressed 9mm out of its holster with his left hand and showed it to Roper.

"I hear you call out, make a sound, I'll kill you here and disappear into the woods before anyone can figure out what's going on. Use the rest of the night to make your plans, not try to alert anyone."

With that Jason switched the knife out for the pistol and got out of the Humvee.

"Do the right thing with the opportunity I'm giving you."

And then he was gone in the night.

Larry Roper sat back in the Humvee breathing heavily, sweat soaking his clothes.

Chapter 51

"Did you enjoy your midnight excursion?"

Father Gregory was sitting next to Jason in the dining hall the next morning. Jason looked over at him with some surprise.

"Not much goes on in the monastery that I don't know about."

"I guess I should explain—"

"Only if you think you need to."

"I'm working on a way to end this standoff without endangering the monastery more than I already have."

"I appreciate that. I would appreciate it more if you would keep me in the loop. I don't like having you act unilaterally."

"I apologize for that."

Jason went on to explain his plan to the Abbot.

"I'll depart tomorrow night, after Roper leaves with his men. Vincent will have just one Humvee and probably only four to six men. He'll wonder why Roper changed his mind, but his explanation makes enough sense to be believed.

"Things are unstable back in Charlotte. Something Vincent is also aware of. After you let him in and he confirms I'm not here, he'll head back to the city right away. He needs to make sure he's not outmaneuvered by any of the other capos. It'll be civil war in the family for a while."

"How does that help Charlotte?"

"It doesn't in the short run."

"Just Hillsboro, that it?"

"No. Hopefully this opens up an opportunity for the civil leadership in Charlotte to regain the control they ceded to the mafia. That will help the city in the long run. They actually have a good start at getting things back to normal with the power plant being operational. If the civilian authorities can regain control, they might make more progress and shore themselves up against the criminal element."

"And the mafia will just step aside? That doesn't sound realistic."

"The militia is key. The outcome of any revolution rests on which side the military supports."

"Power and guns always seem to go together," Father Gregory said.

The day went by without any interaction between the monastery and those outside. Jason took the time to talk with Ernie and Ruth. He gave them directions and a wrote a letter of introduction to present when they got to Hillsboro. Ernie and Ruth had decided to informally adopt Jack and Bobby.

The boys seemed happy with the arrangement. Bobby and Tom, Ernie and Ruth's son, were already best friends. Jack had a crush on Jennifer who was a year older than him, which at that age, was an almost unbridgeable gap. However, he seemed determined to impress her with his warrior abilities, emulating what he had seen from Jason.

The family would stay until Ruth's ankle was strong enough and then set out for Hillsboro. It would take them two or three days to reach their goal. They would have the luxury of supplies and gear to aid them courtesy of Father Gregory.

"You are going back to Charlotte?" Father Gregory asked Jason.

"I have to make sure Roper does the right thing and leaves on his own."

"Why didn't you kill him? You've already killed others in your quest to sow disruption."

"Maybe I was trying to be kinder, not so much the killer you see me as. It also serves my purpose. Me killing Roper could make him a rallying point for the militia, which could coalesce and keep them together. Him leaving, running off, leaves them in more disarray. Makes it easier for the civilians to get involved and regain control."

"Sounds more like the manipulator rather than the compassionate man."

Jason just looked at the Abbot. He didn't expect his approval, but hoped Father Gregory would see the necessity, the duty that drove him.

"You're playing a complicated game, one you can't control, but one you've triggered with your violence. I hope it turns out as you plan. There seems to be so many ways this could go wrong and hurt you."

"I guess I'd be getting my just desserts. That's what you would think, wouldn't you?"

"What I think is unimportant. What God thinks of your actions is."

Jason smiled. "I don't know about that. I'm just doing my duty as I see it."

"And your conscience is clear?"

"I don't relish being a 'man of violence' as you describe me. I'm just trying to push back tyranny and oppression where it threatens my family and my community."

Father Gregory smiled. "We come from two different worlds so we approach events from different perspectives. Perhaps you do have a legitimate role to play. There have always been defenders of the faith, in the physical sense. Men and women who have fought back forces of chaos and evil...I'll be keeping you in my prayers."

"Thank you, Father. I mean that."

That afternoon more vehicles arrived at the encampment. Jason watched from an upper window with his binoculars as an animated discussion went on between Vincent and Larry. It culminated with Roper ordering his troops to pack up and leave, giving Vincent two Humvees for his remaining six men.

That evening Jason said goodbye to Father Gregory and slipped out of the monastery using the tunnel the Abbot had talked about. Father Gregory placed the rope and ladder at the wall to misdirect Vincent and the others later when he let them in come morning.

When Jason exited the tunnel, he was in the cover of the pines. He worked his way around to the road leading back to Charlotte. He had to move fast. Roper had departed earlier that day and was already back in town. It would take Jason all night, running with short breaks, to reach Charlotte. It was going to be an exhausting effort. Complicating his plan was the knowledge that Vincent and his men would be coming up behind him sometime the next day. He needed to be off the road and infiltrated back into town before they arrived.

His gear was packed up; his M110 disassembled and in its own soft case, lashed to his backpack. He had his M4 slung over his shoulder and his 9mm strapped to his side. Running was awkward, but not as difficult as he remembered when in the army, with an even heavier pack.

Upon reaching the highway, he settled into a comfortable jogging pace; one he could maintain for hours and would eat up the miles. It was going to be a long, hard night. Jason's routine was to run for an hour followed by a five-minute recovery walk, then start the cycle over again. He plodded; his pace did not seem to have the spring it once did. *Getting older.* He had the endurance but realized his body did not have the peak power it once had. *If Father Gregory waits until the afternoon, I should not have a problem with Vincent coming up on my tail.* His goal was to get inside Charlotte before anyone could raise an alert. Vincent might or might not assume he was still heading away from Charlotte. *Better to be inside the perimeter in any case.*

Dawn saw Jason crossing the Catawba River bridge on Rt. 16. Three hours later he was approaching the Charlotte airport. The militia was stationed there, so Jason guessed Roper probably would go there to keep himself safe. Jason had proven he could strike, even in the central part of the city.

He worked his way past the empty warehouses, no longer used, sticking to the woods and brush that was reclaiming the land from concrete and blacktop. At an outlying parking garage, Jason went up to the top level, only four stories high, to locate the nexus of activity in the sprawl of the now unused airport.

When he was in position, he unpacked his M110 and assembled it. After checking the distance to the terminal entrance, he dialed in his scope.

The arms coming off the main terminal, all with an assortment of now derelict planes pulled up to the gates showed little activity. The central part of the terminal, however, showed signs of life. There were militia members moving in and out of the building. Across a runway, the general aviation buildings seemed to house the bulk of the men and vehicles. Jason guessed that the officers had located themselves in the main terminal. *Probably creating rooms out of the shops and gate areas.* There would be restaurant facilities that could be jury rigged to provide food. Jason settled in to watch and wait.

Two hours later, he saw Roper through his binoculars. He had just emerged from the terminal. He stopped and looked around. Then he walked over to a Humvee and got in. He pulled the vehicle over to the main door and backed it up to the curb. Then he disappeared into the terminal. *Preparing to leave? You better be.* Jason had no desire to try to infiltrate the terminal and confront Roper up close. He hoped he had made his point. He was about a third of a mile from the entrance; not an impossible shot if he had to take one. What Jason needed to see was Roper packing his vehicle and preparing to drive south. He'd have to hold position until he could be sure Larry was doing what he had told him to do.

An hour later, Roper reappeared. He was with two other men. He spoke to them and the men walked off to get into a Humvee. They headed out onto the runways, towards the buildings that housed the main force. *What's he up to? Increasing his protection? He should be packing up.*

Jason slid the M110 over the edge of the garage parapet. He got Roper in his sights. Roper was drinking something from a coffee cup. A call must have come over his radio. He put the cup on the roof of the Humvee and reached for his radio hooked to his belt. Jason brought the rifle to bear on the cup, now sitting on the roof of the Humvee. Roper was talking on the radio.

Jason slowed his breathing and heart rate. The reticle rested on the cup. He could see, out of the corner of his eye, Roper talking. As soon as Roper reached down to put the radio back in his belt, Jason's finger closed on the trigger. The suppressed rifle gave a muffled *whoomp* along with a satisfying kick. In the next instance the cup exploded as the sonic report rang out.

Larry yanked his head around to the roof. Pieces of the shattered cup hit him in the face. He stepped back and almost fell. Turning, he ran back into the terminal. *Take the hint, dumbass.* Jason hoped Roper understood the shot could just as easily have hit him. In a few minutes, vehicles from across the runway had started up and were headed towards the terminal. Jason saw Roper come back out with two gear bags and throw them into the back. Others followed him out of the building.

Jason broke down the rifle and packed it away. He needed to put some distance between himself and the airport. There would be a search of high places fanning out from the entrance. It would take them a while to get out as far as he was, but they'd get here at some point. Time to head downtown again.

Chapter 52

Jason made his way east towards the inner city. He'd have to wait until dark to get into the downtown area; the interstate was too open and wide for him to cross in the daylight. The train tracks that he used to exit on the east side also passed over the highway on the west side. At night they would provide a way in. Jason guessed the bridge would not be manned, but barricaded. He'd have to climb over or around but, with caution, he expected he could get past the barrier. If Larry Roper had initiated a search for him, it would center around the airport since he had made his presence known there in a dramatic way.

Dusk found him hiding in the brush near the railroad overpass. He took the time to eat and get some rest. For the moment he was safe in his hide. Word would spread of his being in the city, but no one would know his whereabouts.

After night fell, Jason got up and stretched. He was sore. All the running the previous night had left him with complaining muscles. *Loosen up. You've got more to do.* There was a singular focus in his thinking. Nothing beyond the mission mattered. It was the only way to maintain his drive through this long assault on the mafia and the militia. *Remember, you're one man. You can't do everything.* That small voice kept trying to intrude into his thinking. He kept trying to tamp it down.

Finally loosened up, he left the safety of the brush and started for the rail bridge. It was made of concrete with concrete sides to keep any debris from falling on the interstate highway below. The sides effectively shielded Jason so he could cross in a crouch and not be seen from below.

As he expected, near the end of the bridge, piles of concrete rubble had been placed across the span forming a loose, sloping wall about ten feet high. With limited ability to see, it might be dangerous to climb. He could initiate a slide which, although it might not harm him, would be noisy enough to attract unwanted attention. Jason stopped, took off his pack and studied the situation.

He decided he would have to chance the climb. There were no real handholds on the outside of the concrete sides to allow him to climb around the obstruction. The added instability of his backpack would increase the danger of climbing around the sides. He didn't want to risk falling to the roadway below, some twenty feet down. Such a fall, if it didn't kill him, would injure him severely enough to end the mission.

With great care, Jason put his hands on the lower pieces of debris. He tested them to see how easily they moved. If firm, he stepped up on them and proceeded to reach up and test other pieces. Finding handholds and footholds was not the problem, Jason needed to make sure each piece was solidly in place. If he found a piece that seemed loose, he tried to gently move it down without letting it fall or loosening more pieces. If he moved a piece, the resultant gap gave him a firm place to put a foot and continue upward.

In this painstaking manner he inched upward. He kept as low to the pile as he could so his profile would blend in with the rubble. At the top, he had to reach over and reverse his procedure. A half hour later he was on the rails, now inside the barrier.

Now try to connect with Daniels or Luke. They can give me a good read on the situation. Going to the high-rise was out of the question. Jason really didn't know where Luke had set up his own living quarters in the building and he didn't have time to check all forty floors. And he had no idea where Daniel's lived. His office seemed the best bet, although going there would be entering the hornet's nest. Jason was pretty sure it would now be impossible to get into the building.

Find a place to hide and keep watch. If Daniels or Luke are in the building, I can follow them when they leave.

He started for the city offices. The grounds around the building had probably been thoroughly searched after he had shot Big Al. Those who suspected he had returned would focus on the airport. Jason was betting he'd be safe enough in the brush where he had hidden on his first foray into the downtown area.

The park-like grounds across from the city building were a dense mixture of trees and thickets. He could worm his way into the brush and not be seen. If he kept still, one would almost have to step on him to discover his presence. It might not be comfortable, but being that well-hidden, so close to his objective, was an ideal advantage for him.

Dawn found him snug in a nest deep in the bushes. He had crawled through the undergrowth, pushing his pack ahead of him—there was not enough clearance for him to wear it on his back. With the daylight, Jason broke some twigs, pulled off some leaves and made an irregular opening, just large enough for him to see through with his binoculars. Through it he could spy on the main entrance across the street. Now he lay back, relaxed as best he could, drank some water, and ate some beef jerky. *Time enough to watch when people start showing up.*

That morning Jason saw both Daniels and Luke. They walked up together. *Luke must be staying with Daniels, wherever that is.* Now he would have to watch throughout the day to make sure he saw them when they departed. There were military types around the city building. The way Jason was dressed, neither in a militia uniform, nor looking like a mob member, he risked standing out when he emerged to follow. Hopefully the pedestrian traffic would thin out by the time the two men left the building.

They had come up from the south. Jason decided he would work his way down the street using the overgrown areas to cover him. Maybe when they left, he could attract their attention farther down the block and meet with them. If Daniels could tell him where he lived and how to get into the building, Jason could wait until dark and then make his way there. He smiled. It was a plan. That always helped, even it was a bit sketchy.

By late afternoon, Jason had been able to move south to the next block. He was now hidden in front of a police headquarters of some sort which made him nervous. But he had good cover near the road. He was close enough to be able to call out to the men when they passed without alerting everyone on the street. Now the wait began again.

When people began to emerge from the buildings, Jason went on high alert. He'd have only one chance. It had to count. He watched up the street. People passed by within twenty feet and didn't see him. Daniels and Luke wouldn't see him either. They'd have to hear him calling to them. Time passed; it got later; there were fewer people about and dusk was coming. Jason strained to see up the street. Finally, he spotted two men walking together. Through his binoculars he could see it was Daniels and Luke.

They were on the opposite side of the street which put them about fifty feet away from where he hid. Just before they got abreast of his position, Jason called out, "Daniels!"

The two men looked around.

"Daniels! To your left," Jason said a little louder this time. He couldn't keep shouting for too long without attracting others.

Now the men looked over in his direction.

"Cross the street. I need to talk with you."

The looked at one another and walked across the road.

"Come forward ten feet and stand around as if you're talking with each other," Jason said, now in lower voice. "Don't look into the bushes."

"Is that you, boss?" Luke said.

"Not so loud," Jason replied.

"What do you want?" Daniels asked in a low voice.

"I need to talk with both of you. Tell me where you're staying and how to get in your building. I'll make my way there tonight."

Daniels looked around. The few people walking past were on the other side of the road and paid no attention to the two men.

"I'm in an apartment building. It's three blocks west of here up next to the ring road. It's large and white. You can't miss it," Daniel said.

"How do I get in?"

"There's a parking garage underneath. Go in the south end. I'll jam open the door nearest the car entrance. I'm on the fourth floor, number 457."

"I'll be there. It'll be late, wait up for me."

"What else would we do?" Luke asked.

Daniels grabbed his arm and they started walking again.

Chapter 53

Michael Daniels opened his door when Jason knocked on it. He stood there for a moment as if in shock. Jason pushed inside and Daniels closed the door.

"My God, man. You look terrible," he said.

Jason gave him a sour look.

"I'm sorry. It's just that...well, look at yourself in the mirror."

He pointed to the wall of the living room area where a decorative mirror hung.

Jason walked over as Luke entered the room.

"Hey boss," he said in a loud voice. "Wow, you look like you've been through the ringer."

Jason didn't answer. He stared at his image. His hair was sticking out at odd angles, dirty and unkempt. His face was not only reddened by the cold and wind but covered in grime. He had dark shadows under his eyes which gave him a haunted look. His clothes were rumpled and stained from grass and mud from sleeping outside and crawling on the ground.

"You look like you've been through hell," Luke said. "Or delivering hell."

"I have some large plastic buckets of water," Michael said. "You can wash up."

"Thanks." Jason took off his backpack and coat and sat down on the couch, happy to be off his feet. "First tell me what's going on."

"It's only been five days since you left, but we've made some progress," Michael said. "I've got the mayor on board and he's rounding up the council members who he thinks have the courage to try to step forward in opposition to the mob. Luke here has been a surprise. He's quite an orator. He's worked his way through the militia and talked with senior leadership. He's convinced many of them of two things. One, that Roper is an outlier, not a Charlotte native and so may not have our city's interests at heart. And two, that Roper is under the thumb of the mafia which means they are as well. Those two facts are not sitting well with the local officers. They're mostly home-grown and have a loyalty to the city. He's been quite convincing...and subversive.

"Michael wanted to send me to Atlanta to get help from FEMA," Luke said. "The last thing I wanted to do was go out on the road with lots of supplies and gas. I'd be a target for every highway bandit out there."

He broke into a broad smile. "Besides, that would have wasted my true talents."

"You are the showman," Jason said.

"He's more than that," Michael said. "He goes on about loyalty to our city. How Charlotte's nickname is 'the queen city'. How gracious and beautiful it is and that we should live up to our name. Do we want our fair city to be a den of thieves and murderers? Or do we want our city to lead the way towards the rebuilding of the country? He's gotten people thinking about where this ends with the mob running things. And, he's sown doubt in the minds of many of the officers about Roper."

"Questions were raised about the assassinations," Michael continued. "We said we don't know who did it, but we saw the opportunity to take back control. Hell, Luke even stiffened the backbone of our mayor."

"Imagine you, influencing the mayor," Jason said. "Quite a change from being the Duke of East End."

"Hey, that's no small thing. Plus, it gave me my training. The mayor wants me to help out as his spokesperson. He'll want to take all the credit, but, if we turn this around, I'll have a position of influence throughout the whole city." Luke now beamed at his sudden rise to fame.

"Looks like shaking things up is working for you. Let's hope it works for everyone."

Michael now looked serious. "Vincent Bonocchi may be a problem. It seems like he may emerge as the strongest capo and take over leadership. If the mob reorganizes quickly it'll start rooting out the opposition. We'll be uncovered and the support from the politicians will evaporate."

"It's all going to come down to the militia," Jason said. "They have the firepower. Which side they support will determine who wins."

He hunched forward on the couch. The other two men grabbed chairs and pulled them up.

"The militia was probably directed by the mayor before. Even after the mob got control over him, they did what they were told. Now you've introduced doubt in their leadership. What you need to do is get your mayor to man-up and meet with the officers. Tell them that the mafia has to go. That Charlotte has to go back to civilian control. He's a politician, so he'll be able to come up with some story as to why he let this happen. He can also position himself as the crusader, the savior of the city.

"Meanwhile," Jason turned to Michael, "you have to get connected to the engineers, the technicians that make things work. If the militia supports the civilian government, you need to show some advancements to solidify yourselves with the general population. They want normalcy and will support whoever can deliver it. That's how the mob was able to exercise their brand of leadership. Even though they used brutal tactics at times, they made things work, and so everyone put up with them."

"That's a tall order," Michael said.

"You're a bureaucrat. You know how to work with organized systems. Use that to identify those who make things run, then use that skill to prioritize and organize them." He pointed at Michael. "You've lived a quiet life making a small part of a large system work. Now you've been called to a larger task. But it's the same in kind, just not in scale. Remember that."

He turned back to Luke.

"Look how Luke is using his skills but now on a larger scale. You do that as well."

The night passed as the men talked about plans and actions; things that had been done and things that still had to be done quickly to stave off any counter attempts by the mob to regain control. They worked out a "to do" list for both Michael and Luke.

"You two go to work on that list today." Jason sighed. "I've hit the wall and need to rest for now. I'll stay here. When you get back, we can decide on whether or not Vincent needs to go. I also want you to find out if Roper has departed."

He had told them of his arrangement with Larry Roper and the warning he had given him at the airport. The men nodded gravely and got up to ready themselves for the day. Jason lay back on the couch and fell into a deep sleep. He hadn't yet washed up. He'd do that later, he promised himself. The security of the apartment allowed him to relax for the first time in days and he reveled in it. *Tonight...or tomorrow, I'll get back in action.*

Vincent immediately met with his crew when he got back to Charlotte. Tony had done well, working the others in the family, making alliances.

"Some of the other capos tried to pin this mess on you," Tony said, "saying Jason came from our crew, so you're responsible for Big Al and Joe. I turned that around with some of them. I said you were skeptical of him from the start. Put myself on the line and said I was his biggest promoter. That he fooled me, but not you. I told them that you advised Joe against giving Jason more influence, putting him in charge of the power project."

"How'd that go over?"

"Like I said, some bought it. It's mostly true. If you cautioned Joe about Jason then it's on Joe, not you. He fooled a lot of us. Plus, I said he attacked our crew, killing Gino. And I pointed out that you were the one who went after him with Roper."

Tony paused for a moment.

"Then I stuck my neck out and asked them what they were doing while you were chasing the son of a bitch down. That pissed some of them off and I got warned about not showing respect. But the point got made."

"Good job, Tony. I'll remember that."

"One problem though, boss. You didn't get him. Where is he? Did he get away? Do we need to go all the way to Hillsboro to get him? The others will still want revenge."

"And what the hell are they doing about it? If I get control we can talk about revenge. We can send Roper to Hillsboro like Big Al and Joe planned. Jason's probably got family there, roots. We'll get to him through them."

At that moment Ears burst into the room. Vincent looked up in irritation.

"Sorry to interrupt. A militia guy just came by. Someone took a shot at Roper, out at the airport."

"Is he alive?"

"Yeah. The shooter missed. The guy said Roper's freaked out by it. No one knows who did it or where the shot came from. They're trying to figure it out now. He says Roper mentioned something about a Jason Richards."

"Damn!" Vincent said in a loud voice. "There's your answer," he said looking at Tony. "The bastard's returned."

"He wants to kill Roper?" Tony asked.

Vincent shook his head. "No, he's trying to send him a message. I think if he wanted to kill him, that shot would have done it. They didn't know where it came from because the guy's a sniper. Hell, he could have been a half mile away." He paused to look out of his window. "What the hell does he want? What message is he trying to send?"

He shook his head and turned back to his crew.

"The guy took out our two top men. He wants to cripple the family, get us fighting among ourselves. Probably so we don't go after Hillsboro. Is that the message he's sending Roper?"

Vincent got up.

"Ears, we got to go out to the airport and find Roper. The rest of you get out on the streets and keep your eyes out for any sign of him."

The meeting broke up and Vincent and Ears headed for the airport.

Chapter 54

The main terminal at the airport was still in a state disruption. Ears drove up to the entrance. The militia had their guns at ready, aimed towards the car when Vincent got out.

"What are you doing?" Vincent shouted to them. "I'm here to see Commander Roper. I'm one of Big Al's men, put those rifles down."

The men lowered their weapons and Vincent and Ears walked through them, into the building. They headed to Roper's office and living quarters. It was located in a section of the American Airlines Admiral's Club. There was a guard at the door.

Roper opened when they knocked.

"What are you doing here?" he asked.

"Finding out what the hell is going on."

"You get Jason?"

"No."

"I didn't think so," Roper said.

"Why is that?"

"He took a shot at me this morning. From a long way off."

"And he missed?" Vincent's voice evidenced his disbelief.

"He didn't miss. It was to warn me. He shot my coffee cup. It was sitting on the Humvee roof. Do you know how hard that is to do from a distance?"

Vincent ignored the question. "What's the warning about?"

"Not to go to Hillsboro."

Vincent looked around the room. There were boxes out, some packed, some partially packed. Roper turned back to that work.

"What's going on?"

"I'm changing my location. He knows I'm staying so I'm changing it."

"Where are you going?"

"Not sure right now. I'll let you know after I've decided."

"This all seems a bit hurried."

Roper stopped his packing and turned to Vincent. "You didn't get shot at."

"I can't have you run off to who knows where. I have to be able to get in touch with you. Your men have to get in touch with you."

"My men will know how to reach me, don't worry. As for you, I'd worry more about the other capos than me, if you want to survive. Jason was a part of your crew."

He stepped up to Vincent. Ears tensed up. Roper put his finger on Vincent's chest.

"Don't think you can tell me what to do. You're on my turf now. I'll let you know how to reach me and I'll decide how and when to go to Hillsboro. Got it?"

Vincent didn't budge. "You better remember who's in charge. We put you in power, we can take you out."

"Sergeant!" Roper shouted. "Come in here."

A burly militia officer stepped into Roper's room. He was armed with a 9mm sidearm.

"These men were just leaving. Please escort them out of the building and into their car."

Ears gave the sergeant a hard look which the man returned.

"I'll be back. I'm going to come out on top and you're gonna wish you had helped me. It's not too late to get on the winning side."

"I prefer to wait and see who actually wins. Then we can renegotiate my deal since things have changed. Jason represents an escalation in the situation I'm facing...personally. That calls for new terms. You win your fight, come see me. I'll be waiting. But until then, the militia stays on the sidelines."

"I'll be back. Then you'll sing a different tune." Vincent and Ears turned to go.

After they had left, Roper finished his packing. He got into his Humvee and drove out of the airport. After putting some random miles between him and the facility, he pulled over to think about his situation.

Jason couldn't stay around forever. He'd be hunted down eventually. Roper calculated that if he went into hiding for a while, Jason would not be able to find him. He could wait him out. There was still a chance that he could remain in power, but Jason had said that the mob would have leverage over him, something Vincent had pointed out as well.

His officer's families. If they used them to control his senior officers, they would control his fate. There were six men that were key. What to do? He could head to the storage facility and pull his loot and go. That's what Jason said to do. Or, he could talk with those key officers and determine the threat the mob presented. *Damn.* He was under attack from two sides.

If he could neutralize the mob though, maybe he could maintain his position. Jason had to go back to Hillsboro sooner or later. If he changed plans and didn't attack Hillsboro, maybe Jason would forget about him. It *was* possible.

But, if the mob did have leverage over his senior officers, that put him under their control; something he didn't relish. There would be no renegotiating his arrangement and they could even confiscate the loot he had collected.

His loot. Over the year, he'd been given as much scrip as hard value items—gold, silver, precious stones. It didn't seem like much of a problem when things were going well. He anticipated being able to steadily convert the scrip into something more portable. If he bugged out now, that wasn't possible. His hard goods would be the only thing of value that he could use on the road.

His mind began to swirl with his options, most of them not very good. *Begin with my officers.* That was the way to go. He started the Humvee and headed back to the airport.

Later that day, Michael and Luke returned to Michael's apartment. Jason had rested, washed and looked much more presentable.

"We got a problem," Luke announced after they had walked in.

Jason looked at him, waiting for an explanation.

"The key militia officers were put on notice that the mob knows all about their families. Some of the mob sat down with them and mentioned each of their wives, girlfriends, children, parents by name. And they knew where they all lived."

"Did they threaten them?"

"Didn't have to. The information was threat enough. Now they're saying they might not be able to stand with us."

"Jesus!" Jason said in anger. "Don't these men think? If they support you, the mob can't do what they threaten."

"They don't see it that way," Michael said. He'd heard the officers' objections and knew they were scared for their loved ones. "The mob could get to them before things get under control.

They were standing in the kitchen. Jason pounded his fist on the table. "Are these the senior officers? The ones who are supposed to lead troops?"

Luke and Michael nodded.

Jason shook his head in disgust. "What's going on is an insurrection. We're starting a revolution. Restoring civilian control back to the city. Get these men to move their families out to the airport and put them under guard. Immediately! They shouldn't take no for an answer. I'll go take out Vincent and the other capos, if I have to. Cut off the head and the snake dies. I thought I did that, but if I have to cut more, I'll do it."

There was silence in the kitchen. Then Michael spoke up.

"You're right. It's time for action. Not sitting on the sidelines."

"I can tell them what you said," Luke offered.

"I have a thought," Michael said. "Instead of you doing more killing, if we convince these officers to act, I'll have the mayor order the arrest of Vincent and the other capos. Five men in all. That cuts off the rest of the head. The crews will be leaderless. They'll still be dangerous, but not able to threaten the town's leadership anymore."

Jason looked at Michael. "That's pretty good for a bureaucrat. Sends a message that law and order are back." He paused for a moment. "Better put the mayor and all the council members who side with him under protection along with their families. They should be sequestered at the airport like the militia families until the violence dies down. Then the mob won't have any targets."

"We've got to go see the mayor right now. I know where he lives," Michael said. "Jason, you should come with us. Then we have to get to the officers. We can put this into action tomorrow if we can get everyone on board tonight."

"Going to be up all night," Luke said. "I guess this is how revolutions work. Never participated in one before."

"They're dangerous," Jason said. "You unleash chaos, destroy order, and then try to keep control over events that are moving too fast. The goal is to be able to reestablish order on the other side of the chaos. Often things go wrong in the middle and the outcome is not what was expected."

"So, the faster we move, the better chance we have to maintain some control." Michael said.

"That's right. Now before the night's over, I have to pay Vincent a visit."

"You're not going to kill him, are you?" Michael asked.

"No, but I have one piece of unfinished business to attend to. He should be arrested, like you said."

Chapter 55

The visit to the mayor went better than Jason had expected. He was a cautious man, but if the three of them, Jason, Michael, and Luke could get the militia fully committed; *and*, if they could provide security, he'd be on board and get his council members to stand with him.

"If we create a no-risk situation, the stalwart mayor will come on board," Jason said with some irony later. "I'm sure after it's all over, he'll be talking up how brave he and his council were to stand against the mafia and regain control over the city."

"Like you said, he's a politician," Michael said.

"Jason, you have to come with me to talk with the militia officers," Luke said.

"I thought you were going to handle that."

"I was, and can. You know by now that I enjoy the spotlight. But it's too important to not bring everything we can to make our case. And that means you. You're the catalyst that started this. They need to hear from you."

"I have to agree," Michael. "You'll have to delay your meeting with Vincent."'

"That means going out to the airport?" Jason asked. "If so, they may have been informed that I tried to kill Roper. That message I sent to him will be interpreted as an assassination attempt."

The men fell silent for a moment.

Finally, Luke spoke up. "We'll get around that. Roper is an outsider in the sense of not coming from Charlotte. We can vouch for you, especially since you took out the mob leadership. They now know the mob is a threat to them."

"All right, let's go," Jason said.

After his meeting with the senior militia officers, Roper left the airport. He headed to the storage warehouse. There he loaded all the gains from his time in Charlotte. It was two suitcases of gold and precious stones. He looked at a third suitcase holding the scrip he'd been given. A sour grin crossed his face. He picked up a handful of the paper, worthless outside of Charlotte, and scattered it on the ground. The gold and jewels would have to do.

If he couldn't maintain control over his officers, he couldn't control the larger events he saw brewing, and he didn't know how to evaluate the threat of Jason. The man seemed to be an unstoppable force. Roper wouldn't put it past him to remain in Charlotte, eluding capture, to ensure he left. He wasn't going to remain exposed like that. Jason's threat felt formidable.

He didn't have family here. No roots. It was time to go. At least he had more than the last time he was forced out.

Roper loaded his suitcases in the Humvee. The fuel tank was full and he had ten, five-gallon jerry cans full of additional fuel. He could go a long way. He had weapons, ammunition, fuel and valuables. Was it enough to make his way out of the country? He didn't know, but it was time to try.

He got into the Humvee and headed out on the highway, south, to an uncertain future.

Jason, Daniels and Luke drove out to the airport. There was a security checkpoint in place. Jason sat in the back and Michael covered for everyone using his FEMA credentials to get them through. Luke and Jason were explained as assistant and personal security. Roper hadn't given anyone more than a verbal description of Jason and now, in civilian clothes and cleaned up, he passed without notice.

"I know where the officers are quartered," Luke said. He directed them to the main terminal. Again, Michael's explanation got the three past the security at the terminal doors. Luke led them to the left, past the Admiral's Club that Roper had abandoned earlier that day. They walked towards the far end of the wing which expanded to include shops and restaurants. There workers had subdivided the space into apartments. Small, but well appointed, with the luxury of a full working bathroom facility in the vicinity. The quarters were close to the Admiral's Club which not only housed Roper, but the militia Command Center and meeting area.

"Roper stays there," Daniels said as they passed the entrance to the club. There was no guard at the door. "He's probably not there. Usually there's a guard at his door."

"Hiding...or departed," Jason said.

"Wait here," Luke said to Jason when they got near the end of the corridor. "Michael, come with me. Let's round up the officers."

The two went ahead and Jason sat down in a corner trying to be unobtrusive. He could hear multiple voices as Luke and Michael roused the senior officers and convinced them they had to come to a late-night meeting.

After a half hour, they returned with five men looking tired and irritated. Jason sighed and got up. He realized that talking took as much out of him as action. If he was honest, he preferred the action. But now was the moment for talking. Maybe with enough words said, he wouldn't have to take more drastic steps to secure this insurrection that he found himself nurturing.

Introductions were made, not altogether friendly, and the group of eight men went to the club. They entered the command center and all sat down at a conference table.

"Before you begin," one of the men said. "Commander Roper talked with us today. He's under threat. This man," he pointed at Jason, "has threatened to kill him on sight, even tried to do so earlier. So, I'm not sure what you've got to say, but you're not going to get a very sympathetic hearing."

"The situation is complicated, so you need to hear us out, including Jason," Luke began.

Jason put a hand on his arm. He needed to cut through side issues and make his point. Direct and without any gloss.

"Let me get to the heart of the matter. Why we came out here to talk with you. First, I don't give a crap what you think of me. My beef is with Larry Roper. I haven't attacked any of your men, except in self-defense when under attack by Roper. But he's planning on attacking Hillsboro. That's where my family lives. I will protect them with my life and that involves protecting the town. Many will die in any attempt to overrun us. That's why I'm here. To stop an attack before it begins. To save lives."

He paused to eye each one of the men.

"Your city is run by the mafia. Maybe you didn't know that before, but I think you do now. They've threatened your families and loved ones. I understand that. Mine are threatened by them as well. That's why I killed Al Tagliani and Joe Nicoletti. It was to take out the mob's leadership."

Jason hunched over the table.

"Along with decapitating the leadership, I set into motion the possibility of Charlotte's civilian leaders retaking control over the city. Taking it back from the mob. It's called a revolution, gentlemen. Some of you come from Charlotte. This your chance to get your city back.

"In a revolution, the outcome depends on which side the military goes with. That's you. You command the troops, not Roper, so it's in your hands. Now I hear that you've gone soft on Daniels and the mayor. That you're worried about your families."

Jason now leaned back and scowled at each of the officers.

"I'm not impressed. With that attitude. Maybe you deserve the mob running your lives."

"I'm not going to sit here and be insulted." One of the officers stood up.

"Sit down!" Jason said in a loud voice. The man looked at him for a long moment. Jason pulled out his pistol and placed it on the table. "You'll sit and listen to me, or else."

The officer sat back down.

"If your group wasn't a threat to Hillsboro, I'd let you suffer under the mob. We overthrew a small-time gangster in our town because his rule got more and more dictatorial and violent. That will happen here."

Jason now stood up, putting his pistol back in his coat pocket.

"Do you think you're dealing with civilized people? The mob has its own rules and they don't exclude killing, especially outsiders." He pointed to the men. "That's you. You're not family, so anything goes if you cross them."

"We don't need a lecture from you on how to get along with the mafia," another officer said.

Jason turned to stare at the man. His anger clearly rising.

"Apparently you do, since you're all acting stupid." He put out his hand as the man started to respond.

"Shut up and listen. They've threatened you. The mask is off. You know what you're dealing with. Now, stop being so goddamned stupid and cowardly. Go get your families and bring them here for God's sake. Put them under protection. The mob can't get to them if your men are worth anything. The mayor will arrest the capos and the mob's leadership will be cleaned out.

"What you'll have left are leaderless gangsters. You can pick them up when they cross the line and do something stupid. Round them up and put their asses in jail. That's how you take back this city."

Jason paused to look at each man in turn.

"Are you in?" he asked. "Because if you're not, you become my enemy and you don't want that. If you think the mob is violent, try me when my family is threatened."

He sat down. No one moved. The room was silent. Finally, one of the officers raised his hand like a schoolboy. Jason nodded to him.

"Commander Roper came over to meet with us earlier today. He asked us whether or not the mafia had threatened us or our families."

"What did you tell him?" Jason asked, now in a calmer voice.

"We told him they had and we weren't sure what to do about it. We agreed that we would follow his orders but we needed to be sure they were in synch with what the mob wanted."

"And what does the mob want?"

The man shook his head. "That's the problem, we're not sure. They just seemed to want to make the point that they were in charge, not Roper or the civilian government. They let things go through Roper, but he had to follow their direction."

"How'd Roper take that?"

The man looked around at the other four officers. "We're not sure. He understood it, but didn't comment on it. He did say that he was going to relocate because of your attempted assassination. He'd let us know where later."

"It wasn't an assassination attempt. If I had wanted to kill him, he'd be dead. I don't miss. His plan is to bug out to somewhere like South America when he has enough loot. He's not loyal to Charlotte. I'm trying to convince him to go now so I don't have to kill him."

The officers began to talk with each other. One of them looked over at Jason.

"That puts things in a different light."

"Maybe. The main issue for you to understand is do you want to do the smart thing, the right thing and get your city back?"

"Can we talk about this among ourselves? You've given us a lot of information. Can we have a few minutes alone?"

Michael looked over at Jason. The officers weren't armed. Jason nodded.

"We'll be right outside. You have five minutes to decide what you're going to do."

He got up and the three men went left the club.

When they were outside the door, Luke asked Jason, "What are you going to do if they don't agree to help?"

"Kill every damned one of them if I have to."

Luke looked at him with alarm.

"We have to have the militia on our side. If a change in leadership is necessary there, I'll bring it about."

Chapter 56

Within the five minutes, the door opened and Jason and the others stepped back into the room.

"We're on board with you," one of the officers said. "

"Good choice," Daniels said. He didn't want Jason to say anything to upset the newly achieved agreement.

"You all make me proud to be a citizen of the Queen City," Luke said with enthusiasm. "As a spokesman for the mayor I am happy to welcome you on board."

The officers looked at him. They knew who he was but didn't seem sure of his official position. Luke's stating that he represented the mayor caught them off guard.

The three men got up and left the room.

"Still a lot to do," Michael said as they left the airport."

"We live in exciting times," Luke said.

"Like the old Chinese curse," Michael said looking over his shoulder at Luke who now sat in the back seat.

"Not sure it's accurate," Jason said. "In any case there's some truth to it. Just don't let the chaos monster get out of control."

After the officers ended their meeting, one of them wrote a note and gave it to one of the security men at the front door.

"Take this to Vincent Bonocchi," he said, showing him the address on the folded paper.

The man nodded, got into a Humvee, and headed out from the airport. The officer then went back to his quarters and put on his full uniform to go round up the squads under his command.

Dawn found the courier waiting at Vincent's office. When the mobster arrived, he gave him the note and waited to see if there was a reply.

Vincent read the note and told the man to just thank his officer. The man nodded and left.

Vincent's crew had assembled. He sent Rocco and Carlo out to contact the other capos and have them come to his office. They would be suspicious but wouldn't stay away, not wanting to be left out of any scheming that might go on in their absence.

"We got a problem," Vincent said after the capos had arrived.

They came with their bodyguards. There were nearly twenty men in the outer office and hallway including Rocco and Carlo.

"Roper's nowhere to be found. And somehow Jason and the FEMA guy have convinced the senior officers to support them and the mayor. They may be going out to arrest all of us. They're trying to take back control of the city."

"The mayor'd never approve of that. He knows we'd whack him and his family," one of the capos said.

Vincent shrugged. "My guy in the militia thinks otherwise. If the militia goes with Jason and the FEMA guy, the mayor will too. Jason's convinced them that now's the time to strike. While we're disorganized."

"Whaddaya think we should do?" another capo asked.

Vincent noted that leadership was ceding to him. Information had tipped the scales in his favor. The militia officer sent the note to him, which indicated he thought Vincent was the next in line.

"We strike back. I don't want to sit around and wait for some militia pukes to arrest me. Do any of you?"

He looked around the room. The capos were all shaking their heads.

One of them spoke up. "What's this guy who gave you the info want? He on our side?"

"He's trying to play both sides. He'll go along with the others. But he wants to be sure if we win, he won't get whacked."

"So...what?"

"We grab this FEMA guy. I know the building where he lives. We grab him along with the mayor and the militia families. We do it now, before they can protect themselves. With them in our hands, the militia will cave."

The capos left Vincent's office to round up the families. Two cars were sent over to Daniel's apartment building. Eight men in all. They parked along the entrance to the garage to wait. Without knowing which apartment he lived in, they'd have to wait outside to catch him coming or going.

The three men drove back to Daniel's apartment. They had the militia on board and they had the mayor on board, after many assurances of lowering his risk factor. Now they had to wait for the militia to secure the families. Then the militia would start rounding up the capos.

"We did it," Luke said with enthusiasm.

"It ain't over yet. Better wait to celebrate," Jason said.

"You still want to see Vincent?" Daniels asked.

"Yeah. There's someone in his crew. I owe him something. I'm going give him the opportunity to do the right thing, get on the right side."

"But not kill Vincent, right?" Daniels said.

"Right. And don't worry, I won't give away the game."

As they turned on the road to the apartments, Jason saw two cars parked outside, near the garage entrance. He could see some heads through the windshield.

"Something's not right," he said.

"What do you mean?" Daniels asked as he drove forward.

"Those cars, there's men in them..."

"So?"

"Stop. Something's wrong."

"We're almost there," Daniels said.

"Stop!"

Daniels brought the car to a stop in the middle of the street.

"I don't see an ambush," he said.

Jason didn't answer he just watched the cars. Nothing moved.

"Is there another way into the building?"

He was feeling naked. He only had his 9mm. His M4 and M110 were in Daniels' apartment.

Suddenly the two cars started up and accelerated towards Daniels' car.

"Back up! It's an ambush." Jason shouted.

He pulled out his pistol as Michael put the car in reverse and stepped on the throttle. The car started swerving as Daniels fought to keep it under control. Someone stuck a pistol out of the passenger window in one of the cars and started firing.

"Shit!" Luke shouted and dove for cover in the back seat. Jason leaned out of the passenger side and fired at the closest car. Two of his shots went through the windshield. The car swerved and hit the curb. The other car kept coming. More shots came from it and now from the stopped car as men poured out of it.

"Ow, I'm hit," Daniels cried out. The car swerved to one side and backed into a light pole. Luke opened the back door and began to crawl out.

"Get out," Jason yelled at Daniels as he opened the passenger door and returned fire again.

"You go," Daniels said. "I'm hit in the shoulder. Can't get the door opened."

Jason reached back in and tried to pull Daniels to the passenger side. The man's feet were caught under the pedals.

"Go. I'm stuck."

Jason fired two more rounds, keeping the attackers at bay. The intensity of the return fire increased. Their position was untenable.

"Go, go," Daniels said again.

Jason looked at him and tried to pull him again. He didn't budge.

"Surrender. Maybe they want to take you hostage. I'll come for you."

With that he dropped to the ground. Luke was cowering at the rear corner of the car.

"Follow me," Jason shouted.

He ran in a crouch, keeping the stalled car between him and the shooters. Luke followed in his footsteps. They made it around a corner. The shooting behind them stopped. Jason looked around. They needed to find a place to get out of sight but not trapped. Halfway down the side street which dead ended at the freeway, was a storm drain pickup.

"Stay with me," Jason said and took off towards the storm sewer.

He pressed himself under the concrete canopy that covered the opening and slithered into the vertical shaft. There were iron rungs on the side and he used them to climb to the bottom.

"Hurry," he called up to Luke.

When Luke got to the bottom, they took off in a crouch splashing along through the four-foot high drain. Jason kept them running past the next vertical shaft. After what he estimated was two blocks of running through the sewer, he climbed the next shaft they came to. It had a grate on top. With some effort Jason managed to pry it open and scanned the area. They were still inside the downtown, in a low, grass-covered swale that collected the storm runoff and directed it into the sewer.

There was no one around. He put a fresh magazine in his 9mm and got out, keeping watch while Luke climbed after him.

"Holy crap," Luke exclaimed. "Do you think they killed Michael?"

His eyes were still wide with fear. He was panting from both the run and the adrenaline. Jason kept scanning the area as he caught his breath.

"Maybe not. The shooting stopped after we rounded the corner. They were shooting at us, not Michael. Hopefully they want him as a hostage. Probably wanted all of us."

"Bargaining chips?"

Jason nodded.

"Now we're going back," he said and started off towards the apartment building.

Luke ran after him.

"We can't go back there. They'll be looking for us."

"You're right. Out on the streets like here. Not back at the apartment building. My guess is they've already gone."

Just as he spoke, they heard a car coming down the street they had just left. They hid in the bushes next to a building, well off the road. The car cruised slowly down the street. It stopped at the storm sewer. The grate was clearly misplaced. Two men got out with their AR-type rifles. They scanned the area and approached the drain. After checking down the shaft and looking around, they went back to the car. It turned around and headed back up the street.

"They think we continued away from the ambush point. That's in our favor."

"Why go back? Shouldn't we go to the mayor's office, or back to the airport?"

"I need more than my pistol. And the mayor and the militia won't be of any help if the mob has captured some of their families. That's what I'm worried about."

"But how would they know?"

"Someone might have tipped them off. That's why they came for Daniels."

"Who would do that?"

"One of the officers." No one else knew. We have to take care of this ourselves."

"You know I'll help. I'm your man. But I'm a player, a gambler, a schmoozer, not a fighter. I don't do guns. I make my way with my wits and words."

"Well now you're going to have to stretch yourself. 'Cause I need your help. Even if you can't shoot."

"Isn't there any other help we can find?"

"We don't have time and I can't be sure which one of that group sold us out." Jason shook his head. "No, it's on us. Let's go."

Back at the apartment building, Jason took a fire extinguisher and broke open the door to Daniels' apartment. He gathered his gear, checked his ammunition and they exited the building.

Chapter 57

"W here are we going?" Luke asked when they were back on the street.

"Vincent's headquarters. Know where it is?"

"Of course. It's a hike. Should we try to take a car?"

"We can take Michael's. If it still runs. But it's shot up. That could raise suspicions."

"The militia guard the checkpoints. I can talk my way through them. Some rogue gang tried to shoot us up. That's why you're along, for protection. We have to report them to Vincent Bonocchi. I can do this. It's what I'm good at."

Just as Luke said, he talked them through the checkpoint to get out of the downtown area. Luke avoided the main roads where they might run into any of the mob. Two blocks from Vincent's office, Jason directed him to pull into an alley with the car aimed for a quick exit.

"What now?" Luke asked. "You do have a plan, don't you?"

Jason shook his head.

"You're going in without a plan? That's crazy. Worse, it's suicide."

"Can't plan when I don't know what we're facing. We just have to adjust on the fly. The thing is, I know what I want to accomplish."

"What's that?"

"Find out if the mob's taken any hostages and where they are. Then we go free them."

Luke grabbed Jason's arm. "All by yourself?"

Jason stopped and turned to him. "No, I'll have you with me."

"Oh, that's some comfort."

Jason screwed his suppressor onto his 9mm. His M4 was slung over his shoulder. He left the M110 in the car. "Come on. Stay close."

They were crouched a half block away from the office entrance behind some concrete steps. Jason scanned the block, checking the rooftops, doorways, and windows. While they were watching, four men with their bodyguards came out and got into cars and drove off.

"Must be the other capos. Looks like a meeting just broke up," Jason whispered. "I didn't see Vincent. That's good. He's the one I want to talk to."

He waited a few more minutes. Nothing moved on the street. Jason pulled the charging lever back on his carbine. "Let's go."

They walked down the street and entered the office building. Inside, Jason unslung his M4. Leading the way, he quietly climbed the stairs to Vincent's office. He could hear voices inside. He motioned for Luke to stand back from the door. Luke happily nodded in agreement.

Jason stepped inside. Rocco and Carlo looked up with shock, seeing Jason with his rifle leveled at them. Rocco started for his pistol. Jason shot him in the chest. He swung the rifle towards Carlo who froze.

Jason stepped to the side of the inner office door. It swung open and Vincent stepped through with a .45 semi-automatic in his hand. Jason swung the butt of his carbine down hard on his wrist. The gun flew from his grasp.

"Shit." Vincent exclaimed as Jason stepped back to cover both men.

"Get on the floor, both of you. Sit with your hands on your heads."

The men did as he instructed, giving him surly looks.

"Luke, come in here," Jason called out.

Luke's face appeared in the door way. Slowly he stepped inside staring at the damage done.

"Take off your belts," Jason instructed Vincent and Carlo. "Luke, take Rocco's belt off of him. He's the one in the chair."

Luke hesitated, staring at Jason. Without taking his eyes of Vincent or Carlo, Jason repeated his order.

"Go around the far side of the desk. Don't get near these two."

Luke moved in slow motion and gingerly undid Rocco's belt from his waist. When he pulled it loose, the man slumped sideways in the chair.

With a suppressed cry of shock, Luke jumped back. He tried to hand the belt to Jason.

"You hold on to it."

Jason told Vincent and Carlo to push their belts across the carpet to Luke.

"Now lay down on your stomachs with your hands behind your back," Jason instructed.

"You're a dead man," Vincent said.

"Not yet. Do as you're told or *you* might be one."

When the men were in position, Jason gave Luke instructions to kneel down behind each man and tie their wrist with the belts.

"Either of you try to move, I'll shoot you dead. Just like Rocco."

When Luke was done, Jason shouldered his carbine and pulled the two gangsters into a sitting position.

"You stand behind them," he told Luke. "Watch their wrists. If they try to loosen the belts let me know."

When Luke was in position, Jason pulled up a chair and sat it in front of the two men.

"Now we're going to have a talk. You ambushed me and my two friends. I think you captured one of them. We want to know where he's being taken. I also think you may have captured some of the militia families. I want to know where they are as well."

"I don't know nothing," Carlo said.

"You better hope that's right. But I know Vincent does. I think he's the heir apparent. The next boss. The capos coming here to meet with you tells me that. They come to the boss. The boss doesn't go to them."

"I don't know what you're talking about. I told you I'd kill you when I saw you next," Vincent said.

"And here I am, and there you are. Not a very good position for you."

"What the hell do you want? Haven't you done enough already?"

"I want to finish what I came to do."

"What the hell is that? Kill everyone?"

"If I have to...yes. I want to make sure Hillsboro is safe."

Vincent looked up at Jason. Vincent's eyes were full of anger and hate. "If that's all, you could just negotiate with us. We'd be happy to leave that dump alone."

"It didn't sound like it when Joe showed up at our town. It didn't sound like it from some of Joe's statements back here either."

"You trying to take over things. It won't work. The militia won't support your crazy revolt. The mayor won't either. You're done, you hear me? Done!" This last he said with an angry shout.

"That's because you have some of them captive. You'll hold them hostage. That's why I want to know where they are."

"I ain't telling you crap," Vincent said.

Jason turned to Carlo. "How about you? You know where they are?"

Carlo shook his head. "I told you no. I wasn't in the meeting. Vincent arranged it with the other capos. They sent out a team. Rocco and I weren't on it."

Jason stared hard at him.

"It's the truth, I swear."

"Ears go with them?"

Carlo nodded. "Vincent told him to go along, make sure things were done right."

"Shut up you fool," Vincent said.

Jason turned back to Vincent. "I guess it's up to you to tell me. You're the boss now."

"Go to hell," Vincent said. His voice like a growl.

Jason got up and went over to the desk. He grabbed a letter opener and slid his hand along the blade.

"Not sharp enough."

He put it down and took out his sheath knife.

"I guess I'll use this."

He pushed back the chair and squatted in front of Vincent whose legs were stretched out in front of him. Jason held the knife up to Vincent's face.

"You know about pain. You've dealt some out in your career. Now I'm going to ask you again where they are. If you don't answer, I'll deliver you some pain. It won't be lethal. I've got plenty of options until you decide to talk. It's up to you how far I go."

Vincent sat with his lips pressed closed in a sharp line across his face. His eyes burned with hate.

"No answer?"

Without waiting a second more, Jason plunged his knife into Vincent's thigh.

"Aaahhh! Jesus!" Vincent cried out.

"Oh my God!' Luke said from behind. He stepped back with his hand to his face.

The knife plunged two inches into Vincent's leg. Jason pulled it out and blood spurted out of the wound.

"You won't bleed out. We'll try this again. Where are they?"

Vincent sat still, his breath coming in raw gasps through his clenched teeth.

Jason stared into his face.

"Still no answer? Making it hard on yourself. Vincent, I'm going to get an answer, sooner or later. Where are they?"

Vincent kept his mouth shut tight.

Jason plunged the knife into his other thigh.

He cried out and started to fall backwards.

"Hold his shoulder," Jason said to Luke.

Luke caught him and kept him upright. He was making soft, almost mewing sounds while Vincent gasped for breath.

"Next time I go in, I turn the blade. More tearing, more pain, more damage. You sure you want to continue?"

Jason moved the blade over the first leg. Vincent shook his head.

"No, no," he murmured.

"Where are they?"

Vincent was panting. "Catch my breath," he said in between gasps. "In a warehouse. North of here."

"Got a street?"

"Near where you killed Gino. Four warehouses, off Brookshire Freeway. They're in the second one from the end, south end."

"How many men holding them?"

"Maybe a dozen, not sure. Damn this hurts."

"I'll help that later. Ears with them?"

Vincent nodded. "What's so important about Ears?"

"I owe him a favor. I'd like to repay it before I go."

Jason stood up.

"Luke, go into the inner office and find a bottle of whiskey or any other hard liquor. Bring it here."

Luke came back with a bottle of bourbon. Jason tore open Vincent's pant legs and poured the whiskey over the wounds.

Vincent almost screamed as the alcohol bit into the punctures.

"Now, go get my backpack from the car and bring it here. Be careful on the street."

Luke looked at him and hesitated.

"Go now!" Jason said in a loud voice. Luke jumped and ran out of the door.

When he returned, Jason bound up Vincent's legs and jabbed a morphine injection into one of them.

"That'll help for a while. You won't be walking any time soon. Luke, pull him back so he can lean against the wall."

After Vincent was in position, Jason had Luke help Carlo to his feet. Rocco was pushed to the floor and Carlo pushed into the chair. Jason tied Carlo firmly to the chair with the extra belt.

"I think that's all we can do here for now. Time to go to the warehouse."

He looked at Vincent who stared back with dull eyes. Without a further word, Jason turned and left the office with Luke in tow.

Chapter 58

W e need some glass bottles and some gasoline," Jason said when they were back at the car.

Luke was staring at him. He seemed to not have gotten over the trauma of Jason's interrogation.

"Did you hear me?" Jason asked.

Luke nodded. "What are you going to do? Make Molotov cocktails?"

"Exactly. We'll need pieces of rags and something to light them. I expect you can find this while we're on our way?"

"Yeah, I can." Luke paused for a moment. "How far would you have gone back in there?"

Jason turned to him. "As far as I had to go. We needed the information and he had it."

"But you could have crippled or killed him."

"That was up to him."

Luke shook his head as if to clear it. "I guess I just don't understand such violence."

"Sometimes it's called for, no matter how distasteful."

Jason turned to Luke, "Do you know how to get to the reservoir? There's an industrial section out there with a few stores and a bar. I met someone out there who rebuilds old cars from the junkyard. He may have what we need."

"I can find it."

Luke drove them to the area and, after some scouting around the local streets, Jason saw the bar.

"There. Let's get some bottles. We need four of them."

Luke went inside and negotiated for four empty liquor bottles.

"Now, head up the road a couple of blocks. It's on the left. It's a garage with a big yard out back. Like a junkyard, only he 'resurrects' cars as he describes it."

They pulled up and Jason got out. He walked inside and called out, "Harry."

A man came out from behind an old Plymouth.

"Jason. Is that you?"

Jason nodded.

"What are you up to these days?"

"I'm on a mission now. Some people have been kidnapped and I have to help them."

"Kidnapped? By who?"

Jason shook his head. "Better not to know any more."

He held out the four liquor bottles.

"I need you to fill these with gasoline. And I need some rags to stuff in them."

"You making what I think you're making?"

Jason nodded. "The less we speak of this the better. I appreciate your help. No one will know where this came from."

"Follow me." Harry turned to go back into the garage. He pumped some gas from a 55-gallon drum. Then he tore some strips from an old sheet and stuffed them into the mouths of the bottles.

"I use old sheets. Tear them up to use as rags."

"Thanks Harry." Jason shook his hand. "A piece of advice for you. The mob is going down. I know all about how it runs the city. Those days are about to end. I want you to have a heads up, so you can make sure you're on the right side of things."

"This have anything to do with the shootings?"

"It's complicated, but yes. Changes are going to be coming pretty fast. Just make sure you keep your head down."

Harry gave him an appraising look. "I always do."

With the bottle bombs safely nestled in the back seat, Luke drove them to the warehouses. Jason had him park a couple of blocks away.

"We wait until night."

"Do you have a plan? More than the last time?"

"The last time didn't go so badly."

"For us. But there were only three of them. Vincent said there were a dozen men guarding the hostages."

"Let's reconnoiter the area and then we'll talk about a plan."

Jason reloaded all his magazines. Then he grabbed his backpack along with the M110 strapped to it, his M4 and 9mm. Luke carried the Molotov cocktails. They started for the warehouses and settled into some brush across a parking lot from the buildings. There were four cars parked in front of the second warehouse, probably belonging to the gang.

Nothing stirred. As dusk approached, two men came out and, after walking around the building, they climbed to the roof and took up positions.

"Lookouts," Jason said. "They'll have a long field of view up high like that. But they're sitting ducks for a sniper."

"Someone like you," Luke said.

Jason nodded.

"But the others inside will hear the shots, won't they? Won't they also think somethings wrong if they don't hear from them?"

"They may not hear the shots. The rifle is suppressed. They'll be a general sonic crack. The bullet goes supersonic, but they may not react to it. And I don't see radios on the lookouts, so they're not in regular communication with those inside."

"But it's only two. You'll still have ten to go."

Jason looked over at Luke. "It's a start."

"Oh my God. Do you just wing everything you do? We're talking about lives here. Yours, mine to begin with. Then there's the hostages, not to mention the gangsters."

"I'm working on a plan. The two on the roof are easy. I'm trying to work out what to do about the rest."

The coming night was clear and cold. The moon would not rise for some hours to light it and the stars would only give faint light to the dark. Jason would have to take his shot before it got too hard to see.

"Here's what we do," he said.

"I'll take out the two men on the roof. Then we approach the warehouse. I'll take up a position near the door. You throw the firebombs on the cars. It doesn't matter if you hit all of them, just hit some. When the fire starts, I'll yell out 'fire'. That should draw most of the ten out of the building. I can take them down when they emerge."

"But there'll be some left inside."

"Yeah. I'll have to go in and take care of them. You'll wait outside for me."

"The hostages could get killed."

"They could. Hopefully there'll be enough confusion for me to neutralize the guards before they can threaten the hostages."

Luke gave Jason a concerned look. "I assume by 'neutralize' you mean kill?"

Jason just stared back at him. "You ready?"

"Never for stuff like this. But, yes, as ready as I'll ever be."

Jason slipped the M110 through the bushes. He placed his backpack under the rifle for a shooting rest. He settled the scope on the rooftop, moving from one man to the other, gauging the shift in aim he needed to switch targets and get off two effective shots.

"Got to get both before the second one can dive for cover," he almost mumbled to himself.

"Not much cover up there."

"There's the rooftop AC unit. I'll take out the man closest to it first. The one nearer to us, has fewer options for hiding. Get ready to move."

Jason narrowed his attention, dismissing all outside distractions. He slowed his breathing and waited for his heart rate to respond. The scope's reticle settled on the guard who had no idea that his life would shortly be over.

In between heartbeats his finger closed on the trigger. The rifle gave a muffled bark and kicked back at him. The man on the roof disappeared. Jason swung the barrel in a smooth motion to the other man who had heard the guard's fall and turned around to see what had happened. As he turned Jason fired again. The man's head exploded and he crumpled to the ground.

Jason laid the rifle down on his backpack and picked up his M4. "Let's go," he said.

The two men trotted down the slope from their hiding place and started across the parking lot. Jason stopped Luke thirty feet from the cars. He was near a light pole with a wide, concrete base which would provide a good hiding spot after he threw the fire bombs.

Jason ran to the side of the building and found a place with some scrappy volunteer trees growing out of missing chunks of pavement. It wasn't good protection, but it offered concealment. He signaled Luke to light the bombs and throw them.

Luke hurled the flaming bottles, one after another. The flames splashed out when the glass broke as they hit both cars and pavement.

Jason ran to the door, opened it, and shouted "Fire!" inside. He closed the door and ran back to his position. Within seconds the door burst open and three men ran out.

"What the hell?" one of them shouted.

Another ducked back into the building. Jason could hear him calling for help. Soon more men came out, some with blankets. They began to beat at the fires, trying to smother them. Two emerged with some fire extinguishers. They began to spray the fires.

Jason put his M4 on automatic and opened up on the men. One burst took out the three near the door. Another burst and two men went down. Two more pulled their sidearms and started shooting in Jason's general direction, but they weren't sure of where he was. Jason dispatched them with another burst.

Then it was over. Jason got up and motioned for Luke. He counted the bodies. There were seven. With the two on the roof, that left three men inside, if Vincent was correct.

"Only three inside. That's much better odds. Let the fires burn. If I don't come out, you head back to the car and get your ass out to the airport. See if you can rouse those spineless bastards to come and try to save their families. Got it?"

Luke nodded. He seemed afraid to speak.

"Get back up to our hiding position and watch from there."

Jason flicked his fire selector switch to single shot and turned to the door.

"I'm going in now."

"Be careful," Luke said.

Chapter 59

Jason opened the door and ran in shouting, "It's an ambush! Help!"

The interior was lit with a number of kerosene lamps. There was a row of shelving and two abandoned forklifts ahead of him. The hostages were huddled on the far side of the space, all sitting down probably with their hands tied.

Where are the guards? He needed to locate them quickly and take them out before he got shot or they threatened the hostages. Two of the guards started towards him with their rifles at the ready. Jason raised his M4 and shot the nearest man in the chest. He went down, crashing to the concrete floor, his rifle clattering across the surface.

The other man opened fire on automatic as Jason dove for the ground. He scrambled for the cover of the forklift. Shots flew over his head with their deadly whistle, others pinged against the warehouse racking. One bullet grazed across his thigh almost flipping him over. The pain was like a hot iron pressed to his flesh.

Jason rolled over behind the fork lift as shots clanged against the solid metal sides. He swung his rifle around the edge. It took a moment to locate the shooter, the other man who had run across the room. He was angling towards the end of the row of shelving, looking to get to the side of Jason and take away his cover.

Jason fired three shots in his direction causing him to drop to the floor. The metal shelving provided little cover but interfered with Jason's aim. He peppered the area with more shots to keep the man pinned down. If he flanked Jason, he'd be trapped. *Where's the third one?* That man could be coming forward from the other side and he'd be pinched between the two shooters.

The second man now tried to move forward and Jason hit him with a shot. He dropped with a shout of pain, not dead, but taken out of the fight momentarily.

Jason turned to find the third man. He heard some screaming from the hostages. A figure, or maybe two figures lurched towards some cover, a tipped over material cart. It had a thick, metal base which would probably stop a 5.56 round.

"Jason, that you?" the man called out.

"Ears?" Jason replied.

"Thought this might be your work. You kill Vincent too?"

"No. he's alive."

"How'd you find us?"

"I persuaded Vincent to tell me."

"Won't do you no good. You kill all the rest, you still got me to deal with."

"That's just it. I don't want to kill you."

"So you say. You shot me, you bastard."

"You didn't give me much choice."

"Fuck you. I'll give you a chance to leave. Otherwise I'm going to start shooting the hostages, starting with this woman I've got with me."

"Ears. You don't have to do this. The game's over. Roper left town. The militia officers are on the side of the mayor. They're going to arrest the other capos. The mob's broken. Done. It's time for you to get on the right side of things."

"Become a rat? Like you? A turncoat, snitch?"

"The game's over."

Jason stood up from behind the forklift. He raised his carbine and aimed it at the cart laying on its side.

"Not for me. And not for you. I owe you one," Ears said.

"I'm trying to help you. You were a good guy once. A boxer. You helped me. I want to help you."

Jason stepped along the isle, keeping the cart in his sights. The metal uprights interfered with his view as he passed by them. He tried not to let them distract his aim.

"You don't get it. It's about family, loyalty. You take an oath. That's something you don't understand."

"I think I do. It's just misplaced."

"You think you've fixed things here?" Ears' voice rose in anger. "Like you're some kind of savior? We'll be back. People want their vice. They want to take a walk on the dark side once in a while. They just don't want to admit it. Why do you think we thrive? People want to gamble. They want sex, sleaze. That's what we provide. We give them what they want."

"Not everyone wants that."

"Enough do. You can't fix that. Come back in a year. We'll be around. We don't go away because there's always people wanting what we offer and willing to pay for it."

"I'm sorry you feel that way," Jason said.

"You don't know shit." Ears poked out from the side of the cart and fired at Jason. He didn't have a good read on his position and his first shots went wide.

He ducked back behind the cart.

"You've got ten seconds to leave, or I start killing the hostages. No more talking."

"Can't do that Ears. I'll let you leave. Just don't shoot any hostages. You can fend for yourself, but the mob's busted."

Without a further word, Ears reached around the cart and opened fire. Jason resisted the impulse to duck and ignored the deadly stream of bullets. There was to be no more talking. He steadied his aim, and pulled the trigger. The bullet slammed into Ears' head, snapping it back.

His .45 clattered to the concrete floor and the man followed, dropping with a dull thud.

Jason walked up to the cart and helped the woman to her feet.

"It's all over," he shouted to the others.

Cries of relief filled the warehouse. Jason went over to one of the lanterns and picked it up.

"Where's Mayor Chambers?" he shouted out.

"Here," came a voice from the group. A man stood up and walked forward. Jason cut him free.

"Daniels, where are you?" Jason called out.

Michael stood up unsteadily. I'm wounded, but alive."

"You take Daniels with you," Jason said to the mayor. "Luke is outside. He'll take you both back to the airport. Get the officers to send men here to bring these people back. They should round up anyone else who's threatened and then go find the capos and arrest them."

He pushed him forward. "I'll wait here with these people until you get back.

They walked outside. Jason checked the dead and wounded to make sure no one would try to take a shot at them.

The mayor and Michael walked across the parking lot. Jason went back inside the warehouse.

Chapter 60

Two days later, Jason was packing to go. His grazed thigh had been attended to and bandaged.

"You sure you don't want a car? We can afford to give you one after what you've done for the city," Daniels said.

"Thanks, but no. I want to walk. Need to clear my head. I've got lots to think about."

"Having remorse over shooting Al and Joe?"

"Not really. Oddly enough, I'm more remorseful over shooting Ears. He was nice to me. He seemed like he was a good guy once. I tried to give him a chance, but he forced my hand."

"From what you told me it sounds like he didn't want to be taken alive."

"He said some things that disturbed me." Jason paused to gather his thoughts. "He said they'd be back. The mob, or some version of them. People want their vice and so the mob exists to deliver it."

"I can't predict what will happen. I'm only a bureaucrat. But whether or not he's right, they can't be given the opportunity to run a city like they did."

"Just make sure you're ready for some pushback. The other mafia families will hear about this and may come down to take the city back."

"We'll be ready for them."

"So, how's Luke doing?"

"He's a natural, even if there's a lot of bull shit about him. That actually works for the mayor's needs. He's going out with my secretary, Suzy. She thinks he's a hero. Of course he doesn't dissuade her of that impression."

"Changed life. Just like yours."

"Thanks to you."

"Time for me to go," Jason said. He shouldered his pack with the M110 broken down and strapped to it. He grabbed his M4 and started for the door.

"Let me drive you to the edge of town at least. I insist."

They got into the car and drove off.

"Stop at the sausage guy, Russo. I want to say goodbye. He's a good man. You should consider a position for him. He's smart and entrepreneurial. And his daughter is quite the looker."

Jason winked at Michael.

When they finally reached the edge of the city Michael stopped and let Jason out.

"I'd tell you to be careful, but I don't think you need that advice."

"You keep that for yourself. And don't let that mayor go all weak-kneed on you."

He waved and turned to the road.

He walked north, but on the west side of Lake Norman, following the same path he used when he first fled Charlotte. He knew where he was headed. A day later he came to the monastery and walked up to the gate.

One of the monks let him in and, after putting his weapons down, he was led to the Abbot's office.

"Jason," Father Gregory called out. "It's good to see you again. I wasn't sure if our paths would ever cross after you left that night."

"Things got pretty hectic after that, but I survived, as you can see. The mob's been broken and Charlotte has civilian rule back. For now, things are good."

"You can tell me after you've eaten. Let's go over to the kitchen and see what I can round up for you."

After eating what was the most satisfying meal Jason had enjoyed in a long time, they went back to the Abbot's office. He poured some brandy into two glasses and sat back.

"Brandy?"

"We fortify some of the wine we press. It's a secret recipe."

"Add moonshine?"

The Abbot smiled but said nothing.

"I appreciate you stopping. But you're headed somewhere. Going back to Hillsboro?"

Jason nodded.

"Back to your family?"

Jason nodded again.

"But something's still bothering you. I sense it."

Jason gave out a long sigh. He began to relax in this sanctuary. More than he had even after the events in Charlotte had concluded.

"Yeah. Something's bothering me."

The Abbot waited.

"I had to shoot one of the mob members. It's not like I hadn't killed some of the others earlier. But this one was someone I liked. I tried to give him a chance to change sides, step out of the battle. He rejected it. Said I would lose in the end. Said there'd always be vice. People would clamber for it and the mob would wind up providing it. He said they'd be back."

He took a sip of the brandy.

"I'm wondering if all I did was for nothing."

The Abbot paused for a moment before speaking.

"We live in a fallen world. That's a core part of Christian doctrine. And we're fallen creatures. I told you there are no utopias, no perfection this side of heaven. Not until all of creation is healed."

"Then what's the use?"

"We're called to stand against evil, to do what we can each day in some small way to move ourselves, our families, our communities towards the higher good. If we do that, in some small way, we move all of creation towards the higher good. For me that would be towards God."

"What you describe is like a drop in the ocean."

"Maybe. But consider, if everyone acted that way. Everyone on the planet striving to be the best they could, aiming at their highest good, what could be achieved? The mind can't imagine it."

They kept talking late into the night.

"Jason, remember I told you how you are a man drawn to the fight, to slay the dragons? I said you stalk the no-man's land between order and chaos."

Jason nodded.

"I want you to know that you are in danger. An existential danger. A danger to the soul. If you continue to be the warrior, the dragon slayer, you risk losing yourself. You risk turning into a full-blooded killer. There is a price to pay for all the killing and it's a deadening of one's soul or spirit. You risk quenching that voice within that helps give you course corrections. Do it often enough and you won't be able to hear it."

Jason looked at the Abbot. "What I do is for a righteous purpose."

The Abbot continued. "If a man sticks his hand in a flame, what happens?"

"He gets burned."

"It hurts, doesn't it?"

Jason nodded.

"What happens if he does it over and over?"

Jason looked at the Abbot with some confusion. "I don't know what you're driving at."

"If he does it repeatedly, at some point he won't feel it any more. The nerve endings die. He'll be dead to the pain. Kill enough and it will deaden you to God's plan. To see the higher good and aim at it. You will lose that voice and your way."

"I kinda thought I was aiming at a higher good."

The Abbot stood up. "Sleep on it. And give it some thought on your journey."

The next morning after a large breakfast of porridge and eggs washed down with cider, Jason walked to the gate with the Abbot.

"You're a good man, Jason. Think about the finger and the candle. Spend too much time in the world of chaos, slaying dragons, and you may get lost. Go back to your wife and family. Nudge creation, reality, a bit towards the higher good, starting with your family. Focus on the smaller things and don't aim at always playing a part in the large events. You have something of worth. Don't lose it. Nurture it."

He gave Jason a hug and sent him out of the gate with a wave.

Jason walked down to the road. The pale winter sun was up. The sky was clear. It was cold and the frost sparkled in the early sun. It would soon melt, but now everything had a sliver shine to it.

In spite of his leg, he walked with renewed vigor. He was going home. Home to his wife. The woman who gave him companionship and purpose. Home to his family; the girls he had helped to survive and grow through this apocalypse. Home to his son, part of a new generation born in the post-apocalyptic world.

Maybe the Abbot was right. Maybe he needed to take his family and go back to the valley. The girls could come if they wanted. Sarah was now married to Tommy. They had futures in Hillsboro, but maybe they'd come back with him and Anne. There were abandoned farms and fields to work. Good houses, un-looted, stood ready for someone to inhabit them. The few inhabitants that remained there were all close with a friendship forged through the heat of battle. They would welcome him and his family back. They would relish the company and help.

He interrupted his flight of fancy. *It's not about them, it's about you and Anne and Adam. You don't want to lose them.* His daughters and their husbands now had their own lives to lead, their own futures to decide.

The weight of his mission began to dissolve as he walked along. Charlotte's future was up to the people of Charlotte, not him. Hillsboro's future was up to its citizens, not him. There would always be challenges. The world was an unstable place since the EMP attack. But the Abbot might be right. Maybe what he needed to do was just concentrate on his small family. Make that right. Make that better in some way.

His mind began to clear. He smiled as he marched through the morning towards home, towards family, towards a new future to build.

The End

Afterword

Undercover is the fourth book in the *After the Fall* series.

If you enjoyed this tale, please consider writing a review on Amazon. Reviews do not have to be lengthy and are extremely helpful for two reasons: first, they provide "social proof" of a book's value to the reader unfamiliar with the author, and second, they help readers filter through thousands of books in the same category to find choices worthy of their time investment. You provide an essential service to other Amazon readers with a solid review. I very much value your support.

Other novels published by David Nees:

Jason's Tale, book 1 in After the Fall series
Uprising, book 2 in After the Fall series
Rescue, book 3 in After the Fall series
Payback, book 1 in the Dan Stone series
The Shaman, book 2 in the Dan Stone series
The Captive Girl, book 3 in the Dan Stone series
The Assassin and the Pianist, book 4 in the Dan Stone series

For information about upcoming novels, please visit my website at https://www.davidnees.com or go to my Facebook page; www.facebook.com/neesauthor. You can also sign up for my reader list to get new information. No spam; I never sell my list and you can opt out at any time.

Thank you for reading this book. Your reading pleasure is why I write my stories.

Made in the USA
Monee, IL
15 September 2020

42652996R00219